Wreckage Road

By Barbara J. Barker

Dedication: To my mother, who would absolutely travel with her canine friends no matter how difficult the journey.

Thank you for always believing in me.

****

Contents

4

Chapter One

Newport, OR: May 19, 3:03 p.m.

The ground shuddered beneath the surface, a low, rumbling vibration like the distant growl of a train moving away. The few who noticed the disturbance hesitated, waiting for the movement to end. Then, as abruptly as it had started, the shaking stopped, leaving an unsettling calm behind.

Scattered over Newport, squirrels paused mid-scurry, tiny paws frozen on branches. Birds sat motionless on swaying limbs, feathers puffed, eyes wide, still as statues in the unsettled calm. On the cliffs near the coast, hikers exchanged quick, nervous glances, waiting to see if the tremor would be a prelude to something worse.

Just a stone's throw from Yaquina Bay sat the Oregon Coast Sea Sanctuary, overlooking the bay waters and the graceful arch of the Yaquina Bay Bridge. On the wet deck, part of the upper floor, Linda Jarvis and Rick Demotte suited up in their diving gear, preparing for their daily maintenance routine. Beneath them, the shark tunnel—affectionately called "Shark Alley" by locals—was calm, the water clear, and the creatures within it gliding like shadows beneath the surface.

Linda peered into the tank, her blue eyes following the dark silhouettes of sharks as they swam, their sleek bodies slicing through the water with effortless elegance. The slim marine biologist made a note to check the coral on the right side of the tank later. She liked to keep the vibrant colors in sharp contrast to the muted tones of the sharks. She also closely monitored the many types of feathery seaweed planted throughout the chamber, ensuring they were healthy and thriving in the controlled environment.

Rick gathered tools—microfiber cloths, algae scrapers, and plastic spatulas—to clean the tunnel's curved acrylic walls. He moved with the confidence of a man who has done this hundreds of times, checking his equipment as Linda visually examined the coral. They exchanged a few casual words, their conversation light and easy.

Neither Linda nor Rick felt the first tremor. When the ground shifted again, dust motes danced in the light of the overhead LEDs. Linda laughed at one of Rick's jokes, her fingers pulling her blonde hair back into a ponytail, her focus still on the task at hand. The room felt warm, the hum of the aquarium's systems steady, and she was unaware of the subtle tightening of the space around them.

A third tremor, barely perceptible, rippled through the wooden beams of the aquarium, the faintest groan of the structure joining the sound of the water as it shifted. The framed pictures in the halls rattled gently, their glass surfaces catching light in the reflections.

Inside the tank, the fish were on alert.

The catfish and rays darted through the water with a sudden urgency. Sleek bodies cut through the currents fast, the bubbles rising in quick bursts behind them. The sharks, always so calm, glided restlessly. Their large bodies twisted and turned as they swam in erratic patterns.

There was tension in their movements, a kind of anxiety that flowed through the tank. Their bodies were tight and alert. They could sense even the slightest shifts in the water, even the tiny tremors caused by the foreshocks of an impending submarine earthquake. Each subtle oscillation made them dart and weave, an instinctive response to their growing unease.

Outside, leaves fluttered as if stirred by an unseen hand, and a small dog barked once, confused by the sudden shift. The distant hills to the south settled uneasily as cracks appeared in the earth, unnoticed by any except the few hikers out for the day. The forest fell silent, a heavy stillness settling over the landscape.

***

Miranda Smart and her younger sister Melinda had hiked these hills for years. The two girls, healthy outdoor types with long, russet brown braids down their backs and slender forms hoisting sizable backpacks, had noticed the tremors but dismissed any concern because they were so faint.

As they climbed along the winding trail in the cliffs off the Oregon coast, the scent of salt and pine rode the breeze, mingling with the earthy aroma of damp soil. Sunlight filtered through the trees, casting dappled shadows on the path. Miranda paused to admire the breathtaking view of the rugged coastline, watching the waves crashing against the walls thirty feet below.

"Hey, Miranda. . ." Mel's voice trailed off.

"Hmm?" Miranda was barely listening, hand over her brown eyes as she studied the sun glinting off the water. It was beautiful.

"Look at the ground off the trail. It looks like something smashed it. It's all broken."

Reluctantly, Miranda turned her back on the view, her boots scuffing the path underneath her feet. "What are you talking about…" her voice died off as her eyes widened in confusion. As far as she could see right and left, the ground running along the trail was cracking, chunks of soil and rocks splitting right before her eyes.

***

Inside the Sea Sanctuary, Linda and Rick had slipped into the water, swimming down to the bottom of the tank. The tunnel, encased in thick acrylic, rose below them in an underwater world, surrounded by the shimmering blue of the ocean.

Above them, the surface rolled, tiny waves spilling over the deck, reflecting another disturbance. Agitated leopard sharks and rays shot back and forth, skimming off the walls and around again.

Finally, the marine biologists noticed their behavior. Puzzled, they watched the fish react.

***

Miranda squatted, trying to figure out what was going on. The wind whipped through her hair, carrying the salty suggestion of the sea.

Mel shook her hands anxiously. "Maybe we should head back down the trail?"

Without warning, a violent shudder jolted through the earth. The trail beneath them buckled, rocks tumbled, and a deep crack appeared, splitting the path in a jagged line. They each took a quick step back toward the ocean. Miranda's heart raced as she watched in horror. The cracks exploded into wide fissures, dust choking them.

Melinda gripped her arm with a squeak of fear, and they clung to each other, confused, as the ground beneath their feet vibrated. Suddenly, a sharp snap split the air, as an irregular crevice snaked its way through the earth, widening with alarming speed. Small stones burst from the gap as pops of breaking rock echoed all around them.

The cliff shuddered violently. The crevice grew larger, splitting the ground apart in a three-foot gap. It ran the length of the path, as far as they could see in either direction. The girls fell backward, scrambling to get away. Too late, Miranda realized they had nowhere to go. The edge of the precipice blocked their retreat.

Panic set in as she grasped what was happening. "It's a landslide! The cliff is shearing off," she yelled as she struggled to maintain her footing. "We have to get off of here!"

She tried to gauge the width of the fracture in front of them but quickly recognized they couldn't jump it. She pushed Melinda to the left, hoping they could outrun the slide.

Before they took three steps, the earth convulsed with the largest jolt. A deafening roar burst out as two thousand feet of the cliff sheared off, breaking free from the land.

In a heart-stopping instant, Miranda felt the solid rock giving way, and she was tumbling toward the tremor-fueled waves below. Melinda screamed, but it was too late. The force of the collapse sent them plunging into the churning ocean, swallowed by the chaos of water and rock.

The cliff's remnants crashed into the depths. A towering spray erupted, momentarily veiling the face of the newly revealed bluff.

***

Linda scanned the tank, alert to trouble. On either side, vibrant schools of fish flashed by, their scales glinting like jewels against the backdrop of the deep blue walls. Colorful corals and rocky outcrops lined the bottom, providing a habitat for various marine creatures. While she watched, the coral trembled around her.

She turned toward Rick, surprised to see he was swimming toward her. He reached her in a second and, grasping her arm, pulled her up, his movements urgent. They broke the surface and swam to the deck, climbing out fast. A pack of spiny dogfish sharks, irritated and aggressive, were on their heels. They swerved just as Rick pulled his fins from the water.

"What's going on?" she panted.

Before he could answer, the ground beneath them trembled. A low rumble escalated into a strong shake that rattled the structure, the deck creaking as the tank water sloshed up and over them. They tried to stand, realizing that this was no ordinary occurrence. Waves roiled and swirled, sending swells that sped across the surface.

"Earthquake!" he shouted.

As the quake intensified, a shudder swept through the aquarium, and the sound of crashing water grew louder. Screams rang through the building, thumps echoing up the halls. The biologists gripped the railing, eyes wide, watching as the sharks within the tank swam erratically, confused by the surrounding commotion.

LED lights flickered overhead, casting eerie shadows as equipment rattled. Waves rolled over the deck, and vibrations kicked up through the floor. The platform rocked, and suddenly, Rick wondered if it would hold. Massive tremors slammed through the building, knocking them both to their knees.

Just as quickly as it had begun, the quake peaked, a continuous juddering that snapped their necks, flinging them against the railing and holding them there while the tank water poured over them. Then it stopped.

For a few minutes, neither moved. Linda helped a dazed Rick to his feet. The goose egg on his forehead was hot and red, but a gash down the side of his face was bleeding freely. She wiped at it with the sleeve of her wetsuit. Helping the biologist to a chair, she unclipped and slid his arms out of the BCD, stopping quickly to do the same for herself. She left the equipment at their feet while she worked on Rick.

Suddenly, the afternoon filled with a shriek as tsunami sirens blared through Newport, a chilling warning echoing off the cliffs. Panic surged through the streets as those who were able raced to higher ground, eyes darting toward the ocean, where an ominous darkness swelled. The muffled screech pierced the walls of the Sea Sanctuary.

Then, from the horizon, a colossal curtain of water—sixty feet tall—rose, a monstrous wave cascading toward the shore with terrifying speed. Its surface glistened in the light, a blend of deep blues and frothy whites, reflecting the sun as it grew. The ocean roared, a deep, rumbling growl that drowned out all other sounds.

In the Sea Sanctuary, the lights flickered as staff scrambled to evacuate the guests up the stairs, the urgency palpable. The ground trembled beneath their feet. Linda tried to pull Rick up, but he was semi-conscious, and his dead weight was more than she could handle. With no idea how close or tall the wave was, she did the only thing she could think of.

She pulled Rick to the floor and wrestled him back into his BCD jacket. Pulling on his goggles, careful of the gash, she lightly smacked his face, trying to wake him up.

"Rick, there's a tsunami coming. We have to stay in our equipment." She pushed his regulator into his mouth, then snatched up her BCD.

He lifted a hand blearily, and she hoped he understood. She was pulling on her goggles when the wave crashed over the aquarium, engulfing it in a torrent of water. Seawater gushed through doors and windows, pouring in like a king tide. The pressure built rapidly, cracking several tanks and shattering walls as the building struggled against the deluge.

The aquarium had hundreds of tanks of all sizes. Some of the acrylic fronts held, even the huge plates that made up Shark Alley. But water surged inside each habitat, flooding the exhibits and sweeping the marine life into the maelstrom. Thousands of fish swirled helplessly in the currents, the only color in the dark, tumultuous water.

As saltwater exploded up through the hall and onto the deck, Linda, sitting and bracing herself against the rail, hung onto Rick and the railing, her eyes wide with terror and her fingers white. The overhead lights flickered once and then went out, plunging them into darkness. None of the emergency lighting winked on.

The massive pressure of the onslaught anchored them both against the metal rails, and she gripped the regulator tight with her teeth, hoping Rick was doing the same. She couldn't see anything but foam and bubbles as the water rushed past.

Abruptly, she felt the railing shift beneath her grip. A sense of dread shot through her as the metal fence gave, the bolts popping free against the force of the surging waves. Panic strafed her body, and she realized the railing was detaching from the deck floor.

The railing gave a final, desperate spasm, and suddenly, they were no longer tethered. The water swept them off the deck and into the tank, dragging them into a washing machine effect as the giant tank swirled with the force of the tsunami.

Linda lost her hold on Rick, and he spun away. Crashing against the acrylic tunnel, she glimpsed water surging through the lighted passageway, usually filled with happy tourists. Something that felt like a rip current pulled her in another direction. Grimly she sucked a puff from the regulator, grinding her teeth into the plastic and rubber piece.

The desperate marine biologist pressed one hand against her goggles, and the other held out to keep her from bouncing off coral and rocks in the display. A shape whipped by, and she realized it was one of the leopard sharks. Then she remembered the gash on Rick's head. One of the aquarium's strictest rules was staying out of the tanks if you had a wound.

Froth surrounded her as the water seemed to boil. Terrified for Rick, she started searching, bumping a ray and smaller fish as she tried to feel her way around. The lights in Shark Alley failed, and now she swam in total darkness. Finally, she found a wall. Sliding her hands along the slippery sides, she eventually came to the emergency box she knew was there.

The current slowed as she worked on unclipping the door, and the water settled a bit. She was no longer fighting the flow. The door swung open, and she felt inside until she located a flashlight. She swept the tank with the torch and found Rick on the bottom against the coral. A dogfish shark, small and quick, passed over him.

She swam down, reaching him in seconds, and pulled him around. The regulator was in his mouth. He lay still in her arms, and with limited options, she gave him a shake. The flashlight illuminated his white face, and she pulled him close, trying to see his eyes. After a few breaths, he moved slightly. Relieved, she relaxed her hold. His brown eyes opened behind the goggles, blinking slowly. When he saw her, he tried to sit up, raising his fist in a thumbs-up. At least he had his wits about him.

Linda patted his shoulder, giving him a minute to orient. She hoped he didn't have a concussion. But she was worried another tsunami wave would come through, and she hadn't forgotten about the sharks. Rick's wound wasn't bleeding as far as she could see, but it looked raw. A glance told her they didn't have oxygen to waste. Already, the gauge was under the halfway point.

Slipping herself under his arm, she swam up, pulling them both. The deck area was still flooded. She rose to the ceiling, stopping before they bumped. She hated the thought of trying to swim out of the building but couldn't see any other option.

With one hand pointing the flashlight and the other dug tightly into Rick's collar, she moved across the deck and into the hall. Something bumped her, moving fast, and a leopard shark passed. Grateful the big fish didn't care about her, she kept swimming.

With only the beam of her flashlight cutting through the murky darkness, she navigated the flooded halls of the sanctuary. The water was icy, pressing against her wetsuit. She shivered, gliding silently through the remains. Shadows quivered along the walls, illuminating sights of destruction.

The glow revealed shattered tanks empty and bare, with acrylic shards strewn like fallen stars across the floor. Sadness clutched her chest as she swept the light across the ruins. Heartbreaking glimpses of twisted corals, piled on the floor in deformed piles made her want to cry. Their vibrant colors were now dulled under layers of silt and trash.

In the distance, she heard the faint sound of water moving, a reminder of the power that just surged through the building. The back exit leading into the outdoor exhibits was closest. She steered to what was once the aquarium's centerpiece—Shark Alley—its acrylic walls dim and muddy as she swam hard for the doors. Fish shot in and out of the shadows, their scales glinting briefly in the flashlight's beam.

A soft thud broke the quiet as rubble shifted, and then the muted splashes of struggling creatures caught her ears. The light revealed more devastation: overturned benches, smashed displays, and the remnants of educational exhibits now submerged. A lone sea turtle, disoriented but determined, navigated the building's halls. And then, as she crossed into the back lobby, she saw the sight she had been dreading.

Human bodies floated together in the murk. The tsunami caught her colleagues and tourists climbing the steps, their eyes wide open and terror etched on their faces, as it tore the back doors from their hinges and poured in. She didn't want to move forward and couldn't stay where she was. Choking back a sob, she thrust herself forward, dragging Rick with her, ignoring the bodies that bumped her.

Rising through the gap left by the missing double doors, she ascended higher than the building, at least thirty feet. She broke the surface with a gasp, almost immediately pulled by a rogue current toward the bay. She floundered and then pulled Rick's head up. He finally seemed to wake, sweeping his arms out to steady himself. They huddled together, trying to see through their goggles. There was no sign of the Sea Sanctuary above the waves.

She struggled, disoriented by the lack of familiar buildings, signs, and streets, until she caught sight of the Yaquina Bay Bridge still standing. Then, realizing the sun was at her back, she turned west. Her blood went cold.

A massive wall of water was rising in the distance, towering higher and higher—another wave. Her ears roared as her pulse raced.

"Rick!" She caught his shoulder and pointed. With a glance at her oxygen gauge, her hope faded. They clung together, respirators in their mouths, as the water crashed down and the swirling currents caught them.

Everything went dark until there was nothing.

Reed - Albany, OR: May 19, 4:45 p.m.

Reed Walker finished hosing down the last of the cages, the steady hiss of water punctuating the quiet afternoon. He shut off the nozzle, the last task of his shift done, and stacked the metal boxes with soft clinks. Watson, his golden Labrador, trotted beside him, tail wagging in that constant, happy rhythm. The dog had been with him for years, a companion in a life that often felt too solitary.

Reed cut a lean figure, in his forties, with dark brown hair the same color as his eyes. His face was narrow, and his cut was clipped short by preference. In his line of work as an EMT for the Albany township, the last thing he needed to worry about was strands of straight hair falling into his face.

Overall, he cut a pleasant, if somewhat reserved stature, friendly with everyone and close to no one except Watson.

Inside the shelter, the muted glow of a small television lit the office, casting shadows across the worn furniture. Rose and Terry Marple huddled around it, leaning forward in that eager way they had, their words tripping over each other as they watched the screen.

Reed wasn't surprised. They were always excited about something, whether it was a stray dog showing up or a news report about a random event somewhere in the world. Rose and Terry's faces, crinkled and familiar, were animated with their usual zeal. Terry's curly hair was tight to his scalp, save for the thin patch on top, while Rose's gray curls bounced as she nodded eagerly in conversation.

"Hey, Reed!" Rose called out before he could duck back out the open door. "You gotta hear this!"

Terry chimed in immediately. "It's big! Really big, Reed! Just wait 'til you hear this—"

He barely had time to wave before they pounced on him. Their words rushed together, like a river sweeping him along, but the crux of it came quickly.

"There was an earthquake," Terry blurted, pointing at the screen. "And then a tsunami—right in Newport. Right when we felt that little shake earlier!"

Reed blinked, surprise making his mouth feel dry. Newport? He had also felt the tremors, but it hadn't seemed like more than another minor shake-up.

He shushed them gently, more to regain control than quiet their excitement, and turned the volume up on the small Sony set. The anchor's voice was calm but edged with something else—urgency, maybe fear.

17

"Breaking news from the Pacific Northwest. This is a repeat of today's catastrophic events in Newport, Oregon. A powerful 8.2 magnitude earthquake struck just sixty miles off the coast of Newport, sending shockwaves through the region..."

Reed bit his lip, leaning in. He'd brushed off the tremor, but 8.2? That was a full-bore quake, and the loss of life and damage could be considerable.

"Twenty minutes later, a devastating sixty-foot tsunami hit Newport and the nearby South Beach. Eyewitnesses described a massive, overwhelming wall of water surging inland and obliterating everything in its path."

Reed's heart picked up pace as the images flashed on the screen—pictures of overturned cars, collapsed buildings, the rushing wall of water swallowing buildings and streets whole. His throat tightened, but he kept his eyes locked on the screen, unable to look away from the destruction.

"Newport... ten thousand people..." The anchor's voice faltered as he continued, *"...left in ruins. Buildings, vehicles, trees... and even people swept away."*

Reed's mind raced. The sheer magnitude of what had happened was too much to wrap his head around. He hadn't thought it would be anything this serious.

Reed nodded absently, already heading for the door, reaching for his phone. Watson cut around him, quick to find a patch of grass to sniff, not worried yet about the tension building in the humans.

"I better check in at dispatch," he threw over his shoulder as he stepped out. He could already feel the pulse of adrenaline kicking in. There was no telling what kind of response they'd need from the EMTs. Newport or the nearest emergency center, maybe?

Outside, the yard was still warm, the late afternoon sun sinking lower, casting long shadows over the yard. Watson's tail swept through the grass in a golden blur as Reed stood in front of the building, waiting for the call to connect. He glanced up at the US 20 highway and saw the "ANIMAL RESCUE" sign right off the road. Traffic was light, and only a few cars passed.

Today was his day off. Otherwise, he would have been at the station when the alert came in. A bachelor with no family or close friends, he had started volunteering at the shelter last year to get out of the house on the days he didn't have a shift scheduled. It was a warm May afternoon, but he enjoyed spending time with the dogs. Their gratitude seemed sincere, which is more than he could say about his fellow man.

His Bronco sat under a massive, hundred-year-old pine with wide, green branches. As the sun dropped in the west, the big tree cast a shadow across the yard and over the shelter. Standing in the cool shade between his SUV and the animal shelter, he waited for his phone to connect.

"Albany Dispatch, this is Mary. How can I direct your call?"

Without warning, the ground erupted in a series of colossal jolts. Reed scrambled to keep his footing, shock freezing his thoughts.

Another earthquake!

Chapter Two

Chloe - Albany, OR: May 19, 4:45 p.m.

Chloe Cooper lifted the baby girl into her arms, feeling the warmth of the tiny body press against her chest. Mollie Wendel, just two months old, curled against her, her dark lashes fluttering as she nuzzled into Chloe's lap. Her soft, delicate skin smelled faintly of baby lotion, and Chloe couldn't help but smile as she stroked the baby's fine hair, so dark it almost shimmered against her pale pink onesie.

Moni Wendel, her friend, and Mollie's mother smiled, the corners of her upturned eyes crinkling as she caught the expression on Chloe's face.

"You need kids, Chloe," she told her friend.

"It just never worked out," Chloe said, running a finger gently over Mollie's soft head. "First, you need a daddy, and I never found one I liked enough to talk about children."

"A good dad is important," Moni agreed, her voice tinged with affection. "Did I tell you that's how we picked out Mollie's name? M-O for Moni and O-L-L-I-E for Oliver. M-O-L-L-I-E, Mollie!"

Chloe rolled her eyes with a smile, her lips curling in amusement. "Only a hundred times," she teased, though her tone was warm and fond. "But it is a great way to pick a name," she added, not wanting to spoil her friend's excitement. It was her first time meeting Moni in person since she started maternity leave, and the joy in Moni's voice was unmistakable.

Moni was on leave from North Albany High School over the spring term. Chloe, a tenth-grade biology teacher, was working the summer session this year, and she was here at the school today getting ready for the students who would arrive in a week.

When Moni texted her she and the baby had a pediatric appointment that afternoon, they agreed to meet in the school's Teacher Lounge afterward. Most of their fellow teachers had already left for the day, giving them the time and privacy to catch up.

"So, how does Oliver like fatherhood?" she asked.

Moni taught Home Economics, and Chloe had met no one as suited to their job as she was. She was the ultimate example of blending work and home. Oliver was a lucky man to have married her.

The young teacher giggled, her long black hair swaying as she moved. "He complains, but he loves it. He gets up with her most nights and always wants to make her bottles. She's definitely going to be a daddy's girl."

"How are you doing, then?" Chloe asked, her voice gentle as she stroked Mollie's soft tummy. Tiny strands of dark hair, just like her mother's, rested on the baby's head like a cap. Dark eyes blinked up at her, curious and wide.

"Good. I am so happy!" Moni said, her voice full of joy. Her smile was so wide it seemed to light up her entire face.

Chloe smiled back, her eyes bright. "It's pretty obvious," she said. "I'm so happy for you."

"Thanks, Chloe, and thank you for listening when I doubted I could do this. Mollie is a lot of work but so worth it! You're a great friend."

"*We* are great friends," she replied, a smile filling her face as she gazed down at Mollie, then up at Moni.

"Well, I should let you get home," Moni said, pushing herself out of her chair. "I know how hard you worked today, preparing for next week. And Oliver is waiting for us."

Moni lived in Lebanon, a small city next to the South Santiam River on the eastern edge of the Willamette Valley and about thirty minutes southeast of Albany. Her house was a small, vintage single-family home, but she worked hard to make the most of what they had. Chloe thought it was charming the few times she had visited. It always smelled like cookies and incense. Delicious.

Chloe nodded, rising to her feet and helping Moni tuck Mollie into the pink stroller, her tiny hands curling up to brush at the soft fabric. They began walking down the quiet school hallway, chatting about the coming school year and when Moni would return to work. The sound of their voices carried through the empty halls.

Suddenly, without warning, the entire building seemed to lift beneath their feet, and the world fell apart.

***

Seventeen-year-old Brett Clark slid out from under the 2015 Honda HR-V after removing the bolt to let the oil drain. He patted his first repair of the day as he stood. The sable-colored hood felt cool under his touch, smooth and easy. Cars are better than girls, he thought. At least they don't leave you guessing.

He thought about his date last night. Cindy Shepherd was a nice girl, but she definitely came on strong in the end. Just as he was really enjoying what she was offering, she shut down cold. A quick peck on the cheek, she slid out of his car and ran into her house.

What was he supposed to think about that?

I don't get it, Brett thought, rubbing his ear, trying to make sense of it. Maybe Uncle Jess has an answer. His uncle always did.

Jess Tate, owner and operator of Tate's Used Cars, wasn't just family; he was Brett's mentor. As a kid, Brett had been obsessed with engines, and his uncle quickly recognized it. Jess had taken him under his wing, letting him spend hours in the garage, learning the ins and outs of cars and mechanics. Brett's ability to fix almost anything on four wheels made his uncle proud. Brett was counting down the days until he graduated high school so he could work full-time at Tate's Used Cars with his uncle.

His mother's only brother, Uncle Jess, had been there for the Clark kids as long as he could remember. His parents divorced when he was eleven, and his mom had moved them from the small town of Sweet Home thirty miles south of here to east Albany.

"Brett!" Jess's voice interrupted his thoughts.

He turned at the yell and saw Uncle Jess run into the garage, his face ruddy and flushed with sweat. Brett was surprised to see him in the bays. His uncle spent most of his time on the lot, selling the cars.

Jess was as laid back as anyone Brett had ever met. Today, his stride was uncharacteristically urgent. "What's up?" Brett said with a quizzical expression, rubbing the oil on his hands over a cloth and crossing the bay. Suddenly, he felt the tension in his uncle.

Jess seized his arm and yanked him toward the open garage door, his grip tight. "An earthquake hit off the coast an hour ago, a big one. Newport's a mess. A tsunami hit right after. You need to go home and make sure your brother and sisters are okay. I'll go pick up your mom from work and meet you there."

Brett's chest tightened. Matthias, twelve; Piper, fifteen; and Winnie, ten—his siblings were all at home. His mom worked on the other side of Swan Lakes, the industrial park near the northeast end of Albany. It was in the opposite direction of their house, less than ten minutes away.

"Here, take the F-150," Jess said, thrusting the keys into Brett's hand.

"I can take my car," Brett protested, his mind racing. His car was nearby, parked under the canopy of the lot, ready for the drive home.

"The F-150's got 4x4 and off-road tires. Better to be prepared."

"Prepared for what? What's going on?"

"Just go. We'll talk after I get your mom. Tell Matthias to get the go-bags out."

"Okay." Brett frowned as he headed over to the big truck. The go-bags were really just four knapsacks Uncle Jess had brought over. For weeks, his uncle and Matthias had worked on them, packing, double-checking, and ensuring they were ready for anything that could happen. It wasn't just about food or water. They'd thought of everything, from first-aid kits to emergency blankets. Uncle Jess had always been a stickler for preparedness, encouraging all the Clark kids to be ready for whatever life might throw at them.

Jess had also encouraged Matthias to join the Boy Scouts. Now, the Boy Scout code ran through the kid's veins like it was second nature. Brett teased him sometimes, but truthfully, a small part of him envied his younger brother's ability to be so sure of his place in the world. If Brett told

Matthias to grab the go-bags, it would be like the starting shot at a racetrack. Even if it were just a drill, Matthias would be thrilled.

Brett tossed the keys in his palm, shoved them into his pocket, and crossed the last section of the employee parking area. He climbed in, the truck's heavy doors smooth as they closed behind him. The engine rumbled to life, and he pulled off the lot, glancing in the rearview mirror at Uncle Jess in a black Wrangler, now speeding east in the opposite direction.

He wondered what had Jess so worked up. He looked ahead and noted that traffic seemed lighter than usual. With the window down, he realized he could hear dogs barking wildly, Sharp, yipping barks, wild and panicked, echoing down the quiet street. He frowned and slowed, scanning the houses. There was nothing to see, but the barking seemed to come from all directions.

Just as he pulled onto his street, a flock of birds suddenly flew up in a frantic flurry, forming erratic patterns overhead. The sky darkened with their wings. They circled like something had disturbed them and were too frightened to land.

Now, he was getting spooked.

Brett's heart pounded as he pulled up in front of his house. The truck jerked slightly, the suspension barely absorbing the uneven ground as he hit the brakes and parked. He jumped out of the truck.

Before he could even lift his foot to step up onto the curb, the ground beneath him trembled and jerked violently. The neighborhood vibrated with the force, and the buildings around him groaned like they were stretching and cracking. Asphalt broke under his feet, throwing him off balance. The world went silent for a split second. Then the sound hit: the deafening, earth-shaking rumble of the quake as it tore through the city.

Brett's pulse thundered in his ears. His hands scrambled to catch the truck to stop his fall, but the ground bucked again, sending him sprawling onto the asphalt, his breath knocked from his lungs.

The entire world felt like it was breaking apart around him.

***

Jolene Clark skimmed the last set of numbers, confirming that the document was prepared correctly. As an auditor and a mother of four, she had an eye for detail and keen observation skills. But even with her mind firmly planted in the numbers, she couldn't ignore the buzz of unease building in the office. Through the small window of her cubicle, she saw people gathering, speaking in hushed, tense tones. The department crackled with something she couldn't quite put her finger on.

Ruefully, she looked at the stack of folders waiting on her. She really needed to stay focused. Before she could decide, her phone buzzed on the desk. It was her brother.

"Hey Jess," she said, tucking the phone under her chin as she reached for the next folder.

"Jolene, meet me in the parking lot. I'll be there in ten minutes."

A chill slid down her spine. "What's wrong? The kids. . ."

"They're okay. Brett's on the way home. Did you not hear about the earthquake in Newport?"

"No," she gasped, her hand halting mid-air. "Was anyone hurt? How bad was it?"

"It was bigger than an eight with the epicenter on the Cascadia subduction zone." Jess's voice was grim. "There was a tsunami, too. Newport's wrecked. The news is warning people to stay away from the coasts."

Jolene's stomach flipped. "Okay, that makes sense. But why are you headed here?" She set down the folder and caught the phone from her shoulder.

"Paul Baxter was at the lot picking out a car for his kid when we heard about the quake. You know Paul, right? Works for the USGS?"

"I've met him," Jolene answered cautiously. "What about him?"

"He went white as a ghost when we heard about the earthquake. Mumbled something, ran to his car, and sped off like the devil himself was after him. I don't know what he knows, but we need to get the kids. We're heading east— Ochoco National Forest, maybe to camp out for a few days. Get to safety."

Her heart pounded. Jess didn't panic, not like this. If he was worried, she had reason to be, too.

She snatched up her purse, her fingers trembling slightly, and hurried through the office. The noise hit her like a wave as soon as she opened the door. People were speaking faster now, all tuned to the same channel—the emergency broadcast on the television, showing footage of the destruction in Newport. The room was layered with tension. Jolene's stomach twisted again as she pushed through the corridor, trying to ignore the hum of frantic conversations, her phone still pressed to her ear.

"Okay, I'll meet you outside," she told him. She spoke curtly, each syllable edging her closer to panic. His urgency had infused her with fear. Living in Oregon and not worrying about earthquakes and volcanoes was impossible. She was almost running when she reached the parking lot.

At the end of the long drive, she saw Jess fishtail his SUV onto the black tar of the lot, heading to her. She took several quick steps toward the oncoming Wrangler when the ground beneath her suddenly convulsed violently, and a deep, bone-shaking blare erupted from the earth.

The ground heaved, a sharp, terrifying shudder that rattled her bones. Jolene stumbled, her heart thudding against her ribcage as the asphalt cleaved wide open in front of her. Behind her, the building trembled, ripping under the strain. The roof sagged, then warped, and metal sheets crashed like a house of cards. Windows disintegrated, sending shards glinting in the sunlight. The walls shuddered, then bulged outward, vinyl and metal framing splintering and snapping apart. Just barely, she could hear distant cries, muffled and terrified.

Jolene turned toward Jess's Wrangler, her eyes wild. Her legs barely carried her as mighty thumps threatened to knock her over. The earth swelled and heaved again, the ground swallowing chunks of foundation, pulling them into the widening chasm. The parking lot split like paper, cars sliding down as the rift swallowed them, their metal bodies crumpling as they piled up and disappeared into the dark void.

Jess's expression behind the SUV's windshield was one of abject fear. With a screech of rubber on tar, the Wrangler skated uncontrollably toward the opening in the earth, its tires grinding uselessly against the blacktop as he tried to brake.

The ground cracked wider.

With each violent jolt, the earth shook, making it impossible to stand. The Wrangler lurched closer to the hole, and for one brief, harrowing moment, their eyes met—his face a mask of terror, hers a reflection of horror—before the earth opened up beneath the vehicle, and it fell away.

The gap widened in a final, overwhelming surge, heading directly toward her, consuming everything in its path. There was nowhere to go. The concrete gave way beneath her, and the darkness pulled her in, burying her in stones and rubble.

Jolene's last action before the world slipped away was a desperate, hollow scream that never left her lips.

Nadia, Sweet Home, OR: May 19, 4:45 p.m.

The first tremor slammed into the earth like a punch to the gut. A deafening crack ripped the floor of the old rock quarry right through the center. The ground buckled, the split spreading with each jolt. Dense, murky water pooled from the rainstorms flooded the gap, only to drain in seconds—then boiled up in a billowing cloud of super-heated steam that hissed into the afternoon.

In a greenhouse, fifty yards east of the abandoned quarry but still within sight of the massive pit, Nadia Petrova staggered, her feet slipping beneath her, arms flailing desperately to find balance. The entire structure trembled before she could regain her footing, disintegrating around her.

Glass exploded in every direction, deadly shrapnel twinkling in the slanted light. Her body hit the floor hard, her breath escaping in a whoosh. Instinct took over. Scrambling, she dove beneath a shuddering table, her heart hammering against her chest, every beat loud in her ears. She winced as glass landed around her, narrowly missing her body.

Outside, more steam erupted from the split in the quarry, a furious column rising hundreds of feet as the billowing clouds hid the late afternoon sun. Below the steam, toxic sulfur gas hissed from the crack, settling in the bottom of the quarry like an invisible, poisonous fog.

But that was only the beginning.

The jolts raged relentlessly. Nadia could feel the greenhouse shudder again as the ground buckled beneath her. The thin aluminum framing twisted and warped, the structure leaning like it might collapse entirely. The heavy tables stacked with sprawling cannabis plants spilled part of their load, the broad, serrated leaves rattling like trees in a storm. Dan had stacked half bales of product, ready for the next run by the door. The plastic-wrapped packages tipped and spilled, bouncing across the rough floor.

Her hands were raw from crawling. The glass hurt her knees, the tiny pieces digging into her skin as she scrambled toward the door. Her breath came in short, panicked bursts as she stumbled out, half-blinded by dirt.

Outside, the world had fractured into pandemonium. Trees from the nearby farm snapped like gunshots, their trunks breaking under the strain of the tremors. The sky was full of smoke and steam, spiraling up from the quarry, white-hot clouds bulging into the sky.

More loud pops of shattering rock echoed from the quarry. She couldn't make out all the details, but even before the quake stilled, she caught sight of a crimson thread pulsing up from within the fractured stone.

Lava?

It spilled from the earth, viscous, bubbling like liquid fire. She could feel the heat as the flow swelled, glowing brighter and hotter, each surge more furious than the last. The ground hissed under its weight, crackling as the molten river met the cool afternoon, sending up small showers of embers. The noise was deafening, a deep rumble vibrating through her bones.

A lava lake was born.

The ground continued to shudder with aftershocks every few minutes.

Her eyes shot to the rows of cannabis plants behind her. The impact tossed several plants from their tables, scattering green leaves across the dirt.

She cursed under her breath, thinking fast. How in God's name could there be lava under the quarry? That earthquake must have broken the ground and released it. Was the molten river going to reach this far? Would it actually fill the quarry?

She turned, looking at the small Cessna, still upright on the makeshift runway. Dan had tethered it down, but the quake had been strong. From where she stood, it looked okay, but she worried that the quake might have damaged it. Luckily, none of the falling trees had landed on the plane.

Rocks tumbled into the growing pool of lava as the western rim of the quarry crumbled. The edges were breaking, and the pit was widening. Nadia didn't trust that the damage would stop anytime soon.

Her heart hammered. She needed to get back to the house. Her feet were unsteady beneath her, the ground still shaking in aftershocks, each tremor making her knees buckle. Stumbling and falling, she pulled herself up again. The echo of the ground splitting apart, the clamor of falling rocks, and the crackle of surging lava drowned out her thoughts.

She had to reach the truck and get to Dan. He should have returned from Sweet Home by now, but what if he hadn't? The thought twisted her stomach. She could load the plants by herself, but she needed Dan. He was the only one who could fly the Cessna. She fell again and again, scraping her hands against the hardpan. The truck was only a few feet away. The hiss of lava seemed louder. Was it creeping nearer?

How much time did they have?

Dan, Sweet Home, OR: 4:45 p.m.

Impatiently tapping his fingers on the steering wheel, Dan Clark lowered his window to catch the light breeze. Outside, the day was losing its warmth, replaced by the coolness of a fading sun. The hum of the Mercedes-Benz engine was a constant undercurrent to his wandering thoughts.

He glanced at the rearview mirror, catching his reflection. His jawline was sharp, his eyes cold and calculating, every angle of his face honed with confidence. A smirk tugged at his lips, just a flash of self-satisfaction. He liked what he saw.

Sitting in the line at the car spa, he ignored the colorful sign flashing directions. He didn't care about the muck on the car—he could've let it sit there for weeks—but Nadia was particular. She liked the luxury vehicle to stay pristine as if its polished black exterior reflected some kind of status symbol about her.

So, he waited, hands drumming restlessly, the smells of soap and chemicals heavy in the humidity. He barely registered the bustle of other customers and cars in the background. He was too lost in his head.

His thoughts turned, scheming. The greenhouses, tucked away between the tree farm and the old quarry, were his latest idea. Two weren't enough. Not by a long shot. He imagined four—maybe five—sprawling beneath the sun, rows of glass reflecting the daylight, the crops thriving secretly. That would double their output, maybe more. His fingers drummed faster at the thought.

He'd have to get Nadia on board. She'd balk at the risk, always worrying about the state police watching them. Like they were waiting to pounce and arrest them for illegal cultivation. Somehow, he'd need to convince her to see the potential, not the danger. He was sure the old rock quarry provided enough cover to hide their operation.

Monday afternoons at Merry Maple were usually a blur of errands—Sweet Home Feed for fertilizer, the market, the dry cleaners, and a series of stops to keep the farm running smoothly and keep up appearances. He knew how to play the game. He was always the charming businessman, flashing smiles, shaking hands, working his angles, schmoozing with the vendors, and flirting with the clerks.

At forty-five, Dan looked like someone who'd spent years perfecting the art of looking good without really trying. His light hair, whitening at the temples, was styled effortlessly. He walked the fine line between rugged and polished. His stride was confident. He liked to say the world was just one big game, and he was always two plays ahead.

Underneath the good looks and confident veneer, something far simpler consumed Dan: money.

More than his kids, more than his ex-wife, more than the hollow relationships he'd burned through. He'd been married to Jolene for years, but it had taken her four kids to figure out that he wasn't really cut out for fatherhood. He was a man driven by the next deal, the next opportunity. When the divorce papers landed on his desk, he barely flinched. His only concern was the alimony he'd have to cough up.

It wasn't like relationships were his strength. He disliked emotions, commitments, or anything resembling long-term bonds. He was far more comfortable with the short-term thrill of manipulation, collecting his due.

Meeting Nadia had been serendipity. A sharp mind and a love for the hustle made her the perfect associate. Together, they made a dangerous duo. Partners in crime, bound by nothing but greed and ambition.

Blowing out a breath, he decided to bring his F-250 truck tomorrow to pick up the bag of fertilizer. The car wash was a waste of his time. Once he got the expensive luxury car clean, he wouldn't drive the Mercedes-Benz anytime soon. Nadia expected him to wash the vehicle by hand but that wasn't happening. He'd use the auto wash and say nothing.

Bored in the driver's seat of the sleek black vehicle, engine idling, the drone of the car wash conveyor slipping into the background, his conniving wandered to his oldest son. Brett looked just like him at that age; he was tall and had that easy confidence that comes from youth. At seventeen, the kid was finally getting old enough to be useful if his mother and self-righteous uncle hadn't ruined the boy with their sanctimonious preaching. He wondered if the time had come to reach out. He could think of some creative ways to use a younger version of himself.

Finally, he was next in line, and his impatient tapping against the leather steering wheel grew fiercer. As he pulled up to the lifting garage door, he caught sight of the huge plastic storage barrels lining the walls. Lots of soap and wax to keep this place running.

The sun was in the west, casting an orange glow across the pavement as he glanced again into the rearview mirror, checking his reflection. Smooth and polished, just like the car he was driving. Everything felt calm, almost serene.

Without warning, the ground roared beneath him.

A gut-wrenching, deafening shudder cracked through the wash bay. The car jolted forward, the front bumper forced into the building, bending him against the seatbelt as the world around him seemed to shatter. Tires screeched as the car behind him was lifted and thrown sideways, landing on the driver's door. The ground trembled violently, a vicious shake rattling the gas station's metal skeleton.

The walls buckled, the washing station grating and some kind of powder exploded into the air. Slabs of concrete pavement fractured beneath his wheels, and water shot into the air like a geyser, spraying so violently that it smacked against the glass, soaking the interior through his open window.

The pumps tore apart with a violent hiss as lines snapped like brittle twigs, water spurting like fire hoses. The giant storage barrels burst as falling struts crashed into them, spraying torrents of soap everywhere. Sudsy liquid splashed over his windshield in frothy waves as the car wash's delicate machinery gave way to the chaos.

Frozen, Dan gripped the wheel with one hand, trying to wipe soap off his face with the other. Heart drumming in his chest, he yelped when tubs of wax sealant burst open, drenching his car in slick, sticky goo. The air blowers—powerful machines designed to dry the cars—ripped free from their mountings and crashed to the floor, leaving Dan ducking instinctively, his face bathed in a shower of wax.

The car quaked again, and with a final, sickening jolt, the turmoil stopped.

Unnerving silence lasted for a few seconds. The wash tunnel was a wreck. Collapsed beams, crushed glass, ruptured pipes, and overturned cars were all that remained. Water poured over the asphalt in rivulets, mixing with soap and wax, pooling in deep puddles.

Dan blinked, wiping the industrial soap and wax from his stinging eyes, vision blurry, fumbling with the wipers. As he swiped away the gunk, a horrifying sight snapped into focus: bodies—some still, some moving in pain—scattered across the wreckage. He didn't flinch. Dan barely heard the muffled cries.

The pungent stench of gasoline, hitting him like a slap, diverted his attention.

The scent was sharp, chemical—heavy, acrid, and nearly suffocating. It mingled with the sour smell of burnt rubber and metal, thick in his nostrils. The gas pumps had ruptured, and gasoline gushed, slicking the ground into dangerous pools.

His hand scrambled for the starter button. Thanking God for German engineering as the engine sputtered to life, he wallowed backward, the tires slipping in a mess on the ground. Twisting the steering column hard, he slammed the car into gear and attempted to force the wheels over the slippery pavement. Face white, and without a second thought, Dan drove off the lot like a drunken lorry. Somehow, he managed not to run anyone over.

He barely reached thirty yards when the earth beneath him seemed to roar again. He heard the deafening bang before he saw it—the station's pumps blew in a violent burst of orange flame. The force of the detonation rocked the street, sending pieces of the infrastructure flying, twisting metal, and consuming the horizon. The sky darkened as dense, black smoke billowed into the atmosphere, choking the light and turning the world into a nightmare.

Then came the fire.

It spread fast, covering everything in its path, flames licking high, casting a peculiar glow that painted the scene in hellish reds and oranges. After the initial blast, each additional concussion sent shockwaves through the haze, their echoes bouncing off the buildings like thunder. With the window still down, the heat was instant, even to where Dan was attempting to drive around the wrecked automobiles in his way. The car's interior was suddenly stifling. The roar of the flames mixed with the screams of terror and frantic cries from fleeing people who had nowhere to run.

Dan's grip tightened on the steering wheel, his foot heavy on the gas. He didn't look back. The wipers continued to struggle, but the road was clear enough for him to pick his way around the obstacles. Another bang rocked the afternoon behind him, but he was already driving into the chaos of the earthquake, the flaming city a horrifying backdrop to his escape.

The world was unraveling.

Chapter Three

Corvallis, OR: May 19, 4:50 p.m.

It came out of nowhere. The first jolt slammed into Corvallis, a violent shockwave that tore through the ground, rattling the earth beneath Big Bob Wilson's truck. Swearing, his foot hovered over the brake, unsure. For ten agonizing seconds, everything went silent.

"What the hell?" His voice was barely a whisper, cracked with unease.

Leaving Corvallis on Highway 99W, his speed quickly dropped to forty mph, but it was enough to carry the eighty-foot tanker truck, hauling a full load of gasoline, up the incline and cross the cement bridge over Mary's River.

Then, the rumble began, rising from deep within the earth, a harsh growl tearing through the dirt. Big Bob's teeth rattled in his skull as the shockwave spread, his body thrashing against the seatbelt, helpless.

The bridge screeched and shuddered, pulling the foundation apart with each thrust. The truck jerked violently, thrown from side to side like a child's toy in a thunderstorm, and Big Bob gasped in fear. His hands scrambled for control as the single-hulled tanker smashed against the concrete parapets, tearing them apart like wet paper. The road split wide beneath him as the bridge's infrastructure fractured.

"God help me!" Big Bob cried out, his voice swallowed by the uproar.

He yanked the door handle, desperate to escape, but the tanker bucked wildly again, the hull ripping open before he could react. Gasoline sprayed into the air in a glittering arc, a deadly mist of fuel that caught the light.

Sparks flew, caught in the wild dance of motion, and then— *BOOM*—the fumes ignited.

A blinding fireball consumed the bridge when the tanker detonated; a burst of heat sent flames to the sky. The shockwave reverberated through the overpass, finishing what the tremors had started. The supports failed, and the entire structure buckled with a final, sickening screech, taking the remains of the tanker truck and Big Bob with it into the river below.

Thousands of gallons of fiery gas poured out, the fire churning over the river's surface, the heat so intense it scorched the air. The blaze seemed to ignite the very water itself. Flames reached the banks, racing along the shore, jumping from tree to tree, a fiery serpent devouring everything in its path.

Before the shaking stopped, the current took over, dragging the inferno under the north lane of 99W. The fire was relentless, consuming everything in its reach. Between the assault from the water and the shore, the steel bridge soon failed, nothing more than twisted wreckage as it sank beneath the water's force. Dead fish, scrap, and the tiny remnants of the tanker floated through the struts, now part of the dark, polluted river.

The rest of the city fared no better.

On the west side, the ground gave way. A massive sinkhole tore open the heart of Corvallis, ripping through downtown and sending whole buildings toppling into the void. Brick facades crumbled, stucco and concrete splintering into particles. The earth sucked down cars, trees, and homes, vanishing in seconds. A thunderclap-like roar of collapsing earth took twenty city blocks in one jolt.

The river had gone wild on the east side of town as the earth ruptured. Surging into the city with unprecedented force, the river drowned hundreds of people and most of the riverfront in seconds.

Water rushed through the downtown promenade, not trickling but crashing like a tidal wave, overwhelming with the fury of a storm. The water consumed the streets. Windows burst from the pressure, doors battered down, and structures failed.

Located only a mile west of the river, the ground tossed beneath the USGS building, a low rumble swelling into a deafening roar. It grew, surging until the noise was deafening, rattling windows and shaking the walls. Papers leapt off desks, spinning wildly like leaves caught in a tornado. The overhead lights flickered violently, painting wild shadows that jumped across the room.

"It's the Cascadia Subduction Zone!" someone yelled as panic shot through the office.

Walter Simmons hit the floor hard, cradling his laptop to his chest. He only popped up again long enough to snatch his monitor and dive back underneath his desk. A soda can teetered on the edge of the desk, then toppled, splattering its contents across a floor that now felt alive, undulating beneath his rear. There were screams around him, but he stayed focused.

Huddled to protect the laptop and monitor, Walter tweaked his model a little more and watched the results on his bobbing screen. The numbers on the screen scrambled, rising and falling in frenzied swirls, until, in a burst of clarity, they lined up—perfectly.

It was happening.

Magnitude 9.4!

So, the quake that created the tsunami off of Newport was just a foreshock. This was the big show.

His heart hammered against his ribs as the realization hit him like a blow. His model—the one he had built from scratch—had predicted this. This mega-thrust earthquake. The one everyone had warned about but no one seriously expected so soon. The Cascadia Subduction Zone was rupturing.

He wondered where Paul Baxter, assistant director and second in command of the office, was at this moment. With Director Santiago on vacation last week, Walter had shared his model with Paul, trying to convince the bureaucrat of the risk. The man had dismissed his data as improbable, even mocking that the odds of a 9+ magnitude earthquake happening today were about as likely as his teenage daughter getting a new car after totaling the last one. Walter wanted to shout, "I told you so." But there was no time for that now.

The numbers flooded his screen, scrolling so fast he could barely track them. His pulse quickened as his eyes widened. His model wasn't just predicting an earthquake along Oregon's coast.

The whole fault was ready to slip. All seven hundred miles!

The ocean floor trembled beneath the cold waters off the northwest coast of the United States and stretching up to southern Canada.

The Juan de Fuca Plate, ancient and relentless, shifted, shoving toward the North American Plate, stealing feet, then yards. The boundary where they met, a jagged, hidden seam in the earth's crust, played out in a violent collision, forcing one plate to slip beneath the other in a grinding descent.

This submerged fault, the Cascadia Subduction Zone, had held the promise of a catastrophic release of energy for decades. Forecasts flashed through his mind. This subduction zone could produce up to 9.0+ magnitude earthquakes and tsunamis that could reach one hundred feet.

The zone varied in width, offshore beginning near Cape Mendocino, Northern California, passing through Oregon and Washington, and ending at Vancouver Island in British Columbia.

Walter had worked modeling USGS data for less than a year and on this side project for the last six months. A twenty-six-year-old analyst with a passion for patterns and a stubborn streak, he had gotten to this point by ignoring his colleagues' doubts and scoffing. But today, in shock, he watched everything his model had predicted unfold before him.

In a short time, he developed some interesting theories about the Cascadia Subduction Zone. Clues about recent seismic activity on what looked like random minor faults, significant seafloor displacement in odd areas, and unusual ground deformation along the Pacific Northwest coast, primarily in Oregon, piqued his curiosity.

He knew modeling the next big earthquake was a fool's errand. Hell, every one of his superiors gave him that line.

No one can predict earthquakes, Walter.

But a few months ago, just stubborn and dogmatic enough to ignore the consensus, especially when it came from anyone over forty, he started a model anyway to see how the data would play out. He spent his free time and some of his sleeping time adjusting the system and using techniques his peers would have discounted as long shots.

The program he wrote surprised him a few weeks ago by predicting an 87 percent chance of a 9.1 earthquake or greater across the Cascadia Subduction Zone within the next thirty days.

Intrigued, he honed the scope by finding and feeding the model more unconventional data and adjusted parameters to include extravagant concepts. Monitoring the output closely, he used a technique involving feedback loops in a novel approach he had refined with one of his college professors, cross-training the model to identify areas to improve and adapt in an endless cycle. Last Friday, the model produced a new prediction. There was a 97% chance of an earthquake of magnitude nine or greater off the Oregon coast in the next ninety-six hours.

He knew better than to share his theory. Although his programming and analytic skills exceeded those of his colleagues, as the newest team analyst, the team ignored him. He had been pretty sure his computer-illiterate boss, Miguel Santiago, would not be interested, but since the old guy was on vacation, it didn't matter. He only shared the prediction with Paul Baxter because he was dying to share it with someone, and the assistant director had stayed late Friday. It was a waste of time anyway. Paul barely listened before he laughed at Walter and left.

His screen flickered, showing seismic data spiking in wild, jagged lines. The colors shifted from green to yellow to red, alarming reds, each hue more urgent than the last. The rumble beneath him grew sharper, a deep, thrumming vibration that seemed to move through the walls and into his bones.

The tremors intensified. The room jerked violently. An almighty crash startled him. It came from outside, he thought, trying to huddle tighter around his laptop.

Walter's heart raced as the data played out in real time. The Cascadia fault was not just shifting—it was shattering. Off the coast, the ocean floor had buckled. The ground sank by six feet in places and shifted east by as much as one hundred feet. In some areas, the earth dropped as far as forty feet. The landscape had just folded under itself.

Panic rose in his throat, but he couldn't look away from the screen. The scale of the destruction was staggering. Hundreds of thousands of people—probably more—were dying at this very moment. If this data was correct, millions of structures were collapsing, sinking into the earth, swallowed by the shifting ground.

Walter couldn't see it, but the entire Pacific Northwest convulsed violently. Unidentified shallow faults gave way, their intense shaking adding to the destruction. Entire mountainsides collapsed, sending avalanches of rock and dirt cascading down, obliterating everything in their path. Old-growth trees toppled, roots torn from the ground, while entire stretches of land seemed to ripple and shift, sliding downward where the ground had given way. Rifts split the terrain.

Suddenly, a shrill alarm cut through the bedlam. Walter's stomach lurched as his laptop flashed **Tsunami Warning.**

His fingers froze. The monitor split into multiple panels, each one showing a different section of the coast, each one displaying the same terrifying pattern: massive walls of water were forming offshore, taller than any wave he had ever imagined. His breath caught as the waves surged higher and higher, crashing toward the shore, each panel showing the looming tsunami's advance. The data ticked forward—faster, faster, the waves growing taller by the second.

His mouth hung open as he watched.

His mind raced, trying to process it all. Just as the fear settled into his bones, his laptop beeped again, signaling an update. Walter tore his eyes away from the tsunami footage, only to freeze, horrified, at what he saw next.

The red lines tore through Northern California's Cape Mendocino triple junction and continued south. If his model was correct, the San Andreas fault was about to break. Walter stared, his pulse beating wildly, unable to tear himself away from the screen.

A full-margin rupture from north to south was underway.

Albany, OR: May 19, 4:50 p.m.

The earth jolted hard to the right, knocking Chloe and Moni to their knees. The floor folded beneath them with a sickening crack, tiles splintering like brittle paper. Desks and lockers toppled, and a deafening crash rang through the hall as the floor sheared open in a huge rip, swallowing half the school in seconds.

Moni scrambled to her feet, clutching the stroller in desperation. Terror flooded her veins as she stumbled back, eyes wide with fright, away from the gaping chasm that was already expanding. What scared her the most was that she couldn't see a bottom.

She snatched at the stroller restraints, yanking Mollie free. The startled infant was screaming now. Chloe pulled herself up and touched her forehead. Dizzy and nauseous, she looked at her red-stained fingers. Blood smeared down her face, streaking her light hair a vibrant red. Beams and drywall sheets were falling around them. With a horrific screech, the second floor on their left collapsed, raining litter.

Then came the next brutal shock. Chloe had barely found her feet before a heavy metal beam jerked free from its mooring, tipping toward them. Moni's eyes locked onto it first. Without hesitation, she lunged, shoving Chloe out of the way with all her might.

But Moni couldn't escape in time. The beam sideswiped her with bone-crushing force, sending her sprawling to the ground, the weight of the falling girder pinning her legs. Pain exploded through her body, a sharp, unrelenting fire.

The chasm widened, swallowing massive chunks of the school, each huge jerk tearing the crevice open further. Moni knew what was coming. The entire school was going to be consumed.

Moni struggled with every ounce of strength she had left, sitting up with a grimace, her body protesting the movement. She reached out, eyes blazing with a fierce, desperate need. "Take her!" she screamed, thrusting the baby toward Chloe. "Get out! Save her and take her to Oliver!"

Chloe's breath caught, heart pounding as she instinctively caught the baby, her hands trembling. "No! We can still get you out—"

Moni's grip tightened on her arm, her nails digging into Chloe's skin, drawing blood. "Get. My. Baby. Out. Of here!" She hissed through clenched teeth. "Go!"

With one last shove, Moni sent Chloe stumbling backward. Her body crumpled as she fell over, leaving her with only the raw hope that Mollie would survive.

The ground trembled, a vast abyss of razor-sharp edges disintegrating like ancient stone. Desks, chairs, and floor fragments cascaded into the darkness below, the air gritty with dust. Chloe clutched the baby tightly, her heart racing, her breath coming in sharp gasps. Every instinct screamed at her to stay, to save her friend, but the school was breaking apart around her. The beam pinned Moni, trapping her beneath its weight, and Chloe could do nothing.

"Chloe, go!" Moni shrieked over the quake's deafening roar. The remaining walls peeled, plaster raining down in bits. The ground tilted beneath them, the building shuddering as the quake tore it apart.

Chloe hesitated, her body frozen between the sight of the gaping void and the wreckage pinning her friend. Her mind raced, trying to find a way to free Moni, to do the impossible. A sharp crack split the air, the floor shifting beneath her feet. The gap opened wider. The quake swallowed Moni's cries as the ground fell away, pulling her in. One last desperate moment, then she was gone, sucked into the gorge.

The earth roared. A staircase dropped, the hole getting wider, ready to consume everything. Chloe's feet were already moving before her mind caught up, her body racing toward the exit. She muffled the baby's cries against her chest, her heart thundering as she sprinted down the hall. The building shook violently, and the walls tumbled like sandcastles in the tide.

Off balance and out of step with the quake's rhythm, only the pounding of her heart was audible as the world disintegrated around her.

***

Earthquake!

The word flared through his mind as Brett hit the ground and bounced hard repeatedly. He felt the quake roll underneath him. The earth convulsed with a low primal rumble that vibrated in his bones. Concrete splitting like glass, the sidewalk webbed, sending jagged pieces flying. A nearby house shuddered violently, its windows popping outward in a shower of sparkling crystal.

A blur of movement caught his eye. Matthias shot out the front door, trying to carry multiple heavy bags and stay on his feet. His usually neat brown hair stood straight up, and his face was pale with shock. He stumbled, tripped, and tumbled down the porch steps, a jumble of bags and limbs rolling over the ground.

"Matthias!" Brett shouted, pushing himself up. The earth heaved again, knocking him back to his knees, the ground quivering like shaking quicksand.

Their house heaved, its foundation giving way as the walls twisted and buckled. Silt darkened the air. He finally reached Matthias, locked his arm around his brother, and tugged him away from the shuddering house, knapsacks and all. The boy clung grimly to the bags, shaking like a leaf.

Brett's heart raced as the ground throbbed again, returning him to his knees. Just then, Piper stumbled out of the house, Winnie in her arms, her waist-length hair whipping around her like a wild storm. She tumbled off the porch, and Brett was there to catch her in mid-fall, pulling them both toward the safety of the open yard. Matthias sat in the grass, gasping for air, his glasses crooked on his face.

The tan house next door swayed like a fragile tree in a storm, vinyl siding shearing off in sheets. The roof lurched, sending shingles cascading to the ground, and the chimney crumbled. Suddenly, a deafening snap split the air. The front porch buckled and collapsed, sending wooden beams splintering into the sidewalk. Grime plumed into the air, an opaque gray cloud dimming the light.

Across the street, another house shivered in time with the tremors. Brett swiveled to see the windows bow outward, spraying glass across the garden. The foundation tore apart, and with a terrifying clap, the house imploded, collapsing in on itself in a cloud of shrapnel. One house after another followed, the neighborhood folding in on itself, walls caving, roofs tumbling down in a deadly rhythm.

Their own house gave a final groan as it tilted, the roof caving in on the front room. The porch pancaked. Pieces tumbled across the yard, so close Brett could feel the ground shake beneath his feet. Fissures opened the yard, and the next tremor tossed the siblings further apart.

Dismay surged through Brett. He seized Piper, hauled her to her feet, and snatched a wide-eyed Winnie from her arms. He pushed her toward the truck, urgency in every movement. Piper grabbed a few knapsacks and shouted to Matthias, forcing him to follow. They piled into the Ford 150, with Brett dropping Winnie onto the front seat, but the little girl immediately crawled to the back, nestling beneath the bags with a muffled whimper.

The engine sputtered as Brett fumbled to steady the wheel and hit the gas. The tires spun on the cracked asphalt, struggling for traction. As he barreled forward, the street around them was a blur of destruction. Houses lurched and fell, their roofs caving in, sending clouds of filth and junk into the air. Brett silently thanked Uncle Jess for sending him in the truck. There was no way his old car would've made it through this minefield of splintered ground.

He swerved around massive fissures, the truck's frame shaking with each violent jolt. The vibrations rattled through the frame as he veered left, narrowly missing another fallen tree, its roots ripped from the shaking ground.

"Where are you going?" Piper yelled from the back.

Brett's heart skipped a beat as he realized muscle memory was guiding his hands, but he didn't know where else he would go. The car lot. It was the safest place he knew. Uncle Jess would have to pass it on his way back with Mom. They could meet there.

"The car lot," he hollered back.

Piper climbed over the seat, squeezing in beside him, eyes darting to the road. Her gaze was sharp even as her hands shook. She studied the asphalt ahead, now a ragged mess of cracks, some wide enough to swallow a tire. Each bump sent the truck lurching, a constant reminder that the ground was tearing itself apart beneath them.

The scene behind him was surreal. Buildings wobbled like reeds in a storm, windows shattering, and roofs caved in with thunderous crashes. The truck jolted again, dropping them as they hit another upheaval in the road. Brett fought the wheel to keep control as the broken ground pitched back.

He wasn't sure if they'd make it.

***

Reed fought to keep his balance as the ground beneath his sneakers shifted away. Standing was impossible. He staggered, his knees buckling as he hit the ground with a violent thud. The phone ripped from his hand, spinning through the air. Watson barked wildly, frantic barks of fear and warning. He could hear all the dogs in the shelter barking madly.

Around him, the world became a blur of motion and sound—shouts from inside the shelter, the low screech of the earth shifting beneath his feet, the sharp crack of trees bending and breaking around him. The air was full of chaff and the sharp scent of earth. The shaking intensified, and he tried to get on his feet, suddenly aware of the loud creaking and a shriek of wood. His eyes shot up, the hundred-foot pines swaying ominously overhead.

Suddenly, with a deafening crack, a massive pine uprooted from the earth, soil flung into the air as the roots tore free. Dirt and wood sprayed through the air like bullets. Reed's heart caught in his throat as the giant fir leaned off-kilter and barely remained upright. The next jolt dumped the heavy trunk in his direction.

Fear surged. The ground heaved beneath him, tossing him sideways as instinct screamed through his muscles. He threw himself to the ground, yanking Watson with him, rolling across the shaking earth, rocks tearing into his skin.

A wind rushed past as the branches wider than his arm crashed to the ground, narrowly missing them. The deafening impact of the trunk landing on the shelter sent a shockwave through his body, rattling his bones.

Dirt engulfed them, choking the air. The pungent smell of pine sap and the musty scent of soil made him cough.

Reed's body tensed, his eyes squeezed shut as the ground trembled with shocks. Pine cones jerked free, flying through the air, and long, sharp needles lashed across his face and arms. Gnarled branches buried them.

The quake finally slowed and stopped.

Reed lay there, face buried in Watson's fur, the dog's body shaking beneath him, both of them gasping for breath. The low growl in Watson's chest vibrated through Reed's ribs, the sound a raw mix of fear and anger. Reed lifted his head, blinking against the dust, his chest heaving. The air still smelled rich with pine, and a kaleidoscope of green covered them. After the roar of the quake, the peace was almost deafening.

Then Reed remembered Rose and Terry.

Battleship Rock, CA: May 19, 5:05 p.m.

Miguel Santiago flipped open his notebook, his fingers itching to add another entry. He'd been waiting for years to see this place up close. Now, standing seventy feet above the ocean, on a hillside overlooking Cape Mendocino, he felt a deep satisfaction. Cape Mendocino was one of the most seismically active areas in the contiguous United States, and as a geologist, he hoped to feel one of the many light tremors that happened every day.

While he waited for the earth to move, he scanned the rugged cliffs, eyes drawn to the jagged rock formation below. Battleship Rock rose against the deep blue of the Pacific. Named by the locals because the huge rock formation bore a striking resemblance to a WW11-era battleship. The imposing stone had long been on his to-do list to visit. It was exactly as he'd imagined: dark, formidable, and as striking as the locals had claimed. The sea churned at its base, waves crashing as if the stone had suddenly set sail.

An ocean breeze washed over him, lifting the scent of salt and damp earth as it tousled his thinning gray hair. His lips curled into a smile as he scribbled the words *Battleship Rock* onto the page. The black sand beaches, the tectonic activity, the greywacke outcroppings—everything here had drawn him in, and the geologist in him was hungry to see. Now, here he was, enjoying what he considered a well-earned break from his job as Center Director at the USGS in Corvallis.

The sound of the waves, rhythmic and steady, soothed his mind. Below him, the ocean surged again against the stone, sending up sprays of mist that glistened like tiny diamonds in the afternoon sun. Miguel felt the weight of years of hard work slip away. His bucket list, filled with his favorite places, was slowly emptying. He'd never married. His work had always come first. Now, at fifty, he still had no regrets. This was his reward.

He paused, inhaling deeply, letting the briny air fill his lungs. His eyes lingered on the horizon, where he knew the three tectonic plates met just beneath the water. A rare triple junction he had studied for years. The faults were responsible for the daily activity, a reminder of the restless forces beneath the surface. Miguel couldn't help but smile, knowing he was standing on a living, breathing piece of geology.

He sighed, prepared to start back. It would take the rest of the daylight to hike to his camp near the small municipality of Capetown, but it was well worth the walk. He didn't have to be back in the office until next week.

Before he could start, a sharp ring sliced through the tranquility—sharp and insistent. He frowned, pulling out his phone. His office in Corvallis.

Before he could swipe to answer, the ground suddenly shuddered, slabs of dirt around him breaking and folding. A tremor!

He stumbled, gripping a nearby boulder, feeling the earth pulse beneath his feet. The cliffs on the left cracked, sending a cascade of rocks and dirt tumbling into the sea with a thunderous roar. Surprised, he stood back up. That was stronger than he expected from one of the daily light tremors.

Trying to convince himself that the worst must have passed, Miguel was shocked when the hillside convulsed again, a violent shudder heaving through the earth. Sand kicked up, filling the air with a choking cloud. Rocks slid down both flanks of the hill, a torrent of earth crashing toward the water. The sight was both breathtaking and terrifying. Miguel clutched the boulder tighter, knowing that if it gave way, so would he.

The ocean, calm a few minutes ago, writhed as waves surged and recoiled. He had a minute to wonder which of the plates converging beneath him had ruptured when the sea pulled back, revealing the sandy bed beneath, glistening in the harsh light. Unnerved, he watched as far out on the horizon, the water rose, a monstrous wall of blue towering ominously. He knew what was coming, but there was no time to react.

The tsunami hit with a deafening roar, a fifty-foot wall of water that smashed against the shore, tearing everything in its path. The hillside trembled violently beneath Miguel's feet as the wave surged up, pushing against the land.

He braced for the impact, the ground trembling beneath him, fully expecting to be swept away. Yards below his boulder, the wave stopped, hung for a long second, and fell back. The water retreated until it met the surface, now only thirty feet below his position.

Miguel felt a wave of relief flood through him. He was alive, spared by mere feet. He would not have had a chance if he had been standing on the beach.

Glancing back toward the ocean, Miguel found the grab handle of his knapsack and headed up the hill behind him. No telling how high the next surge would be or the one after that. He wouldn't feel safe until he was at the highest pinnacle these cliffs could offer. He didn't realize he was still clutching his phone until his fingers numbed. Tilting the screen so he could see it, he confirmed it had been his USGS office in Corvallis calling.

He wondered if they had called to warn him. But that was nonsense. Accurately pinpointing the earth's movement was impossible.

New kids in the analyst pool always thought they could predict earthquakes. When he was a young geologist, he had been the same. He was sure the answer was around every corner. But, forty years in, they had never pinpointed a single event. Predicting earthquakes was far beyond technical capabilities, no matter how hard the kids tried.

Below him, more water arrived at a terrifying speed, rising high into a liquid wall. The second tsunami rolled over the drowned shore with an unimaginable force, crashing into the cliffs with a deafening roar. The water completely submerged Battleship Rock. He climbed faster.

Chapter Four

California: May 19, 5:10 p.m.

For decades, scientists had speculated about the Big One—a massive earthquake along the Cascadia Subduction Zone that could set the San Andreas Fault roaring to life. Scientists met the idea with caution. Such a catastrophic chain reaction could rip apart the entire West Coast. No one wanted to believe it could happen in our lifetimes, not really. Too much was at stake.

But today, the ground beneath them would prove the potential wasn't just a nightmare. It was a ticking time bomb.

***

Martha Nahale had always loved the isolation of Manchester, California. Nestled in Mendocino County, five miles north of Point Arena, the tiny town hugged the rugged northern coast of California. She'd traded the bustle of city life for expansive views, a spacious home, and the quiet hum of nature that only the most remote places could offer. In her fifties now, she couldn't imagine living anywhere else.

As she stepped onto the front porch to soak in the last slivers of the afternoon sun, she smoothed down her black hair and gave her clothes a quick once-over. Paint stains on her shirt and pants were never an option. As a prominent artist, her agent never let her forget she had to present a polished image—even if she was just stepping out on her front porch for a tea break.

The warm cup in her hands, the faint scent of star jasmine from the flowers by the porch, and the distant hum of the ocean were a comforting backdrop to her solitude. But just as she sank into her favorite chair, tea in hand, the world shifted.

A terrifying, guttural rumble of tectonic plates colliding beneath the town seemed to echo from the earth's core. Houses shook violently, and the streets split into massive gaps. The porch jolted with a terrible jerk. Windows blew out, glass spilled across the porch in a deadly shimmer, just missing her. Screams filled the air as the town tore apart.

Martha's cup flew from her hands, crashing into the ground, the sharp sound drowned by the noise all around.

The next jolt sent her flying forward, throwing her through the wood railing with a sickening crack. She tumbled into the dirt, heart racing, pulse pounding in her ears. Panic spiked. Even if she could move, she didn't know which way to go. Everything was moving, shifting, breaking.

She glimpsed people spilling from their homes, faces pale and eyes wide with fear, as the tremors turned into a ferocious quake. The madness suppressed voices as houses cracked open and streets split. Tree trunks splintered, and a fissure sliced through her yard like a deep wound, stretching across streets and under the collapsing houses. She knew she had to move, but the ground shook so violently that crawling felt impossible. Each tremor tossed her around like a ragdoll.

Grasping the danger, she tried to crawl away from the ever-widening tear, but the shaking made that hopeless. The ground separated further with each jolt until the gap was three feet across. The tremors bounced her back, and before she could stop herself, she was sliding down into the earth, the cold, sandy dirt crumbling against her body as she dropped.

Desperately, she dug her feet in the sides, trying to find rocks, roots, anything to leverage herself. Only her fingers, pressed tightly into the ragged edge, remained above ground. Panicked, she tried to think, to figure out a way back up the side of the trench. She was slipping. The world was spinning, shaking, falling apart. She could barely hang on.

The shaking deepened, and she felt herself slipping. Suddenly, the earth gave a deafening crack, and the sides of the rupture slammed shut with terrifying force. There was no time to scream, no time to brace. She didn't have time to register what was happening before she died.

All that was left was an inch-long scar through the yard and Martha's fingers poking up through the dirt.

***

A few miles south, in Bodega Bay, the sun-spangled water lapped gently against the pilings, the fishermen and boaters unaware of the destruction moving closer. All at once, the soaring, cawing seagulls interrupted their graceful flight, agitation silencing them. Their wings beat frantically, their bodies twisting as they veered inland, the sky above suddenly heavy with their agitation. Below, no one noticed.

On the water, Rocky Johnston lay asleep in the berth of his Yellowfin 54 Cabin Cruiser, a crumpled sheet knotted around one leg. The other was propped on a pillow in a cast.

The boat sat securely at Spot Point Marina, his temporary home since a fall a week ago left him with a fractured ankle. Painkillers dulled his senses. With no other obligations, he gave in to the fog of drowsiness, letting the slow afternoon pass him by.

Suddenly, the ground convulsed, sending fishermen and visitors scrambling for safety. Boats bobbed hard in the harbor, their anchors struggling against the relentless tide. The shoreline cracked, fissures spider-webbing through the sand as the ocean roared in response. Waves crashed higher, drenching everything in salty foam.

Rocky groggily awoke to the violent pitching of the boat. Something wasn't right. He blinked, trying to clear the fog in his mind. The waves were unnaturally high, crashing against the pier, the boat shuddering like a storm was tossing it. But no storms were in the forecast. His head spun, and he couldn't quite grasp what was happening.

Screams echoed somewhere distant, car engine sounds revving as if racing through the confusion. After a few minutes, it felt like the boat was sinking, but that couldn't happen because they were docked. He wondered if he was dreaming.

Pushing himself upright with difficulty, Rocky balanced on his one good foot, his crutch under his arm. His frizzy brown hair stuck up on one side and flat on the other, his bright white cast contrasting against his dark skin. Tugging at his shirt, he glanced down to make sure he was still dressed properly—no need to freak out the neighbors.

Carefully, he took a step, trying to steady himself. Just as his crutch hit the deck, the bottom of the boat slammed into something hard. The shock sent him sprawling, crashing to the floor with a grunt of frustration.

Lying in a tangle of arms and legs, he cursed. "Shit, this day really sucks."

But the boat didn't stop moving. Tipping a little, the unsettling sensation grew. Alarm flared in his chest. He caught the edge of the bunk for support just as the boat slanted hard to the right. The shift was slow initially, but it moved faster as it fell until the boat leaned at an unnerving angle. It felt like he had been dropped on the floor of the bay minus the water. He knew something was wrong, but minutes later, when he pulled himself out of the cabin and onto the deck where he grabbed the railing, he couldn't believe his eyes.

The bay was empty. The water had retreated, exposing the mudflats, shimmering in the late afternoon sun. A few fish flopped helplessly in the shallows, their silver bodies flickering in the puddles. Boats of every size sat stranded on the sand—his included. No one was around. The silence pressed against him, the wind picking up with a new, unsettling force.

He turned toward the marina and froze. The buildings were flattened. The parking lot was barren of cars and people, ripped open by massive fissures that snaked through the earth. Trees were leveled, thrown like toothpicks across the ground. The boathouse at the end of the pier, where he sometimes stored some of his gear, was gone. In its place was a twisted heap of wood and metal, its contents spread like discarded toys on the wet sand.

The wind suddenly picked up, and with it, another deep sound. It came from behind him. Rocky spun toward the ocean, swearing as he caught his ankle cast on a bucket, pain flaring up his leg. The tip of the inlet to the north blocked his view of the horizon, but he didn't need to see the wave to feel it.

An enormous wave surged up and over the finger of land, burying it under a wall of water fifty feet high. The wave fell forward, refilling the bay and still a towering thirty-five feet. Rocky had no time to think, no time to react. He didn't even have a chance to scream. The wave hit with a brutal force.

In an instant, the churning maelstrom swallowed his boat, the marina, the bay—everything.

***

Tremors raced toward San Francisco, where the iconic skyline swayed like a pendulum. The ground surged, and skyscrapers twisted and fell. Streets buckled. Asphalt ripped apart. The earthquake tossed cars, sending them crashing to the ground and flinging broken parts into the air. Palo Alto, a hub of innovation, lay in ruins, with buildings crumbling to the ground.

Streetcars rattled violently, their wheels jumping the tracks, crashing into kiosks and pedestrians alike. The F-Market and Wharves Streetcar Line had just made its turn around Justin Herman Plaza, the spot where tourists and regulars often waved hello to Max Edinburgh, the transit operator for Streetcar no. 1077.

Max had driven this route thousands of times and was waving to regulars when the ground started moving. His hands squeezed the wheel, and he felt a chill steal down his back. Lifelong San Franciscan that he was, Max's gut told him this quake was something worse. He didn't have time to warn anyone.

Before he could even open his mouth, the streetcar lurched forward. It jerked and jolted, threatening to tip, rattling like a wild animal trying to escape a cage. A sick realization flashed through his mind: *It's the Big One!*

Then, with a deafening crash, the streetcar tore through the brick front of the San Francisco Railway Museum. The ground heaved beneath the impact, and the clatter of bricks and mortar falling was almost drowned out by the wave of rubble that flooded the space. Max was gone in an instant, crushed beneath the weight of the destruction.

The Financial District and the rest of the city disintegrated. Glass facades shattered into thousands of glimmering specks raining down onto the streets below. People were sliced and impaled, dropping into heaps as the ground shook. The air thickened with the stench of burning remains, choking the few who were still alive. Columns of smoke and concrete powder swirled into the sky.

Market Street transformed into a hellscape. Sirens screamed, but the bone-rattling rumble of the quake and the cries of those trapped beneath the ruins drowned their wails out. Towering buildings shuddered and collapsed. Cars flipped and slid, their wheels spinning uselessly in the chaos, while streetlights tore free from their posts, whipping through the air like deadly missiles. A bus teetered on the edge of a deep fissure, the passengers' faces pressed against the glass, their eyes wide with terror as the ground below them cracked open. The bus teetered once more before plummeting into the abyss, swallowed whole by the earth.

Fruit and pastries exploded out of toppled street vendors' carts, rolling into the streets like strange confetti in the pandemonium. Storefronts blew apart, sending windows and walls into the street. The sidewalks split open, wide gaps snaking through the slabs. Above it all, the neon signs that had buzzed with life flickered erratically, some popping into stillness, others buzzing angrily before disintegrating, their colors doused instantly. The afternoon sun struggled to break through the dust clouds, casting a sickly, surreal glow across the destruction. People lay motionless in the streets, trapped or dead.

Only the iconic Golden Gate Bridge stood steadfast, its cables trembling but unyielding against the mayhem surrounding it. Cars were skewed across the road; some smashed into the bridge itself, and others collided with one another in panicked confusion. But the bridge still stood.

The San Andreas continued to slip, the quake sending tremors along the central fault line, threatening to unleash even more destruction.

***

The ground trembled violently across California, from San Jose to Hollister, and Parkfield—the small town with its seismic reputation—was no exception. The San Andreas fault had slipped countless times in recorded history, but nothing had prepared them for this. Experts had warned that a quake of magnitude six or greater was inevitable. When the earth beneath Parkfield shifted, it unleashed a magnitude 9.

No one had ever experienced such a force in modern times. The screeching of metal, splintering wood, and shattering glass filled the air as homes buckled and businesses crumbled into heaps. Concrete fissures engulfed everything in their path. Too many people were caught in the pandemonium, unable to escape the destruction.

The fault line moved again, this time wreaking havoc across southern California. Los Angeles, San Bernardino, and Palm Springs were hit with the full, brutal force of the quake. The earth shuddered violently, sending shockwaves that tore through the cities, toppling skyscrapers and reducing them to rubble. The iconic Hollywood sign vanished under a cloud of debris, its enormous letters vanishing from view instantly. Turmoil erupted everywhere.

The sound of entire cities abruptly rearranging themselves atop thrust faults was unbearable.

Then came the final, terrifying act: the Salton Sea. The earth split with a thunderous crack, the sound carrying across the barren desert. Rifts snaked through the dry land, eating anything in their path. Water surged, thrashing against the shore before it drained away, leaving behind a barren wasteland. The once-thriving shoreline, teeming with life, was now a lifeless expanse, a haunting reminder of the sea that it had once been.

For those who survived the earthquake, the nightmare had only just begun. The air reeked with the stench of ruin, and there wasn't much left of the cities and homes. No shelter, roads were impassable, and the cries for the lost echoed through the night. Those who lived faced the harsh reality of homelessness, hunger, and the aching grief of the aftermath.

The Big One had more than lived up to its potential.

Battleship Rock, CA: May 19, 6:00 p.m.

Miguel pressed his back against a boulder, the ground still for now. The ocean churned in sickly shades of yellow, brown, and gray. Foamy, scum covered waves spewed in every direction, a smothering ring around the hilltop where he sat. Three waves had hit, but there was no telling if more were coming.

He pulled out his cell phone, hopeful for some sign of communication.

Useless.

The cell towers must be down between here and Corvallis. His mind raced, wondering how far the destruction had spread. Just as he dropped his phone, his knapsack vibrated. Puzzled, he fumbled through it, brushing past the usual gear—pens, a compass—until his hand brushed against something unfamiliar. A matte black cube-shaped device.

The emergency phone! He'd almost forgotten about it, buried beneath the clutter. He'd charged it to prepare for the trip, but it had slipped his mind entirely once he'd hit the road. This was the emergency-only satellite phone designed for disaster zones, with cell towers in strategic locations handling the service. Miguel snapped it open, his heart racing.

Quickly, he answered. "Hello?"

"Director Santiago?" The signal was faint but almost clear.

"Yes, who is this?"

"Sir, this is Walter Simmons." Walter's voice faded, and the signal shredded. Then he was back. "Sir, we've had a major earthquake here in Corvallis."

Walter Simmons! Miguel remembered him. From the analyst pool, too new to be taken seriously. The kid was a tech geek, one of the many who thought they could predict earthquakes with algorithms. Usually, Miguel didn't get involved with their endless data fiddling.

He tried to picture the man. Tall, skinny, messy brown hair, pretty nondescript overall. Miguel wasn't sure if he had ever spoken to him. Then Walter's words registered.

"Corvallis felt that quake?" He did the math quickly. Corvallis was over 350 miles away. Miguel's stomach sank. He'd thought this was a local quake. If they felt it in Corvallis, that changed everything.

"How bad?" Miguel's mind clicked through the implications.

"Sir, the whole Cascadia Subduction Zone ruptured an hour ago. The San Andreas and several other faults were activated at the same time. The entire west coast just went through a magnitude nine plus earthquake!" Walter's voice lifted, his excitement clear.

A magnitude nine? Nothing would remain standing. The whole West Coast? Miguel's head spun. He cupped the phone tighter, his thoughts racing.

What was happening at the USGS office, and why wasn't someone with more authority on the line? He needed to talk to his second in command, the assistant director.

"Let me talk to Paul Baxter."

"He's not here, sir. A few people were still in the office when it hit. We lost some. I moved them to the other side... I'm the only one here." Walter's words rushed out, disjointed. Miguel felt the cold weight of those words sink in.

"Then let me talk to Joe Wilson." Joe was the office manager. He was always there.

Walter paused. "Joe Wilson is dead, sir."

"What!" Miguel stared at the phone. "Who's in charge there?"

"No one is in charge. I'm the only one here." Walter's flat statement left Miguel speechless. The young man didn't even notice. He kept talking as fast as the words could spit out.

"Sir, I called because I needed to warn someone. I am still seeing earthquakes swarming east and south of here. The areas toward Mount Hood, Mount Jefferson, and the Sisters are going crazy! We need to warn someone!"

Miguel's teeth clenched. He couldn't make a decision without data, not when lives were at stake. Walter was panicking. He may be a kid with good instincts, but he didn't have enough experience to understand the big picture. Without seeing the data Walter was looking at, he didn't dare act on it. The kid was raw and had little experience. Earthquakes were precursors of volcanos, sure, but what were the odds that this would all play out simultaneously?

Miguel glanced downhill at the new shoreline. Another monstrous wave curled and surged around his hill. He had to move. He needed to get back to the USGS building. One mile east of here, there was a ranger station. Maybe he could cross the cliffs and get some help there.

"Stay calm, Walter. Watch the data. I'm trying to get back to you. Just hang in there. I'll be back as soon as possible."

"But. . ."

"No buts," Miguel cut him off. "Watch the data. Keep this phone close. I'm coming." He clicked the phone off and shoved it into his bag.

Standing, Miguel pulled on the knapsack and started hiking east.

Albany, OR: May 19, 8 p.m.

Chloe sat on the crooked countertop, her fingers trembling as they clamped down on the chipped ceramic. She contemplated the sleeping baby beside her. Her eyes stung, and she wiped at the tears streaking down her cheeks, only to feel more slip free. She kept seeing Moni's face in the last few seconds, scratched, bleeding, her wide, terrified eyes, determined to save her daughter.

Mollie was wrapped tightly in high school sweatshirts off a fallen display and snugged between the wall and a candy rack. The convenience store they sat in was at least a mile from the school, but she still jumped every time the earth moved. The aftershocks were nowhere as strong as the original quake, but they rattled Chloe's bones just the same. Dampness lingered in the air, pools of spilled soda mixing with something sour, curdling her stomach.

She had never seen or heard of anything like how the earth had opened up and swallowed the school. The parking lot, the street in front of the school, and the houses in the neighborhood just plummeted. As she fled, she kept looking back and saw house after house drop into the void that took Moni. Worse, she heard the screams and knew the houses weren't empty. She wondered where the edge of the sinking pit had stopped and shivered at the thought of it following her here.

The sirens had gone silent during the quake. There were bodies everywhere. Not in the store but outside. A man lay in the parking lot dressed in a Fast Trip uniform, so she assumed he would have been running this place. He must have hurried outside when the quake started.

He would have been safer in here. Most of the product was on the floor, but the neon sign that flew off the top of the building and nearly decapitated him was a lot worse. Multiple people, some limping and injured, all dirty and scared, had passed the store on foot. She imagined they were trying to get home or find their loved ones. If she didn't have Mollie to worry about, she might have walked home, too. It felt like she had stepped into a nightmare, and there was no waking up.

Not one vehicle had driven by. She supposed it shouldn't have been a surprise. Bad fractures marred the roads she walked. Water pipes gushed, and electrical conduits snapped and sparking. And the wrecks. Automobiles of all types, from semi-trucks to mini-coopers, had demolished each other, the twisted metal everywhere she looked. It was a war zone. The carnage choked her, and she tried to look anywhere else. People darted past her, no one stopping, so she kept going, too.

The convenience store next to Kinder Park was a lucky break even with its busted windows and doors. Once she forced herself around the manager's body, she found a place to sit for a few minutes and tried to calm down. She had salvaged a bottle and some baby formula from the mess on the floor. She had been afraid Mollie wouldn't eat, but hunger overcame fussiness. The baby finished the bottle and promptly fell asleep.

Now, she was trying to decide what to do. No first responders or rescue units were out anywhere along the road she walked to get here. A few people had sat on the curbs, dazed and desperate, barely noticing her walk by. Screams followed her, the echoing sound terrifying in the dim light.

Buildings with walls completely gone revealed twisted metal and exposed wires, furniture, and goods thrown into the street. Fires lit up the evening sky. She couldn't tell what was burning or where, but it wasn't far, and it seemed bad.

Her house was miles southwest. Her car was swallowed up with the school, and she didn't have her purse or even a jacket. Despite the quake and the fires, it was growing cooler outside. She thought about walking in that direction, but if she got there and it was all destroyed, what would she do then?

Should she pass Mollie to the authorities? But where would she find them? Maybe a hospital or a police station. She looked at the tiny girl and imagined how easy it would be for her to get misplaced in this mess. She thought about Oliver and what he already lost today. He needed to know about Moni. Sighing, she knew she really didn't have a choice.

Moni's house in Lebanon was about twenty miles from here. Chloe was in pretty good shape and thought she could hike that in a few days. Then, after she returned Mollie to Oliver, she could figure out what to do from there.

Using her phone as a flashlight, she sorted through the stuff on the floor, picking out what they'd need. She found an old orange knapsack in the back; maybe it belonged to the guy outside. She emptied it quickly, dumping clothes and equipment onto the floor and refilling it with baby supplies—formula, diapers, wipes—and food for herself. She needed to be smart about the weight. With Mollie to carry, she couldn't afford anything extra.

It was full dark when she heard low voices outside. They were standing over the manager's body, talking. Hesitating only a minute, she could hear the rough note in the voice speaking and decided in a second to run. She had no intention of trusting anyone in this chaos.

She pulled on the knapsack and picked up the sleeping baby, scurrying through to the rear of the store. The back wall had fallen into the parking lot. She carefully picked her way over the fragmented blocks and rubble, not wanting to make a sound. In the dark, she cut through the trees behind the store. Kinder Park was big enough that she could find a place to hide.

Blending in the darkness, she kept going. The air was cool against her skin, the scent of the trees behind the store mingling with the smoke in the distance. She didn't want

Mollie to wake up and give their position away. Maybe she was overreacting, and the people would have been fine. But with Mollie to care for, she didn't dare take any chances. If something happened to her, Mollie would never get home.

She was grateful she had worn jeans to work that day. The jacket she'd found smelled faintly sour, but it was warm, and she bundled herself and Mollie tightly in it. It was chilly outside but not cold. Thankfully, no rain had fallen all week. She planned to pick her way through the trees until she felt they had found someplace safe, maybe a large group banded together or something, and then they'd spend the night with them.

Tomorrow, they'd head east toward US 20 and start for Lebanon.

***

Piper, Matthias, and Winnie had fallen asleep. The long minutes had dragged on as the siblings waited. He hoped they stayed that way for a while. With no answers to their questions, Brett was glad for the reprieve.

Shifting his position in the truck's front seat, tired eyes scanned the area around him all night. He stayed low behind the wheel, parked near the street at Tate's Used Cars. He'd tried to blend in with the other vehicles on the lot, but most lay tossed and damaged, many on their sides. Some vehicles had slipped halfway into the gaps splitting the cement. He kept his distance, making sure their truck wasn't too close to the deep rifts.

Brett twisted the steering wheel, angling the truck so it looked like the quake had tossed it around, a small detail that might help them blend in with the wrecks. The grime on the windshield made the truck appear abandoned, a dull, gritty gray overall. Low in the seat, Brett kept his fingers tight on the wheel, lifting his head slightly every time a survivor trudged past. It was never his mother or his Uncle Jess.

Dozens of people walked by. He didn't know who to trust, and no one looked official. The many screams and cries echoing through the evening rose and fell as it grew darker. Brett's throat tightened as he tried to ignore the sounds, trying not to feel the weight of their desperation pressing on him. He didn't dare leave the kids but felt bad for not helping. He knew what Uncle Jess would say, though. Stay with Piper, Matthias, and Winnie. No matter what.

He wished his mom and Uncle Jess would drive up, but that something had happened to them was eating at his subconscious. He watched the street with wet eyes. Uncle Jess would have to pass this way with his mom. He intended to stand watch because giving up seemed like a betrayal.

Piper had fallen asleep on the seat behind him, and Matthias and Winnie tumbled together in the back on top of the go-bags, Matthias snoring softly. Every time the earth moved, they stirred, restless and still afraid.

Brett's eyes scanned the road east, the twilight stretching shadows across cracked asphalt and toppled street signs. He knew it had been too long. Uncle Jess and his mom should have returned this way hours ago. If something had happened to them, Sweet Home would be his only option.

A lump formed in his throat at the thought. His father, Nadia, the Christmas Tree Farm—it was all twisted up in a mess of lies and half-truths. A farm that wasn't a farm, a business that hid a secret Brett had stumbled upon last year, one he wished he could unsee.

Last year, he discovered Dan Clark and his partner Nadia were running an illegal grow operation behind the trees on their property. Backed up to forty acres of Douglas and Noble firs sat a derelict, mile-wide quarry. The pair farmed two big greenhouses full of plants in a clearing a short way off the rim of the old pit. He had asked Uncle Jess about what he had stumbled over, and reluctantly, the big man told him the story.

"I wish you hadn't seen that, Brett," Jess had said. "But you can't put the genie back in the bottle. I'll tell you what I know, but this subject is painful for your mom. She hoped you all would be grown before the truth got out."

"I wasn't spying," Brett looked indignant. "I saw Dad go out that way, and I followed to see if he needed help with the trees or something. Back by the quarry, they have a runway and a cargo plane sitting on it! I didn't even know Dad could fly, but he took off while I watched from the trees."

"That old pit has been there for more years than I can remember. It was abandoned in the 80s and has sat there, deserted, ever since. Then, that rich Russian Ivan Petrova, Nadia's late husband, purchased the quarry and the land all the way up to US 20. He was a nice guy, that Ivan. He had grand dreams for the quarry and the trees. You know, he opened the first Christmas Tree Farm in Sweet Home. He said he was going to make it the Christmas capital of Oregon. He had plans for the quarry, too. But before he could get started, he had a heart attack, leaving everything to Nadia."

Jess had shaken his head. He didn't say it to Brett, but Nadia was no Christmas enthusiast. Ivan's love for the holiday meant nothing to her. Where Ivan had been a friendly, jolly man with a penchant for yuletide joy, Nadia was a beauty with a more self-serving nature.

Christmas trees?

She couldn't care less. Wealth was her only true love.

"So, months after Ivan passed, she met Dan in a bar and hired him to run the tree farm. You know your dad. He's an entrepreneur, and he saw an opportunity for quick profits. Although he ran the farm, his ambitions far outgrew the trees." He chuckled grimly at the pun. "Beneath the phony front of seasonal greenery, he turned the job into a cover for a much more lucrative operation—a hidden marijuana farm between the forest and quarry."

"But… the Christmas trees? They sell them every Christmas." Brett's confusion wrinkled his forehead.

"You're right. It's a great cover. The trees grow, but more by accident than design. Meanwhile, in the back, far away from prying official eyes, the true crops flourish. I don't know how much they've made, but it has to be a lot if your dad is still there. I wouldn't be surprised if they had collected millions of dollars over the last five years." He placed a hand on Brett's shoulder.

"These small towns along US 20 are all interconnected, and everybody knows everybody. Your mom doesn't want this to get out and taint your reputation or your brother and sisters' reputations. So, I've gone along with her and kept quiet. I need you to do the same. We keep the custody visits short. That's why you kids never spend the night. Now that you know, keep an eye out on the other kids while you're out there."

Brett wasn't finished. "How long has mom known about the weed farm?"

Uncle Jess sighed. "Jolene figured it out the first year. Things had been bad between them for a while, and it was the final straw for her. She took you kids, came to Albany, and started divorce proceedings. A few weeks later, your dad moved into Nadia's house at Merry Maple. From what I heard, they hired some undocumented workers to turn the flat field around the quarry into a runway. Your dad took some flying lessons and bought a used Cessna with Nadia's money. They've been flying their product out without touching the highway ever since."

"So, my dad is a crook." Brett's voice was bitter. He hadn't always liked his dad, but... a criminal? He thought about his few friends, and then a girl's face crossed his mind. Would it make a difference to his peers?

"The law says you can home grow up to four marijuana plants. Nadia and your dad... well, they call that splitting hairs. Your dad never did mind breaking the law, and he doesn't hesitate to bend or snap rules if it means putting cash in his pockets. He and Nadia are operating in the shadows, thriving off what the rest of us would call illegal, though they see it as 'simply a smart move.'"

That conversation had changed everything. He kept his uncle's words to himself, but he never looked at his father in the same light again. In the last year, he visited Merry Maple Christmas Tree Farms less and less. His dad and Nadia seemed not to notice, or maybe they just didn't care

Despair choked his breathing. If something had happened to his mom and Uncle Jess, he couldn't imagine all they would have left was his dad. It was too big to think about. Maybe Jess had trouble with the Wrangler, and they were walking. He clung to that hope, watching the road.

It sure was a mess. Slabs of streets jutted at odd angles, some split wide enough to reveal the earth below, dark and raw. Pipes must have ruptured because water ran like a small creek on one side. The other side was slick with mud. No streetlights. He couldn't see a light anywhere. People had abandoned cars, leaving them skewed or resting on the curb. Doors were left open. He stewed over how hard it would be to navigate through the wreckage when the time came.

Sweet Home was like forty miles from here. He wondered what his dad would say if they had to head there. He doubted they'd be welcomed with open arms, though Nadia seemed fond of Winnie. She always fussed over the little girl, and they played dress up with Nadia's gowns, furs, and jewels. Winnie loved the bright colors and soft fabrics.

It never occurred to him that the quake could have extended as far as Sweet Home. He pulled his jacket over Piper and returned to watching for his mom and Uncle Jess.

He prayed they'd come by soon.

Chapter Five

Reed, Albany, OR: May 20, 6 a.m.

Dawn broke in a harsh wash of orange light, slicing through the haze of filth that still hung gritty in the air. Reed Walker stood on the corner of the shelter's property, his eyes scanning the damage that stretched out before him. Beyond the building, even the land bore the scars of yesterday's jolts.

Everywhere, turned-over trees concealed the ground. A small pond that shimmered under the sun now sat murky and stagnant, churned to a muddy brown by the tremors. Scattered remnants of the landscape—damaged electric poles and signs, splintered branches, and a few bedraggled bushes—slumped against the bleakness.

The shelter itself was a disaster. The massive pine tree that had fallen during the quake lay across the roof, its heavy branches sprawled out like misaligned arms, needles scattered across the wreck of the building. He knew it would take heavy equipment he didn't have to move that trunk.

Reed's heart tripped as he stood there, staring at the ruins. Rose and Terry... He had tried for hours to reach them, digging through the ruins, calling out, hoping for a sound—anything. But there had been nothing. He tried his best to find a route under the pancaked roof, but in the end, neither he nor Watson made it more than a few feet.

The scent of damp earth and pine hung heavily, mingling with the faint, metallic trace of twisted metal. A few animals could be heard from the back, their whimpers a stark reminder that he would need to do something about the surviving dogs. The empty cages he had stacked late yesterday lay strewn about the yard, some crushed under the weight of fallen branches, while others gaped open, their mangled remains scattered.

There was no sign of his car. Buried under a mass of green branches from the pine, it would take a bulldozer to recover his SUV. The pickup truck belonging to the Marple's had also been crushed though a rear tire poked up through the branches. Too bad it was no longer attached to the truck.

He wasn't too sure how his Bronco would have held up on the highway in front of the shelter anyway. Raggedy asphalt created makeshift speed bumps every few yards. He walked out to examine the deep fissures cutting across the lanes. Some of them were a foot wide. You could lose a wheel running over a hole like this.

Abandoned cars littered the highway, their twisted and windowless metal frames glinting in the early light. Reed had checked every one, but the same grim reality greeted him: no survivors. Some were empty, their occupants long gone. The few trucks that passed through last night had driven faster than seemed safe, swerving dangerously around the hulks in the road, unwilling to stop for anyone.

On the Marple's property, the shed built off the side of the main building stood in disarray, its walls leaning at precarious angles and the roof partially caved in. Reed and Watson had spent the rest of the night on the floor, keeping each other warm against the last standing wall, the only stable structure on the property. Multiple tremors kept him awake, and thoughts of Rose and Terry didn't help. Now, with the sun up, Reed knew he had to decide what to do next.

His phone had no signal, and Albany was likely a mess. He wondered if his apartment building, a five-story brick building on the south side of the city, still stood. It would be a long walk back, but the passing drivers had been going too fast this morning for him to run to the highway and flag down. Some drove on the shoulder when the asphalt grew into hills, blocking them and even driving in the ditch when they had no other choice.

He glanced down at Watson, the big golden lab sitting beside him, his amber eyes watching Reed patiently.

"Well, fella, I think we'll have to walk back to Albany. Maybe we'll find a car on the way." He patted the Labrador's silky head. Watson woofed anxiously. "I know, it's a mess. But we can't help here. It's too late for Rose and Terry. Let's head to town and see what the situation is. First, though, let's take care of the other dogs."

They circled the tree, and the shelter remains, stepping over branches and litter. Only a handful of the outdoor pens were occupied. Between the cages and the dog run, he counted twelve dogs. Charlie, the black and white Borgi mix, looked at them with wide, anxious eyes, trembling. Two of the larger dogs—Bella and Stella—barked excitedly, tails wagging furiously. They were hungry, but Bella and Stella always scarfed their food down first when Reed fed them. He rubbed the Alaskan Shepherd's head through the cage wires.

"Hang on, Bella, breakfast is coming."

Reed wrestled a large bag of dried food out from beneath a collapsed wall. Dirt clung to the bag as he ripped it open, the crisp scent of dry kibble cutting through the air. He filled bowls, moving quickly.

The latches on the pens were stuck, wedged shut by the quake, but Reed pried them open one by one. The dogs surged forward, tumbling out of their cages, paws skidding on gravel. Their barks filled the air with confusion and excitement. Stella nearly knocked him over, trying to lick his face before she dived into her bowl. He fed and watered everyone, including Watson.

After the dogs emptied their bowls, he tried to decide what to do with them. Rose and Terry loved these animals. He couldn't just leave them caged. In the last year, he had become friendly with most of them. They were good dogs. If he put them back in the pens, they'd starve. He looked at Bella's striking wolf-like face as she rubbed herself against his arm. Though loyal, friendly, and strong, she had been returned twice to the Animal Rescue. Reed knew her aversion to cats kept her from finding a forever home.

At least if they were free, they'd have a chance. He watched as the glossy dark Weimador Terry had named Shadow melted into the brush along the perimeter. Even if he wanted to re-cage her, he wasn't sure he could find her, let alone catch her with those long legs. He knew from experience that dog could run.

Mind made up, Reed pulled out more bags of food, ripped them open, and spilled the contents across the yard. It wasn't much, but it would have to do for now. He filled the water bowls, the weak flow of water sputtering. The water mains must have busted, and it wouldn't take long before even this trickle stopped. Coco, a large male Cockapoo, finished lapping up the liquid to follow Reed around the yard, nudging his pockets to see if he had any treats stashed away. Coco loved treats, and he knew Reed usually carried some.

He found a few old jugs from the shed and filled them as well. Watson's tail wagged as he licked at the water, his large, golden body moving in and out of Reed's way as the dogs ran around him. Duke, easily the most energetic of the strays, played with Watson. The puggle was all wrinkles and floppy ears. If he could get past digging up every yard he found himself in, someone might keep him. The other dogs darted under Reed's feet, their movements frantic with suppressed energy.

Reed's stomach rumbled, but the kitchen was a wreck, flattened by the weight of the collapsed roof. He'd have to wait. With luck, he'd find something along the road.

Finally, by midmorning, he was ready to go. His emergency bag was buried in the trunk of the flattened Bronco. As much as he'd like to have that bag, the back of the automobile was under the stout base of the tree. No amount of digging or cutting of branches was getting him near the SUV's rear compartment.

He cursed under his breath as he surveyed what he had to work with, but there was little time to waste. Trash scattered the yard, but he found a few useful items—a battered cup, wipes, and some tools. He took them all, wrapping them in an old, torn blanket he found buried under a pile of mangled boards.

He monitored the road all morning. Not a single car had passed in the last hour. Reed had always preached the mantra of "Prepare to be self-sufficient" during earthquake drills, but standing there now, feeling the weight of the lull, he couldn't help but wonder if this was far worse than anyone had imagined. Rescue teams should have been pouring in by now. That they hadn't sent a chill through him, a knot tightening in his gut. He wondered if Albany was the only city hit.

The water from the hose was down to dripping, and Reed drank as much as he could stomach. He filled another bowl for Watson, the dog lapping it up eagerly. They could carry water, but it would run out soon. If the road didn't yield something better, they'd be thirsty long before they reached Albany.

Looking around, he guessed they were ready to go. The dogs were scattered around the yard, most of them roaming the backyard. He hoped they'd be okay.

"Watson!" he whistled for his friend. Watson came around the corner of the fallen building, tail wagging. Charlie was on his heels.

Reed smiled despite himself. Charlie had been at the shelter longer than any of the other dogs. He was a quirky little thing—part Border Collie, part Corgi—with big, rabbit-like ears and black button eyes that gleamed with mischief. His coat was mostly white, except for the black markings resembling ink splatters.

Rose had dressed him in a red collar with a black and white scarf threaded through. It made him look like a little adventurer ready to head out into the wild. One of the smaller dogs at the shelter, he was only about fifteen inches tall and twenty pounds but all heart.

He crouched and ruffled Charlie's fur, his fingers brushing over the soft pink centers of the dog's ears.

"You keep an eye on everyone, okay, Charlie?" he said to the dog. The dog barked and wiggled in place as if he understood.

Reed stood and motioned for Watson to follow. He hefted the makeshift pack onto his back and started walking toward the road, his sneakers crunching on gravel. Six steps in, he realized Charlie was trailing behind them, his little legs keeping up just fine.

Reed stopped and turned. The wind kicked up a bit of sand around them, swirling the dry earth in little whirlwinds. He set the pack down and knelt.

"You need to stay here, Charlie," Reed ordered. "You can't come with us." Charlie sat and tilted his head, his expression inquisitive.

"No, Charlie, stay here." Reed made his tone as firm as he could. Now, Watson was sitting with his head cocked as if wondering what the fuss was.

"Look, both of you. Charlie has to stay here. It's going to be a long and dangerous journey. I don't know what we are going to find. Charlie could get hurt. He is better off here…" Reed let the words die off. It was very clear that both dogs were humoring him, letting him talk. Short of penning the little dog back up, he wasn't sure what else he could do.

He studied the dog's face, remembering Terry's complaints about Charlie's stubbornness. Maybe that was why he'd never found a home.

"Fine. I'm not putting you in a pen. If you want to follow us, that is on you. If you run off, I'm not looking for you," Reed warned the pooch. He stood back up and took up the pack. Using a rope, he tied it across his back. "Let's go. I hope you aren't sorry."

Charlie didn't look sorry. He just stood up, trotting closely behind Watson. They reached US 20, and Reed stopped, taking a long look east and then west. Smoke rose, staining the western horizon. Must be some pretty bad fires to cause that much smoke. He doubted anything but a 4x4 could get over the uneven peaks of pavement, but he couldn't find a working vehicle of any type among the wrecks in front of the Animal Shelter.

The few buildings he could see in the distance were also wrecked. He didn't see any figures moving around. He could stop by and see if there was anyone needing help.

The road looked bad in both directions. It was only a few hours' walk back to Albany and the dispatch station. Unless they got delayed, they should be there by mid-afternoon. The three of them started walking west.

Chloe, Albany, OR: May 20, 7 a.m.

Chloe hiked through the streets, trying not to look at the damage. Her sneakers crunched over glass and fragments of bricks, the sound loud over the ragged noises of the city. The unmistakable smell of burning wood and plastics drifted from the wreckage, making her throat scratchy and sore.

She shifted the weight of the knapsack on her back, the baby nestled in the borrowed jacket against her chest, and kept putting one foot in front of the other. Moni's face dominated her thoughts. She couldn't outrun the memory, but her feet kept trying

She moved onto 9th Avenue, where the street split into the Santiam Highway stretch of US 20. Cracked asphalt twisted like a serpent down the street. The few buildings still standing leaned unsteadily; the rest were slabs jutted through with heavy beams spilled onto the road. Chloe weaved around the mess, careful not to cut her skin on the spikey, twisted metal, and jagged lumps. The air here smelled bitter—concrete powder mixed with the pungent odor of gas. There was something else, too, something she refused to acknowledge. The scent of death lingered, faint but unmistakable.

Every few blocks, the hiss of escaping gas filled the air, followed by sudden bursts of flame—quick, hungry outbursts that leaped from the cracked pavement like an angry phoenix. She flinched at the fire's intensity. Escaping gases were feeding the inferno. Shadows stretched long and twisted over the ruins, painting the world in hues of hell.

In the distance, voices floated on the wind—calls of people searching, digging, maybe trying to help each other. Then came the screams, shrill and desperate, echoing through the stillness. Chloe gritted her teeth, ignoring the hollow ache in her chest. The discovery of something terrible was obvious.

No sirens cut through the morning, though. She had yet to see a real rescue team. The group she'd left behind in the park that morning had been small—maybe thirty people. No one had followed her. No one had even tried to stop her when she left. Out here, there were even fewer people in the earthquake's wake.

Including the people outside the convenience store last night, she had only seen a few dozen or so people in the streets, the ones this morning hurrying in some other direction. Traffic had been light when the earthquake hit late on a Monday afternoon. She assumed most folks had been home. An hour later, she would have been home, too. Moni and Mollie would have been with Ollie. Just one hour. Her heart hurt at the thought.

Now she was here, passing one destroyed business after another. Most had crumpled vehicles in their lots, and too often, she couldn't unsee the bodies as she passed. She had heard the warnings like everyone else— Albany's old, unreinforced buildings were a death trap. The warnings were now the truth, splattered all around her.

She wondered how much of the city had been swallowed by the huge fissure that took the school. The fatalities and missing were going to be bad. It suddenly occurred to her that if one sinkhole had opened up in the town, there could have been more. She shuddered at the thought.

Dismally, she hoped it was better than it looked, but something about the hush told her this disaster was far worse than it looked here. She forced herself to focus on Mollie.

SE Waverly Drive was next. Waverly was less than a mile from the US 5 Interchange, and then she'd be out of the city. She needed to get out of Albany before the deafening quiet turned into something worse. She tightened her grip on the baby, tucking her closer to her chest. Then, without another glance behind her, she picked up her pace.

Brett, Albany, OR: May 20, 7 a.m.

Tate's Used Cars sat just past the corner of 8th Avenue and SE Waverly Drive on the south side. Brett waited until Piper sat up. Her long hair was kinked up. She looked tired. He knew she had been crying, but he said nothing. Matthias and Winnie still slept in the back.

"Did you sleep at all?" she asked him.

"Not really," he said. His voice was weary. "I was watching for Mom and Uncle Jess."

Her brown eyes welled up, but she didn't let the tears spill. "Did they come back?" She knew Mom and Jess would have returned to the car lot if they could have.

He shook his head wordlessly and glanced back at his two sleeping siblings.

"What are we going to do?" she whispered.

He sighed. He had been up all night wondering the same thing. "The roads are terrible. I don't know how far we can get on them. Uncle Jess's dealership was flattened, and the only people who showed up here were… looters, I think. I parked us against these other two trucks, so it looked like we were stuck together, at least in the dark. Anyway, those guys left us alone. I was hoping the police, first responders, or somebody would come by, but I haven't seen anyone who looks like help. Even the radio is just static. No emergency messages or anything. I don't think we can stay here."

The cocoon of the truck's cab had kept out most of the smoke overnight, giving Brett a false sense of security, but he knew it wouldn't last.

"Do you think… they're not coming back?" Piper could barely get the words out.

He knew what Piper was asking. "If Mom and Uncle Jess were coming, they could have walked back by now," he told her, hating the words. He watched the tears slip down her face, and he choked, refusing to let his tears fall.

"I'm scared," Piper said, her voice barely audible.

Brett took a deep breath, forcing himself to sit up straighter, trying to appear stronger. "Don't be afraid. I'll take care of you. I promise."

Her brown eyes searched his face, hesitant, but she didn't say anything.

"I don't know what's going on either," he continued, running a hand through his short hair. "I don't know why no one's come by to help, but the people I've seen look... unreliable. There's a fire up ahead," he pointed north, at the black smoke billowing in the distance. "More than one, maybe. We're going to have to try to get to Sweet Home."

"Go to Dad?" Piper looked doubtful.

"If I were alone, I'd look for Mom and Uncle Jess. But they'd expect us to get the kids somewhere safe. Sweet Home has to be in better shape than Albany. We have to try."

Piper's brow creased, reservation clear on her face. "I don't know how much help Dad will be, but okay. Are we going to drive in this truck?"

"It's our best bet, but I don't know how far we'll get. This is a Super Duty-150 with 4x4. Uncle Jess keeps it in good shape. Maybe we can make it further than I think."

Brett started the truck as she leaned back to wake Matthias and Winnie. He looked at the gas gauge, relieved to see it was nearly full—thank God for that. He thought the fire to the north had to be a gas station. Steering the truck forward, he tried to prepare himself.

Water from burst mains shot up into the morning, geysers twisting and twirling as they fell back to earth. The road's left side was now a river swirling with scraps and leaves. Haze hung in the sky in almost every direction. It had worsened overnight, along with a weird orange glow coloring the fog, so he knew fires were still burning all over. He hoped they wouldn't have to deal with them.

Brett rolled over the curb and onto the road. The truck lurched as the tires struck a crooked fissure in the asphalt, sending jolts through the frame. He tried to stay out of the water. The dry side of the road was a patchwork of deep cracks and upheavals as if the earth had rolled up in angry waves. Potholes split the ground, some filled with murky water that reflected the morning sky, while others were choked with muck and debris.

He'd take SE Waverly Drive south to US 20 and follow the highway to Sweet Home. It usually took less than an hour, but he had a feeling it would be much longer today.

As Brett steered, a trail of dried mud sprayed from the tires in clumps. They crept along slower than he'd like, but there was no other choice. The road was a minefield. The black rubber struggled for traction. Waverly was barely navigable; the pavement buckled and twisted, forcing the truck to weave like a drunkard through the obstacles. A crumpled stop sign hung from its post at an odd angle.

Deep fissures stretched open, some wide enough to swallow a car, forcing Brett to make fast decisions. He was caught between obstacles and gaps in the road. He ran out of usable road not even a block away from the dealership. He climbed the curb to the sidewalk, the truck rocking in protest.

Uneven patches where grass had given way to chunks of cement and gravel marred the lawns. Broken saplings looked like bare sticks. Fences and houses splintered. The only sound was the engine noise, which somehow worried Brett even more.

"Where are we going?" Matthias asked, yawning.

"Sweet Home. We're going to see Dad," Piper told him.

"What about Momma?" Winnie asked. "Where is she? Did she see what happened to our house?"

"Mom and Uncle Jess…" Piper hesitated, but shock covered Matthias's face as understood what she was trying to say.

"We need to go find them!" he exclaimed.

"No," Brett tried to sound confident like Uncle Jess. "We're going to Sweet Home. Matthias, you know what Uncle Jess would say."

"Get to safety first. You can't help anyone else if you're hurt." Matthias repeated his uncle's words, drilled into all of them. Of the entire family, Matthias was most like his uncle. He scowled but let the argument lapse.

"Maybe you can pull some of those granola bars and water out of the go-bags," Piper tried to distract him.

"I don't want yucky granola bars. I want cereal," Winnie said. "Let's go back to the house."

"The house fell down," Matthias reminded her. They squabbled for a few seconds over the bags, but finally, she accepted a bottle of water. The granola bar lay on the seat between them.

"You should have packed cereal," was her last comment on the subject, but he ignored her and took a big bite out of his bar.

Around a sinkhole that had destroyed a huge section of Waverly, they pulled back out onto the two-lane road only to have to perform the same maneuver repeatedly on both sides. It had already been an hour, and they hadn't even reached US 20 yet.

Brett was sweating from fear and nerves. There wasn't a single house still standing. No one was digging in the ruins. He caught sight of people crossing through the backyards, but they ignored him. Brett didn't know if that was good or bad. He'd love to have an adult step in and take over, but he didn't trust anyone. His Uncle Jess had warned him not to rely on other people. He needed to take care of himself and his siblings.

Consumed with worry and awed by the desolation, they finally reached US 20 and turned onto the main stretch. The light poles were down, and most signs had fallen. The sign that read "Santiam Hwy/US20" was on the ground, and he spent a few precious seconds trying to read it upside down, hoping for reassurance he was where he thought he wanted to be. His focus wavered, drawn to the sign.

Suddenly, a flash of movement caught his eye. A woman walking east on the road, several feet in front of the truck, saw them just as they saw her. She stumbled, trying to scramble out of his path. Her clothes were dusty, her jacket way too big for her, her hair wild, and her eyes wide with fear as she darted toward the shoulder, trying to get out of his path.

Brett and Piper caught sight of the bundle clutched to her chest as her jacket flapped open.

"She has a baby!" gasped Piper, pointing.

Brett slammed on the brake, sliding on the litter. Everyone screamed, and he clutched the steering wheel, terrified he would run them both over.

Nobody moved for a long, stretched-out moment, and then, to the left, he saw her. A lady older than himself, maybe in her thirties, dropped to a seat on the remains of a bent streetlight pole. The white blocks from a concrete building spilled out into a small parking lot behind her. Some kind of neighborhood market, he recalled, his brain muddled by the scare. A good portion of the building was lying across two cars parked in front, the entrance demolished.

The lady's arms wrapped around her body, and she was talking into her jacket. He guessed she was soothing the baby. He tried to calm himself down before he approached her. Her face was dirty and scratched. She had dried blood where her blond hair started, the messy strands falling just below her shoulders.

He jumped from the truck and approached her, trying to appear non-threatening. Carefully, he avoided razor-sharp edges of deformed slabs and the sprawled electric wires, though it was doubtful the black cables were alive.

"Are you okay?" he asked from ten feet away.

She glanced up and frowned at him. "You almost ran me over. How old are you? Do you have a driver's license?"

Brett felt a flush of embarrassment. "Yes, sorry. With all of this," sheepishly, he waved a hand at the wreckage surrounding them, "I didn't see you. Is the baby okay?"

She looked at him tersely, but years of dealing with teenagers allowed her to sum him up quickly. Her eyes softened just a touch. She had a natural ease with kids—especially teens—her voice calm but firm, her presence steady. She knew how to listen and understand the unsaid, a rare skill that earned their respect. He was an average kid. He didn't mean any harm, and if he was as freaked out as she was, it was no wonder he hadn't seen her.

"She's fine." She kept her answer short. Mollie made a few quick peeps but was already settling back to sleep.

Brett remembered Uncle Jess's warnings about strangers, but his mother had always impressed him with her kindness. He didn't see how he could just drive off and leave this woman and baby.

Before he could say anything else, Piper hopped out of the truck. "Hi, I'm Piper. This is my brother Brett."

The young girl had pulled back her long hair into a ponytail and dusted off her clothes as best she could. Chloe smiled at her. She had students like this every year. Young girls on the edge of adulthood, trying to act like women. It was second nature to put them at ease.

"Hi, Piper and Brett. I'm Chloe. No harm done. We are both okay. I'll just stay closer to the sidewalk while I walk. A good lesson for me."

"Where are you going?" Piper asked, already warming up to her. "You should ride with us."

"Piper," Brett hissed at her. His sister was just like their mother. Always helping someone. Not that Brett hadn't had the same thought, but he wanted to ease into the conversation and see what he could learn. Not just blurt it out like that.

Chloe shook her head. "It's going to be dangerous out here. You guys can't just ask anyone to join you. You're going to have to be smart."

Surprised, Brett looked at her with gratitude. She was right, but convincing his brother and sisters was another story. Piper was frowning already.

"You have a baby," she pointed out. "You aren't going to hurt us."

"No, I'm not," Chloe agreed. "But others will. You've got to be careful." She turned to Brett, her voice softer. "Your instincts are good. Keep trusting them."

Matthias and Winnie clambered out of the truck and came over. Before Brett could say anything, they walked right across the spaghetti mess of wire on the ground. Luckily, nothing happened.

"First lesson," Brett said firmly, grabbing their shoulders and turning them around. "These cables might have electricity in them. If you step on them, you could get electrocuted. Watch where you walk, and NEVER step on wires or cable!"

Both kids agreed weakly. They looked traumatized and tired.

"He's right again," Chloe said, standing. Another whiff of ruptured gas lines blew through, the metallic odor nauseating. This wasn't a healthy place to hang around.

Collecting more kids was not part of her plan, but the teacher in her felt compelled to ensure that at least this group was safe. Watching Brett, she couldn't help but feel sorry for the older boy. He was clearly herding cats and was nervous. "Albany is a minefield of ways to get hurt now. You guys have to be careful."

"This is Matthias and Winnie, my brother and sister," Brett said, his eyes appreciating her input.

"Brett, I'm hungry," Winnie rubbed pale cheeks. "Can we have a real breakfast now? I want cereal."

At a loss, Brett looked at the market behind them, but it was clear they couldn't get in there. The café across the road had collapsed, its green and white awning draped over the sidewalk, and the building reduced to a pile of rubble. There used to be a taco place, an ice cream parlor, and a coffee shop right along here, but the signs were gone, and the buildings crushed into each other. He couldn't tell where one ended and the next started.

He bit his lip, wondering what to do. He didn't want to use up their emergency rations if there was another option.

As he turned to look down the street, Chloe took pity on him. Moving beside him, she whispered, "Most of these places are too badly damaged to try anything. I have some breakfast buns in my bag we can share, and then, further down the road, you might find a place less destroyed."

Suddenly, the ground rocked as another aftershock hit. It was a strong one and lasted over a minute. They clutched each other, Chloe holding Brett's arm as the kids huddled close. Mollie whimpered uneasily.

It faded away and stopped, but the brief motion changed the group's dynamic. Riding the tremor together had bonded them, if only slightly.

"Let's get in the truck," Brett told his sister and brothers. "Chloe has some breakfast buns we can share."

Matthias and Winnie perked up, smiles on their faces. Winnie loved pastries. They headed toward the truck, Brett and Chloe gratified to see them carefully avoid the wires this time.

"Can I hold the baby?" Piper asked as they followed.

"Her name is Mollie. I bet she'd be happy to sit with someone new." Chloe handed her knapsack to Brett. "Buns near the top."

"Where were you walking to?" asked Piper, already making friends with Chloe.

"Everyone, this is Mollie," Chloe said. She held up the baby so all the kids could see her. Mollie blinked at them and babbled a little. Chloe put Mollie on Piper's lap once Piper sat in the back. "I am taking her to her dad's home in Lebanon."

"Where's her Momma?" asked Winnie, sliding close to Piper on the seat.

Brett saw the expression on Chloe's face; it was as if she was about to cry, so he hastily jumped in. "Here, Winnie, can you hold a bun in each hand?"

Distracted, Winnie took the pastries, biting into the sweet bread happily. Brett knew his little sister well enough that the question would come back up, but they'd be ready to answer with something vague next time.

Brett climbed up and sat next to Chloe in the front seat, passing the buns to Matthias. "Lebanon? That's like twenty miles away. You can ride with us. We're headed to Sweet Home, and I'll go right through Lebanon. Our dad lives in Sweet Home."

"What about your mom?" Chloe kept her voice low. The other kids didn't hear as they fussed with the baby.

Brett shook his head. "She was working. She's an auditor at one of the places by Swan Lakes. Uncle Jess went to get her, but… they didn't return. They might be…" his voice faded again, and he didn't finish.

Chloe bit her lip. She couldn't just walk away from these kids. Touching his hand, she said. "I'd love a ride to Lebanon. Mollie is a lot heavier than she looks. Let's go before someone else comes along. There will be a lot of desperate people out here soon, and we don't want to be around."

Chapter Six

Miguel, Corvallis, OR: May 20, 8 a.m.

Miguel spent the entire night bouncing between helicopters, each one taking him further north. As a young geologist, he had piloted noisy helicopters to remote outposts, but now, years later, it was a different world. The quiet hum of the modern rotor blades felt alien to him, and the damage below twisted his gut.

Everywhere the searchlight swept, the landscape was a nightmare. All along the coast, cliffs had collapsed into the churning sea, rebuilding the shoreline. The surge had swallowed everything.

Much of Redwood National Park was underwater. Most of the mighty redwood trees still stood, but he knew the saltwater could eventually kill them if it didn't drain back to the sea. Plumes of spray blew high into the air, and the corpses of huge elk and other animals floated on the surface along with uprooted trees and vegetation. The sandy shores had been consumed, and cliffs had hollowed out, leaving boulders jutting from the surface.

Inland, it was worse because there was no water to hide the damage. The towns were unrecognizable—cars overturned, homes swallowed by the earth, and streets twisted at impossible angles. Hundreds of disoriented and stunned people lifted their heads to watch the helicopter pass, but no one waved. Bodies sprawled everywhere. He couldn't fathom how they would gather the dead or where they would put them. As the rotors sliced through the air, he wondered how many bodies had already been carried out to sea, lost forever.

The forests had been razed. Thousands of massive firs had been snapped like twigs, their roots exposed to the open air, the earth around them blasted apart. The light from the helicopter's search beam barely cut through the oppressive darkness, but Miguel felt a strange relief in that. He didn't think he could stomach what lay beyond the light.

After endless hours, Miguel's helicopter finally flew over Corvallis Municipal Airport fifty minutes after the sun had risen.

If he had a car, it would have been a short drive to the USGS, but one look from the helicopter convinced him he would not be driving. The roads looked bad from the air. He peered down, trying to spot the familiar landmarks, but the devastation was so complete that nothing seemed recognizable.

Large chunks of blacktop were tossed, some teetering over gaping sinkholes. In the distance, smoke billowed up from the interchange, black tendrils curling into the sky. The remnants of vehicles lay abandoned, some overturned, others half-submerged in the earth's new folds.

To the west, the ground had simply given up. A massive sinkhole had swallowed entire blocks. It looked like the earth had cracked open and eaten half the town. The ragged edges of the collapse dropped alarmingly into a pit of nothingness. The scale was unimaginable. It stretched for miles, and the depth was anyone's guess. He wondered if the sinkholes resulted from damage to the aquifers under the state.

A fast flyby exposed the rest of the town, now resembling a shattered puzzle, with pieces lost or unidentifiable. The USGS building on 9th Street was barely standing. The east side had been leveled. No structure had escaped the wrath of the quake. The seismic activity had crushed some buildings beyond repair, while it reduced others to smoldering heaps. Fires raged unchecked, sending choking clouds of smoke into the air, coating everything in a grim haze. Miguel's stomach churned as he realized Walter Simmons had understated the damage. The scene before him was far worse than the analyst had described.

Getting past Mary's River would be the first hurdle. Both lanes of 99W were barely recognizable—burned black and crumbling into the river. The steel bridge that once spanned the water now lay twisted, half-submerged. He looked closer, pressing his face against the helicopter's window. A tanker truck, its contents ignited, had fallen into the river. Half on land and half in the water, it was still burning. The liquid fire had spread along the banks, the foliage feeding the flames. The river appeared tainted, contaminated by the wreckage and the fire. Downriver looked bad as far as he could see.

As the helicopter swooped around the airport, he saw the terminal burning, and the runways barely intact. A small group of people had gathered at a safe distance, watching them land, but they made no move to approach. Miguel was relieved. He didn't need any distractions. The pilots, as professional as ever, barely spoke before rushing off to their next mission.

Miguel pulled on his knapsack and stepped forward onto the tarmac. He set his sights on the USGS building. He could make it in an hour if nothing else stood in his way.

He already knew better than to expect anything to go smoothly.

Chloe/Brett, Albany, OR: May 20, 9 a.m.

They passed a few stragglers as they left town, shadows among the destruction. People sat on crumbled curbs, staring blankly, shoulders sagging, their eyes hollow. Some waved weakly, desperate, but Brett didn't stop.

Chloe tried the radio, but Brett shook his head. "It's been static all night," he told her.

The truck bumped over the pavement, the tires screeching as they dodged abandoned cars and clutter. Brett drove, eyes darting around, Chloe's calm voice a steadying presence. "Keep an eye out," she murmured, scanning the road.

The overpass ahead loomed, sagging dangerously. Its concrete and steel piers were losing the fight, threatening to collapse like the rest of the world around them.

Ahead, a group of figures blocked the road on the bridge. Five or six adults, their faces twisted in resentment or frustration, ducking behind guardrails, then popping back up, brandishing chunks of cement and jagged rebar. The wind carried away their angry shouts, but their intent was clear: they wanted Brett to stop.

They were only driving about twenty miles per hour. "Should I stop?" he asked Chloe, hoping for some input.

Chloe squinted through the windshield, trying to see more. "You don't have a completely clear path across the road with those cars in the way, but I think we can make it. Start slowing down, but don't stop. When I tell you, floor it."

"We'll hit those other cars," Brett objected, slowing down anyway.

"Aim between them. We're making space." She sounded grim.

Brett took a deep breath.

"Everybody buckled in?" she asked the three kids in the back without turning.

Three yeses answered her, though the voices were shaky. Lying between Piper and Winnie, Brett had belted a makeshift car seat for Mollie. The baby was sleeping again, and Chloe hoped she would stay that way. At least she was safely restrained.

They were almost to the incline.

"Get ready," Chloe said, her eyes steely.

Brett's hands trembled, but he tightened his grip on the wheel. One of the men in front of them walked toward the slowing truck, his posture aggressive. He held a crowbar in one hand. Blood smeared his face and torn gray shirt. As he got closer, Brett could see the anger and desperation twisting his jaw, and in dawning realization, he knew they intended to take the truck.

"Now!" Chloe snapped.

Brett slammed the accelerator to the floor, leaning into the steering wheel. The engine revved into gear. Lurching wildly, the big black tires charged through the rubble. As he bore down on the man, Brett knew this would end in seconds. The man in the road hesitated just a breath too long—then leapt out of the way, his crowbar smashing into the rear light with a sickening crack as they passed.

"They're just kids!" someone screamed from behind, and to Brett's horror, the group surged forward, desperate. One of them, a hulking bald man, hurled a jagged piece of concrete. It slammed into the cargo tray with a bone-rattling thud, skittering forward and crashing under the back window. The truck shuddered as the kids screamed in fear.

"Go faster!" Piper yelled.

"Through there!" Chloe pointed to a narrow gap between two sports cars, the path barely wide enough for the truck. "Hit them hard. They'll skid away!"

Brett didn't hesitate. He floored it just as the bald guy dropped a hand on the tailgate. The truck jerked forward, and the man screamed in frustration as the tailgate popped open, tearing free from his grasp. He ran a few steps after them, spewing obscenities in frustration before he stopped.

Winnie was crying, and he could hear Piper comforting her. The baby fussed, and a wide-eyed Matthias yelled, "Watch out!" as another piece of rebar shot over, scraping across the truck's roof with a shriek of metal. The truck swerved violently onto the shoulder, but Brett kept his foot planted. Soon, the group was just a blur in the rearview, their figures shrinking, helpless, as the truck tore through the wreckage.

"Slow up, Brett," Chloe panted, her grip tight on the seat. The truck rocketed over another fifty feet of rutted easement before slowing. "Don't stop, but ease up a bit. It's hard to see what's ahead. You did good. Really good."

"Like LEGOs! You're the king of Wreckage Road!" Matthias pounded his shoulder over the seat. "That was awesome!"

Brett swallowed hard, focusing on the road ahead as they navigated a four-car pile-up. "Wreckage Road?" He ignored the bodies in the cars and the splashes of red in the windshields.

"Yeah!" Matthias cheered. "Only World Racers get to compete on Wreckage Road. You're the best!"

Chloe's hand trembled against the seat. "Looks like a wreckage road, all right," she muttered.

Piper's voice wavered as she clutched Winnie close. "What about those people? Why'd they do that?" She looked at Chloe, who had leaned over the seat to check on the whimpering baby. "Why did they act like that?"

"They wanted the truck," Brett said, his voice tight as he maneuvered the truck around another obstacle.

"Desperate people," Chloe shook her head and rubbed Winnie's hand. "They want to get somewhere, and we had a moving vehicle. You did a good job, Brett."

Piper frowned. "Where's the police?"

"I haven't seen any police or first responders since the earthquake last night. What about you guys?" Chloe sat back down and studied the road ahead.

"We haven't seen anyone either. But someone needs to stop those crazies."

"Are those go-bags?" Chloe asked, indicating the bags on the floor under the kid's feet.

"Yes." Matthias held one hand protectively over his.

"Do they have guns in them?"

Piper looked at Chloe, shocked. "Of course not."

"Any weapons? Anything to protect yourselves with?" Chloe pressed.

"No," Brett's face was dark. "You think we'll need weapons, don't you."

"Those people aren't the only ones we'll have to face. I don't have anything either. We'll need to think of something."

Brett sighed, swerving around a semi-truck, trying to see ahead of it. "Let's hope we don't meet any other groups for a while then."

"What's with those burning buildings? Is the fire department coming?" Matthias pointed out the window.

The industrial parks were ablaze on either side, tall flames roasting the steel and concrete. Black smoke billowed into the sky, casting a dark pall over the landscape. The sun was hazy here. Heat shimmered, distorting the view of the buildings, crumbling under the assault of fire and ruin.

"Nobody's coming," Winnie was the only one who answered. She pulled her hand away from Piper's to cover her eyes. It looked like a scene from a movie, all fire and destruction. Their metal shells twisted, abandoned cars cluttered the road and parking lots. Shapes sprawled across the asphalt. Brett tried to drive a little faster so the kids in the back wouldn't have time to identify the bodies for what they were.

Suddenly, the ground shook, another heavy aftershock. The truck slowed and stumbled over split asphalt as Brett struggled with the wheel. A weird ripping noise filled the air.

Chloe didn't hesitate. She hit the down button for the window, and a blast of smoke and filth rushed in as it opened, stinging her eyes and coating her skin with grime. She ignored the soot and complaints from the kids while she slid outside, up on the door's window jamb, trying to get higher, and looking around the buildings and across the fields. Holding tight, she gasped.

Everywhere she looked, sinkholes and rifts opened before her eyes, leaving behind dark edges that dropped into nothing. While she stared, more of the earth collapsed. Faults split the ground, the burning buildings sliding into their depths while the fractures kept moving in their direction. There was nothing to stop them. Soon, this road wouldn't even exist. She couldn't explain how this was happening, but she knew what they needed to do about it.

With a sharp intake of air, Chloe dropped back into the seat and pushed a finger hard on the up button for the window. Her voice was urgent. "Drive faster. We need to get out of here."

Brett looked at her sideways. He was afraid to ask, so he hit the gas without a word.

Miguel, Corvallis, OR: May 20, 12 p.m.

It took Miguel two hours to make a trip that usually took fifteen minutes. Twice, he stopped, hearing faint cries of help, but both times, the voices dissolved before he could find their source. A rustling in the parking area of an industrial facility made him pause. He crouched low, expecting a person, but a sleek cat darted out from the remains, eyes wide, fur bristling. It hissed and vanished into the shadows.

Ahead, the city was still burning. The stench of smoke and smoldering ruins hurt his nostrils. Every so often, a loud *thud* echoed through the morning as another structure crumbled, sending tremors through his chest. Soot muted the city's colors. Chasms broke up the highway. When he couldn't jump over, he skirted around the worst of them, but the earth's damage soon grew more extreme.

Sometimes, the chasms were so wide he was forced to walk off the road and around them. It took a while to catch his attention, but the closer he got to the city proper, the more he noticed the strange activity from the fissures.

At first, he thought the wet areas left near the rifts were just from earthquake geysers. Then he heard a strange gurgling, like water rushing from deep below. He stopped, squinting at the streams of water flowing from the newly formed craters. The terrain seemed to pull apart, releasing groundwater.

Another aftershock struck, and the earth groaned again, a deep rumble that rocked Miguel's feet. Without warning, the geysers erupted again, spraying water in all directions, the mist swirling and clinging to the air. He peered through the haze, his skin damp, the air saturated with the smell of wet stone and mud. More water surged from the cracks. Puddles formed rapidly, spilling their contents and spreading into pools.

Miguel had witnessed groundwater seeping from the earth before but had seen nothing on this scale. Large ponds were forming across the fields.

He picked up his pace, but he was tired. Getting closer to the interchange, he forced himself to press on without a break. The roads here were full of abandoned vehicles, and he wound between them, watching for any threats. None of the half a dozen people he passed tried to stop him. They were all consumed with their own troubles.

A few called out to ask him the same question. When would help arrive? Miguel tried to sound hopeful when he answered, though a pit formed in his stomach. No rescue units had shown up yet, and he feared none would anytime soon.

The lack of support did not surprise him. The damage across Oregon was unbelievable. Survivors in Corvallis would have to help each other in the short run. Yet, he was afraid if he stopped, he'd never get moving again, so he kept walking.

The route felt interminable.

Just before he reached the interchange, the damage became even worse. Great slabs of highway were gone. The fractures were huge. Crumbled edges broke new paths, asphalt, and sod, both victims of the disappearing ground. He got on his knees and looked down into the widening rifts, but even straining, he couldn't see a bottom. Disconcerted, he jumped back up, circling the crevices, and walked faster.

Mary's River came into view, and he got a closer look. The defunct steel bridge poked above the surface, twisted and half-submerged, its jagged edges sticking out of the water. Water swirled beneath it, its surface an oily sheen, like an iridescent floating residue. Dead animals floated past. He wrinkled his nose in disgust.

Taking the bridge was a risk. Many of the struts and beams were gone, and the entire structure was black. But it would keep him out of the water. He did not want to swim in that bitter cocktail of death, tattered wood, and gas-coated water that made each breath feel like it was being pulled through a greasy rag.

Miguel's chest hitched as the steel bridge sagged beneath him. Only the first step and the metal beneath his sneaker shifted with his weight. He reached for the rails, gripping tightly. The bridge felt unstable, as though it might give way at any moment, and vertigo tugged at him, the river below an endless wallow.

Slipping on the wet steel sent a shiver of fear through his spine. The bridge swayed dangerously, creaking as it buckled under the river's current. He steadied himself, hands tightening around the rail, the grip so tight it hurt. The smell of the polluted water was overpowering, like a weight pressing on his lungs. He could taste the foul air on his tongue, and the thought of slipping, of falling into that river, sent an icy wave of dread through his body.

Finally, after what seemed like hours but was probably only fifteen minutes, he reached the other side and firm, if blackened, ground. Miguel walked up the road, climbed over the parapet and onto the grass, and worked his way up the incline to the highest point left on the Corvallis/Newport Highway. He stared west, toward the Willamette River.

Shawala Point was gone, and so were all the lanes heading west. The Willamette River had rolled over all of it.

The river bank had eroded, and while he watched, another new tremor shook the ground. In response, the perimeter gave a little more, sections peeling off and tumbling into the water. He fancied he could feel the pull of it, that heavy, inevitable sinking, the land unwilling to hold its ground.

Standing water covered both sides of the river bank, farther than he could see. A good portion of the shoreline on the west side must have sunk during the earthquake. 99W Highway, once at least one thousand feet from the river, now merged with a much broader Willamette.

Ten minutes later, when he stepped onto the remains of 99W, the water was knee-deep. It smelled awful. Gasoline's stench, raw and pungent, rose from the flood; an oily sheen in various colors slid past him across the cloudy surface. Little waves rolled by as the current followed its new path. Strangely, it was very warm.

As he struggled out of the flooded highway and onto 4th Street, the smell of diesel clung to his skin. He used 4th Street to reach NW Polk Avenue, where he turned left, his sneakers squelching with every step. The diesel odor still clung to his skin and shoes, but he didn't want to waste the little water he carried to clean it off.

Miguel picked up the pace now that he was getting close. He remembered the cat and looked for more signs of life—birds, a dog, or something normal. No one was around, animals or humans, which was the creepiest thing of all. Mixed with the smoke, a faint trace hung in the air, remnants of trash and sewage. The odor caused him to sneeze and spit the foul taste in his mouth onto the road.

He walked fast down Polk Avenue, leading him to NW 9th Street. He was coming up on Washington Park and the Benton Center property when agitated movement on the side street caught his eye.

A peculiar sound, like sandpaper rasping, echoed faintly. Walking over to see what it was, Miguel was astonished to find the sidewalk gaped open, concrete just gone, and a jagged six-foot-by-six-foot chasm that seemed to breathe with life. In that dark abyss, billions of cockroaches swarmed, a mass of glossy exoskeletons reflecting the sun's muted rays. Their frantic activity created a rustling sound, a ceaseless whisper, harsh and shrill.

The stink hit him first—a pungent, musty scent of decay mingled with the faintest hint of something sweeter, almost sickly. It clung to the back of his throat, making him recoil instinctively. The roaches surged and ebbed like a living tide, their bodies glistening, each tiny creature a part of a writhing mass overflowing into the cracks and crevices of the crushed pavement. Suddenly, something surfaced from the depths of the squirming pool.

A human ribcage stripped bare of flesh and blood, the cartilage gleaming as if polished, floated up. With a shout, Miguel fell back, horror etched across his face and a dirty hand to his mouth. He thought he was going to vomit. The partial skeleton bobbed briefly above the tide of insects, pale against the dark swarm, before sinking.

The roaches clung to the bones, crawling over the shiny white surface, a living blanket consuming every strip of flesh. The weird rubbing sound intensified as the rib cage sank with a soft, unsettling squelch. Before he could move, another bone, a femur from a different-sized human, bobbed up, and the relentless movement swallowed it again.

The insects rolled over one another in a frenzied scramble, antennae twitching, legs moving in a blur. Some dropped into the depths of the gap or spilled out on the remains of the sidewalk, only to be replaced by others. He took two steps back, his face twisted in revulsion as more bones rose and sank back. The rhythmic tapping of the roach's legs against the cement edges was insane. He stepped back further, eager to get away from the grotesque sight.

Turning, he almost yelled, the sound jerked from his lungs. Standing behind him, only a few paces away, was a massive figure of a man. His silhouette was stark against the remains of the neighborhood. Dirt and grease clung to his skin, streaking his arms and face like the aftermath of a storm.

In one huge hand, he carried a bulging black bag. His other hand was wrapped around the arm of a body he was dragging across the pavement. Another victim of yesterday's earthquake, the woman, had crushing injuries to her head. The left side of her cranium had a huge dent with blood matting her flaxen hair to the wound. Dirt and soot covered her clothes, and she looked like someone dug from the wreckage. It was clear she was dead.

The giant stood still, patiently waiting for Miguel to move. His hollow and vacant eyes registered nothing. Miguel shifted sideways, trying to get away from this macabre scene. As soon as he was out of the way, the man started moving forward again.

When he reached the pit of cockroaches, he dropped the bag and picked up the woman's body, one hand on her shoulder and one on her thigh. With a grunt, he pushed her forward. She landed with a slurping sound and sank immediately. Picking up the bag, he turned it upside down. Arms, legs, feet, and hands tumbled out. Unidentifiable body pieces and more dropped into the trench and disappeared without a trace.

The roaches grew more frantic, the swarm humping up and then smoothing out as they received the offering. Rolling up the black bag, the big guy shoved it in the back pocket of his old jeans and turned. He stopped and studied Miguel this time. His eyes had the flat look of a shark's gaze.

Miguel had backed off fifteen paces, and fear moved his feet again. He turned and ran down Polk, tripping over the uneven street, catching his balance, and glancing back, afraid to find the guy chasing him. But he just stood there watching Miguel until the street curved, and he lost sight of the gruesome figure.

Relieved to see the USGS Building in the distance, even though it looked like half of it was on the ground, he ran faster.

Reed, Albany, OR: May 20, 12 p.m.

Reed had circled several properties along US 20 before he gave it up as a futile effort. He found no one alive, and most of the buildings were so badly damaged he didn't dare enter the ruins. The bodies he found were crushed beyond anything he could do for them. He hadn't heard a single voice. Smashed cars were all that remained. The only signs of life were the smears of blood, but no one had been there to help. The victims either had been moved or somehow, they had moved themselves. He wondered if the survivors had left during the night.

Watson and Charlie kept pace with him, though it was clear both dogs were edgy. Nose to the ground, Watson knew the drill. He was trying to find injured victims, people they could help. Charlie stuck by his side, probably more hindrance than help. The little dog seemed determined not to be left behind.

Then, the pack grew.

Before he stepped on a property a few miles down from the Marple's— a small house and stables for rent, two more dogs appeared from nowhere. Bella, the Alaskan Shepherd with lush, silver fur, and Stella, her wiry schnauzer-poodle hair in its usual tangle, trotted up alongside him like it was just another day.

He tried to shoo the dogs back toward the Animal Rescue, but in typical stray fashion, they walked around his gestures and sniffed where they wanted to go. Exasperated and with little ability to shift them, Reed let them follow.

By the time he reached the You-Haul-It dealership on the next lot, his small following had grown even more. Duke and Coco, two males happy to do whatever the other dogs were doing, as usual, bounded up beside the group. Now, he had Watson and five other dogs trailing behind him. It was feeling like a circus, and Reed wondered how he'd feed them all in a few hours.

Another aftershock rocked the parking lot. Reed's spine stiffened as he and the dogs rode the wave of energy, waiting for it to pass. He was not going to get used to that motion. The vibration was stronger than before, deeper. The ground shuddered beneath his feet, a deep rumble that seemed to resonate. A low, distant ripping noise echoed across the field, followed by a series of smaller, sharp snaps that seemed to come from the north, but Reed couldn't see past the remains of the structure in front of him. The dogs whimpered, and Charlie pressed himself against Watson, his little body trembling.

Dread made his heart pound. He edged around the dealership and, in the back, climbed up on one of the still-standing trucks, trying to see across the fields.

When he did, the sight stopped him cold.

The ground to the north was buckling. Not just folding but sinking—huge chunks of land falling into massive crevices grinding their way across the field. A fresh fissure tore through a pond, splitting the water into streams that poured into the widening chasm below. Mud and grass followed, the land unraveling before his eyes. The faults spread in every direction, merging into gaping gorges that seemed to stretch endlessly toward Albany, their depths unfathomable from his perspective.

Reed whipped his head west, looking toward the city, but the western sky was covered in darkness. Fires. Something was burning—great pillars of flame reaching into the sky, black smoke billowing high into the air. He couldn't tell where it started and where it ended. The horizon dimmed as smoke covered everything. Now, he knew where the bits of soot riding the breeze came from.

Suddenly, his plan to return to Albany seemed like a bad idea. He felt a primal instinct surge through him as another aftershock sent a fresh wave of tremors through the ground. Trying to hurry and not fall, he dropped from the truck.

His whistle cut through the air, loud and commanding. Watson was at his side instantly, the rest of the dogs following in a chaotic, panting pack. They moved fast, heading back toward the highway, but Reed's mind raced. Where could he go? South?

They reached US 20. The ground rumbled again, this time with a more violent tremor. Reed's sneakers balanced against the bumper as he climbed onto a dented delivery van, using the crumpled car it had collided with to push himself up onto the roof. Higher now, he could see the landscape more clearly. He tried to determine which direction was safest. He already knew the north and west were trouble.

The south was no better. Fractures tore the land apart, spreading like scars across the earth. A grocery warehouse crumbled, its parking lot vanishing into the rift beneath it. Asphalt, cars, shopping carts—all devoured in one brutal swipe. The entire landscape was splintered as if a giant hammer had struck the land, leaving nothing but ruin.

He needed to head away from Albany. It looked like running east was the only option.

Before he could climb down, he heard another kind of roar. He turned so fast he nearly slipped. A big, black Ford Super Duty headed toward him at maybe thirty miles per hour, swerving dangerously around the wrecks, bouncing wildly over bumps and pieces of asphalt. He waved his arms, hoping to get their attention, when a dark gray shape the size of a dog ran in front of the truck.

The driver reacted instinctively, jamming on the brakes, and the big truck skidded across the pavement, catching and knocking aside the dog just at the last second. It only crashed to a stop when it struck a Toyota lying on its side. Wincing when he heard the yelp, Reed scrambled down. The aftershock slowly subsided, and the ground stilled as he ran, Watson ahead of him, toward the fallen animal.

It was Shadow, the dark gray mid-size dog that Rose Marple deemed a Weimaraner and Labrador mix. Shadow was a notorious hunting dog like all Weimaraners and got her name for how silently she stalked her prey. She had probably followed Reed and the pack all morning, waiting to see where they were going. The aftershock must have rattled her, or maybe she hadn't heard the truck at all.

Reed hoped Shadow wasn't seriously hurt. The dog had a great temperament, relaxed and mellow when not on a hunt. Watson and Shadow liked many of the same exercises, and sometimes, he took both dogs on a hike just to give their long legs a workout.

The dog wasn't moving.

He knelt, careful as he ran his hands over the sleek charcoal-colored fur. Watson whimpered and pressed his snout gently against Shadow's soft gray ear, looking for a response. Shadow's chest rose and fell with a soft groan—a low sound that was more relief than pain but still enough to make Reed's pulse race.

The rest of the dogs came running up, Charlie in the rear huffing with the effort. They circled the scene, picking their way over the torn highway. Heavy detonations echoed over the landscape, but the injured animal drew everyone's attention.

"I'm sorry, I'm sorry, I didn't see her until too late," a teenage boy jumped out of the driver's side of the big truck, his face horrified. "Can I help?"

Before Reed could reply, a woman with a mass of shoulder-length blonde hair flying in all directions and wearing an oversized jacket climbed out the window and knelt on the truck's roof. She held a hand to shade her eyes from the bits of soot spinning by, looking to see where the piercing booms were coming from. Each of the blows echoed with a heavy thud across the landscape. Behind them, further down the road, something blasted with a thunderous bang, a fiery building exploding outward, and even those in the truck ducked at the sound.

Whatever she saw, the woman didn't stop to explain. "Brett, get in the truck, NOW!"

Reed's instincts kicked in. He didn't need an explanation. He could already feel the pressure of time slipping away. As an EMT, he knew how to move fast on limited information.

Brett didn't hesitate, either. He slid his arms under Shadow and picked up the injured animal in one smooth motion. "Grab the other dogs," he yelled to Reed and started running.

The woman was already sliding into the driver's seat. Brett dashed to the back of the vehicle, careful of the dog's bleeding leg despite his speed. He placed the dog in the truck bed on an old scrap of cloth, then ran around and climbed into the cab.

Reed nodded, already moving. He scooped Charlie up in his arms, feeling the small body tremble against his chest. He whistled, and Watson, his fur streaked with dirt, bounded toward him, eager to follow. The other dogs were right behind him, and there wasn't time to waste.

He sprinted toward the truck bed, the air heavy with the smell of burning plastic and sulfur. The tailgate was open, and he scrambled in beside Shadow. The world seemed to blur around him as he shoved Charlie toward the back of the bed, just as a piece of concrete rolled over the floor and into his lap. He tossed it over the side, leaning over Shadow to shield her as the rest of the pack jumped in.

The woman hit the gas pedal, and the truck shot forward, clipping the delivery van and almost hitting a Honda before she swerved. Bracing himself, Reed jerked the tailgate up. Metal screeched against metal as they sideswiped more cars than they missed, but the truck picked up speed. They tore down US 20, hitting every bump.

Cracks sliced through the asphalt behind them. The tires screamed as the woman veered left, sending sand and silt spitting into the air.

Miles passed, and gradually, the collapsing earth faded into the distance, the noise becoming an echo behind them. The western sky was still dark as it disappeared behind the pines that were still standing. As the blue horizon opened up ahead, the sound of destruction softened, replaced by a stillness enveloping the truck.

Breathing hard and fearing she was having a heart attack, Chloe pulled over to the side, the gravel crunching under the vehicle's weight as it stopped. She fell back against the seat, breathing heavily. The dogs huddled around Reed, their bodies trembling, the scent of fear mixed with the sweat and dirt still lingering in the air.

Then the rear window slid open with a soft click, and a small face with brown ponytails poked out, her eyes wide with curiosity.

"Oh, he's so cute! Can I hold him?" The little girl's voice was hopeful as she eyed the dog in Reed's lap.

Charlie hopped down, jumped the few steps to stand on his hind legs, and licked Winnie's fingers in greeting. Reed slumped against the steel side, the adrenalin finally slowing. It looked like Charlie had already made a new friend.

The truck started back up, and they were on the move again, disaster still behind them, but for a moment, Reed allowed himself to breathe.

Chapter Seven

Walter and Miguel, Corvallis, OR: May 20, 1 p.m.

Dust and dread hung in the air as Walter paced the small, half-destroyed room, each step echoing the sickness coiling in his gut. He was living in a nightmare far worse than he had ever imagined.

The shock of yesterday's quakes still gripped him, twisting through his thoughts like a vise. He wondered if the first quake, the 3:03 p.m. magnitude 8.2 that generated the tsunami that took out Newport, would be considered a foreshock or if such a strong quake would be considered an event on its own.

The 4:45 p.m. event on the Cascadia Subduction Zone had generated a full-margin rip shattering the West Coast. Reports coming back overnight indicated the massive energy from the second quake had lengthened the faults even further. The fault rupture pattern was complex, but he had spent the night narrowing the magnitude to something closer to 9.6.

He had only seen such events in textbooks and simulations, never in real life. Studying faults, tectonic plates, and seismic patterns over the last few years had not prepared him for the raw, ugly reality of surviving an earthquake. It was a cruel new lesson.

Chills prickled his skin as his mind raced. The quakes had been bad enough, but the model he'd worked on, still running on the corner of his desk calculating grim predictions for the future—told him it could get worse. How much worse? How much more could the earth tear itself apart? The probabilities danced around his mind, each one darker than the last.

Walter hadn't slept. The night had passed in a haze of calculations and leery glances toward the few remaining walls of his office. His eyes were bloodshot from hours spent staring at his screen, his mind racing faster than he could process the data. The generator still hummed quietly in the background, a faint, almost comforting sound breaking the silence of everything lost.

The building shifted, creaking under its weight. Walter flinched, the sound startling him each time. Already half of the structure had fallen. The right-wing was a flattened heap of metal and concrete. He couldn't even bring himself to think about the bodies he had left over there—Joe Wilson, the office manager, and two others.

He had wrapped them in tarps, placing the bodies near an entrance, covered enough to protect them from animals but easily found by recovery teams. He couldn't stand to keep them in this room with him. Although he hadn't worked here long enough to make friends, he knew their faces and names.

If the parking lot was any sign, only a few of his coworkers were still in the facility before the quake. Only half a dozen cars remained, and they didn't look like they were going anywhere with the wrecked building debris from the other wing on top of them.

After disposing of the bodies, he had to decide what to do next. Every aberrant sound fueled his fears, and exhaling deeply, he let anxiety flood his chest. For a moment, he stood there, wide-eyed, caught between relief and the weight of the last several hours.

Then curiosity anchored him. The need to know—*to prove it*—pulled him back. He couldn't abandon the one part of the building that still stood. He needed to decipher his model's calculations. Baxter and Santiago may not have believed his model predicted the earthquake, but Walter was sure it had. Now, he needed to determine if it was a fluke or real science, especially since the model was continuing its predictions.

He cleared a space amidst the disorder, setting up his chair and a desktop. Alone in the ruins, he felt the familiar comfort of solitude. He had no family on the West Coast and had yet to make any friends. A loner by nature, Walter was hoping to find someone who shared his interests in data science, but he had no luck yet. After a quick look outside, he imagined the shape his apartment was probably in and hurried back to his space.

Dark hair clung to his forehead, dampened by sweat. He spoke to himself in a low monotone, piecing together data fragments and connections that spun in his mind.

He ignored the smell of filth mixed with something burnt—a lingering reminder of the collapsing structure. Running a dusty hand through his messy, spiked hair, he left behind a streak of white and gritted his teeth, forcing himself to focus. Many hours later, his thoughts were so deep in the data that he didn't hear someone calling his name.

It was Director Santiago.

"Walter, I'm here!" The director sounded aggravated and exhausted.

His attention splintered, and Walter jumped up, weary, and pulled back into reality. He hurried toward the inoperable entrance.

Director Santiago was trying to squeeze through what was left of the misaligned front doors. Dressed in khakis, a tee shirt, and a denim jacket with a knapsack on his back, he didn't much resemble the staid leader of this office. A suit and tie would have been more familiar. Powder swirled in the dim light, settling across his bald dome as Miguel staggered across the wreckage flung on the floor. The junior scientist helped the older man in.

Miguel's eyes widened when he saw Walter. His clothes were a jumbled mix of dirt and grease. Rips marred his neat dress shirt, and muck caked the edges, turning some of the white a mottled gray. A faint smear of what looked like dried blood soiled the collar. The strain of the last eighteen hours showed on his trembling hands streaked with powder and dirt.

"I'm glad you're here, sir. I've got so much to show you," Walter pulled him by the arm through the collapsing hallway. The young analyst's face was ashen, and a smudge of soot crossed his cheek, framing wide, wild eyes that darted nervously around the room.

"Walter, stop. There's no rush," Miguel resisted, trying to find space to put his feet as the mess on the floor attempted to trip him up.

Walter didn't slow down, his grip tightening. "No sir, you are wrong. We need to hurry and let the right people know. This disaster is not over yet."

Miguel shook his head, his frustration rising, and quit resisting. "We've had the mega earthquake and tsunamis up and down the coast. I get it. What you are talking about."

They reached the small area Walter had set up. Amidst the destruction, his desk stood like an island of methodical chaos—monitors blinking, two laptops stacked on top of each other, their screens lit with incomprehensible data. It was a stark contrast to the mayhem around them.

"Do you have the generators running?" Miguel asked, dumbfounded at how organized and clean this setup was in the middle of all this muddle, especially considering Walter's appearance.

"They kicked on as soon as the quake ended. I just had to reroute some of my wiring to assemble this. But that's not important. Look at this!" Walter's impatience spilled over as he jabbed a finger at the monitors. "The second quake was at least a magnitude nine. I think 9.6, but I know that has to be verified in Reston. Tsunamis flooded the coastline for hundreds of miles! Up the rivers, through the cities, the damage is catastrophic."

"I know. I experienced the tsunami in Capetown and got a first-hand look on the helicopter ride back here." Miguel pushed Walter aside to get a better look at the monitors as the words continued to spill from the frenzied analyst.

"The fracture in the Cascadia Subduction Zone wasn't just a small rupture. It triggered faulting across hundreds of miles. The rock layers are twisting and shattering. We're seeing breaks deeper than anything we thought possible— places where the temperature is over a thousand degrees Celsius. The sensors are going crazy! And maybe it's not just pressure. It could be something we've never considered. Maybe it's fluids seeping in. Or maybe something else entirely! Maybe it's something we've never looked for before."

Miguel squinted at the monitors, struggling to make sense of the data churning across the screen. He wasn't a data jockey, and the numbers made little sense to him. He leaned in closer, his nose nearly touching the screen.

"Walter, intraslab normal-faulting events over 7.6? They've only happened seven times since 1929," he said, shaking his head. "And every single one was tied to bending stresses in the outer-rise region of the subduction zone. I just don't see those conditions here. Plus, think about the San Andreas fault—why did the other faults react?" He crossed his arms, clearly frustrated.

"Wrong question," Walter told him excitedly. "What you should ask is—*Why are the other faults still reacting?* Look at this, and this, look here," the young analyst pointed so fast that Miguel couldn't keep up. "All this yellow is movement. Sure, it's minor compared to yesterday, a lot of 4s and 5s. But, look, Albany's right in the middle of it. The ground's fracturing *now*, not yesterday! What the hell would cause that?"

The yellow pulses on the map nearly consumed all of western Oregon, with Albany glowing like a hot spot. It flickered and pulsed with the ominous intensity of a warning light.

"Watch this," Walter urged, tapping another monitor. "This is a time-lapse from yesterday, right after the earthquake. See how it is all still? No yellow from British Columbia to Southern California. Now watch as it ticks forward. An hour later, *this*—" His finger jabbed again, showing the spreading waves of yellow. "Look how deep it's getting, especially in Washington and Oregon! This is real time!"

Miguel leaned in, ignoring the junk around him, and let his mind focus on what Walter was saying, pushing the world of destruction around them to the back of his thoughts.

Walter hadn't finished. "And check this out—over here," he pointed to another monitor, "this data's suggesting the Juan de Fuca plate *snapped in half.* That's amazing all by itself, but somehow, that event turned into a full-margin break! Do you realize what that means? It impacted the whole North American Plate, setting off the San Andreas down south. It doesn't stop there. We've got hundreds of unidentified faults under Oregon, all of which look to have been activated. You can see how they're spreading toward the east right here."

Miguel rubbed his face, exasperated. "This can't happen. There must be some kind of mistake," He dropped into Walter's chair, the leather creaking under his weight, and began typing.

"I know, right? Yet, the facts are clear. It's happening differently this time. This isn't just an earthquake—it's something else. It's like the faults are all linked—deep, deeper than we've ever seen before. This data doesn't lie. But it's confusing! I think the faults that caused the quake happened in extremely deep parts of the tectonic plate. Look at these numbers. The depth of the rupture in the Juan de Fuca plate was *63 miles.* The temperature in those depths is much higher than usual, and we know the rocky material will break more easily that far down. But the effects are spreading, and the tremors don't stop. The land is actually breaking up and sinking. Maybe subducting under the North American plate? This isn't over yet."

Miguel sat back and looked at him, his face flat. The implications were terrifying. "Walk me through this from the beginning. If I'm calling the governor, I need to understand everything."

"You need to hear the whole story first," Walter insisted, urgency creeping into his voice. "Remember what I said last night? Check this out." He pulled up a new map of Oregon. His finger hovered over a glowing red spot. "See this? My model predicts those tremors we discussed—those still shaking Albany and other areas. It shows them converging right here in central Oregon. Right on top of Mount Hood, Mount Jefferson, and the Three Sisters. If this keeps up, we're looking at major volcanic eruptions across the entire chain."

Walter's words hung in the air, their weight sinking in. The earthquakes and tsunamis—they were just the *beginning* of this disaster.

Reed, Chloe and the Kids, US 20, OR: May 20, 2 p.m.

Ten miles from Lebanon, the road was split open, a gulley-sized rift where US 20 veered south. The crevice veered toward a giant sinkhole on the west side of the road, filled with trees and crumbling soil. Chloe was relieved to see it wasn't visibly growing.

The remains of a "Blue Sky Produce Market" sign lay flat on the east side, and a partially collapsed vegetable mart slumped next to the road.

Chloe pulled into the uneven, dirt parking area for Blue Sky, hoping to circle the rift, but suddenly stopped, her shaking hands needing a few minutes. She exhaled slowly. Silence hung in the air after the engine cut out, punctuated only by the irregular tick-tick-tick of the cooling motor.

Around her, more turmoil reigned. Toppled produce stalls left a collage of crates, half-filled with scattered greens and yellows, abandoned in the dirt. Dozens of ripe tomatoes split open, forming small pools of red on the ground nearest the truck. So much ruined produce was a shame. Very little remained intact, and she saw no people.

The rumbling earth had calmed several miles ago, and hopefully, the ground-eating rifts they had fled were also miles back and had stopped destroying Albany by now. She thought about her friends and her students. She prayed they were okay, refusing to admit anything else.

They were probably ten miles north of Mollie's home. Chloe rested her head on the steering wheel, the tremors of fear and adrenaline still crawling beneath her skin, the weight of exhaustion settling in her bones. She ached all over.

The soft gusts of wind stirred silt across the cracked pavement, bringing the faint sting of sand over the group in the truck bed. Reed knelt over Shadow. The dog whimpered softly, her fur matted with blood. One look through the rear window, and Matthias jumped out of the back seat, dragging a go-bag, and was around and in the pickup bed before Chloe could muster a clear thought about the group they had just picked up. Dropping the tailgate, the Boy Scout climbed in as the rest of the dogs jumped out. Matthias knelt beside the man, exchanging names and asking questions about the injured animal.

"You okay?" Brett's voice broke through her thoughts. His light brown eyes, almost golden with concern, searched her tight face.

"I've had better days," she said drolly.

"Me too. I can't believe I hit a dog. I think I feel the way you look— like you'll be sick."

"I don't think being sick is a luxury we have time for. I'm okay," she mustered up the smile she used in class when it had been a tough day of teaching. She watched as one of the dogs, a moppy-haired mutt, sniffed along the ground and headed around the broken-down pavilion, stepping over the fruits and vegetables scattered everywhere.

Reed could have told her that Stella, the pooch she was watching, didn't look like much with all that wild hair, she was one of the smartest dogs he had ever met. She was also mostly well-behaved, so something must have caught her attention if she had taken off.

Winnie was leaning out the small rear window in the seat behind them again, patting a happy Charlie. The little Borgi licked her fingers as she giggled. Piper had freed Mollie from her restraints and whispered soothing words, changing her diaper while her eyes kept track of the activity in the back. She squeezed her fingers into a fist when she saw how much they trembled. Luckily, Mollie didn't care.

"Let's talk to the new guy really quick before we go on," Chloe said to Brett. She let go of the wheel and opened the door. Brett joined her from the other side.

Matthias had his bag open, and the first aid kit spread out. The big guy worked quickly, applying pressure to the wound along the dog's leg, his hands steady despite the wild ride. Winnie was rubbing the Borgi's big black, silky ears, and clearly, the pup was enjoying her attention. Looking around, Chloe counted five more dogs besides the injured patient and the one that took off around the pavilion.

"Are you from a pet shop or something?" She asked the guy. His face was narrow, with sharp features framed by a stubble that hinted at days without time for a proper shave.

"Animal Rescue. You passed it on your way here. Well, what was left of it. I let the dogs out after the quake. They followed me, some of them."

Reed never looked up. He kept his tone light and continued to stitch the four-inch gash along the gray limb. Shadow lay still, only an occasional twitch giving away her nerves.

"Reed, do you want to put some petroleum jelly over the wound before you bandage it?" Matthias asked, pulling out a jar. He pushed his glasses back up his nose. "It might be more comfortable for Shadow."

"That's a good idea," Reed told him. He finished stitching the wound and tied off the knot. "Shadow is lucky you had this first aid kit. The lidocaine made this way easier for her."

Matthias beamed, his dirt-streaked face lit up with the compliment. "I'm glad I'm working on my Health Care Professions badge. My Uncle Jess is helping me..." his voice faltered when he thought of his uncle.

Reed noticed his face shift and smoothly deflected. "Do you want to bandage her leg?"

"Sure!" Diverted from his fears about his uncle, Matthias carefully unwrapped the bandages and slid closer for better access.

"Reed," Chloe emphasized the name she heard Matthias use so he'd give her his attention. "Can we talk over here?"

She indicated a spot several feet from the truck, next to the collapsed stands. Brett joined her as Reed jumped out of the truck bed, Watson following. The man moved with a purposeful calm, his lean frame exuding quiet strength, the kind that comes from years of hard work and steady discipline. His dark brown hair, the same rich shade as his eyes, was clipped short at the back and sides, leaving little more than a shadow against his scalp.

She liked what she saw so far but kept her face neutral. Everyone knew serial killers could pull off normal, and the way the last twenty-four hours had been going, it would just be her luck.

Brightly colored peppers, bruised and battered, spilled from a smashed crate at her feet, their glossy skins marred by dirt. The sweet aroma of ruined fruits grew stronger by the stand. Chloe could feel the spooky quiet. There were no birds, no chatter, just the wind and the rustling of leaves. The hush was oppressive.

"My name is Chloe Cooper," she said, holding out a hand, which he shook, a little amused by the formality. She moved confidently, belying how she looked with her blonde hair mussed and dirt all over her face. Her tone was crisp, not friendly. "This is Brett Clark. The truck belongs to him and his siblings."

"Reed Walker," he answered. "Thanks for pulling us out of whatever was happening back in Albany."

"I'm sorry I hit your dog," Brett said, the words falling out in a rush.

"Well, circumstances were less than ideal. I'm guessing you're a better driver when you aren't driving through an earthquake, and the ground isn't cracking and dissolving around you." Brett and Chloe smiled at the irony.

"This is my dog, Watson." he continued. Hearing his name, the golden lab perked up and squeezed between the three to sit in the middle.

"Watson likes attention," Reed told them with a wry smile. Watson barked, the sound loud in the stillness.

"So, what will you do with all these dogs?" Chloe asked, her eyebrows raised. Her blue eyes were observant, weighing the man and his answers.

"Like I said, they are all residents of the animal shelter I volunteered at. The quake demolished the place. I let the dozen dogs that made it out of their cages, and these guys," he indicated the other dogs, including Charlie, who was now curled up in Winnie's lap, "followed me when I left. I'm an EMT and was headed back to Albany to see if I could help. Then the ground started shaking again, and it looked like it was collapsing into giant sinkholes."

"Something destabilized the ground," Chloe agreed. She seemed to relax a little. "I'm a sophomore biology teacher at Albany High School. I know a little about earth displacement and the large number of faults under the ground in this region, but I never expected this. One of those earth tremors swallowed Albany High School. That baby Piper is holding, and I barely got out of there." She hesitated before rushing on. "Her mother didn't make it, so I'm taking her to her father in Lebanon. Brett and his brother, Matthias, who you already met, and his sisters, Piper and Winnie, are giving me a ride on their way to their dad's house in Sweet Home."

"I'm sorry about your friend," he told Chloe. "The way things look, I don't think there is any chance of returning to Albany soon. If any of the city is still standing, US 20 between here and there is gone. Do you think that ground destabilization will spread as far east as this?" He pointed to where they stood.

Chloe shrugged. "I don't know. This is not my area of study."

"Do you think everyone in Albany is dead?" Brett asked in a low voice.

"I don't know that either. I am guessing this is unprecedented, and probably very few people understand what's happening."

At her words, they looked around and then back the way they had come. The ground under their feet no longer felt stable, a reminder of the earthquake that had just unraveled Albany behind them. High on the horizon, over the trees, they could see the smoke billowing, painting the western sky in dark colors.

They all felt it—the urgency mixed with the weight of dread. Watson nudged Reed's hand restlessly. He even felt the threat.

The gentle rustle of leaves fluttered in the faint breeze, one of the few signs of movement. A half-tipped basket of kale swayed slightly, and big yellow onions rested against a cracked piece of pavement. Over near the front of the pavilion, a cooler box had tipped over, spilling bottles of water on the ground. Looking at them, Chloe realized she was thirsty. She bet the kids were, too.

Piper and Winnie were fussing over Mollie, who was awake now. The baby sat in Piper's lap, and Winnie, her brown ponytails bobbing as she played with the baby's fat hands, giggled at Charlie's attempt to lick the little girl. It was the most normal behavior Chloe had seen since this disaster started yesterday.

"Can we keep her?" Winnie asked Piper.

"No, she has to go to her daddy," Piper explained, laughing a little.

"I think we should keep her. Momma loves babies. She told me she misses us all being little. She'll want to keep Mollie." Winnie's lips thinned to a stubborn set line.

Piper wrapped an arm around Winnie, enclosing Mollie, Charlie, and her sister in one big hug. She didn't want Winnie to see the tears in her eyes. Brett had told her of his fears—her mom and Uncle Jess were probably gone, and she was praying he was wrong. But deep inside, she knew it was true. They could have and would have walked back to the dealership overnight if they had been able to.

Brett stared nervously at the western horizon, and that's when the barking started. Reed looked around fast. Stella was the only one missing, and he couldn't see her. Before he could speak, the other dogs, including Watson, took off toward Stella's frantic alarm. Only Charlie remained. Winnie held the little Borgi tight and didn't let go. Reed ran after them, Chloe right behind.

"Stay here," Brett told his siblings, then chased after Reed and Chloe. He jumped over spilled produce as he followed the barking around the leaning open-air pavilion, its wooden beams fractured and failing under the weight of the roof.

The sweet, earthy scent of crushed herbs drifted through the air, mingling with the sharp flavor of squashed citrus. He hurried around shattered glass jars of honey, pooling like amber in the dirt, reflecting glimmers of light. The sticky mass spattered in all directions.

He finally caught up with the others in the back and stopped short, shocked.

The fire or explosion that had torn through this part of the market was unmistakable. An ancient row crop tractor, paint peeling and the lower half charred, sat at the end of a field stretched east in jumbled rows of vibrant green, some of the small plants uprooted by the earthquake and others shaken and battered. Lopsided power poles edged the field, their wooden posts another victim of yesterday's quake.

It looked as if the massive machine's tires had blown out, and the rig had caught fire immediately—or maybe the other way around. Either way, the bottom of the machine had burned until the tires melted into rubber strips, and a charred ring around the machine showed how far the fire had spread before it burned itself out.

A black electrical line draped the cab.

"It's a live wire!" Reed held up a hand, preventing Chloe and Brett from moving forward. The crackling line threw sparks, the bright bits leaping through the air, popping and sending flashes of light over the smoldering wreckage. "The wire landed on the cab. It looks like it caused a fire."

The cab door was wide open, and several feet away on the ground lay the driver, unconscious or dead. Brett couldn't tell.

With her thick, wavy hair standing straight up, the Schnoodle edged toward the body, a jumble of long limbs and frantic tail, barking endlessly. "Stella!" Reed yelled. "Get back here."

The shaggy pooch ignored him and darted forward just as the ground started to vibrate again. She bit into the jacket covering the man's shoulder, trying to drag the body herself.

Brett heard Winnie screaming behind him as the ground trembled. Heart pounding, fear gnawing at his insides, he stood rooted to the spot. Sweat dripped down his back as the crackling sound intensified. Scared, he realized the tremors were jerking the electrical wires, and they could come loose at any moment.

Every instinct screamed to rush forward to help, yet caution held him back as he realized more wires could fall. Who would take care of his siblings if he died here? Before he could decide, the big golden dog— Reed called him Watson, darted forward, joining Stella. Teeth sinking into the fabric, together they pulled hard, and the man slid over the dirt. Then Reed was there. Grabbing the guy's arm, they pulled the man out of reach of the sparking wires together.

It was an older man, maybe in his fifties. Soil clung to his jeans and denim jacket, starkly contrasting the bright yellow of his work shirt, frayed and grimy at the neck. He groaned when they let go, trying to free an arm to rub at his face.

"What the hell happened?" His voice was confused, and he squinted his eyes, looking around.

Brett was suddenly happy to remember Reed was a medic. He wouldn't have known what to do next, and he thought maybe Chloe was thinking the same thing. The ground stilled, stopping its erratic movements, and slowly, the wires still attached to the standing poles stopped quivering. But the wire over the row tractor continued to spark and jump.

Winnie had stopped screaming. He hoped Piper and Matthias had the situation at the truck under control.

Reed checked the man's airway and ensured it was clear and he could breathe. Pushing back the sleeve, he felt for a brawny wrist, pleased to find a pulse beating strongly. "Sir, can you hear me?" he asked.

Suddenly, the injured man jerked violently, scrambling back in panic. "The utility wires, look out," he yelled, throwing an arm over his head.

Reed grabbed him by the arm before he could pull himself further away, yanking him back. The guy was big, but so was Reed, who was at least ten years younger. Chloe stepped in then and captured the man's other hand. Kneeling and speaking in a level, composed voice, she said, "You're safe. The wires can't reach you. Please calm down, sir."

His body trembled under their hold, and for a moment, he stared at Chloe, confusion and fear still swimming in his eyes. Slowly, his breathing steadied, and he finally relaxed, his words spilling out in a rush. "I was in the cab," he told her. "The quake hit, the pavilion started falling apart... then the wire snapped, came straight for me. I never would've gotten out if I hadn't already opened the door." His voice broke. "I fell, and the electricity... I must've got shocked."

"Do you hurt anywhere?" Reed asked him.

The man blinked as though trying to process the question. Then he looked at Reed as if he'd lost his mind. "I hurt everywhere," he told the medic. "That really hurt."

His face was pale, his gray hair matted with dew and dirt, and his features frozen in shock and relief. A fine sheen of sweat beaded on his forehead, and his eyes—wide and unfocused—betrayed the adrenaline still pumping through his veins. His body felt stiff and sore, every muscle trembling, and he was acutely aware of the ache that blossomed in his arms and legs from the impact of the fall.

"I'm fine," he growled, shoving Reed's hands away. "Just let me catch my breath."

"You should go to a hospital," Reed's eyes narrowed. He didn't push the point. "But I don't know what facilities are still standing after the earthquake."

"The earthquake!" The words slapped him out of his daze. His eyes cleared, and he stared around, suddenly aware of the devastation. "How bad was it?"

"Bad enough," Chloe leaned out so the man could see around her to the skewed pavilion. "It hit Albany, and the damage there is really bad. What's your name?"

He stared at the crushed market. "Albert Frost." A quiver shuddered through him as he looked at the destruction, a sinking realization creeping in.

"Albert, we are going to Lebanon. Maybe you should come with us, get checked out."

He jerked his gaze to her, but his response was swift. He leaned back, his shoulders stiff. "I'm not going anywhere." His voice rose slightly. "I've got my own place to get to."

Stella appeared out of nowhere, sidling up beside Reed, her scruffy curls a patchwork of mixed-up black, gray, and white. She padded between Reed and Chloe, her soft whine barely audible as she settled down beside Albert, resting her head on his leg, her warm body providing an unexpected comfort.

"What's with your dog?" Albert looked at her, a frown turning down his lips.

"She pulled you over here. I think she's worried about you. Sorry, she's a stray and does whatever she wants, right Stella?" Reed stroked her tousled coat.

"Huh, Stella was my wife's name. She passed two years ago." Albert's brow crinkled as he stared at the big dog. She wasn't much to look at. Her coat clumped up unevenly, some sections matted together, others frayed at the edges like an old blanket. He reached out a trembling hand and rubbed her bulky fur. Stella chuffed as if agreeing with him.

"Albert," Chloe drew his attention back to her. She spoke gently but with an edge of urgency. "The quake was a bad one. Some bizarre aftershocks hit back in Albany. The ground was literally breaking and collapsing into rifts. I know it sounds crazy, but we all saw it happen. Your pavilion and the vegetables are a loss. You should come with us to Lebanon."

"My house is just east of here. If I go anywhere, I'm heading there." He ignored her protestations. "My pickup truck is on the other side of this field. I don't need any help."

He struggled to stand, contradicting his statement, but Reed and Chloe didn't argue. They couldn't make the old man go with them.

"I appreciate your help," Albert gave Reed a weak but sincere nod. "If you think it's worth your time, help yourself to whatever's left. The produce is a loss."

"Thank you," Reed said. "Would it be okay if we also took some of the water? We have three young kids with us, plus the dogs, and everyone is thirsty."

"Huh. Yeah, whatever," Albert waved his hand dismissively.

"Thanks again, and good luck." Reed whistled Watson to his side, and most of the other dogs followed.

"Remember what I said about the ground breaking up and sinking," Chloe told him. "It could start again. You need to get away fast if it happens. It may not reach this far, but keep an eye out."

"Will do. Thank you, ma'am." He gave a grim nod and turned toward the cultivated field.

The remaining wires swayed overhead. Albert cast them a dark look.

The farmland was a jumble. The plants were still small enough that even though most of them were lying in the dirt, he could still walk between the rows easily. He took six steps onto the soil before he noticed he wasn't walking alone. At his feet was Stella.

"Hey, call your dog," he called back to Reed.

"I told you, she's a stray. She goes where she wants to."

He scowled. "I'm not feeding her."

"I can't make her come with us. Maybe after a while, she'll turn around," Reed offered.

Albert gave the dog a stern look. Around her ears, a welter of darker fuzz spilled to her eyes, and each step she took seemed to send a puff of dust drifting from fur that hadn't seen a brush in days. She stared up at him placidly.

"I'm not feeding you." He told her. "And I'm not going to brush all that crud out of your coat either."

Stella just waited for him to start walking. Grumbling, Albert headed through the field, the mutt at his heels.

"I don't have time to take care of a dog. My house is probably destroyed, and there isn't any place for either of us to sleep. I don't have dog food..." the complaints continued as his voice faded while they walked away.

"Boy, he sure is grouchy," Brett remarked with a grin as the group watched Albert and his resolute canine companion cross the field.

"Now you're down one dog," Chloe said to Reed.

He shook his head. "I told you, they're following me. I tried to leave them at the Animal Rescue. But if they stayed—" he stopped picturing the fissures and sinkholes. "You saved all of us by coming along when you did."

"Thank Brett, I was just another passenger. He was headed to Sweet Home and offered us a ride. If he hadn't, Mollie and I would have still been in Albany when the ground broke across US 20. We would have never made it this far."

Reed clapped Brett on the shoulder. "Thank you, Brett!"

The young man blushed. "It would have been better if I hadn't run into Shadow."

"Nothing is ever perfect," Chloe told him. "At least we're all alive and still moving forward. Lebanon is only ten miles from here. With any luck, I can still get Mollie to her dad today."

They looped around the weakened pavilion to the truck. Along the way, they snagged a few baskets and filled them with any undamaged produce they could find. There wasn't a lot. Chloe's eyes scanned the row of crushed vegetables, and she took what she could—radishes, beets, a few peppers, and some onions that were still in good enough shape to eat.

Winnie and Matthias stuck their noses up at the onions and peppers, but Chloe was worried about food in general. They ate all the breakfast buns before leaving Albany. Although that filled their stomachs this morning, she knew how much teens and children could devour. The protein bars in the go bags wouldn't last long. Everyone would be hungry soon.

Keeping that in mind, she picked up a big, aluminum, dented pot and some gardening tools she could use to cook. Hopefully, things would be better down the road. If not, she could wing a pot of soup in the wilderness.

Reed helped himself to a few apples, eating them fast. His stomach stopped growling by the third one, and he thought apples had never tasted so good, even if these were last year's apples pulled from storage. Most of these vegetables were probably greenhouse grown but they'd still taste great.

Everyone gathered around the water, and though it was warm from sitting in the sun, they drank like they hadn't had a drop in days. When they finished, they piled the remaining bottles in a box and stacked the box in the back of the truck.

After Reed examined and complimented Matthias on his bandaging prowess with Shadow, they all piled back into the truck. Chloe and Brett fiddled with the radio again, but all they heard was white noise. If anyone was broadcasting, they weren't receiving.

Brett wondered if the radio stations were out of commission, but he still twisted the dials in vain. Matthias had stayed where he was in the truck bed, his knees drawn up, still cradling Shadow's head in his lap. Reed and the dogs settled in next to him.

The landscape ahead was calm. There were no signs of the destruction that had torn apart Albany, no signs of the giant rifts that had ripped through the outskirts of the city.

Hopefully, the next stop would be Lebanon.

Chapter Eight

Miguel and Walter, Corvallis, OR: May 20, 4 p.m.

The ground vibrated again, the fourth time in the last hour. Twice, Miguel heard a reconnaissance plane fly over. The first time he hurried out, he was more worried than surprised to see the water in the streets. The second time, he was stunned to see how far the deluge had risen. Oily chemical smears stained the swales where water flowed like a creek overtopping the curbs.

A few people wandered by but didn't stay. Haggard with haunted looks on their faces, they melted back to wherever they were hiding once the plane flew away. After running into the crazy guy pulling the dead from the wrecked houses on his way here, Miguel didn't blame them. He wondered if any of them saw the roaches.

"Did you know who he was?" Walter asked as he set down another armful of snacks and bottled drinks he had pulled from the wrecked vending machines. It wasn't nutritious, but the crackers, cookies, and bars had kept the hunger pains away. Miguel had told him the bizarre story about the body disposal earlier.

"Never saw him before," Miguel shivered with the memory. "He was big and terrifying. And those roaches. Disgusting."

"We should probably figure out how to barricade ourselves in tonight."

"I've been thinking," Miguel rubbed his face. He hated to say the next words. "Your model may have some merit."

Walter's face lit up. "Of course, my model has merit! I told you so!"

Miguel held up a warning hand, trying to temper Walter's enthusiasm.

"I don't understand the science behind it enough to know how solid it is. We need to get your model to Reston. They've got the resources to—"

Walter cut him off, typing on his keyboard fast, still standing. "I think our best bet is to upload the data file to the USGS cloud storage server and then include a link to the file in an email. But that's not going to get my model sent. It's too big. I can't get the USGS file transfer service up at all. Even if we weren't worried about security, I'm not having any luck with open-source FTP solutions either. Internet access is sporadic at best."

"We need to get your laptop out of here and into the hands of specialists. I think it's time to call the governor."

"Finally!" Walter snatched Miguel's emergency phone from the desk and started punching keys. Walter was familiar with emergency phones, using his as a receiver and letting them follow the chatter of emergency responders while they worked. While he tried to find a viable number to reach the governor, they listened to the latest updates.

The news was bad. One quake on one fault was devastating enough. With the whole West Coast letting go simultaneously, the impacts were catastrophic. From San Diego to Prince Rupert, buildings and bridges failed.

To everyone's shock, the San Francisco-Oakland Bay Bridge had collapsed, taking hundreds of vehicles with it. Skyscrapers crumbled and fell, smashing into each other and bringing down the city center. Old City Hall and the Figueroa Hotel in San Francisco disintegrated into masonry clouds, and in the Mariana District, it was like the ground transformed into quicksand. Sidewalks buckled and dipped, revealing a shifting, muddy soup that swallowed everything it touched. The quake left behind a patchwork of sinking structures and swollen puddles, thousands dead and many more missing altogether.

Before anyone could gather their wits, enormous tsunamis had swept in, then partially drained back out, leaving a landscape torn apart. Sixty-eight percent of the population of California lived on the coast, even though coastal counties comprised only twenty-two percent of the state's land area. Some of the first responders were reporting entire communities wiped off the map or drowned. There was no way to count how many were lost between such devastating events. This scenario was repeated all up and down the coast.

The I-880 Viaduct and Nimitz Freeway were destroyed. Most other highways, railways, and bridges were severely damaged or destroyed. In California, authorities were preparing for casualties in the millions.

In contrast, only six percent of the population lived on the coast of Oregon. But one hundred-foot tsunamis rolled ashore up and down the coast. Initial estimates were bleak; less than one percent of the coastal population was expected to have survived. But even that wasn't the worst. Multiple reports of land subsidence, especially through the Willamette Valley and the Western Cascades, kept the alarms ringing nonstop.

Walter and Miguel were overwhelmed by the disaster. Neither Walter's model nor Miguel's experience could explain what was happening in Oregon.

To the young analyst's frustration, getting the governor on the phone proved next to impossible. So, he tried alternating with the call Miguel had been trying to make all day with no answer.

The phone line crackled, a sharp, static-laced hiss cutting through the air. This time, the USGS office in Reston picked up.

"USGS, this is Vancris," a voice barked. Though the voice was distorted, Walter understood what he said.

It was David Vancris! The Deputy Director was well known, even out here in Oregon.

Walter pressed the black cube harder to his ear, stumbling, trying to say the right thing. "Uh, Deputy Director, this is Walter Simmons from the Corvallis, Oregon office."

"Corvallis! We... trying... reach... what's your status?"

Status? He looked around him, his little oasis of clean in a wrecked world.

"Our building is mostly flattened. There is only Director Santiago and me here."

"Let...talk to Santiago," Vancris snapped.

"Director Santiago!" Walter called. Miguel was in another room, trying to unearth the handheld radios from a storage unit. His flashlight bobbed erratically as he hurried back to where Walter waited.

"It's Deputy Director Vancris. I was able to get through," he told Miguel as he handed over the phone.

"David? This is Miguel."

"Thank...you're still alive... staff ... too?"

Miguel's face creased. He could barely make out the words. "There's only Walter and me here. Listen, David, I hope you can hear me. I don't know what you are seeing in D.C., but our systems here tell us this disaster is still unfolding," Another burst of static drowned him out, making his words fizzle into nothing. He pressed his free hand to his forehead, trying to steady himself against the headache gnawing at him from the tension and the noise.

He tried again: "We sent you our data, but we have a model you need to see. We can't transmit the model; there is too much damage or something."

There was a long pause before Vancris's voice fought its way back through, distorted but clear enough to catch the words. "Sending… helicopter… Wash… Park, meet…" The call cut off again. The line snapped with a final, quick break.

Miguel stared at the device and then looked at Walter. "Pack everything. They're sending a helicopter for us. We'll meet in Washington Park."

"When?" Walter started grabbing notebooks and paper.

"I don't know. That part got lost. Let's go now and wait in the park until they show up. This is one ride I don't want to miss."

They hurried to pack, with Walter pulling the laptops into shock-resistant and waterproof sleeves and then the knapsacks. He stuffed bottled water and some snacks into his pockets as an afterthought. There was no telling how long they'd be in the park.

The floor shook beneath them several times, and Miguel worried about the effects of the tremors on the ground beneath their feet. He found himself afraid as they hurried out the back.

Oliver's, Lebanon, OR: May 20, 6 p.m.

The fragments of US 20 sprawled in all directions, like a jigsaw puzzle scattered carelessly on the ground. It sure looked like a wreckage road. Abandoned vehicles bunched up here, forcing Brett to slow down. He had to pick his way across between the fallen trees and the mangled highway. Chloe wanted him to push forward, to get closer, but the twisted wrecks blocked their way.

She glanced back at Mollie. Moni's face flashed in her mind's eye, and tears choked her throat. She'd get that baby home, but was home even still standing? The possibility of Oliver being caught in the quake terrified her. She clasped her hands tightly. As a young lawyer just starting as a junior partner, she didn't know if he would have been home when the quake hit. She sent another prayer and kept her fingers crossed.

She still had four bottles of formula and a handful of diapers left. If she could get Mollie home today, that would be enough.

As they neared the small city, the truck choked, and a metallic scraping sound ground under the hood. Brett didn't say anything, but she knew the increasingly erratic noises from the engine were troubling him.

A faint scent of smoke lingered in the air. It was the odor of buildings reduced to rubble, of destruction still smoldering— a mixture of burnt wood, scorched earth, and charred metal. The asphalt of US 20 buckled beneath them, the cracks rippling like water, shifting with every mile.

The side streets looked worse. The bigger structures were crushed, concrete bent in impossible angles, with empty window frames gaping open. A few more people walked the roads here than they had seen back in Albany, probably gathering, searching, hoping to find survivors. Chloe knew the grim truth: some people wouldn't be found. They were buried beneath the wreckage.

When they reached Oak Street, they were stopped by a makeshift barrier—a slab of wood spray-painted with the words "BRIDGE OUT!" and a hastily drawn arrow pointing west.

"There's a canal that cuts under the road. The bridge must have collapsed," Chloe said.

"It cuts over twice, a second time about a mile further," Reed had climbed out of the back and was pacing alongside the passenger side of the black truck. "I've driven this way multiple times. How far down US 20 to Mollie's house?"

"Just after the highway veers southeast but before Cheadle Lake," Chloe said, her fingers digging into her snarled hair, trying to pull out the grit. Piper offered her a hair tie, and she took it gratefully, pulling the mess into a ponytail. "Maybe a couple of miles? I don't know if we can get through."

"Let's follow the detour and see where that gets us."

Nobody had a better idea, so Brett shifted into gear, the truck grinding again in protest, and they turned left. Chloe glanced back at the baby and then at the other three sitting on the seat. Everyone was grimy, tired, and scared. The younger kids had dark circles under their eyes. But spirits were better than she would have expected. The dogs had made the difference.

Winnie sat with Charlie curled in her lap, running her fingers through his hair and whispering to him. The dog snuggled close to her, his black eyes watching her face. Duke, with his wrinkled face and floppy ears, lay on the seat next to

Piper, with the girl resting one hand on his soft, brown coat and the other on the sleeping baby. The rest of the dogs were in the back with Reed and Matthias.

She caught a glimpse of Reed in the side mirror as Brett jerked the wheel to the right, avoiding another hole in the pavement. They had been lucky to run into an EMT in these conditions. He was leaning against the side of the bed, his dark head turned away, his eyes fixed on the road behind them. He wasn't easy to read, she thought. He kept to himself, his eyes always assessing, but there was something about him—something Chloe couldn't ignore.

She wasn't one to trust easily, especially after too many broken promises made in the past. Men lingered too long, their smiles never reaching their eyes, and Chloe had learned to keep her distance. She'd become good at relying on herself, deciding maybe that was all she needed.

Shadow was still sleeping in Matthias' lap, but the other dogs were awake, their faces turned to the wind, eyes closing against the cool evening air. They made for an odd convoy—six dogs, four kids, two adults, and a truck full of tension.

The road was a battlefield here, the asphalt torn apart like paper left out in the rain. The truck's tires climbed over split pavement, the sound of their slow crawl punctuated by the occasional pop as the truck navigated around sinkholes that could easily start growing again. Only a few brave vehicles dared venture down these side streets—mostly SUVs and trucks, their engines whining as they dodged the craters that marred the landscape.

The neighborhoods they circumvented were a little better than the buildings off of US 20. More houses stood, though no one escaped with minor damage. People lingered in the yards, waving at them, but Chloe told Brett to keep going. They waved back but didn't stop. They couldn't have helped anyway. The kids were already hungry again, and the protein bars were long consumed. They had nothing to share besides their vegetables.

When they passed Lebanon High School, Chloe was saddened to see the crushed building. She'd spent countless hours with the biology teachers there, and now the building was nothing but a pile of rubble. She hoped no one had been at the school when the quake hit. The parking lot was empty, which was a good sign.

From Brett's perspective, he had ridden through neighborhoods like this when they started earlier today. He utilized the same process of dodging sinkholes and fissures that were too big to drive over by climbing curbs and riding down what was left of the sidewalk. He threaded through the wreckage in this fashion, following Chloe's directions. But the clicking sounds the engine was making had him worried. Something was vibrating, too, and he could feel the pull through the steering wheel.

By the time the sun sank low and dusk crept in, they had reached their destination. The street was nearly as bad as the road leading up to it. The pavement was like a rough sea, rising and falling unevenly, the truck rocking with every bump. The dogs barked in the back, unsettled by the rough ride. The yards were a patchwork of ruins—fractures splitting the earth open, crisscrossing the grass like trails in an old map.

No lights and no people in the yards here. Chloe's heart sank. She had no idea how they'd find Oliver if he weren't home. A little voice whispered— 'or if he were dead,' but she forced the thought away.

The cozy white cottage was still standing, though it was barely recognizable. A skeleton of wood and metal sprawled across the yard, half-collapsed into the grass. It was the remains of the porch. Glass splinters glinted in the faint glow of the truck's headlights, scattered across the ground like fragments of fallen stars. The front door hung lopsided, clinging to the frame by a single, twisted hinge.

The dogs jumped out when the engine cut off, excited to be on the ground again. The engine clinked loudly as it cooled, the only sound they could hear. Chloe got out slowly, and Reed joined her, scanning the area for any sign of danger.

"It seems quiet," he said softly. "Are you sure this is the place?"

"Yes," the word caught in her throat, and she suppressed a quiver. Oliver had to be here. "Oliver!"

Her sudden call made everyone jump. But she got a reaction right away. A man came around the house at a run. She recognized him immediately despite his torn clothes and the dirt on his hands and face. She flew across the yard, jumping over damaged debris, meeting him halfway.

Reed and Brett couldn't make out the words, but they all heard his cry of anguish as Chloe kept talking. He half turned and nearly fell on the grass. She caught him close, and they hugged as she finished.

Brett came up behind Reed. "Should we do something?" he asked, his voice barely above a whisper.

Reed shook his head, mouth turned down. "Nothing we can do. Let them talk. Let's get the kids and the dogs watered while we stop."

His siblings and the dogs had gathered near the back.

With hands on her hips, Winnie was arguing with Piper, who was holding the baby. "I don't want to give her to him. We should keep her."

"Winnie," Piper caught her hand, holding Mollie with the other. "You know she has to go to her daddy."

Winnie's pouted, and she started to cry. "I wish Momma were here. She wouldn't let you give Mollie away."

"You know mom would not take a baby away from her daddy, even if we loved the baby," Piper whispered. "You know that, Winnie."

Winnie pushed Piper away, putting her little hands over her face and turning her back on her sister. "Momma wouldn't let you. She wouldn't let you give Mollie away."

Charlie whimpered and stood on his two back legs, leaning against the little girl. Winnie only cried harder and pushed him away. Charlie's ears folded, and he trembled, belly in the dirt. Brett knew his little sister understood they couldn't keep Mollie. She was missing their mom, and losing Mollie was one blow too many for the little girl in such a short time. His heart ached for them all.

"Go pick her up. Let her cry on you. I'll help Piper and Chloe with the baby," Reed told him in a muted voice and gave him a little push.

Brett nodded, scooping his sister into his arms. She fought for a few seconds and then collapsed against him, sobbing. "I want Momma," His chest tightened as he held her, the weight of his grief pressing down on him. He wished he could fix everything, make it all better, but he couldn't.

He settled in the truck's front seat, cradling Winnie. She clung to his neck and cried. He should have been more aware of her feelings; he berated himself. Of course, she was confused and wanted their mother. He was nearly twice her age, and all he wanted to do was cry for his mom and Uncle Jess. He sat that way for a while, cradling Winnie. Her sobs slowly faded into soft hiccups. He patted her back and said the soothing things he had heard his mom say in situations like this. She finally fell asleep in his arms.

Out in the yard, Oliver was crying too. His face was streaked with dust and blood, torn clothes clinging to him. A gash ran along his calf, the blood congealing and mixing with the dirt. His eyes were red from crying, his body trembling as he held onto Chloe.

An older couple appeared at the edge of their yard, their faces worn with grief as they approached Chloe. Brett watched Reed walk over with Piper and the baby, and the girl handed the child to the weeping father. Tears Brett had held back until now slipped down his cheeks, and he cried for his mom and uncle, hiding his face in Winnie's hair. Nothing would ever be the same even after they got to his dad's. The loss of his mother and uncle was like a physical ache.

He thought bitterly that earthquakes didn't just devastate the land and cities; they tore families and friends apart, dooming them to loneliness and loss. Brett cried until he felt empty, and then, sitting there, he pulled himself together. He had to be strong for the kids. He wouldn't let his mom and uncle down. They'd be at Dad's soon. He could stay strong until then.

Darkness folded over Lebanon. In the rearview mirror, he saw Matthias kneeling with the dogs, the boy's head bent. He better make time to talk to him as well. They all needed comfort tonight.

Reed joined Chloe a little later while she was gathering Mollie's meager supplies. Before he started speaking, she stiffened, expecting to hear him say he was striking out on his own. After all, he owed them nothing except a truck ride out of Albany.

"Hey, listen," he started awkwardly. She wasn't very friendly, and her expression did little to make conversation with her easy. "If you think you should stay here with Oliver and Mollie, I can make sure the other kids get to their dad in Sweet Home."

Nonplussed, she stared at him and then looked away.

"Trying to get rid of me?" she shot back, the bite in her voice unexpected.

He never understood women. Reed froze, caught off guard. "No, not at all," he stammered. "I just... I wanted to make sure you had options."

Chloe let out a long breath, shaking her head. "I think the last thing we have right now is options. I appreciate your offer, but Oliver has his neighbors to help with Mollie, and I'd like to keep going. Make sure the kids are safe."

Trying to save the conversation, he kept his tone light even though he wasn't sure what he had done wrong. "Okay, I'm going to suggest to Brett we stay here tonight and leave at first light. Is that what you were thinking?"

"Sure," she pulled the orange pack from the back seat. "Uh, sorry I was a little harsh. I didn't expect you to want to hang around."

"Not a problem," Reed stepped back just as someone called his name. As he went over to help, he wondered why Chloe was so prickly. He sighed internally. He never had luck with women. He always managed to say the wrong thing. Worse, he wasn't even sure what the wrong thing was.

Chloe watched him walk away. Whenever she trusted a guy, he showed her who he was, and she reflected that the picture was never attractive. She doubted an earthquake had improved her luck.

They'd get the kids to Sweet Home with their dad. Then she'd figure out what to do next.

Dan and Nadia, Sweet Home, OR: May 20, 7 p.m.

It took all day, but the last of the cannabis bales and most of the plants were loaded into the Cessna. The ground had been cleared, and all the fallen pines dragged off the runway. Scraping the blacktop smooth enough to handle the plane's takeoff was the worst part, and even now, it looked more like a patchwork than a flat surface.

Nadia wiped the sweat from her brow, leaving a smear of loam across her skin. Her hands were raw, and the smell of the earth and plants clung to her clothes, mixing with the heavy sulfuric stench that made her stomach churn. She hated manual labor, but she hated losing money more.

The relentless heat weighed down on them. Their only luck was the wind direction. It blew south all day, carrying the worst of the heat with it. Sweat beaded her brow and ran in rivulets down her back, soaking into her top. The air tasted grainy with its weight, making each breath feel like inhaling smoke.

Dan banged the Cessna's cargo door shut with a grunt, his face smeared with grime, his shirt plastered to his body, sopping and sticky. He glanced toward the quarry, blinking with nervous tension. The molten lake of lava had spread fast, a shifting mass of black, red, and orange that pulsed in the evening air.

The ground beneath them vibrated with a low, constant hum. Now and then, the earth crackled with an eerie sound, followed by the deep rumble of the lava, echoing like thunder.

The wrecked greenhouses were behind them, their skeletal frames leaning, and the floor littered with broken plants, their leaves torn and crushed. The tables were empty, and the plants were packed into every available inch of the plane, ready to be flown to Montana. There was barely room for Nadia and Dan.

An old prepper buddy of his had some land in the Big Sky state and a safe place to store the crop until they figured out what came next. One thing was clear, though—they weren't coming back to Oregon. Not that Dan cared. There was nothing for him here.

He didn't have time for more worries. The lava was climbing, filling the quarry at an alarming rate. The molten rock, glowing hot and bright, crept toward the Christmas tree farm, a smoldering tide that could soon swallow everything in its path. His stomach churned—not from the sight of the lava—but from the gnawing urgency that pushed him to hurry.

He had told Nadia this morning to stay back at the house and pack up the money and the rest of her stuff, but she insisted on helping him with the plants and the runway. Everything had to be her way. She always had to be in control. Now, they had to return to the house and pack it all up. It'd be dark by the time they finished, so they had no choice but to wait and fly out tomorrow. Even with this disaster, he wasn't willing to risk a night flight since they had been too cheap to add lights to the runway.

He wasn't leaving without the money. Not after all this. The stash was buried in the cement basement floor. It was nearly five million, all in one-hundred-dollar bills, packed tight in a safe. They'd worked for years to build up that fortune and with whatever was happening with the earth around here, he wasn't losing that cash.

He glanced around, eyes settling on Nadia, who was standing a few feet away by the edge of the tree line. Her back was to him, her body tense. She stood motionless, staring at the lava, her eyes narrow, lips pressed tight. The heat from the quarry reached her even at this distance, the air shimmering in waves.

"Nadia, let's get back," he hollered, heading for the truck.

Nadia didn't respond. The sulfurous air was abrasive, a harsh bite that scraped at her throat with every breath. The sky above had turned sickly yellow, the haze swirling like a weird fog that clung to the earth. Nadia's anger simmered, just as hot as the lava creeping into the quarry. Earthquakes and lava. It was so unfair.

They hadn't discussed warning anyone—Sweet Home, the neighbors, the town—they were all on their own. The only thing that mattered now was getting back to the house, grabbing what they needed, and getting the hell out before the lava wrecked the runway.

She ran over to the truck and clambered in the passenger side. "Let's go," she said, her voice heated, like the air around them.

Dan didn't hesitate. He yanked his door shut and started the motor. The rumble of the truck's engine drowned out everything else—the clashing of the earth, the hiss of the lava, the sickly smell of sulfur—but it couldn't drown the gnawing feeling in his gut. They needed to hurry.

Reed and Chloe, Lebanon, OR: 7 p.m.

The night stretched long across Oliver's front lawn. A tangle of folding chairs and makeshift bedding littered the grass. Across the street, a guy with a bushy mustache had set up his ham radio on the curb, wires trailing to his setup from a battered shed, which leaned unsteadily in the backyard. Oliver called him Carl. Brett stuck close to the amateur operator, hoping to hear something positive about Albany.

By dark, a soft hum of static filled the air as Carl twisted the dial, searching. When the first crackling voice came through, everyone stopped talking, and quiet fell over the group, breath held as the words filtered through. The conversation was brief, but the news was grim, with the scale of the disaster unfolding in slow, terrible pieces. It was the first real sense they'd gotten of just how bad things were.

"All the way to San Diego..." Chloe's voice was a whisper, the shock clear on her face as she stared blankly into the dark.

A woman beside her gasped. "Earthquakes and tsunamis all the way up to British Columbia! My sister lives in Vancouver..."

"No wonder we're not seeing rescue units," Reed shook his head as the scope of the devastation dawned on him. "It's the whole west coast. And with that quake we ran from this morning in Albany, maybe it's not done yet."

"What do you mean?" Oliver asked. He cradled a sleeping Mollie, anxiety wrinkling his youthful face.

"What happened at the school, those rifts that split the ground in north Albany didn't just happen yesterday afternoon. We had aftershocks all night," Chloe told him.

"When we tried to drive out on US 20 this morning, another quake hit," Brett added. "Split the ground wide open for miles, tore the road apart. We barely made it away."

"You teach science. Is that possible?" Oliver asked Chloe. Several people drew in to hear what she had to say.

"I teach biology, not earth sciences. I don't know how it's possible, but it sure happened." Stress lines tracked over Chloe's brow.

"Are we safe here?" Carl asked the question everyone was thinking.

"I don't know. I don't know what is going on. There has only been one aftershock since we arrived tonight, and it was nowhere near as bad as the activity this morning. I think if the tremors here increase in strength or volume, we should not take any chances; just leave and head south down US 20."

"Oh, I don't want to leave Lebanon," an older man with a cane cut in. 'My daughter has a house across town. She'll be here to check up on me."

"Maybe we can get more answers from the radio," Chloe said.

I'm trying," Carl said. "I don't think the problem is the radio. I think there just isn't a lot of chatter." He tried for hours, but the news was sporadic. The only thing they knew for sure was that this was bigger than Albany and Lebanon.

With the ruins spread around them, the collapsed houses created a jagged profile against the dark sky. Their windows were gone, roofs buckled inward, and walls cracked open. No one dared to sleep inside. It was safer on the lawn, where at least the world couldn't fall on them.

A dozen neighbors joined them and sat in the yard in a loose circle on the grass, hands stiff from the cold, minds numb with exhaustion and disbelief. They were here, waiting. For rescue or daylight. In the dark, it seemed insurmountable.

Reed moved through the group, checking on the wounded, though the supplies were meager. The bandages from the kids' go-bags had been used up quickly. He cleaned and wrapped the gash on Oliver's leg. It didn't need stitches, but antibiotic ointment was going fast. The cuts and bruises were minor compared to the scale of what had happened. Luckily, there were no major injuries among the group.

Reed's hands moved with practiced ease, offering what comfort he could—a soft hand on a shoulder, a gentle word, though they all knew there wasn't much more to say. Helicopters had flown over all day, but if any landed, they weren't in this suburb. No rescue teams. No signs of help. He wondered if they had sent all the aid to Portland.

Chloe pulled the vegetables from the truck, grateful she had picked up the large, dented pot from the fruit and vegetable stand. Matthias helped her build a fire with sticks and scraps, pulling matches from his go-bag. The crackle of flames soon filled the air, cutting through the tension.

Together, they prepared a hot soup, rummaging through the pile of produce—carrots, tomatoes, onions, and some green and yellow squash—and dropping them into the pot.

One of Oliver's neighbors provided extra bottled water. Chloe poured the water over the produce, watching the liquid pool around it, grateful but uneasy. The woman had been lucky, she said—just came from the market when the quake hit. She had not yet entered the house and was standing on the sidewalk when the first tremor hit. The quake flattened her home and crushed her car under a tree, but at least she had the bottled water.

Chloe glanced toward the street, eyeing the dirty puddles that had formed in the gaps where the pipes had cracked open, grayish streaks of muck floating on the surface. She didn't say it out loud, but the worry gnawed at her. There wasn't enough clean water. Not nearly enough.

The fire popped and crackled, sending a smoky trail into the air. The soup steamed, filling the night with the scent of the simmering vegetables. Using whatever they could find for makeshift bowls, everyone ate. They sat around the fire, the conversation muted. The soup was more of a stew, but it was hot—and for most of them, that was more than they had had in a day.

She ensured the kids ate a full meal, even a quiet, resentful Winnie. The little girl glared daggers at Oliver. But Charlie wormed his way back into her lap, looking for his dinner, soon distracting her. Eventually, the two of them curled up by the fire.

The rest of the hungry dogs ate the cooled stew without complaint, and Chloe was amused to see Shadow lick her dish clean while still leaving every carrot at the bottom. Duke came in behind her and finished off the orange bits quickly.

The ground would shift beneath them every so often, a light tremor that sent ripples through the soup, making the pot rattle on the fire. Both men and women flinched, but no one panicked. They were getting used to it by now, reminders of how fragile everything had become.

Each time the ground moved, Chloe looked for Reed. She'd catch him looking for her, and they'd exchanged glances, thinking the same thing. Would the aftershocks turn into the terrifying disaster of this morning? But nothing more happened.

So the night wore on, cold, dark, everyone on edge.

A sudden, frantic burst of barking sliced through the midnight air, the sharp sound of Bella's growls carrying on the cool breeze. Her bark was frantic with anger, threat laced through her snarls. Reed's heart leaped into his throat as the dog's voice echoed off the house and into the darkened yard. He rushed toward the noise, Brett and Carl following, trying not to trip over the remains of a tattered fence tossed all along the property.

As he rounded the corner of the house, the beam of his flashlight swept over the scene. Bella, usually the most placid of the dogs, was in a frenzy, teeth bared, lunging and clawing at the broken wall. Her fur bristled, her body trembling with wild energy as she dug furiously into the rubble. Dust and small rocks flew as she tossed the earth aside in desperate attempts to uncover whatever was hidden behind the boards.

Reed called her name, his voice cutting through her anger, but she ignored him, focusing solely on the unseen object. She barked again, louder, every inch an Alaskan Shepherd. She was all muscle, teeth, and fur. Reed had a fleeting thought that maybe her forebears would stand up to a polar bear with this kind of courage. He couldn't imagine what was causing this reaction in Lebanon.

The air around them stank of damp earth and smoke. The wind caught the fumes of hundreds of fires, blowing it over the yard. Reed's heart pounded in his chest as he got closer, flashlight in hand, the beam dancing over the cluttered yard.

With effort, Reed got a rope around Bella's neck, pulling her back as she fought against him. Her growls turned into frustrated whines, her body straining against the leash. She was relentless, eyes wide and focused, her barking still echoing through the yard. Brett took the leash, trying to calm the big dog to no avail.

With Bella held back, Reed carefully approached the pile. More flashlights lit up the wreckage as a few others joined, cutting through the darkness. A pair of wide eyes gleamed back at them in the shadow of the collapsed house wedged into a crawl space. A brown tabby cat, covered in dust, huddled in the corner. The cat's thin body quivered, but its green eyes spit fire.

Before he could move closer, the cat hissed and lashed out, its claws flashing in the dim light as it scrambled to defend itself. Reed flinched back, but Carl quickly threw his heavy coat over the cat, pinning it long enough to pry it free from the rubble.

The moment it was out of the rubbish, Bella's restraint snapped. She lunged again, her growls rising in pitch, desperate to get at the animal. The tabby twisted and snarled, its back arched, and before anyone could react, it sprang free from the coat, its lithe body twisting like a shadow, vanishing into the night.

Bella bolted after it, barking madly, but the cat was already gone, now part of the darkness. Reed exhaled sharply as the dog continued to bark into the empty night.

He looked at the others apologetically. "Sorry, Bella hates cats. We never knew why, but she always goes nuts when she sees one. It's the main reason we couldn't get her adopted out.

Brett had run after her and recaptured the rope. With much persuasion, he finally coaxed the wolf-like dog back to the front yard. She sat by Carl, almost as if she suspected he'd bring the cat back, but she was quiet for the rest of the night. Carl tied her rope around a signpost as a precaution.

The truck became a refuge as the night wore on, and the fire burned low. Piper carried Winnie inside, holding her close, wrapping them both in the truck's blanket. Charlie, small and dark, curled into Winnie's lap, his tiny body a comforting weight against her. The rhythmic thumping of his heartbeat seemed to soothe her, and soon, her breath slowed, heavy with the exhaustion of her tears.

Matthias climbed into the front seat, his body slumping as he sat down, but he reached carefully for Shadow, the dog's paws skimming the seat before settling against his side. Matthias adjusted Shadow gently, making sure the dog was comfortable before leaning back, his eyes heavy, his body pulled by the gravity of exhaustion.

Across the yard, Oliver sat on the ground, cradling Mollie in his arms. He didn't wipe away his tears. He didn't need to. His neighbors sat with him, but even their presence couldn't ease the raw ache in the air. It was a long night, a subdued silence interrupted by distant rumbles of falling ruins and the occasional aftershock.

Chapter Nine

Miguel and Walter, Corvallis, OR: May 20, 7 p.m.

Washington Park was submerged, its rolling expanse of green swallowed by a murky lake. The fading light of twilight barely revealed the outlines of soccer nets and baseball fences, now lost in the swirling brown water. The low, flat fields where kids ran and played yesterday were now an unrecognizable stretch of water.

Walter's mouth fell open. "What the hell is going on with all this water?" he blurted as they stood at the crest of a hill, its six-foot rise offering only a temporary respite from the encroaching flood. The chill of the evening air cut through them, the cold seeping through the damp fabric of their clothes. The faint beam of their flashlights sliced through the shadows, illuminating ripples in the water but little else.

They had exited the USGS building through the back, picking their way through a maze of fallen birches and the deformed parking lot so the analyst had missed seeing the river flowing in the streets. The water had surged in quickly, but after years of living in Corvallis, Miguel had known to worry about the park's low elevation the moment Vancris had declared it as the meeting point. Sure enough, subsidence between here and the river sank the ground enough to flood the whole area.

The river was still rising, inch by inch. From the east, it had rushed in, rolling across the edges of the field like a tide until it covered everything. It reeked. As the ripples moved, the earth beneath them seemed to shift, a silent reminder of the instability gnawing at the city's foundation. A nasty-smelling mist hung over the surface, obscuring their view.

"We're not landing a helicopter here," Miguel said, scanning the area. The visibility was near zero, with the water still creeping up, and the mist only made things worse. There was no place flat enough and no solid ground to land on. They'd have to find another way.

"Well, the Benton Center's out," Walter said, reading his mind. "That old brick building collapsed yesterday, and the new one didn't hold up either."

"We need to get someplace high and flag down the helicopter. If we use the flashlights, maybe we can draw them to us."

"Yeah, but where?" Walter's voice was flat, tinged with frustration. "We can barely see past the waterline." It was nearly full-on dark by now, and only the soft lapping of the water broke the stillness.

Miguel squinted through the growing dark. "Corvallis High School is six blocks from here. They have a big track field. Maybe the water hasn't reached that far, or maybe we can find a building along the way to stand on."

He adjusted the weight of his pack, pulling it tighter across his shoulders. Before they left the USGS building, he had changed into the sweatpants and sweatshirt from his knapsack but they offered little warmth against the brisk air. His sneakers, still damp from the river earlier, were cold. But something nagged at him, a memory from earlier. He dropped his bag at his feet.

"Hang on a minute," Miguel said, heading toward the water.

Walter watched as he carefully stepped down the incline until he reached the water's edge.

"What are you doing?" Walter asked. Anxiety wrinkled his forehead.

Miguel crouched down and dipped his fingers in the oily water. Surprised, he pulled them back. The water wasn't just warm, it was hot! "Something is heating this water," he told Walter.

Walter scrambled down to stand next to the director, swishing his own fingers in the muddy lake. The look of surprise on his face was comical. "What is this?"

Miguel straightened, scanning the water's surface, where the ripples seemed to shudder instead of roll. "Something along the line is heating this water. The land by the river is sinking with the tremors, but something's pushing heat into the water."

"This is a lot of water to heat," Walter looked out over the dark lake. "Are you thinking we're standing over a pocket of subsurface magma? Like a hot spring?" He scanned the lake. "On this scale, it would have to be enormous."

"I don't know what to think, but let's try to get to the high school."

They climbed back up the incline, and Miguel retrieved his pack. Their flashlights flickered erratically as they made their way toward NW 9th Street. The street was a mess—water had spilled over the curb, running along the swale. He didn't know if rescue efforts were happening in other parts of the city, but everything was dark and still here. The sound of the moving water echoed around them. He thought about the big guy feeding bodies to the roaches again and shivered.

"Can we cross that?" Walter asked doubtfully, eyeing the torrent.

"I think we have to. Let's take it slow. The ground's probably a mess under the water." They stepped forward carefully, the water creeping up to their shins, its warmth still unsettling. Beneath their feet, the pavement was anything but smooth. Cracked asphalt stuck out of the ground, waiting to trip them.

Walter sneezed as he tasted and sniffed the foulness. The water swirled around them, tugging at their legs with every step. The heat was strange; it was not enough to burn, but it was uncomfortable. They crossed as fast as they could.

"We need to warn people to leave," Walter said, his thoughts zipping.

"And send them where? How far do we evacuate? If we're right, sending people in any direction could be just as dangerous. We don't know enough."

Frustrated, Walter stopped. "We know. You just don't want to believe my model. At the very least, anybody in Corvallis should get to the other side of the river. Best case, they get on the west side of Interstate 5 and head south until they get to California."

"That's hundreds of miles. Injured people, folks with kids can't just pick up and head south!"

"They can if the alternative is staying here and dying!"

Miguel didn't answer. He wondered if Walter was right, but dismissing the practical knowledge gained from years of experience was foolhardy. It seemed impossible that a disaster of this magnitude could still be unfolding.

They moved on, leaving the street a twisted mess of flood and rubbish behind them. Passing between businesses and houses, they tried to keep to high ground. The land trembled continuously, water filling the low elevations to the south as the ground sank in that direction. The air felt heavier as the light faded completely, leaving only the piercing beams of their flashlights cutting through the darkness.

Stepping across parking lots of mangled concrete, Walter kicked the pieces away. Miguel was breathing hard and trying to keep up. Walter barely noticed. He kept scanning the skies for the helicopter. It got darker and spookier.

"Hey, look at that." Walter stopped and stared at the building in front of them. The corner had collapsed, and the recessed entry and big double-sided display windows had frames of jagged glass fragments all around. A faint, flickering light spilled from the inside. It was an electric light.

But it wasn't the light that caught Walter's attention. He aimed the beam higher, over the cluttered roof. A methodical pattern of sleek, professional-grade antennas covered it. Thin, silver rods gleamed faintly under the glow of their flashlights. Coaxial cables snaked down the sides, disappearing behind the walls.

"This guy has electricity, and he's broadcasting," Walter exclaimed, his voice rising with the realization.

"Could we use that to reach either the governor? Or Reston?" Miguel asked anxiously.

"If he can broadcast, we can too. Let's go in."

The sign out front was long gone, but it didn't take long to figure out what kind of store this was. The strong scent of animals, pet food, and cleaning products filled the air. The floor was littered with overturned shelves, bags of kibble scattered like confetti, chewed-up toys, and half-empty grooming supplies strewn in chaotic piles. Brightly colored collars and plastic bags of treats lay jumbled together; tipped-over water bowls held the remnants of fresh water.

"It's a pet store," Miguel said, stepping carefully over a display of fallen leashes.

The animals seemed unharmed by the quake. The cages were upright, though not in their original spots. Rabbits munched on hay, guinea pigs shuffled nervously in their pens, and the birds, agitated, talked and squawked, their feathers puffed up, their chests heaving with nervous energy. Even the fish tanks were intact, only three-quarters full. The water was murky but calm.

Lizards sat perched, their bright eyes watching the men as they moved. A few puppies and kittens poked their faces through the bars of their enclosures, soft whines and mews filling the air. The noise from the animals masked their footsteps as they made their way deeper into the store.

At the back, near a small, dimly lit office, a man sat hunched over a cluttered desk. A dirty cap pulled low, casting shadows over his face. The brim was green, but Miguel couldn't make out the logo—likely the Oregon Ducks, though it didn't matter. What mattered was the man himself, his attention fixed on the notes scattered before him.

The guy didn't notice them.

He wore a faded green and yellow Oregon jersey, loose-fitting over his thin frame, sleeves rolled up. His eyes were wide, darting over the notes in front of him. His lips moved rapidly as he spoke into a microphone, his voice crackling over the speakers.

"...And, folks, if you're just tuning in, let me tell you, this is no ordinary quake. No, we're seeing tremors coming in waves, like the ground itself is... *shifting*, like it's *settling*—but it's not settling, it's *breaking*, pulling itself apart piece by piece!" His voice rose with excitement, unfazed by the damage around him. "The river? It's tipped west, rolling into the city! And no, this isn't a coincidence, people. It's the seismic activity. That's right. The river banks? They're *unstable*. The *ground's* sinking, people! That's why it flooded, why the ground is sinking. The water's... well, it's *hot*, too, I felt it! It's thermal runoff! Do you think it's just the earthquake? No, this is deeper. The earth's heat is rising, *literally*."

His voice was erratic. The guy was almost giddy with the thrill of spinning theories. His hand gestured wildly, occasionally tapping the mic to emphasize points as though speaking to a live audience. "And what happens next? I'll tell you what happens next—more tremors. Bigger ones. We're talking about all the *damn* fault lines under Oregon, people. They're going to snap. It's only a matter of time before the entire city—*this* city—goes under."

He paused for a breath, his eyes glinting with excitement. He didn't see the two men walking up the aisle. They were barely a few feet away, standing beside the glass tanks holding the mice, geckos, and frogs. Busy broadcasting, the guy didn't seem to notice, lost in his own frantic updates, shaking his head as though unraveling some grand mystery.

"...And we're not done yet. Aftershocks? They're not random; they're part of a *pattern*. A signal. The earth's got its own radio station now, broadcasting—whether or not we like it." He chuckled to himself, tapping a few keys on his laptop, eyes darting from the screen to the microphone as the conspiracy theorist continued, oblivious. "Corvallis is doomed. The rest of Oregon isn't far behind. This isn't a fluke! We've been living on borrowed time; now it's time to *pay the price*. The West Coast? Every damn thing could go up in smoke! The volcanoes are restless—Mount Hood? *Mount St. Helens?* Don't get me started on Mount Shasta! They're *primed*, sitting on the edge, just waiting for the signal and the tremors. That's the signal. It's happening now."

The man shifted his weight, his voice trembling with the energy of his own words. "The Ring of Fire's a ticking time bomb. It's not just one eruption. It's a *chain reaction*. When one goes, they all go. And this city? This *entire* coast? It's going down, and it's gonna happen fast. The earthquakes are just the warm-up. When the volcanoes blow, it's gonna be over in the blink of an eye."

His voice grew louder and more frantic as he drove his point home. "If you're hearing this, you need to leave. *Now.* Don't wait. Don't think you have time to pack. You don't. Run while you still can! Because when the Ring of Fire goes—*and it's coming*—you won't have another chance. The West Coast will *sink*." He laughed a high, tense sound. "Literally, people! The ground's already cracking open, the water's boiling, and the air's weighted with something else— *destruction*. So, if you're still in the city, you've got maybe— *maybe*—a few days before it's too late. Get out! Run while you can!"

He leaned closer to the mic, his voice barely a whisper like he was telling a secret. "It's over. And we're not just talking about a flood or a quake. We're talking about the end. The Earth is shifting, people. *Everything* is coming apart."

He jumped to his feet, pacing around the desk, when he almost ran into Walter, stopping short with surprise. Standing up straight, his frantic expression relaxed, and the craziness faded away. He pulled off the headset and sat it on the desk.

"Hello. Did you want to buy a pet?" he inquired, his voice shifting to a calm, professional tone.

"Uh, we heard your podcast," Walter told him cautiously.

The guy brightened. "Pretty good, huh? Maybe you've listened before? Emmet Shale is my name, and my podcast is called '*The Big One Any Day Now*.' I'm also an author, inventor, and fringe geologist. I coined that term because academia doesn't believe me, but I ask you, who is right now? For years, I've warned people along the West Coast that these quakes were long overdue. But I knew the time had come last week, and we were only days away from the biggest earthquake yet. The west coast is going to be remade!"

"I'm Walter Simmons," the analyst introduced himself, his tone skeptical. "So, where did you get your information?"

"Cape Cove Beach. Last Tuesday, several dozen oarfish washed up on the shore. Some of them were over fifteen feet long! Once I heard about the doomsday fish, I knew it was only a matter of time."

"Doomsday fish?"

"Sure, doomsday fish or oarfish live in the deepest part of the ocean. They only wash ashore when a big earthquake is imminent. Last week, they started rolling in. Washed ashore along Cape Cove and north of there. I rode down to see myself. They were big mothers, like fifteen-twenty feet long! When you see one, it's an omen. I guess a couple of dozen is a lot bigger omen."

"Omens, o-kaaaay." Walter shook his head.

"Not just the oarfish, man. Why do you think I own a Pet Store? Animals can predict earthquakes. Everything got real quiet in here fifteen minutes before the first jolt, and then they all went crazy seconds before the quake started. It gave me enough warning to strap down and ride it out safely." He pointed to a makeshift contraption that looked like a steampunk overstuffed armchair along the wall.

Built sturdy and solid with a reinforced frame, it had stocky wooden beams at the base and heavy, wide-set legs to keep the chair grounded. Beneath, steel anchors jutted from the concrete to reduce the shaking. An old blue cushion, frayed at the edges from years of use, was held tightly by a full-body harness, the straps crossing over it. Above, a canopy of brushed aluminum arced high, its surface catching the flickering light in bright reflections.

Emmet looked proud. "You can't see it, but I built a vibration-dampening system underneath, like shock absorbers for a chair. It worked a treat! Thanks to the early warning from the animals, I had enough time to get strapped in and rode that quake out as slick as you please."

Walter shook his head, but he had to admit he was a little impressed. The few minutes he spent under the desk weren't comfortable at all. "You were lucky," he said.

"Luck, nothing," Emmet laughed. "I knew Sunday night it was going to be yesterday. The ants out back didn't go back into their mounds when it got dark. It's a proven fact that ants will stop their normal behavior before earthquakes. They stay outside their mounds instead of going to sleep at night. They knew the quake was coming. It was Ant-icipation!"

The science geek in Walter didn't know how to respond to that without being rude, so instead, he gestured toward the broadcasting equipment to change the subject. "How are you generating electricity after the quake?"

Emmet waved his skinny arms, his head bobbing up and down like a chicken. Walter noticed his cap matched his jersey. "I've been ready for the big one for years. I have a commercial backup generator in the back parking lot, and I powered that puppy up as soon as the quake ended. This building is retrofitted for an earthquake, and my antennas and the rest of my equipment are tied securely down. My audience needs to hear from me."

"And you're telling them to leave Corvallis?" Walter shot a look at Miguel. The Director just rolled his eyes.

"Not just Corvallis, they should leave all of Oregon! This isn't just your basic earthquake, guy; this is the *BIG ONE*!" He emphasized the last two words, pumping his fist. "The quakes haven't stopped, and those aren't just aftershocks. This is spreading, Corvallis, and most of the west coast is going to sink, and then," he stopped short and poked at Walter with a finger, "then it's prime time, and we'll be looking at Volcano Alley!"

"Hmm, volcano alley," Miguel stepped around the cages and held out a hand. "Mr. Shale, I'm Director Miguel Santiago with the USGS. We're in the building about three blocks over. Do you know it?"

"Sure, over by Washington Park," Emmet said.

Tired and edgy, Miguel got right to the point: "We need to get a message out as soon as possible. Can we use your equipment?"

"What kind of message?" Emmet looked suspicious.

"The USGS was sending a helicopter to Washington Park for us, but the park is flooded. We hoped to use your equipment to reach the helicopter and tell them to pick us up at the high school."

"The park is flooded. I knew it! The land is sinking." Emmet rushed to the front of the building and peered out. He called back, "I'm ready; I just have to get the last of the animals on the boat."

"Boat?" Miguel was bewildered.

Emmet hustled back and started picking up cages.

"You know how to use that equipment?" he asked Walter, indicating his broadcasting setup.

"I think so," Walter said.

"I've got a duplicate setup on my boat out back. You can use this rig to contact your helicopter, but you had better hurry. Just before you guys showed up a guy up near Portland called in. He said over the last twenty-four hours, the groundwater levels rose, flooding the whole of the upper Willamette Valley where he is. He was on top of his barn trying to get someone to fly in and rescue his family."

Miguel frowned. "That's not possible."

Walter slid him a side-eye. "Maybe you should stop saying that, Boss," he said. "I think today will rewrite just what is and is not possible."

Cages under his arms, Emmet laughed out loud. "Better listen to the kid, Director. I think he's right. You know that huge aquifer under us that's been supplying water to this state? Well, that guy I talked to said it has ruptured in multiple places. He said liquefaction during the quake forced water and soil up through these massive cracks. The ground is breaking away, sinking, and a flood is heading this way. So, make your call. I need to finish loading my boat."

Yanking open the back door, the metal screeching against its frame, Emmet disappeared into the darkness.

Walter sat down and started working the switches. He tuned into several channels, calling out for the USGS helicopter. Miguel's eyes stayed on him, but his mind was elsewhere, thinking furiously. What was going on under their feet?

His thoughts delved up Reelfoot Lake, in the Mississippi Valley. One of the most famous examples of groundwater flooding after an earthquake was the creation of that lake in Mississippi. It occurred after a series of powerful earthquakes near New Madrid, Missouri, in the early 19th century.

At that time, the earth itself had shifted, and in doing so, it created a lake out of nowhere. But that had been a small, contained event. What Emmet had described was *massive*—a hundred and fifty miles of disrupted land. The thought gnawed at him, impossible yet plausible. His head throbbed; his thoughts clouded with exhaustion.

Walter stood, grabbing his gear. "Okay, the helicopter is only a few miles out. There's nowhere to land around here, and they don't have time to wait for us to get to the high school, so they'll hover and drop a ladder. Let's get out back."

Miguel didn't like the sound of the ladder. His stomach flopped as he followed Walter outside through the back door and onto the asphalt. In the dim light, a vintage Chris Craft Capitan Cruiser loomed like an old ghost.

Sitting haphazardly hitched to a pickup; its worn wooden hull took up the lot. "THE BIG ONE" was etched across the exterior hull, and the letters on the side were the only fresh paint on the boat. Stains from years of exposure streaked, cracked, and faded the rich mahogany. The varnish had long since peeled away, leaving behind weathered, raw wood, its surface rough like dry skin.

The dull gray rope that was tied around the pitted chrome fittings swayed gently in the faint breeze. Rust had crept in, claiming the fittings and the brass cleats, which now bore a tarnished green hue. Above it all, the long, whip-like antenna reached for the sky, its thin metal frame catching the weak light from the building. The sagging canvas canopy, battered and torn, clung to the boat like a memory rotting with time. Cages of all sizes sat piled on the deck. Emmet took everything but the fish.

"The fish will just swim away when it floods," he told Walter. "They're all freshwater fish, and the tanks are open on the top."

"Where are you going?" Walter asked him. He could hear the helicopter approaching from the distance. Miguel had his flashlight out and was waving it in the air, trying to catch the pilot's attention.

"I'll follow the river south until I hit Eugene. My buddy there will help me get out of the state. Here," he shoved a small card at the man. "That's my website. You can follow my podcast directly on my site. I don't mess with those government-run hosting services. You know the ones I mean."

Bemused, Walter looked at the card as the helicopter hovered over them. A bright search beam centered over the parking lot. Sure enough, it had the 'The Big One Any Day Now' address.

"You sure you don't want to come with us?" he asked Emmet as the man clambered up the trailer and then onto the boat. He tucked the card in his pocket as the whipping wind tried to snatch it.

"Not a chance, boyo! Good luck to you both," he called, hanging on to his cap as he vanished into the cabin. A metal ladder dropped between them. His knapsack strapped tight on his back, Walter held the ladder steady, sending Miguel up first.

He couldn't see any water from where they stood, but somehow, he believed the crazy pet store owner. He hadn't trained his model to detect anomalies in historical flood data related to earthquakes, oarfish sightings, animal behavior, or insect activity. What would he see if he did?

As soon as he settled in his seat on the copter, he pulled out the laptop and got to work.

Albert Frost, US 226, OR: May 20, 7 p.m.

Albert Frost's hands rested on the steering wheel as he drove home, his aches and pains from falling out of the tractor and then being electrocuted by those blasted lines still bothering him. Beside him, Stella, a mop-head mess of a dog, sat perched on the seat, her wiry coat ruffled by the breeze coming through the open window.

"Damn dog," Albert muttered under his breath, his voice rough, "I don't need you. Don't need more trouble. There's always something."

She gave him a sideways glance, her dark eyes unreadable under the curls, while her ears perked up at every unfamiliar sound.

The old truck rumbled along the paved driveway as they approached Albert's ranch—a sprawling estate with manicured lawns and towering oaks that seemed out of place in the dusty landscape. The house was a massive, elegant structure nestled amid acres of land, its stone exterior glinting faintly in the fading light.

Albert sighed, his thoughts drifting. He had made the money and built this place for her, his wife, Stella. She had been everything: beautiful, spirited, and full of life. He loved her so much. There was nothing he would not have done to make her smile. He spent his life giving her everything he thought she deserved. In the end, the only thing he couldn't give her was good health. The unfairness still ate at him every day. He couldn't see past the bitterness.

Trying to stay busy since his loss, he cultivated and managed the Blue Sky Vegetable Market and the adjacent farm because that was the one business Stella had loved. He left the rest of his farms and businesses to tenant managers. The money kept rolling in, but it sure didn't mean much anymore. A team of gardeners and maids kept the house nice because he wouldn't let her house look anything less than perfect.

He dressed simply in worn jeans and a yellow shirt, the kind of attire that made him look like he had nothing, even though his bank account said otherwise. And he wearily made it through each day.

Stella woofed softly as they drove up the black pavement to the house, passing huge green shrubs just developing bud heads. He gave her a look. "What? It's too early for the hydrangeas to be blooming."

Stella chuffed and stuck her nose in the air. Albert grumbled under his breath. Now, the mutt was complaining about the landscaping.

Once inside, the large, spotless kitchen stood quietly. The maids knew to leave before he got home. He preferred solitude. Albert ignored everything and walked over to the pantry. Hundreds of neatly stacked cans, each label facing forward, lined the shelves in the big room. The maids shopped and stocked the pantry. Albert appreciated their help, though he rarely told them.

Moving stiffly, he prepared a quick dinner, nothing fancy. He opened a few cans, their sudden metallic pop breaking the stillness, the aroma of seasoned meats and vegetables blending in the air. The clink of a can opener was the only sound as Stella sat quietly on the floor, eyes fixed on him, her tail swishing lazily across the gleaming hardwood floor.

Dinner was simple, nothing to get excited about. Just the same food, day after day. Albert shoveled it into his mouth without tasting it, still gnawing on the bitter thoughts of the past. He had opened a can for Stella, too. They ate together. It wasn't until he washed the few dishes that he realized he had spent the meal talking to the dog and enjoyed sharing with someone. He couldn't even remember what he talked about. It was a long time since that had happened.

Afterward, they settled into the den. Albert dropped into the old recliner—a sagging, ratty chair with frayed upholstery that had seen better days, its springs creaking under his weight. Stella, however, curled on the plush luxury rug at his feet, a striking contrast to the worn chair. The rug, a rich blend of deep reds and intricate patterns, was the last piece of decor his late wife had chosen before she passed. Albert had not changed a thing in the house.

The air seemed still. The only sounds were the low hum of the furnace and the soft click of Stella's nails against the wooden floor as she adjusted her position. Albert leaned back, resting his head, trying to relax. But it was a momentary peace.

The ground trembled beneath him. At first, it was just a subtle vibration, a whisper that sent a chill up his spine. Then it grew. The floor bulged, throwing Albert forward in his chair. Stella barked, her body stiff, ears pinned back, her eyes wide with fear. Walls creaked, a deep, bone-rattling sound, followed by the harsh snap of wood splintering. The ceiling groaned in protest, powder trickling from above. The lights flickered, and the air grew dense with the smell of snapped wood and drywall.

Albert tried to rise, but another quake hit, stronger this time, throwing him back into the recliner. The walls cracked, and plaster rained down, filling the air with a musty odor. The room spun as the house seemed to collapse inward, the entire structure shaking violently, the sound of breaking beams and snapping wires deafening. He remembered the pretty blond, Chloe, this afternoon and her warnings of potentially more quakes.

Stella was at his side in an instant, her nails pulling at his shirt as she nudged his arm, her low growl urging him to move.

"I'm fine," Albert grunted, struggling to his feet, his legs unsteady. As he reached for the door, the entire house shifted again. The hardwood buckled beneath him. He fell, crashing onto the floor runner, a hard landing on the powder sprinkled rug.

Stella was already there, her smaller frame darting around him, her body vibrating urgency. She pulled at his sleeve with surprising strength, whining softly as if telling him to get up, then her teeth gripping his jacket. Albert pulled himself upright with another grunt, his legs weak and trembling. Together, they stumbled into the hall, but as they stepped from the den, the boards beneath them gave way again, this time with a violent crack, opening a wide hole in the floor. Stella yelped as she fell, disappearing into the blackness below.

"Stella!" Albert screamed, his heart skipping a beat. He dropped to his knees, reaching for her, but the space between them was too deep. His heart pounded in his chest as he leaned over the edge of the gaping hole, looking down into the darkness below. From the couch she landed on, Stella's eyes locked onto his, wide with fear but still steady. The lights flickered on and off, making it hard to see. More of the roof caved in, and another jolt buried the kitchen behind him.

Panic surged as he grabbed longboards from the side tables knocked over in the hall. He braced them on the remains of the first floor that now resembled a long ramp leading into the basement, with the end resting on the old couch. Albert limped to the living room windows and jerked free one section of the long drapes. Rolling it up like a makeshift rope and holding the fabric over one arm, he dropped back in front of the hole and slid down the ramp until he could wedge himself. Splinters dug into his skin, but he ignored the pain, inching down into the basement.

Winding one end around his wrist, he tossed the rest of the roll down to Stella, who was waiting on her forelegs on the back of the couch.

"Grab the curtain," he yelled.

He didn't know how, but Stella knew just what to do as if she were reading his mind. She bit into the heavy-weight cloth with her teeth. Struggling up the incline, her paws slipped, but she leveraged the cracks to gain a toehold, with Albert hauling on his end of the crude rope. The platform beneath him shuddered in time with the tremors, and the shaking made the whole procedure even more precarious.

Trying to reach Albert, she crept up the wooden section a few inches at a time, paws slipping, but thanks to her grip on the drapery, she made it far enough for him to grab her hair by the neck. Pulling hard, he boosted her up the remaining incline. Rolling her onto the solid floor, he lunged after her, his arms and shoulders barely clearing the ramp before the battered wedge of flooring completed its collapse beneath him.

Hanging from the rim by his elbows, aching and sneezing, he was shocked when Stella, still holding the improvised rope, backed down the hall, dragging him onto the solid first floor again, panting and disoriented. The ground trembled harder.

Albert scrabbled to his feet, tugging Stella close. They wobbled down the hallway and found the front doors gone, ripped from their hinges. The ground outside was splitting, geysers of dirt and rock bursting from the earth in blasts. The sound of the eruptions was deafening, each blast creating new craters.

Albert and Stella hurried to his truck, the engine revving as it tore down the driveway, the earth crumbling beneath them. Albert's thoughts flashed to Chloe again, to her seemingly impossible warnings. He slammed the truck into gear, tearing east on US 226, praying to find somewhere the earth wasn't collapsing.

Chapter Ten

Reed and Chloe, US 20, OR: 5 a.m.

When the sky changed to a bruised purple, and the sun finally rose, Reed found himself hoping for a better day. As he picked his way down US 20, he wondered if that would be possible. If the streets out of Lebanon were any sign, it wouldn't be easy.

They loaded up while Chloe kissed Mollie and hugged Oliver.

"Are you sure you don't want to stay here until help arrives?" Oliver asked her. The scrapes on his face had crusted over, and he looked worn.

"It's hard to say goodbye," she said, rubbing Mollie's soft cheek. "But I want to get these kids safely to their dad's place in Sweet Home."

He nodded, but his eyes were dark and sad. "Be safe, Chloe, and remember, you have my everlasting thanks for bringing Mollie home. If you hadn't made the trip…" he choked on the words. "Anyway, if you ever need a lawyer, you have pro bono service for life."

Chloe smiled at him. "I'll remember that."

Now, on the road, she tucked that memory away for later. She hoped that one day, their paths might cross, and she could see Mollie again—maybe tell her about her mother. The thought made her smile for a minute, and then her fingers locked on the door handle as she braced herself, sitting upright, her eyes scanning the roadside for any sign of trouble. A few cars passed, but more people were on foot than there had been yesterday.

The truck jolted as Reed drove, trying to control the vehicle as it lurched over another stretch of torn-up road. The engine groaned, and a low knocking sound came from beneath the hood, followed by a dull rattle, as if something loose had been tossed into the works. Reed winced, praying the engine wouldn't seize up completely.

US 20 ahead wasn't an improvement. Blowholes had shattered the asphalt, stretching to the south, leaving sand and rocks piled around the craters. The F-150 bounced and jerked as he swerved to avoid damaging the tires. The engine sputtered again, a sound that made his stomach tighten. He glanced at the dashboard—too many warning lights lit, especially the one he dreaded—Check Engine. The strained thrum of the motor was the only constant sound the truck made.

Brett had already worked on the engine this morning. About a mile out of Lebanon, they had stalled. Rolling one minute and dead the next. The young mechanic had checked under the hood, with Matthias holding the flashlight. For fifteen minutes, the younger man had worked with what little he had—twisting, tightening, and cursing softly until he found the trouble—a loose coil wire. He reattached the wire, and the engine turned over. It sounded rough, but it ran. They could drive, for now.

But that wasn't Reed's only worry. The smoke ahead thickened, a dark, suffocating curtain hanging over the horizon. His unease grew as they neared the growing haze. The air in Lebanon was still heavy with the remnants of small fires that had mostly been contained, but the smoke here felt ominous. The earthquake must have devastated Sweet Home. He worried about what that meant for the kids and their father.

In the truck bed, the dogs shifted restlessly, their paws scraping against the metal floor, adjusting to the truck's rough ride. Brett and Matthias crouched low, their bodies bouncing as the vehicle jolted, straining for balance.

In the back seat, Piper and Winnie huddled together, the older girl's arms wrapped protectively around her younger sister. Winnie nestled Charlie comfortably in the crook of her lap, his head resting in her arms and his big ears twitching. The girls whispered, their voices barely audible over the truck's rattling.

Beside Reed, Chloe sat with her spine stiff, her eyes fixed on the smoky horizon. Her silence spoke louder than words, the weight of her thoughts pressing down. He could feel her gaze even without looking. Her lips were pressed tight, her chin set. Since their brief exchange the night before, she hadn't said much to him, and he got the distinct sense she didn't particularly like him.

On the other hand, she sat with Watson at her feet at the end of the evening, and he watched her fondle his golden lab, stroking his fur. Everyone liked Watson. Reed figured he might need to take notes from the dog. With a shake of his head, he refocused on the road.

The quake left its mark everywhere, warping the land into something unrecognizable. The truck hit another stretch of road that felt like it had been chewed up and spit out. They swerved to avoid chunks of asphalt that were too high to drive over. Some side roads were completely blocked, buried under piles of junk that even a tank wouldn't get through. Reed kept to the highway, fingers crossed, hoping for smoother terrain.

They weren't even halfway to Sweet Home.

Miguel and Walter, Portland, OR: May 21, 5 a.m.

By the time the sun rose against the hazy horizon, Miguel and Walter's heads were pounding from hours of constant noise and disjointed radio chatter. The journey had stretched through the night, the crew making repeated stops to drop off supplies and extract rescuers from the most critical areas.

The steady hum of the helicopter blades pierced the cool morning, stirring the smoke into a smothering haze. Below them, the city of Portland lay in ruins, a scene of unimaginable destruction.

The landscape was unrecognizable. Thousands of buildings were destroyed. The Forest Park USGS office was no exception, located just outside the park in Northwest Heights and three miles west of the Willamette River in Portland.

The building looked like it had been flung from the sky, the structure sagging, cracked, and crumbling. Gaps split the walls, exposed wires hung in the morning air, and the smell of crushed stone and burning rubber clung to the air. A small area had been cleared, but the pilot took one look at the cluttered patch and refused to land. Miguel and Walter had to climb back down the ladder, their legs aching from the descent.

Inside, bedlam reigned. People darted between pieces of broken furniture, and scattered papers lay everywhere, blown by the wind snaking through the gaps in the walls. Frantic conversations rose and fell. The scent of scorched electronics permeated the rooms, mingling with the odor of sweat and fear. Techs rushed around, trying to salvage what little they could, pulling equipment from the rubble, but most of it was beyond saving.

Miguel and Walter exchanged a quick, frustrated glance, speaking in hushed tones as they tried to make sense of the madness. Talking to their colleagues, Miguel and Walter painfully realized that the usual processes of scientific inquiry had been upended. Nothing about the earthquake made sense. Nothing fit into the patterns they had studied.

Even the aftershocks, which should have been diminishing, were growing stronger and more violent. The rupture zones were too deep and too far-reaching for anyone to comprehend. Conversations erupted in fragmented bursts of confusion, with voices rattling off data points that seemed to defy logic. No one had answers—only more questions.

"We're seeing things that don't make sense," an analyst ranted to Walter, his voice shaking. "These numbers—they're impossible."

Walter grunted in agreement, staring at the readouts that offered no answers. The numbers lined up without rhyme or reason, just like the ground beneath them, which refused to stop shaking. The fissures were deepening, spreading like a disease through the landscape.

Corvallis was still sinking—every second a reminder that no one knew how long it would remain above the rising waters. Some were already calling it Willamette Lake. The thought lingered in his mind, dark and unsettling. Whatever had caused this was far bigger than anyone could grasp. Emmet Shale's warnings now felt less like paranoia and more like a grim prediction.

The tremors showed no sign of letting up, some more violent than any so far. The earth kept biting back, swallowing cities whole. Albany, Crabtree, Lacomb—all gone, erased without a trace. The dense forests of Santiam were the next in line, though no one could say if the ground would settle in time to spare what remained. The central towns were all in danger, their fates uncertain.

There was no explanation for why the earthquakes surged eastward, why the earth refused to quiet, and why the tremors seemed endless. No one had answers. The data on the screens was a blur of incomprehensible numbers, relentless and cold. Forty hours of this. Mountains buckled, forests cracked, and the earth seemed to breathe in confusion. There was no pattern, no logic behind any of it.

Then, Gemma McMan appeared. Her tall frame cut through the noise, her graying hair pulled back tight, her face drawn with worry. Behind her, a younger man—a techie barely in his twenties—was glued to his laptop, his focus so intense it was as if the rest of the world had ceased to exist. He barely acknowledged other people as Gemma guided him through the frenzied halls, but his eyes never left the screen, fingers typing furiously.

Walter watched him, almost envious of how the guy could lose himself in the numbers and work. He wished he could do the same, find some solace in the data, in something that made sense.

"Miguel," she said, extending a hand. "Glad to see you made it."

Miguel shook her hand, his grip firm but tired. "Gemma. I hoped things would be better here."

She grimaced. "No luck there. Portland's in pieces. Vancris said you're bringing something critical that might help us understand what's happening?"

Miguel nodded. "Meet Walter Simmons. He's an analyst on our team. He's built a model that seems to match what's going on. I thought we could get it to some senior technicians and see if it means anything."

The young man—Tau—looked up from his screen, his almond-shaped eyes sparking with interest as they studied the tall analyst and his laptop. "I'm Tau Wang," he said quickly, offering Walter a handshake.

"Walter Simmons." He shook the other man's hand, noticing how Tau's hands returned swiftly to his laptop, fingers tapping even as he listened.

"Tau is a senior data scientist visiting from the Reston USGS office. He got here Monday afternoon, just in time for the earthquake. Vancris asked him to look at what you have." Gemma stepped back, giving Tau a little push. "Could you gentlemen work together, please?"

Without waiting for further pleasantries, Gemma turned to Miguel. "You need to come with me. We've got a critical situation with the CEI Hub tanks. I could really use your expertise."

Neither Walter nor Tau noticed them leave.

The two men found a corner in the building's wreckage, scrounging up connections to the generator to maintain batteries and boost their internet link. The noise of frantic workers and distant shouts faded away, irrelevant, as they sat down together while Walter laid out his findings.

Tau scanned the program on the screen, nodding occasionally, the tech talk flowing between them in quick bursts. Their world shrank to numbers and data, to trying to understand the chaos they couldn't control. They had no time for the crumbling building or the disasters unfolding outside.

They were consumed by the puzzle beneath them—why the earth kept shaking, why the damage spread so wildly. It was all they could focus on. Outside, the world went on.

Oregon's largest city was in ruins. Already torn apart by Monday's massive quake, Portland was about to sink deeper into hell. More than half the population had perished before the quake ended, victims of pancaked buildings and blunt force trauma. The survivors wandered all night, cold and injured, trying to dig through the collapsed buildings for anyone alive. Now, the situation would grow more dire.

Though Director Gemma McMan and the authorities had known for years that the ground beneath the Critical Energy Hub was unstable and that the tanks rested on unreliable fill dirt, they had done little to prepare. The costs were simply too high, and the odds of a major earthquake were not compelling enough.

Less than half of the 600 fuel tanks were retrofitted and prepared for a major earthquake. The hub, precariously positioned on the six-mile peninsula along the Willamette River's west bank, sat on poor soils, including loose silt and sandbanks. Some tanks were over 100 years old. The hub had a combined storage capacity of 350 *million* gallons.

When Monday's quake hit, raw screeches echoed as the tanks were shoved in all directions, metal scraping against metal with terrifying consequences. One by one, the tanks tore apart. The quake's force slammed them back together, sending them ricocheting off each other like oversized marbles, their sides crumpling and splitting with every violent collision. There was the sickening sound of cracking steel, followed by the hiss of pressure releasing. Fuel splattered out in toxic, oily streams, darkening the earth and the surrounding water in a swift, suffocating blanket. The stench of gasoline and chemicals stung the air, mingling with the dampness of the river and the sharp, metallic odor of shredded metal.

With each tank's collapse, the disaster grew. More shocks smashed through until the entire complex buckled under the earth's power. The sound of the collapsing metal and concrete rolled through Portland as portions of the facility crumbled into the river. Ten minutes after the quake stopped, almost every tank was damaged, from slow, steady leaks to massive tears or warped walls releasing a hundred types of liquid fuels, the chemicals pouring from the ruptured tanks. The worst-case scenario had arrived—and no one had a solution.

Mangled, unidentifiable objects drifted on the churning waters. All six miles of the CEI hub failed, releasing dangerous environmental toxins with names that most of Portland's population had never heard of. Lethal gases swirled above the water.

A tidal wave of fuel surged across the riverfront, engulfing streets and buildings in a slick, poisonous flood. The sheer scale of it was staggering—190 million gallons of fuel pouring out with a force that dwarfed even the most infamous disasters. In comparison, the Exxon Valdez disaster had released only 11 million gallons of crude, a mere fraction of this deluge. The BP Deepwater Horizon spill, before now the largest in U.S. history, had unleashed 134 million gallons into the Gulf of Mexico. But this was different, this was a land-locked disaster. The stench of diesel, gasoline, and toxic chemicals saturated the air.

At sunrise, the river, now slick with a dark, oily sheen, shimmered like a cursed mirror. Drifting off the water, the sharp aftertaste of sulfur created a fog so strong it seemed to settle on the skin, staining everything it touched.

Constant tremors chipped wedges of soil away at the riverbanks, each shock sinking the shore and widening the river, pulling toxic fuel into the city's heart. It wasn't a question of if the fire would ignite but when. A spark was all it would take.

For the thirty-six hours after the quake, the city held its breath. Aside from the aftershocks, no immediate disaster struck. In those precious hours, evacuation could have begun. But there was no time to spare with survivors to rescue, the injured to treat, and basic supplies to scavenge. The looming threat from the CEI chemicals simmered in the background, but with each passing hour on Tuesday, other worries overshadowed it.

Wednesday morning, cool and hazy, a few hours after Walter and Miguel started working in the Forest Park USGS office, potential became a reality.

A sharp crackle sliced through the air, faint but unmistakable, as sparks from falling steel rods and beams sputtered against the slick surface of the Willamette River. For a moment, there was only a stillness. Then, with a violent hiss, the vapor above the water reached a flash point, igniting in a burst of flame that seared in all directions. The fire spread rapidly, tongues of orange leaping high as the foul black oil that coated the water began to bubble and seethe, holding the heat in a slow, relentless burn.

The hiss grew louder and more strident, the air crackling with every burst of gas that erupted from the water's surface. Each pop reverberated through the air like a warning shot. Flames spread with horrifying speed, crawling across the slick, greasy surface and consuming everything they touched. The heat slammed into the shores, immediate and stifling, an invisible weight pressing down as everything consumable burst into flames, sucking the oxygen from the air.

Above, the sky quickly turned into an angry swirl of smoke and ash, dark as tar. Willamette River had become a churning, boiling river of fire and fuel. The hiss of a million tiny flares filled the air. Teeming with the stench of burning fuel and chemicals, the atmosphere blended into a toxic stew. The disgusting odor clung to everything.

At the USGS building to the west, Walter's head snapped up, eyes scanning the room. Tau's face mirrored his unease, a look of alarm creeping across his features. His nostrils flared as the air shifted, an overpowering stink of burning plastic, charred wood, chemicals, and scorched fish cut through the space. The reek burned in his throat, stinging his eyes with its intensity. Whatever this was, it was blowing in from the outside. Suddenly, he knew they were in trouble again.

Instinctively, he searched the room for Miguel. He couldn't see the short director among his colleagues, who were jumping to their feet and moving toward the back of the building. Without hesitation, he stood and yanked his laptop from the desk, snapping it shut. A tug at his arm spun him around. Miguel was there, pulling urgently, his grip tight as he yanked Tau up, too, a wordless panic in his movements.

"We have to get out. Grab your stuff, and come on," Miguel told them, his tone curt, and Walter was sure he heard a note of fear.

"What's wrong?" Walter jammed his laptop back into the bag, tense enough not to argue. Tau hesitated, but Walter had seen enough in the last few days to expect anything. He snatched Tau's laptop and shoved it in next to his own.

"Don't you smell that? Fire! We have to get out of here!" Miguel pulled both men toward the back of the building.

"What's on fire?" Walter asked, clutching his bags with one arm. Tau seemed confused, so Walter pushed him between Miguel and himself. Their momentum kept the other man moving.

"Everything." Miguel reached the back wall, where a large hole split the concrete. Multiple people were waiting to climb through, and the line was moving quickly. As soon as the line cleared, Miguel pulled them through the gap and back out onto the lawn they had arrived on. Only this time, there was no helicopter to pull them out.

The entire view to the east vibrated with flames, a giant red and orange curtain sweeping their way.

"Run," Miguel told them grimly. Shocked, even Tau needed no coaching to flee to the west, scores of people at their heels.

Reed and Chloe, US 20, OR: May 21, 8 a.m.

Reed's eyes shot to the fuel gauge again, watching as the needle inched closer to the red line. The engine sputtered slightly, already anticipating the empty tank, and Reed's stomach tightened in response. He drummed his fingers on the steering wheel, the rhythm steady but forced. He had already checked the gauge half a dozen times in the last hour as if doing so might change the outcome. It didn't.

Yesterday, they had passed station after station—each one either crushed by rubble or flattened in the quake. Rubble buried the gas pumps, and wreckage covered their tanks. Today had been no better. He kept scanning the roadside, but every familiar sign of a filling station was a memory or a wreck. There was nothing left, nothing that could keep them moving.

Chloe's eyes were fixed on the road ahead, her face drawn. She didn't bring up the fuel, but Reed knew she was thinking the same thing. The longer they went without finding accessible gas, the more urgent it became. But there was little to be done except keep driving, keep looking.

Before they left, Reed asked Brett to mark the spot on Matthias's map where his father lived. The boy had done so without complaint, but Reed had noticed the hesitation in his response.

"You sure this is the right way?" Reed asked, trying to keep his tone friendly.

Brett nodded but didn't meet his eyes. "Just off US 20. Before you hit Sweet Home. There's a Christmas tree farm called Merry Maple. My dad provides security there. He lives with the woman who owns it."

The name *Merry Maple* tugged at Reed's memory. He'd passed it a few times and remembered the rows of snow-dusted trees, the carved sign swaying in the winter breeze. But he'd never stopped. Never needed to.

"Okay, great! That's good," Reed said. Relief, fleeting as it was, slipped through him. After passing through Lebanon—seeing the warped streets, the crumbling buildings, the stench of burning—he hadn't expected Sweet Home to fare much better. It was a larger town and larger towns always seemed to suffer more. But maybe they wouldn't even have to enter the city limits.

Now, a little after nine a.m., he relaxed a little, thinking they might have enough gas to make it the whole way. They passed a sign that read 'MERRY MAPLE CHRISTMAS TREE FARM – 1 MILE'.

It was as if his positive thinking had jinxed them. Their luck ran out one minute later. The engine sputtered, a fitful, uneven cough, then fell silent for a second before sputtering again, weaker this time. Reed's hands squeezed the steering wheel. He knew without looking what the gas gauge would say. The needle was buried in the red, the little amber light blinking at him like a warning.

The truck had been fighting him for miles now. A few of the dashboard lights that still worked flickered. Reed cursed under his breath.

"Not now," he whispered. He had hoped to get the kids dropped off to their dad before the truck died on them.

"Reed?" Chloe's plea or warning— he wasn't sure what she was trying to say in that one word that hung between them.

Another protesting growl came from the truck. A low, grinding noise rumbled through the floorboards. The engine coughed one last time and died. They coasted for a few feet before stopping in the middle of the road.

Reed's foot hovered over the pedal momentarily, then dropped. The engine was dead, refusing to be coaxed back to life with a push of a button. He pushed the button anyway, but the only sound that followed was the soft click-click-click of the starter, turning in vain.

Nothing. The gas tank was bone dry.

"Shit," he muttered under his breath, sitting back with his hands still on the wheel, staring at the road ahead.

"Just another mile," Chloe said, her frustration clear. Reed felt it, too. Every inch of that mile now felt like a hundred.

Well, he wasn't one to avoid the inevitable. "Okay, it looks like we're walking from here," he said, opening the door as the kids grumbled in the back.

The air outside was mild and dry. The wind rustled through the quake-weakened trees along the roadside, sending leaves and small branches scattering across the rutted pavement. It was sunny, almost warmer than it had been in days, and the temperature was a strange contrast to the desolation around them. At least it wasn't raining.

The road stretched ahead in ravaged pieces. A toppled pine sprawled across the easement, crooked limbs reaching out like a fallen giant, and other trees rested awkwardly against one another, like an unstable game of pick-up sticks.

As he stood on the uneven asphalt, a whiff of something caught Reed's nose, like sulfur or matches burning. It was distant, but it made his skin prickle. The others didn't notice it as they climbed out and gathered their stuff.

But Watson growled low, his head against Reed. Reed rubbed his ears, looking around. There was nothing to see. "Alert," he told the dog softly.

Watson stiffened in understanding. The canine would be prepared and ready for anything now that Reed had given that command. He turned and caught Chloe watching him with narrowed eyes. She nodded briefly, and he realized she heard what he said to Watson. Good, she'd be alert, too. Hopefully, they'd reach the Merry Maple without trouble but if not, better to be prepared.

Winnie bent down to straighten Charlie's black and white scarf. He panted happily, letting her fuss over him. Piper had wiped away most of the girl's tear streaks, but Brett remained close, his gaze constantly shifting, watching his siblings. Matthias and Piper pulled on their go-bags, and Brett slung Winnie's bag over his back with his own. It wasn't heavy, but she skipped along with Charlie, and he wanted to keep her smiling.

He hesitated to approach Reed, but he had a suggestion as everyone packed up. Already, the big man felt like their leader. He was that type of man, like Uncle Jess. "Hey, Reed."

Reed looked up from tying his blanket.

"I know it would be heavy, but what do you think about bringing the tool kit with us? If we found another car or truck with gas, maybe I could get it started."

Reed thought it over. Brett was thankful to see that the EMT was much like Uncle Jess. He treated Brett like an equal. "We're only a mile from your dad's place. That tool chest probably weighs thirty pounds. Do you think it's worth the work?"

"We can take turns. And who knows what we'll find in the next drivable car?"

"Okay," Reed stood and clapped him on the shoulder. "I know the basics, oil changes and stuff like that, but your knowledge far outstrips mine. I don't know if I could have started this truck back up this morning. Let's go with your idea."

"I wish we could have found some gas." Brett stared glumly at the truck. "My uncle loved this truck. I wish we didn't have to leave it."

"Maybe we can work something out when we get to your dad's," Chloe offered.

"Maybe," Brett didn't sound like he believed it.

"What's all that brown smoke from? Is Merry Maple on fire?" Matthias asked Chloe.

"I don't know." Chloe turned to look toward the southwest, at the sky above the Christmas Tree Farm. It was a grim canvas of swirling brown and gray. The smoke rose in ghostly plumes, layered and ominous, stretching high into the air, blotting out the blue. It didn't look like a fire.

She glanced back to the dark skies further south and then at Reed. "Good thing we don't have to walk all the way to Sweet Home," she said.

He agreed. Sweet Home looked like an inferno. He figured they were five or six miles out of the city. As they had gotten closer, the horizon had settled into a solid mass of black smoke. The low whistle of the wind, the sound thin and dry, added to the creepiness.

Everyone was ready, but no one was excited about where they were going. They all started walking.

Chapter Eleven

Miguel and Walter, Portland, OR: May 21, 8 a.m.

Miguel's breath rasped through his throat, his chest heaving as his sneakers slapped against the cracked asphalt. The air was thick with smoke, a bitter cloud that scratched his lungs with every breath. His eyes burned, tears mixing with sweat as the flames behind them pressed forward. He could feel the sweat trickling down his neck.

Walter's footsteps pounded beside him, Tau's lighter feet echoing the tension as they veered sharply north onto NW Laidlaw Road. Around them, the cries of others fleeing the fire headed west, but Miguel's mind was elsewhere—on the industrial building he'd glimpsed that morning as they had flown in. That quick look had given him an idea. He shared the option with the other two. Walter didn't look enthusiastic but Tau just turned and jogged up Laidlaw. They followed him.

Miguel didn't know what business the building housed, but it didn't matter. What mattered was the helicopter on the landing pad behind the building. If the craft was intact and if they could find the keys, he thought he could fly it out. The closest USGS building was north in Cook, Washington, hopefully far away from this madness.

His heart hammered as he pushed on, the world around him narrowing to just the road ahead. The haze felt like it weighed on him, pressing down with each step. They were getting away from the fire, but the dread gnawing at Miguel's gut didn't let up. Walter's model—they had to get it to USGS experts. He still didn't know if it had any worth, but he grew increasingly desperate as this disaster continued. What if the model held the key to understanding what was happening?

As they jogged, a fence emerged ahead, its steel frame looming like a dark, twisted barrier. The sign above the gate was barely legible through the smoke, but Miguel could make out "INFINITE BIOLABS." A guardhouse sat inside the fence, a sagging structure with no glass in the windows and a roof that seemed about to cave in. The guard was gone, probably fled after the earthquake. The gates lie half-crushed on the blacktop. Firs, oaks, and cottonwoods had fallen across the fence, leaving a gap wide enough for them to slip through.

"You think it's safe?" Walter said, leaning back doubtfully.

"One way to find out," Miguel picked up a stick and hurled it against the fence, watching it clatter to the ground. Nothing happened.

Then, without warning, Tau bounded forward, a burst of energy and noise. He sang loud and fast as he rushed forward, like an Asian Kenny Loggins. *"Highway to the danger zone, ride into the danger zone!"* He scrambled through the mangled fence with surprising agility, his feet kicking up dirt and leaves as he vaulted over fallen branches. On the other side, he whirled and whooshed out his fear, bending over and leaning on his knees.

Cautiously, Miguel and Walter followed, squeezing past the right side gate, the metal catching their clothes. Once through, they hurried past the guardhouse, stepping into the shadow of the building. Bits of tree and leaf clung to them.

"Kenny Loggins? Are you crazy? What if that fence had still been live?" Walter asked him.

Tau's grin was wide, his breath still coming fast. "Do or do not. There is no try," he shot back, quoting Yoda with a smirk. His black hair blew in the wind. They could smell smoke again.

"Yoda! That's who we need right now." Walter laughed despite himself. This guy was funny.

Miguel just shook his head, not appreciating the humor. "This is not a movie. Next time, wait until we're sure."

"You think we'll have to go through another electrified fence?" Walter stopped laughing, horrified.

"I don't know. We need to keep moving. This fence won't stop the fire," Miguel pointed down the road. They started again, Tau in front. Their footsteps echoed against the blacktop as they ran, the sense of urgency driving them forward. The road ahead seemed deserted.

Walter kept moving, but a smile crossed his lips. Tau was all right. He had friends back home who weren't as cool as the Asian man.

A hulking mass of concrete and steel, cold and industrial, emerged as the trees parted, its geometric shape a stark contrast to the surrounding nature.

The Infinite Biolab Building.

Only a few small, dark windows remained. Multiple security cameras lined the exterior, watching the abandoned grounds. If their black eyes were any indication, they were probably dead. No lights anywhere.

The air around the building carried a faint, unpleasant odor mixed with the urgent hint of smoke drifting from the distant flames. Sparse landscaping—barren patches of dead grass and leafless shrubs—encircled the entrance. The torn-up parking lot contained a few scattered cars, a sign that not everyone had escaped.

The building's structure had clearly taken a beating from the quake. The edges had been twisted. The upper floors had pancaked in on themselves, leaving the building leaning forward awkwardly like it had been caught in a slow-motion collapse. The entrance was annihilated, the door frame bent and crumpled, the glass gone, shards scattered across the pavement. It clearly wasn't safe to enter.

Everything about the place screamed danger, destruction, and desertion. Miguel hoped the doors to the helicopter were unlocked. He did not want to enter the Infinite BioLabs building and look for the keys.

"This looks like the labs on Resident Evil," Tau commented. "A little more wrecked, but you get the idea."

Walter understood perfectly. "Like maybe in Retribution, in that underwater simulation with the facility in Russia?"

"I don't know what that is, but I am seriously hoping we don't have to go in there. Let's see if we can find the helicopter." Miguel pushed past them both.

Tau and Walter exchanged understanding looks and then followed him. It looked like an Umbrella Laboratory. Now, they were both watching for the iconic logo featuring a stylized red-and-white umbrella split into eight segments— four white and four red. The symmetrical umbrella would give this place the final sinister touch, not that either one of them needed more malevolence. This place was creepy enough.

They circled the building, moving quickly past a broken courtyard that might once have been an employee break area. The earthquake had cracked the benches and toppled a shelter. But the paths were long overgrown with weeds, and dead plants filled the gardens. Maybe Infinite BioLabs didn't employ landscapers. The grounds had an air of neglect. Like management trying to save money at the employee's expense. The trio barely took notice, their eyes fixed on the landing pad ahead.

Just as Miguel remembered, the helicopter was still there. He was happy to recognize the make. It had been a long time since he had flown a Westland craft, over twenty years ago, before the British company merged with Italian helicopter manufacturer Agusta. Now, they called these Leonardo AW139. This helicopter was matte black with no side logos.

The doors were locked.

Disappointed, Miguel stepped back. "The keys must be inside the building."

Tau scanned the back of the building. "The exit doors are nearly ripped off, so we can get in, but that building…" He shook his head.

Although the back wasn't as crushed as the front, it was still a mess. Twisted walls were webbed with cracks. The ground lay covered in slabs of cement that must have sheared off during the quake. Rebar poked out of the walls.

The steel back doors were partially torn from their hinges, the dead weight barely clinging to the frame. There was just enough room to squeeze by.

"This is a bad idea," Walter said.

"It's either finding the keys or we run again," Tau pointed out. Subtly, he nodded at Miguel with his chin. Walter got the message. Miguel was in no condition to keep running.

"You two stay out here. I'll go get the keys." Miguel didn't want to risk everyone's life. But Tau wasn't staying behind.

"I wonder what they do here?" He fell in step with Miguel.

"Tau, this isn't an expedition. I am ordering you to stay out here," Miguel insisted, stopping.

Tau wasn't raised to dump all the risk on the older generation. He kept walking. "Yes, sir," he said smartly but didn't stop.

A deep, metallic scraping noise echoed out from the heavy doors as the slim man reached them. Tau leaned in, trying to see.

"No electricity," he reported, ignoring Miguel's frustration.

Miguel gave up arguing with him and rummaged in his bag for a flashlight. He knew they had to hurry.

Walter sighed. He reached into his knapsack and pulled out a flashlight. "My flashlight, I lead," he told the others. He didn't want to go in but squashed the feelings of fear.

Miguel, Tau, and Walter stepped through the battered remains of BioLab's back doors, their sneakers uncomfortable on broken glass and bits. Tiny specks floated in the air, the narrow beam of Walter's flashlight sweeping across the particles. A sharp crackling sound echoed from somewhere deep within the building. Despite himself, Tau froze.

He was a lot more scared than he let on to the other two, but his dad had taught him to meet fear head-on. The old man would say it is better to die trying than to live as a coward. Would his dad be proud or call him crazy like Walter did? He took another step, trying not to hold his breath.

The darkness pressed in around them, interrupted only by the dim beam of Walter's flashlight, which danced over the cracked walls and twisted steel girders.

The flashlight flickered as Walter turned it toward a doorway ahead. A crooked sign read, "Security Office." Tau shoved the door, but it didn't budge. The slab wedged in the halfway open position, stuck at an awkward angle. The door jamb was warped and splintered, but they could just squeeze through.

Once inside, they found the office space even worse— tiles missing, chunks of plaster fallen away, wires dangling like dead vines. They could hear no industrial humming or buzzing noises, air conditioning, or mechanical whispers. An odor hit them fast: a sour stench that tightened their throats.

Suddenly, their feet locked up, and they were all too apprehensive to move.

Nadia and Dan, Sweet Home, OR: May 21, 8 a.m.

The house felt claustrophobic, the air strong with dust, hot wax, and the faint whiff of sweat. Nadia's curses in Russian were sharp and impatient as she shoved items into the go-bag, trying to make everything fit. They had been up all night. Nadia hated working by candlelight.

Jewels, furs, and designer clothes spilled across the floor, their soft fabrics and sparkling stones tangled together in a mess. Two bags already bulged with cash—five million in worn, unmarked bills—and the zippers strained as though ready to burst. Nadia muttered another curse under her breath as she crammed the last items into a third bag—perfume bottles, makeup, and a collection of shoes she couldn't bear to leave behind.

It was clear they would not fit. The cargo plane, already weighed down with cannabis plants, had little space for her luxuries. She looked at what she'd have to leave behind, briefly tempted to toss a few plants aside to make space for her things. But she couldn't.

Her gaze shifted to Dan, who was already dragging the money bags toward the truck through the door. He didn't look back. His silence was colder than any reprimand, his indifference sharper than the argument she wanted to start. She swallowed the bitterness. There was no time for that.

They had no time to sleep. The rising lava lake limited their options. By 8 a.m., three full go-bags were in the back bed. Dan started the engine, but the quick start wasn't enough to quiet the tight coil of anxiety in Nadia's chest. They bounced down the trail toward the back of the property, the truck tires sliding over gravel.

In their rush, neither Dan nor Nadia looked back. The noise of the truck's engine drowned out the sound of the group running up the main drive. Until now, Dan hadn't even given a thought to his four children. He would have assumed his ex-wife was dealing with them if he had.

Before the truck even reached the quarry, the hiss of the lava lake reached their ears, a low, ominous sound. The heat rolled in with it, broad and stifling, even inside the truck. She could feel it pressing against her skin, stifling.

Dan's grip on the steering wheel tightened until his knuckles blanched. Purposely, he drove the truck near the quarry's edge. He started calculating how much time they had left, trying to get a good look at the rolling, molten surface in the pit. The wind was still blowing mostly to the south, but a shift to the east would make their escape even more dangerous. Over ten yards of the quarry's lip had been eaten away, and the sight of it made his stomach tighten. He didn't trust the stability of the ground beneath them.

Driving over to the plane, he parked and jumped out of the truck, his hand grazing the door. Jerking back, he was shocked to find the door metal hot enough to burn his palm. His sneakers barely touched the tarmac before he glanced around, checking that the plane parked on the runway was far enough away from the seething lake. He was already moving fast, adrenaline taking over as he climbed the ramp to the plane. The metallic taste of fear lingered in his mouth. He didn't like what he saw.

Climbing up the ramp, he swung open the door and hurried to the front. Reaching the cockpit, he yanked open the door and slid into the pilot's seat. The switches clicked under his fingers as the engine hummed to life. He checked the oil pressure and the engine temperature, but his thoughts kept drifting back to the heat. Would it mess with the plane's systems? He shoved the thought aside. There was no time for doubts now.

"Load the bags on the plane," he yelled to Nadia.

Back at the house, Reed stood with his hands on his hips, irritation creasing his forehead. "They must have seen us. What the he…" He bit back the curse, finishing with, "Heck."

"Where's daddy and Nadia going?" Winnie asked Piper as the truck disappeared into the trees. A confused frown furrowed her brow. Charlie jumped on her legs for attention. She rubbed his head absently, fingering his silky ears.

"I don't know," Piper said. "Brett?"

The boy glanced at Winnie, watching her pick up the persistent dog, but he said nothing. He set down the tool chest and tried to catch Reed's eye.

But Reed was too distracted, moving forward a few steps, following the fading sounds of the engine down the path.

"Wherever they're heading," said Chloe, her hand shielding her eyes. "That's where all that brown smoke is coming from."

"Reed," Brett cleared his throat and looked ashamed. He moved beside Reed and talked softly so Matthias and Winnie couldn't hear. Chloe stepped closer. "There are greenhouses back there. My dad is a weed farmer. He sells it. No one knows. My Uncle Jess said to just stay out of it."

Reed's brows shot up, his mind working through the pieces. "He grows and sells marijuana?"

Brett's face flushed.

Chloe was more practical. "So, the greenhouses are on fire?"

"No," said Reed, frowning. "Way too much smoke. Something's off. Maybe the trees are on fire."

Matthias, meanwhile, had wandered toward the black BMW parked by the house. The door was open, and the keys dangled from the ignition. "Hey, look. The keys are in Nadia's car."

"Under any other circumstances, I would say let's just stand here and wait for them to return. Today, I think we should follow and see what's going on." Reed ran a hand over his face, then joined Matthias by the driver's door.

"What about the dogs?" Matthias asked, glancing over at the pack.

Reed let out a long sigh. "Normally, I'd leave them here, but splitting up is too dangerous. We squeeze everyone in."

The hum of the BMW's engine was barely perceptible. Usually, he would've appreciated the smooth, controlled power beneath his hands, but the bumpy, uneven trail ruined the experience. The car rattled over the ground, the screech of metal catching loose branches and the stink of something burning permeated the air.

Chloe rested one arm around Watson as he pressed against her for balance, the dog's muscles taut with tension. The kids and dogs huddled in the back, their nervous energy palpable. Shadow leaned heavily on Matthias, her sore leg stiff from the hike on US 20, still intelligent and watchful. She knew something was off. Watson's ears flicked at every rustle in the air, his body coiled with unease.

The tree farm evergreens pressed in on both sides, blocking most of the light, their green silhouettes swaying slightly in the wind. As they drove deeper into the woods, the dirt road seemed to shift beneath the tires. Reed's focus narrowed, avoiding the deeper gouges that threatened to jar them further. The conifers that had fallen across the road in the quake had already been cleared, leaving behind scattered branches and the scent of crushed needles.

"We don't know what we're walking into," Chloe said, her voice subdued, trying to watch the rearview mirror and the road ahead simultaneously.

"I know," Reed replied, his jaw tight. He looked back in the rearview mirror, seeing the kids' anxious faces. "What else can we do? He is their father."

Chloe's eyes narrowed slightly, her lips a line. "That doesn't always mean what you think it means." She glanced back at Brett, her eyes lingering on the worry etched into his features. Her stomach rolled uneasily.

The air felt heavier every minute, an oppressive heat growing around them. Then, an intense, metallic smell, like rotten eggs, cloying and sour, seeped through the gaps in the car frame. The sulfur was stifling, and the kids wrinkled their noses, complaints rising from the back.

"What is that smell? It's gross!" Winnie asked, burying her face in Charlie's fur. The little dog sneezed and groaned.

"It smells like burnt matches—like a million of them lit at once," Matthias said. He tried to peer out the window but pulled back sharply when his nose touched the glass. "The glass is hot!"

Chloe touched her window, drawing back her hand when she felt the heat. She glanced at Reed, her expression uneasy.

He gave a curt nod, his gaze fixed on the evergreens. "Look at the trees," he said.

The fir trees lining the path were a sickly brown, their needles dry and brittle, hanging loosely from the branches. The further they drove, the worse the damage. This wasn't just the aftermath of the earthquake. These trees hadn't dried out from the tremors. They were dying, and the cause was something worse.

Watson growled low in his throat, his ears flat against his head. His eyes locked on the windshield, eyes alert as the trees thinned.

Then, in a heartbeat, the car burst through the last of the forest, and Reed stiffened as he hit the brakes. His mouth went dry. The sight in front of them took his breath away.

The landscape stretched out wide and open, the trees gone, leaving nothing to block the view. A massive rock quarry sprawled across the land, its crumbling edges spikey against a bright, hellish glow. Lava, intense and rolling, churned within the pit inches from the rim. Its surface splashed like liquid fire, sending bursts of red and orange streaking upward. Above the quarry, heat shimmered as plumes of brown, choking smoke shot into the sky, twisting in the sulfurous wind that clung to everything.

The ground beneath the trail seemed to pulse. Reed's stomach turned as his eyes tracked the powerful, swirling columns of gas and the loud hiss of the lava. He could hear it through the closed car windows.

"Reed…" Chloe's voice was barely a whisper, her hand squeezing his arm. Her fingers were trembling. The kids were mute with fear. Watson let out a low, frightened whine, his body rigid beside them. Duke barked, and Piper tried to shush him.

Tearing his eyes away from the terrible pit of lava, Reed looked both ways and saw mangled greenhouses to the left and the gray F-250 they had been chasing, two hundred yards to the right, parked next to a cargo airplane. A woman struggled with hefty bags in the bed, fighting to pull one over the side, presumably to load it on the plane. It was too heavy for her.

"There," he pointed to the truck. "Let's get out. Approach slowly."

"That's Nadia!" Winnie said, lighting up.

Everyone climbed out. At the last second, Brett grabbed the tool chest and carried it along with them. The heat hit like a wall.

The woman didn't notice them, her back to their approach while she fought to pull the black bag out. It caught underneath the inner lip of the tailgate, and she struggled in vain to free the fabric. The noise from the quarry and her swearing masked their approach.

"Nadia!" Winnie's voice rang out, high and clear. Before Piper could stop her, she ran forward, Charlie in her arms.

Truly, Winnie liked Nadia more than she liked her dad. When she and her siblings visited, Nadia would pull out her fancy dresses, pretty shoes, and jewelry, and they would play dress-up. The older kids were always busy with their own stuff, but Nadia liked her, and they would play for hours. She was sure the older woman would be happy to see her.

Nadia spun around at the cry, her breath coming in sharp gasps. Her usually immaculate hair now cascaded in disarray around her flushed face. She blinked, eyes briefly meeting Winnie's before snapping to the others. Without hesitation, she dropped the bag, half hanging over the tailgate, and turned back toward the plane, her movements frantic.

Brett hadn't seen much of the woman in the last year, but her disheveled appearance shocked him. Gone was the composed, polished woman who owned Merry Maple, always impeccable, her hair neat, her makeup flawless. In her place stood someone unrecognizable, her wild appearance reflecting the chaos around them. The grace that defined her was nowhere to be found today.

"Winnie," she gasped out and then ran up the ramp to call into the plane's open door. "Dan, your kids are here!"

"What the hell!" Dan's voice bellowed from inside the plane, and then the children's father appeared, stumbling down the cargo ramp. Sweat soaked his shirt. His hair was wild and greasy, and dirt streaked his face. The frantic energy of the night before was written all over him.

Charlie squirmed free of Winnie's grip, shot up the ramp, and past Dan with a yelp, his short legs carrying him between the man's feet before Dan could stop him. Winnie was right behind him.

"Winnie, grab your dog. Get him out of here," he yelled at her.

Only ten years old, she flinched at his harsh tone but continued past her father to follow Charlie, who had now darted around Nadia and was on the plane. Nadia caught hold of Winnie's arm before she could slip through. The little girl struggled, her small body wriggling, but Nadia held her firm.

"What the hell is this?" Dan cried.

Reed stepped forward, cutting the distance between them in half. Brett right behind. "This is your kids coming to you after a damn earthquake." Angry at the reception, the EMT's voice was rough.

"Mom and Uncle Jess never came back after the quake," Brett said, his face stiff. He dropped the tool chest and his knapsack on the ground. "I don't think they made it, so I brought the kids here. I thought... hoped you would help."

If anything, Dan got angrier. "Your mother wanted custody, and she got it. Don't come running to me every time something happens."

"These are your kids," Chloe snapped, her voice rising. Watson growled low beside her. Shadow yelped, shrill and threatening. Bella and Coco's barks joined Duke's in a rising chorus.

Dan's face twisted, his lips curling into a sneer. "Looks like you've got enough protection for them. Now get off my land."

He made it two steps up the ramp when the lava lake started belching. The fiery pool erupted, spitting iridescent bubbles of gas that popped violently. Splashes of molten rock landed over the quarry's edge. The earth beneath them groaned, shuddering, and another aftershock hit, knocking Dan off balance.

"Get inside," he screamed at Nadia.

With one hand firmly gripping Winnie's arm and the door with the other, Nadia pulled the girl toward the plane. "Let's take her," she yelled over the lake's crackling.

"No," wailed Winnie, struggling against her. The fabric of her shirt tore as she fought to free herself.

Dan didn't care either way. If Nadia wanted the girl, she'd be small enough to sit on the floor with the plants. He hurried up the ramp. "Whatever, just move it!"

"No," Brett yelled, sprinting forward, Reed hot on his heels. The ground rumbled beneath them, throwing them off balance. Chloe grabbed Piper and Matthias, keeping them steady and holding them back from following. The already agitated dogs barked frantically as they ran alongside the two men.

Another tremor rippled through the earth, and before anyone could make it to the ramp, Charlie shot out the door, his small body launching toward Nadia. His teeth clamped onto her wrist in a sudden, furious snap. Nadia screamed hysterically, slamming the pup against the side of the ramp to shake him off, letting Winnie fall from her grasp.

The impact sent Charlie flying through the railing, his tiny body spinning in the air before colliding with the ground below. He didn't move.

Winnie screamed as she saw Charlie fall, her small hands reaching desperately toward him. "Charlie!" She crawled through the rails, her eyes wide with fright, her body shaking.

Nearly underneath her, Brett yelled at her. "Winnie, jump, I'll catch you."

Winnie squeezed her eyes shut, heart racing, and leapt, trusting her big brother who never let her down. Dan lunged toward her, but she was already airborne, and Brett caught her mid-fall, swinging her into his arms with a breathless exhale.

"Damn it, forget them. Get inside!" Dan yelled. He shoved Nadia through the door, followed her, and leaned back out to heave the ramp away from the plane. He slammed the hatch shut. Twenty seconds later, the engine shifted, and the plane moved. Reed scooped up Charlie, whistling brusquely at the other dogs, and everyone fell back.

The quake's rumble deepened, building to a terrifying crescendo. Then, a massive evergreen tore from the ground with a deafening crack. Reed spun just in time to watch the tree plummet, its roots snapping violently as it pulled free of the soil. The giant trunk crashed onto the BMW with a sickening crunch, the roof caving under the tree's crushing weight.

At the pit, incandescent spatter blew in a high arc. The ground cracked multiple times, and the rock sheared off, disappearing into the orange and black lake. The quarry was expanding, the molten lava rising, burying everything in its path. Reed knew they had to get out of there now. He glanced back. The plane was twenty yards away, its engines roaring louder as it taxied.

Five steps put him at the truck's driver door, and relief washed through him as he caught sight of the keys hanging from the ignition. He dropped Charlie onto the back bed. The little dog whimpered when he landed, and Reed felt a second's relief that the pup wasn't dead.

"Get in the truck," he yelled.

Chloe pushed Matthias and Piper toward the back of the cab, urging them into the F-250 as Brett scrambled into the truck bed with Winnie. Matthias snatched up Brett's knapsack and the tool chest, struggling under the weight. He managed to shove both into the back of the pickup before pivoting to find Shadow.

Brett clambered over the black bags, pushing them to the sides to make more space. The dogs bounded in after him, paws sliding over the smooth liner.

Brett reached back, yanking the tailgate up, and felt the bed liner shift slightly under his weight. It wasn't fastened down. A quick glance told him it looked new. Maybe his dad hadn't gotten around to finishing the installation. It didn't matter now. He positioned himself in front of Winnie, his body a shield, hoping and praying the lava spatter wouldn't reach them.

Matthias scooped up a whimpering Shadow, who tried and failed to jump onto the tailgate with the other dogs. Together, they rounded the side and dove into the backseat. Chloe closed their door with a thud, yanking her door open and swinging into the front seat. Her voice pierced the air as she screamed, "Go! Go!"

To the side, great gouts of lava shot up in the center of the lake as the ground beneath vented more of the boiling rock. The lava gushed over the rim, a thick flow oozing across the ground, spilling toward them in a widening wave. Chloe froze for a second, the sheer force of it paralyzing her. She'd never seen anything so terrifying in her life.

Reed smashed his foot on the gas, gravel spraying in all directions as he rocketed forward, the pickup truck chasing the plane down the runway. The aftershock had stopped, but the flowing lava grew stronger, swelling up from the depths in surges.

The path they had arrived on was completely blocked with the massive pine and what was left of the BMW. With the molten rock now rolling behind them, the only option was to go forward. Reed leaned a bit, eyes raking the tree line, praying for a break in the trees to escape and veer off into the forest before being trapped.

Dan flicked a few switches, pushing the throttle forward with a firm hand. The engines hummed louder, the plane's belly vibrating beneath him. He leaned back, focused ahead, waiting for the runway's edge to creep up. It wasn't the longest stretch, and he knew from experience he'd need to be quick to catch the airspeed just right. He adjusted the rudder and checked the ailerons—everything perfectly synced for lift-off.

As the wheels finally broke free from the tarmac, his heart skipped a beat in relief. The ground dropped away beneath them, the trees below growing smaller as the plane rose. He circled, scanning the land below, looking for any sign of his kids. His pulse quickened when his eyes landed on his gray truck racing down the runway.

"They took my truck," he complained to an exhausted Nadia, who sagged in the navigator's chair. She waved a hand dismissively, a gesture that barely registered as concern.

"Wait, what the hell!" he screamed, sitting up straight.

Nadia jerked upright, her eyes wide with alarm. "What, what's wrong?"

"The go-bags!" he snapped, his mind racing. "They're still in the truck bed. They have our money!"

He stared, eyes narrowing in fury as the Ford truck barreled toward an obscure backroad. The wheels kicked up dust before the truck made a hard right and disappeared into the impenetrable green of the forest.

"My jewels, my dresses!" Nadia flushed red, eyes like flint. "Go back down. Land this plane. We need to get our bags."

She pressed her nose against the window, scanning the ground for any sign of the truck's retreat. Before she could spot it, a series of deafening blasts erupted from the quarry. The ground seemed to shudder, sharp cracks split the air, and a thunderous roar rattled the plane's metal frame. The noise was deafening.

"The fuel tanks just went," Dan's voice was tense. "Lava must have reached the greenhouses and set the aviation fuel off."

Flames spat and climbed as massive columns of black smoke billowed from where the mangled greenhouses once stood. They were gone.

The tanks stacked near the ruins had ruptured, their contents igniting in an enormous blaze. Gases of bright orange and red rushed upward, crackling and popping as they devoured anything left in their wake. Twisted metal, glass fragments, and the smoldering hunks of trees burned, distorting the air around like a mirage.

The entire area, trees, everything was a raging fire as the lava continued its advance. It had already reached the runway blacktop and continued to eat its way forward.

"I can't land." The words wrung from his lips as if they hurt. He'd circled the area again, but the reality was clear. "The runway's gone. If we try to land now, we won't be able to take off again."

"Then land on US 20!" Nadia's breath came out in furious gasps. She couldn't believe they had lost everything except the plants. Five years' worth of work—it wasn't fair!

Dan flew a rough grid over Merry Maple, scanning the area below. There was no sign of his gray truck. He couldn't see the trails that wound through the tree farm in too many places. The highway spread out beneath them, but his gut tightened as he saw it. There was no way to land. Between the abandoned cars and trucks and the damage to the road, they'd wreck the plane landing on it.

Swearing a streak now, he circled the area again, his eyes scanning the roads below.

No truck.

Finally, he knew they had to go. Even though he had filled up the plane yesterday, their gas wouldn't last forever, and with their cargo, they couldn't take the chance of being stranded just anywhere. Fury choked him as he turned the plane west.

They'd stop in central Oregon at a little airfield he knew of, refuel, and return. He glanced sideways at Nadia. Her face was a storm—her eyes wild, her mouth a tight line of fury. But he felt the same way. He wanted those bags back, and nothing was going to stop him.

Chapter Twelve

Reed and Chloe, Sweet Home, OR: May 21, 10 a.m.

The trails were a maze. It didn't help that so many trees had uprooted, falling across the dirt roads, forcing them to repeatedly backtrack, looking for US 20. Reed's mind churned with more dangerous thoughts—could the quarry blow, sending a surge of molten rock through the woods? Or just as bad, would the eruption spill over, drowning everything in its fiery flood?

"Matthias, do you know the way to the highway?" He asked over the seat.

"I've been on some of the main trails, but I don't recognize this one," the Boy Scout told him. He pushed his glasses back up his nose and wrestled with his knapsack for a minute, pulling something out. "I've got my compass. You're heading north. We need to go east to get to US 20."

"I know where we are." Piper sat up and pointed over the seat. "There's a trail coming up on the right. Take that one. Matthias, it will lead to the stream, and we can follow it out."

"Piper hiked all this last year," Matthias told them. 'She did a mapping project in school. If she says this is the trail, she's right."

"Good enough for me," Reed said, turning fast as the trail came up.

"Did you see that quarry pit?" Chloe's voice was shaking. "I know the Cascades are on the ring of fire, but I've never heard of activity like that around here."

"I don't know what's happening, but we need to get out of here." Reed pushed the truck harder, skidding in the dirt.

"And go where?" Chloe wrung her hands, trying to think.

"Let's get to Sweet Home and warn the authorities about that lava lake. Then we'll figure it out."

Twenty minutes later, a cheer broke from the group as the highway finally came into view as they crested over a rise. The fence lay in ruin, its metal bent and broken, so Reed eased the vehicle over it. They didn't stop long, just long enough for Winnie and Charlie to scramble into the backseat with Piper and Matthias before they took off south.

Chloe leaned over the seat, eyes scanning the young girl, her fingers brushing through the tangled mess of mousy brown bangs. The child seemed untouched—no bruises, no sign of injury where Nadia had clutched her. She was as filthy and worn as the rest of them, her face streaked with dirt, but she looked unharmed. Piper pulled a brush from her bag and started pulling through her sister's hair, the act calming them both. Chloe exhaled, leaning back into the seat, the cool glass pressing against her temple as her thoughts raced.

Reed gave her a sideways look. "What are you thinking?" he asked.

"We do need to warn someone in Sweet Home about that lava pit," she said slowly. "I don't know that they'll believe us; it seems incredible. But we have to try."

"I think they'll believe us," Reed told her, eyes fixed on the road ahead. "That eruption is going to start a forest fire. You could smell the gas that the pit was releasing. If the wind picks up, it could blow straight into Sweet Home. No idea how dangerous it is." He let out a frustrated breath. "The real issue? Tracking down someone who actually has the authority to do something about it. Then we figure out our next move."

"You mean…" she tipped her head toward the back.

"Yes. Hey, Piper, do you kids have family anywhere?"

"No, just my mom and Uncle Jess." she hesitated. She had finished retying Winnie's curls and was pulling her long hair into a ponytail. She stopped as if thinking before her fingers slowly finished. "Well, and my dad, but he's a jerk. What are you going to do with us?"

"Don't worry. We're not abandoning you. Let's get to Sweet Home and warn them about the new volcano in their neighborhood, and then we can figure out the rest. For now, if anyone asks, we're all family." He caught her smile in the rearview mirror and smiled back. Chloe studied him from under lowered lashes as he followed the highway, dodging abandoned cars and fissures. This guy was certainly different from the men she was used to spending time with.

Matthias also smiled at his words and sat back, stroking Shadow. The dog arched under his touch, clearly enjoying the attention. Reed was a great guy, and his dogs were awesome, too.

Reed glanced at Chloe. "Do you have family in Albany or Oregon? Is there anyone you need to contact?"

She shook her head, ponytail swaying in time with the motion. "I never thought I'd be happy to say it, but I have no family at all. My mom passed away five years ago, and my dad has been gone a long time. No siblings, grandparents, aunts, uncles or anything. How about you?"

His forehead creased. "Just my dad. He has a farm in Kentucky right off a bend of the Mississippi River, so he's far away from all of this madness. Like you, I have never been so glad to live alone. I never married or had children. It's just me and Watson."

"And all of his furry friends," As if reacting to Chloe's words, Coco chose that minute to poke his head over the seat and tried to lick her cheek, breaking the tension and causing everyone to laugh.

"I didn't expect to travel with this menagerie. But here we are," he jerked the wheel, missing another giant pothole.

It was slow going, but finally, they were close enough that the wall of black haze spread over the highway. It was like driving through a shroud.

It was clear the quake had hit hard here. Sweet Home looked like it was unraveling, its problems too many for what was probably dwindling resources. Reed didn't even need to veer off the Sweet Home exit. A State Trooper was already there, parked in the first lane with his patrol car blocking the ramp. He raised a hand to stop them, his uniform streaked with soot, goggles fogged, and a mask covering most of his face. His hat was gone, but the gun still hung at his side, a grim reminder of this nightmare.

Reed parked the gray truck on the easement and went to talk to the officer. The haze swirled around them. In the back, Brett started coughing, and the dogs whined.

"Piper put Winnie on your lap and tell Brett to get in here," Chloe ordered. "This smoke could have anything in it." She jumped out, calling the dogs. She crammed them into the cab wherever she could fit them until the small space was filled with fur and people.

Brett leaned over the seat and tried the radio. This time, it worked. A recorded emergency message was playing. *"...devastation stretches from the shore to the interior along the entire west coast. Powerful tremors continue to rip through the region, and millions are feared dead. Massive rifts and sinkholes—miles wide—are swallowing land. The situation is dire. If you are in western Oregon, evacuate immediately. Go to your nearest evacuation site. Each town has designated departure points. If you can't get to a departure point, head east to safety. Do not wait. Leave now. Stay tuned for further updates. The following is a list of designated evacuation centers..."*

Someone read off a long list. Chloe wasn't sure, but it sounded like the closest one to them was in Bend, a larger city maybe an hour or two away. The message repeated, and she dug for pen and paper in the glove box to write the names. Everyone watched her anxiously.

"What about Mollie?" Winnie asked, little wrinkles marking her smooth forehead.

"They just called out Lebanon, Winnie," Piper hugged her. "Her dad will get her someplace safe."

Chloe fiddled with the dial, trying to switch stations and get more news. When FM didn't work, she tried AM channels. Finally, the static broke, and she heard a voice, a man talking excitedly.

"Okay, okay, listen up, people! This is Emmet Shale, and I know some of you out there think I'm just some guy with a tinfoil hat, but what I'm telling you is REAL. I've been watching the numbers and checking the reports, and if you haven't noticed yet, we're in the middle of something big here, something bigger than anyone's prepared for!

"The earthquakes, folks! They're not stopping. They started, what—two days ago? And they're only getting worse. I'm not talking about the usual tremors we get from time to time—no, these tremors are spreading like wildfire, opening the earth beneath our feet! I'm telling you—sinkholes, massive

rifts, and the ground just splitting apart! Corvallis—gone. That's right, people, GONE. What the sinkhole didn't consume was swallowed whole by the Willamette River. Drowned. I know because I was there! I sailed my boat right out of the heart of the city on roads that turned into rivers, and even the rivers flooded! And that's not all! Albany's down, too. Millersburg and Riverside! The ground just cracked wide open and fell away—cities vanishing before our very eyes!"

Chloe hastily twisted the knob back to FM, cutting off Emmet Shale. Nobody said anything for a long minute.

"He's probably just a quack," Chloe said, trying to sound firm.

"Yeah, lots of crazies come out when disasters happen," Brett backed her up. The kids were quiet. Chloe returned the channel to the emergency broadcast, the previous message still repeating.

When he returned, Reed was using his arm to cover his face. He was coughing, and worry etched across his face. He listened to the emergency message before he started talking.

"All this black smoke," he indicated the cloud over Sweet Home with a sweep of his arm. "The earthquake caused a gas station to blow up, creating a fire that swept through the north half of the town. There's no entrance from the highway until they can get this under control. The military is evacuating what's left of the town from the south side."

"It's been burning since Monday night?" Chloe leaned forward to see more as Reed started the truck. Though it was warm in the truck, he left the AC off.

Reed coughed again. "Yeah, he's praying for rain. I told him about the quarry. He'll get the message to his superiors, but I don't know what they can do about it."

"So now what?" Brett asked.

"The news isn't good. Like we heard on the radio, that weird ground sinking we ran from in Albany spread east. It wasn't just Albany that sank. At least Crabtree, Scio, and Lacomb have also fallen into giant sinkholes. It's still happening."

"Oh my god, it's true," breathed Chloe. "Do they know what's causing this?"

"The trooper didn't have any idea. But there's more. Powerful earthquakes are rattling Mount Hood. The USGS is sending out warnings of an imminent eruption." His voice was grim.

"This is insane. Maybe we should get out of the state until someone can figure this out." Chloe shifted Watson over a little. "I wish we had our phones and could track what's happening."

"The trooper said there's a big evacuation effort in Bend. He suggested we head there. It's only about seventy-five miles from here. I think it's our best bet." Reed pulled onto US 20 and waved to the trooper as he drove by. The man held up a hand.

"Will we see Mount Hood erupt from here?" Winnie half climbed the seat, trying to see out the windshield, and started giggling as the dogs shifted into one another to accommodate her.

"Maybe we'll see the smoke. It depends on how large the eruption is. But the flows won't reach this far." Brett pulled her back onto his lap. "It'll be a bad day for anyone close to the mountain, though."

Miguel and Walter, Portland, OR: May 21, 10 a.m.

Inside the security room, darkness swallowed the space. They entered cautiously. The room was a maze of overturned desks, dented filing cabinets, and monitors with cracked screens. Walter's flashlight cut through the gloom, landing on a desk standing a few feet inside. Papers lay scattered everywhere. Among the mess, a few ruined brochures lay half-buried beneath broken ceiling tiles, their bright, glossy covers now far from their former vibrance.

Miguel had finally found his flashlight, and a second beam pierced the darkness. Tau stepped closer to the desk, swatting the air, attempting to dispel the nauseating odor that clung to the room like a sickness. He picked up a brochure, holding it gingerly as if it might fall apart in his hands.

"This place... what were they even doing here? It smells awful," His voice was tight with unease.

Walter joined him, picking up another pamphlet. The light from his flashlight caught the cover as he turned it over. Miguel stepped deeper into the room, flicking his flashlight over the dark corners. Sparks crackled from exposed wires, bright and erratic, flashing like tiny lightning bolts in the silence.

Each spark made Walter flinch, his hand trembling ever so slightly as he angled the torch to read the inside of the brochure. A few words stood out in the harsh glow: *"Innovative, Cutting-Edge, Safe."* The words felt out of place in the wreckage of what was supposed to be a high-tech facility.

No Umbrella Logo, that was reassuring.

The reassurance didn't last long. Inside the brochure, glossy images of pristine laboratories filled the pages. At the edges, small thumbnails of animals bordered the text. Walter squinted, his stomach sinking as he recognized the creatures.

Reptiles.

"They're working with genes from Komodo Dragons. Looks like they are trying to solve multi-drug resistant bacteria in humans." Walter said, reading the captions.

"Komodo Dragons!" Tau looked shocked. He had never seen one in person, but he knew how dangerous the lizards could be.

"Yeah, maybe some other reptiles too. It says here that Komodo Dragon venom prevents blood from clotting. They are trying to find a way to use it as a blood thinner. Snakes, too. Apparently, some snakes, like Burmese Pythons, can rapidly regenerate their organs. They also have studies here that are working on that."

Tau dropped the brochure he held with a shudder. "Great. Snakes and dragons. Let's get the keys to the copter and get out of here."

Meanwhile, Miguel moved through the room with slow, deliberate steps, his flashlight beam sweeping across toppled chairs and desks skewed at odd angles. His eyes scanned the walls as the light flickered over glass and debris.

Nothing.

He exhaled, the hope of finding a key box or a hook with a set of keys slipping further from his grasp. The humidity was stifling in the security room.

Sweat beaded on his forehead, and he wiped it away with the back of his hand. The keys had to be here somewhere. But with each passing moment, his optimism was draining, and he felt the weight of it as he made his way toward Tau and Walter.

His flashlight flicked over the desk, and that's when he saw it. Something... out of place. A faint, unnatural shadow against the floor. He stepped around the corner of the desk, his heart picking up pace. He pushed the chair aside with a soft squeak, his breath caught in his throat as his light followed the motion. Behind the desk...

There was a body.

Miguel froze, his stomach flipping violently. The flashlight lingered on the figure sprawled on the floor, limbs missing. The man's face was pale, almost ghostly in the dim light, his eyes wide open but glassy, staring blankly at the ceiling.

His throat was gone, and the rest of his body ripped apart, a dark stain spreading underneath him. Strips of fabric clung to the wounds, the raw edges of flesh bitten and tugged free by the mouthful. One arm from the femur down and both legs from the kneecaps were gone. The other arm was thrown back over his head, most of the tissue and muscle gnawed off.

Miguel had never seen anyone mauled before, but he imagined this was what it would look like. Something made a meal of this guard. A deep, metallic scent rose above the body—blood mixed with a rotten odor.

"Miguel?" Walter's voice broke through the fog in his mind. He sounded distant, cautious. Miguel's legs cramped, his posture changing as the realization sank in.

They weren't alone here.

His fingers tightened around the flashlight, and the beam shook as he stood there. Tau and Walter circled the desk, Walter's flashlight bobbing as fear took control. Tau's breathing was quick and shallow. The body looked even worse in the illumination of two flashlights.

"What...*chewed* him like that?" The horror was clear in Tau's voice.

"I don't know, some kind of animal. Maybe a bear or a cougar?" Miguel kept his tone low.

"We need to leave. Now." Walter said, trying to sound firm. But his voice cracked.

"Wait, look," Tau leaned forward, using the desk for leverage, and reached over the man's head. Walter followed his fingers with the flashlight. The corpse's remaining hand was half under the head. Maybe that's why it still had skin. Now they both saw what Tau's quick eyes had found. A big, silver ring of keys lay next to the open palm. Holding his breath, the slim scientist reached down and seized the metal circle. It was sticky from the pooled blood.

Tau gagged slightly, holding the ring out to Miguel, who took it and wiped it with paper from the desk.

"Is that it? Will those keys open the helicopter?" Walter asked.

"Maybe. Let's see." He turned, intending to hurry out the door, when his foot hit something metallic. A handgun slid a few feet across the floor. Sucking in his breath, he grabbed it and pointed his flashlight, examining the weapon.

"This revolver was recently fired," he told Tau and Walter, their eyes wide, staring at the piece in his hand.

"How can you tell?" Walter looked around fast.

"Burnt gunpowder on the muzzle," Miguel said, sniffing the front end of the gun. He handed his flashlight to Tau and opened the cylinder. Two bullets had been fired. He looked back at the unlucky security guard, then, snapping back the cylinder, he settled the piece tightly in his grip.

"Let's go."

"Are you keeping that?" Walter tilted his head.

"We might need it," Miguel answered shortly. "Better to be safe than sorry."

"Do you even know how to use it?" Walter asked skeptically. He would have never taken Miguel for a marksman.

"I know how to shoot," Miguel told him.

"It sure didn't help that security guard," Tau's voice echoed a bit too loudly.

"Think positive and move faster," was Miguel's only answer. Tau's face twisted in concern, but he moved faster.

With flashlight beams sweeping the hall ahead of them, Tau and Walter led the way out. Walter's sneakers snagged the splintered bottom of the doorframe as they crossed over, and the air outside rushed in to meet them with a smoky bite. Even with the smog, it was great to be outside.

Miguel squinted into the haze, his pulse quickening. The fire was getting closer. He could feel the heat, stronger than when they went in.

"Move," he urged them again as he broke into a run toward the landing pad. Tau was right behind him, his breath shallow, eyes darting around, shoulders tight with anxiety he couldn't hide. Walter loped after them, his feet heavy in the oppressive air. There was no time to waste on the winding path. They cut straight across the courtyard, the dry brush crunching beneath their sneakers, the sound loud and unsettling.

Walter stole a glance at the ruined courtyard as he ran, his gaze catching on the twisted, overgrown plants—wilted and frail. They spoke of neglect, not the hand of nature. But the crumpled and broken fountain and the cracked stone benches were marks of the quake's power. He tried to picture the place before the earth had rattled it to pieces, but the destruction around him blurred the image.

A soft rustle stirred under the overgrown landscaping, where the crushed shrubs and leaves lay like a blanket. The faint smell of damp earth mingled with a musky, reptilian scent, lingering unnoticed in the smoke-clogged air. Beneath the dried foliage, a massive Burmese python lay camouflaged, its tan and brown scales blending seamlessly with the dead grass and fallen leaves. Its sleek, sinuous body stretched out, a blur of dark blotches hidden in plain sight.

The python had only just escaped its strange and sterile captivity. A violent tremor had torn through the vivarium, ripping cages apart, shattering walls, and splitting the floor. Corpses, both human and reptile, littered the ruins, and those who had survived the quake found themselves facing other freed creatures, aggressive and untamed.

It had taken the python hours to find its way out of the debris, a dangerous journey through the destruction. Now, it basked in the weak sunlight, still and patient, soaking in the warmth, though the smoke annoyed the creature. Its tongue flicked in and out, tasting the strange dry irritant.

Suddenly, the snake realized there was a new threat. As the men drew closer, the snake's muscles tensed, coils tightening slightly in preparation. It froze, sensing the movement coming toward it.

Miguel and Tau jumped over the tan and brown log-like obstruction in their path, but Walter's foot came down with a sickening crunch, landing squarely on the snake's body.

The python jerked, aggression surging through its muscles as its scales rasped harshly against the ground. A frantic hiss split the air, sending a shiver down Walter's spine.

His eyes widened in horror as he realized what he'd just stepped on. His foot was still planted firmly on the snake. The terror of the moment stole his breath. He lurched instinctively, off balance, and stumbled backward. The weight of his knapsack yanked him over, and flailing; he fell, his head smacking into the dirt with a dull thud. The impact knocked him senseless for a few seconds.

The python, now fully alert, uncoiled with explosive speed. Its muscular body snapped through the dirt, the rough scrape of its belly scales against the ground barely audible as it shot forward. In the blink of an eye, it was between Tau's legs, its massive form brushing against him.

Tau choked, saliva catching in his throat as his heart slammed against his ribs. The world seemed to slow, every heartbeat stretching into eternity. He couldn't tear his eyes away from the creature's shifting muscles, the sheer size of it overwhelming his senses.

Before he could react, it was gone—vanishing into the forest with the quiet swiftness of a shadow. Tau's body reacted before his mind could catch up. He let out a strangled scream, his feet propelling him away from where the snake had been, each step fueled by sheer panic. His legs pumped furiously as he bolted toward safety, not stopping until he was sure the serpent wasn't following. His pulse pounded in his ears, his breath ragged.

Miguel stood, his mouth open, the key ring hanging from his hand. He couldn't process the size of the creature that had just zipped past. He blinked, trying to catch up to what had just happened.

Walter groaned and rolled over, trying to push himself up. Miguel took a step back, then turned to rush over and help Walter from the ground.

"Did you see that freaking snake!" Walter shouted, his voice high-pitched and shaken, face flushed red with adrenaline.

"It's gone, Walter. The snake is gone," Miguel urged, trying to calm him down, his own heartbeat still racing. "It's gone."

Tau's second scream shattered the air, high and raw, a sound of pure terror. Miguel and Walter snapped their heads toward him just in time to see a massive Komodo dragon stalking across the courtyard.

The dragon's body rippled with muscle. The creature, nearly six feet long and moving with terrifying fluidity, held its flat, broad head high, nostrils flaring as it sniffed the air. Its thick, bowed legs struck the ground with a resounding force, each movement slow but packed with raw power, while its long tail dragged behind like a heavy anchor.

The Komodo's forked tongue flicked out, tasting the air with quick, darting motions before retracting, curling upwards to press against the roof of its mouth. Its eyes, cold and calculating, fixed onto Tau with a predatory focus that sent a chill straight down Miguel's spine.

"Don't move! Stay perfectly still!" Miguel's voice was a whip, the command sharp and urgent, slicing through the tension.

Tau's breath hitched, his chest rising and falling in shallow, ragged bursts. His entire body was stiff and trembling as he fought to remain motionless. His eyes were wide with terror, locked onto the advancing reptile.

Miguel's hand shot out to grab Walter's arm, his fingers digging into the skin. The cold of his touch sent a jolt through the younger man. Miguel thrust the keys into Walter's palm, his movements incisive with urgency.

"Find the right key. Get that damn door open!" he growled, pushing him toward the helicopter. "Move slowly."

Walter's pulse thundered in his ears as he took the first step, the movement attracting the dragon's terrifying gaze. The reptile's attention shifted, its head snapping toward him, the powerful body swiveling in his direction, its gaze now fixed on Walter.

Miguel, struggling to keep his breath even and controlled, tightened his grip around the cold metal of the dead security guard's gun, steadying himself before he moved forward. Now the dragon was watching him. Cold eyes gleamed, its tongue flicking once more as it weighed its options.

Then, something caught Miguel's eye— a dark trickle of blood running down the dragon's back, a runny, slow stream that dripped onto the dirt. It was fresh and vivid against the creature's scaly hide. Maybe the security guard had shot this animal.

Tau remained motionless, his face as pale as the smoke that blew through the courtyard, eyes wide but unblinking, not daring to make a sound.

Miguel's mind raced, but there was no time for second guesses. His heart lurched as Walter's feet kicked up dirt, his figure now sprinting toward the helicopter. The dragon's head turned, eyes tracking Walter's every movement, a low, rumbling growl vibrating in the creature's throat. Too many targets.

Miguel's heart lurched. He was about to yell something, but another aftershock vibrated the ground before he could. As the rumble faded, a deep, guttural hiss split the air. The sound was raw, hungry. Miguel's choked, his eyes jumping to the forest.

Another Komodo dragon emerged from the trees, its massive frame nearly twice the size of the first. The beast's body was a muscle wall, each powerful step sending shockwaves through the ground, a thundering force bearing down on them. Unblinking, its eyes locked onto Tau with a deadly focus.

The earth shivered beneath this beast's weight, and the air seemed to split in front of it. Its tongue flicked out as it closed the distance, tasting the air with quick, darting movements. Miguel shook, a cold knot of fear in his chest.

One was terrifying enough—two?

They had no chance.

Zigzag Falls, Mount Hood: OR, May 21, 10 a.m.

The ground beneath Ramona Wellington's boots vibrated faintly, sending an unsettling ripple through her spine. She squinted at Mount Hood's towering form, its once-pristine summit now hidden behind a rising cloud of dust and smoke. The mountain's face in front of her was marred with deep cracks. Lines snaked down the slopes, a sight far more terrifying than anything produced by the top so far.

Ramona quickened her pace and braced against the uneven trail. The evergreens to her left trembled—not from the wind, but from the restless ground beneath them. Crossing the old wood beam bridge, she glanced at her surroundings and knew where she was, recognizing the path. She was about six miles from the parking lot.

Years ago, runoff carved a gulley down the hillside, and tremors from previous activity sent large boulders tumbling, choking up the cleft. The park rangers patched up the gap with lumber hauled up from the foothills, a rough but functional bridge.

She shifted the weight of her knapsack, settling it across her back, and thought about what she was doing. For thirty years, she had been a park ranger in Oregon. She knew these trails like the back of her hand. Alerts for Mount Hood weren't new, but this was different. They usually had days to clear the area before things got dangerous, not hours. This could get bad, fast. She hoped the equipment she carried would be enough to make a difference if the summit erupted.

Ramona and a few other rangers volunteered to hike in and search for stragglers who hadn't answered their radios or phones. Records showed two hikers climbed this trail two days ago but hadn't been accounted for during the evacuation. She'd hoped to find them on their way back, but she knew that would take more luck than she usually relied on.

So, when two figures appeared around the next bend, her heart skipped. The young men—boys, really—couldn't have been over twenty. She let out a breath she hadn't realized she'd been holding and broke into a run, her legs pumping faster as she jogged up the trail to meet them.

"Don't you guys feel the tremors," she yelled as she dashed to them.

They both looked anxious; she had to give them that.

"What's going on?" The blond one asked, his bangs falling into his eyes.

"The USGS issued a volcano alert for Mount Hood. We are evacuating the park." She started hustling them down the trail. "I'm Ramona. You're Barry and Sam?"

"I'm Sam," said the dark one, his brown eyes flashing with fear. "We came down because of the tremors. They haven't stopped all night."

"It's called an earthquake swarm. The USGS raised the level alert overnight. Let's get you off this mountain."

Unfortunately, that was easier said than done. They still had several miles to go before they reached the parking areas, and the ground deformations were growing stronger. A deep crack split the air with a violent *boom*, followed by the sound of rock crashing down the slopes. The ground buckled beneath them, making each step harder, forcing them to fight for balance.

Ramona glanced up, horrified by what she saw. A column of fire and molten rock shot up into the air, a blast so deafening it felt like the very air was being torn apart. And, worse, the cloud of black swirling smoke wasn't just rising, blotting out the blue of the sky; it was sinking fast and spilling in their direction.

Skidding to a stop, Ramona understood what she was seeing. Multiple lava domes near the top were exploding. Grabbing the hoods of the two young men, she yanked them back with her. "We'll never make it. Follow me!"

They scrambled after her, panicked too much to protest. The howl of the eruption filled the air, deafening and relentless. Ramona dropped over the side of the trail, under the bridge, diving between the jagged boulders. She dug into the soft earth, the boys beside her, their hands frantic as they worked. Together, they created three shallow niches deep in the mountainside.

"Get down on your stomachs! Now!" she shouted. The boys obeyed, trembling but moving fast. Ramona jerked three pony air bottles from her bag and tossed one to each of them, keeping one for herself, followed by Mylar emergency blankets. "Cover yourselves with these," she ordered.

Like moles burrowing into the earth, they quickly settled into the niches, pony bottles clutched over their noses, heat-resistant blankets over them. Ramona took a few extra seconds to pile loose dirt over the boys' blankets, trying to add another layer of protection. Then, with a final glance at the young men, she dug deep into the earth herself, pulling her blanket tight and pressing her face to the ground.

If this doesn't work and we die, she thought, eyes squeezed shut tightly, face in the dirt, *no one will ever find us.*

A deafening roar filled the air, drowning out everything else. The wind hit like a blast furnace, searing and suffocating. It came in a sudden rush, bending the trees with a violent howl that carried the scent of sulfur and charred earth. Clumps of ash rained down, coating everything in a grimy gray dust. Rocks rattled above them on the timber bridge.

The ground vibrated beneath them; the heat was unbearable. Ramona's heart raced, her mind repeating a desperate prayer—please, let them be on the edge of the ash flow, and let some ridge or rock divert the molten river barreling down the volcano. If not… if the lava came for them, there was no escape.

The flow surged down the mountainside in multiple streams, ruthless and all-consuming. Trees were devoured in an instant, rocks melted, and the ground itself seemed to burn beneath the ferocity of the flow. Everything in its path was reduced to ash and ruin.

As the super-heated streams continued down the sides, the wind picked up behind them, howling through the smoke-filled air, carrying with it the sound of shattering stone and cracking trees. The ash clung to the mountain like sticky soot, and the world vanished into a haze of gray and orange—a hellscape of fire, destruction, and choking heat. The world bent under the intensity of the destruction, everything warped and distorted.

Chapter Thirteen

Miguel and Walter, Portland, OR: May 21, 11 a.m.

It seemed as if everything happened at once. A series of violent bangs detonated from the east, and the deep, thunderous sound ripped through the air, unmistakable to Miguel.

Mount Hood was erupting.

Simultaneously, Walter screamed as he swung the helicopter's door open, punching his fist skyward in excitement. The smaller of the two Komodo Dragons seemed confused by the loud noises coming from different directions, and he swung his heavy head in one direction and then the other.

The larger dragon, the darker one, didn't hesitate. With a sudden burst of speed, it charged forward, its massive body propelling itself toward the smaller dragon and Tau, who stood frozen. Miguel leveled the gun, ready to use all the bullets in defense of the analyst, but knew it wouldn't be enough.

When the giant Komodo Dragon hit, it was like a freight train. The smaller lizard didn't realize the danger until the bigger beast plowed into him. They rolled, squealing and snapping at each other, saliva and blood flying. Miguel suddenly realized the leaking blood on the back of the first reptile must have attracted the larger animal. Maybe it viewed the weaker, wounded dragon as an easy meal.

Tau, too afraid to run for fear of attracting either lizard, was right in the path of the behemoths. He tried to dodge the huge ball of muscle and scales, tails whipping, but they sideswiped his slim form, tossing him across the courtyard, nearly at Miguel's feet. He lay in a heap, groaning.

The animals ignored him and focused on their brutal clash. Rearing on their back feet, standing six feet tall or more, claws ripped, heads bobbed, straining as they bit each other, scales and flesh flying, before they fell over. The larger one immediately straddled the smaller one.

Miguel reacted with self-preservation. He shoved the gun in his knapsack, hoped he wasn't adding to Tau's injuries, and grasped the wounded scientist under the shoulders. He half-carried, half-pulled the man, his head on swivel the whole time, eyeing the fighting dragons and, on the other side, the distance left to the helicopter.

More booms rattled the air, and the trees and smoke whipped into a frenzy, probably from whatever was happening at Mount Hood. Miguel stumbled, Tau's weight pulling him down, but he rallied, found his feet, and pushed them both forward.

Suddenly, Walter was there, grabbing Tau from the other side, and between them, they carried the half-unconscious scientist to the helicopter. Walter lifted Tau into the back, strapping him in as Miguel dropped into the pilot's chair and started the liftoff procedures.

The dueling dragons paid them no attention. Back on their hind claws, they clasped each other in a death grip, the larger dragon's teeth sunk into the shoulder of the smaller animal. Roaring with pain and anger, the creature viciously tore at its aggressor's back, trying to get away.

Miguel flipped on the battery and strobe switches, his hands moving with practiced ease. He twisted the throttle, easing it to idle. It had been years since he'd flown, but the motions were as familiar as if he'd never left. With a quick glance at the ignition switch, he flicked it to "start" and pressed the button, holding his breath. The engine sputtered, then roared to life with a sharp pop before settling into a steady hum.

A triumphant whoop escaped him, but he quickly snapped back into focus, checking the mixture and adjusting the engine RPM. He engaged the clutch, watching as the blades began to turn. Reaching up, he flipped on the alternator switch and timer, heart racing, readying himself for lift-off.

The dragons had fought savagely. Now, they were both bleeding and clearly injured. They faced off, growled, and then lunged ferociously at each other, refusing to quit. Bloody drool dripped from their mouths; their red-stained teeth bared for another bite. This was a battle to the death.

It was time to go. Miguel increased the speed of the rotor blades and adjusted the pitch. The helicopter lurched forward just a bit and lifted vertically off the ground. Seconds later, they were ten feet off the ground, then twenty. In front of him, Miguel could see the dragons slam back into each other through the big glass bubble front, a prehistoric scene out of a nightmare. He shuddered at the thought of those bites and knew the sight of what was left of the security guard would haunt him for a very long time.

He lifted the craft over the trees and sucked in a breath of astonishment. The top third of Mount Hood, the beautiful white crown, was gone. Covered in clouds and burning particles, he couldn't tell if the cone had disintegrated or was just hidden behind the curtain of blackness. Lava ran down the sides in streams, bright glowing lines standing out against the ash-covered slopes. Even from here, he could see the broad lines of mud lahars choking the rivers.

The smoke seemed to be drifting southward, and the winds were weakening for now. That was a slight relief. Miguel didn't need any of that shit getting into the helicopter's engine. He knew just how dangerous it could be—abrasive enough to tear through machinery in seconds under the right circumstances. Gripping the cyclic with one hand and the collective with the other, he pressed the foot pedal, rotating the chopper north. He pushed the collective lever up, lifting them higher as they veered away from the mountain.

They swung wide around Mount Hood, making sure to stay clear. Cook, Washington, lay to the east, but Miguel wasn't about to risk cutting it too close. He'd take the long way around.

Below them, the mountain continued to erupt in a furious display while wildfires ravaged Portland and the Willamette River burned. It was a scene pulled straight from the depths of Hell.

Reed and Chloe, US20, OR: May 21, 12 p.m.

The damage along this stretch of US 20 felt different. Fissures still crisscrossed the highway, but there was more space to navigate with fewer cars and fallen trees in the way. Even so, progress was slow.

Every few minutes, loud snaps or cracks from somewhere ahead or behind reminded them just how unstable the road was. They navigated around new rockslides and sinkholes that seemed to pop up without warning, the earth itself unpredictable. The only other vehicles they'd seen were headed west toward Bend. Their drivers were too focused on getting away to spare a glance or a word. Brett didn't expect them to stop, even if they could. He couldn't trust any of them anyway—not with what they'd been through. If it wasn't for Chloe and Reed...

As they rounded a curve past Upper Soda, surrounded by steep hills, Reed suddenly eased off the gas, slowing the truck.

The kids sat up, jostling with the dogs, trying to see what was wrong. "What is it?" Matthias called out, his glasses slipping off and landing in his lap. Duke stepped on them. Luckily, they didn't break. Matthias snatched them up with a frustrated sigh and leaned around the wriggling puggle to push them back on.

"Food?" guessed Chloe. The kids cheered behind her, and the dogs, catching their excitement, barked. Everyone was hungry, stomachs growling louder than the truck's engine. Reed shifted in his seat, glancing toward the others and then at the spilled food scattered along the roadside.

A fifty-foot bakery truck lay sprawled on its side, blocking nearly everything but a sliver of the easement. Its back doors were wide open, one resting awkwardly against the truck's side, the word "FRESH BREAD" only partially visible. The other door had fallen to the ground.

"Looks like there's still some stuff left. I know everyone's hungry. Let's see what we can find." Reed shifted the truck into park and killed the engine.

Before he could finish, the kids were already out, darting across both sides of the truck. Chloe's concern cut through the rush. "Do we have time?"

"We'll hurry." Reed stepped out, leaving the door open. A tangle of branches, rocks, and random bits of metal littered the area, but Reed moved quickly, weaving through it toward the back of the truck. When he peered inside, it was a jumble. Packages were tossed around, scraps of bread and plastic wrappers carelessly discarded.

The faint smell of yeast and sugar wafted inside, mingling with the dust from the road. Bright red plastic carts, once filled with fresh pastries and loaves of bread, had toppled against what was now the truck's floor. Some of the carts had been flung from the truck and now lay empty across the road.

Dozens of packages, half their contents missing were strewn across the cracked pavement— flattened croissants, their golden layers smeared with dirt, baguettes crushed underfoot, pastries that had lost all shape and purpose. Loaves of bread wrapped in plastic were twisted and abandoned where they'd fallen. It was clear others had already stopped, picking through the spoils—some packages lay crumpled or stepped on, a haphazard trail of hunger and carelessness.

"Why would anyone waste what might be the last baked bread for who knows how long?" Chloe said, anger sharpening her words.

"Maybe they were scared of the eruption warning and were in a hurry," Piper, who always saw the good in people, defended those who came before.

Brett laughed at Chloe's expression and rolled his eyes. "She's just like our mom. She always has something nice to say." A look passed between the teens, part sorrow and part fondness, as they both realized how he worded the comment. At some point, they knew they'd have to acknowledge their mom was gone.

Chloe, chastened, looked at the girl ruefully. "You and your mom are right. I need to be more like you. Let's hurry, too."

Together, they picked up armfuls of bread, their colorful plastic wrappings ripped in places, but the loaves mostly unharmed. The scent of fresh bread rose in the air, and Matthias couldn't resist—he pulled off a few slices, stuffing them into his mouth as he worked. Plain bread, he thought, wish I had some peanut butter and jelly.

The dogs eagerly circled the back of the truck, sniffing the air, their tails wagging as they scarfed up scattered chunks, licking the torn packaging. Reed quickly scooped up anything with chocolate or raisins, his eyes scanning the ground for any leftovers that might cause trouble. He tossed the forbidden scraps out of reach, making sure no eager canine mouths found them. A sick dog would only slow them down.

After the dogs had eaten their fill, he ensured the rest of the food stayed safely away from their prying noses.

They worked fast, sharing their finds, their excitement with the food only diminished by their need to hurry. Winnie and Charlie picked their way across the cracked easement, following a clear path over the dry gravel, their eyes scanning for pastries. The bread was fine, but pastries—she could almost taste the cherry filling. A sigh escaped her lips as she thought of it, the sweet, tart bite of it.

Then, her eyes caught something off to the side, near a cluster of scraggly shrubs. It had a bright red filling, unmistakable: cherry danishes.

"Look, Charlie!" She pointed, excitement flaring in her chest. She scrambled over the rubble, eager to reach them, Charlie beside her.

They didn't see the bobcat.

It crouched low in the dry, withered grass nearby, its tawny coat blending almost perfectly with the earth's faded colors. Its green eyes locked on the pair—unblinking and intense. Its ears twitched, and its tail flicked slightly, disturbed by the irregular tremors, but its focus was locked on the little girl and her dog.

The bobcat had been moving south, avoiding the worst of the quakes. It had circled the group, sizing them up for several minutes. The humans were too large to eat and wouldn't be a threat if he left them alone. But the girl and the dog, separated from the others, were a different matter. It began to creep forward, slow and deliberate, its paws barely making a sound as it slinked over the rubble-strewn road.

Bella had stopped by the gray truck, her nose close to the ground, methodically cataloging every scent. She scratched at her ear, stood, and was about to head back to the others when a new scent hit her—a faint trace of pine and earth, but something stronger lingered in the air. Her nose twitched, and her eyes scanned the surroundings, alert.

Suddenly, her fur bristled, and she whipped around, hackles raised. Her deep bark cut through the air. The sound startled everyone, sending Brett's arm jerking as he dropped the bread crates he held. Reed spun, his eyes searching, and Winnie's head snapped up, ponytails bouncing in surprise at Bella's alarm. She turned to Bella, not seeing the bobcat behind them.

The bobcat's lips curled back in a silent snarl, and it rose, muscles coiling, claws outstretched. It was ready to pounce. Its green eyes locked onto Charlie, unaware, just a few feet away. One swift leap and she and her meal would be gone.

But Bella didn't hesitate. With a burst of speed that seemed to defy logic, she shot across the cracked highway, her paws barely touching the ground. Her eyes locked on the cat, and before it could react, she was there. The bobcat hissed, ears flat, but with the fluid grace only a wild predator possessed, it sprang to the side and darted up the hill, vanishing into the trees.

Bella wasn't done. She gave chase, her barks and snarls echoing over the hills, a blur of fur and muscle, driven by instinct and adrenaline to catch the despised cat.

Reed and Brett reached the pair just as the bobcat disappeared into the forest, their hands grabbing Winnie and Charlie, pulling them back to safety. Neither the child or the pup understood the danger that had passed so quickly, but they didn't need to. Reed ushered them back into the truck without a word. They tossed the last of the baked goods into the truck's bed and loaded everyone quickly.

Bella, panting roughly, trotted back toward them, her eyes bright with the rush of the chase. Her tail wagged furiously as she leapt into the truck's back seat, settling by Brett's feet. Her chest rumbled with low, continued growls, the sound unmistakable.

They took off down the road, circling the bakery truck and leaving the wild cat behind. The weight of the near-miss hung in the air.

Chloe handed out bread and pastries, her hands a little unsteady as she passed them back. She regarded the little girl over the seat. Internally, she shuddered at what might have happened. The razor claws of that bobcat could have taken an arm off such a small child. It could have been so much worse.

"Winnie," she said in a level tone, handing her a cherry danish. "It's really important you stay close to the group from now on, okay? Things are different, and after the earthquake, it's just not safe to wander off."

Winnie wrinkled her nose, looking up at Chloe with a hint of defiance. "I didn't step on any wires."

"No, you didn't," Chloe agreed evenly, using her best tone of authority. "But this is a new rule. Everybody stays close. No wandering off. Promise?" She held Winnie's gaze, waiting.

Piper nudged her sister. "What would Mom say?"

"Listen to the teacher," Winnie said with resignation. She broke off a piece of her pastry and fed it to Charlie before meeting Chloe's eyes again. "Okay, I'll stay close. Sorry."

"You're good with them," Reed told her without taking his eyes off the road.

Chloe shrugged. "I've been a teacher for fifteen years. You learn a few things about getting kids to listen." She smiled a little, the tension easing. "A lot of direct eye contact helps with cooperation."

"Well, let's hope we can make Bend tonight," Reed said, his voice more determined now. "No more stops. Can you put the radio back on? Maybe there's been some updates."

It was the same recording. Chloe left it be while they pressed ahead, opening packages and making lunch from the bakery goods.

Miles later, when the emergency message changed to a live announcer, it startled everyone. Reed braked hard, rolling to a quick stop, trying to understand what the broadcaster was saying. They sat still on the side of the road, listening to the update.

"—This is a special emergency broadcast. A little after noon PST, Mount Hood erupted in a series of violent explosions. The USGS reports that multiple lava domes on the summit gave way, sending torrents of molten lava and pyroclastic flows surging down the mountain and into nearby communities. Tremors continue to shake the ground, and the sky is impenetrable with choking ash clouds.

At this time, authorities have been unable to reach the affected areas because of the dangerous conditions. The disaster is far from over.

In a terrifying development, the tremors have now spread south. Mount Jefferson is also rumbling, and an eruption warning has just been issued for that area.

If you are within the evacuation zone, you must leave immediately.

This is not a drill. Evacuate now. Your safety is the highest priority. Stay tuned for further updates."

"Is that Mount Jefferson?" Winnie, perched on Piper's knees, had her face glued to the window. Way in the distance, a huge pinnacle rose over the trees. Reed glanced at it and then up ahead. Closer to the road and coming up on the left, another narrow ridge squatted. This one looked withered, a jagged summit of rock looming over the highway. Reed recognized Three Finger Jack.

"You should put that Emmet Shale guy back on. He might know more. Hey, where's Mount Jefferson's snowcap?" Matthias asked, trying to see out the window around Winnie.

"They're glaciers," Chloe automatically corrected Matthias. She sucked in a breath. "Drive, drive now!" she urged Reed.

He didn't argue; he just shoved the truck into gear, pulling fast onto the road. US 20 was not so heavily damaged along this portion. He kept his fingers crossed they could make it to Bend without incident.

"There are five glaciers on Mount Jefferson," she explained as he sped up. "If they've melted that fast…" her voice trailed off.

"Mount Jefferson is probably twenty or twenty-five miles from here," Reed told her. "You don't think it could reach this far, do you?"

"The blast from Mount St. Helens extended almost twenty miles from the volcano," she said, her eyes worried. "I don't know what to think anymore. Nothing we've seen makes sense. Let's just get to the evacuation site and figure it out there."

"We're passing Three Finger Jack now. If Mount Jefferson goes, Jack will act as a shield."

"Maybe," Chloe's face was dark. "But anyway, drive as fast as you can."

The road struggled ahead, skirted by dense forests that gave way to rocky terrain after they passed Santiam Junction. The truck wound through the curves, Reed pushing the vehicle faster to cover more ground. Then, without warning, another aftershock shook the earth violently. The truck lurched sideways, the tires screaming as they fought for traction.

A low growl rumbled from deep within the earth, the sound vibrating through the truck's frame. The steering wheel jerked hard in Reed's hands as the vibrations intensified. He slammed his foot on the brake, but the truck slid, its momentum carrying it off the road. They hit a rotted stump, the impact jarring them to a halt.

The earth shuddered again, this time with even more force.

Three Finger Jack towered, its outline sharp against the sky. Then, with a grinding screech of shearing rock, boulders the size of small cars broke loose from the mountain, tumbling down the slope in a rush of volcanic stone. Gravel and dirt spilled across the pavement for a long city block in a dense, choking cloud.

To the right, giant cedar trees crowded the easement, acting as a buffer. The broad trunks shook violently, their massive, irregular, spreading branches flapping as the earth slammed against them, sending splinters and cedar bits scattering through the air like green snow.

The tremors slowly died. Everyone sat still, frozen in the aftermath, eyes wide, waiting for something to happen. But nothing came.

Reed vaulted out and crossed the gravel, Watson at his heels, the dog's claws clicking against the stones. Brett and Chloe quickly followed, their eyes scanning the highway ahead. Black boulders, remnants of ancient lava flows littered the road. Some were as tall and wide as the truck itself. It was barely passable. But the long cracks that split the asphalt were even worse—some as wide as the trunk of an old spruce tree, deep enough that the mountain's fill couldn't even bridge the gap.

The ground suddenly trembled again. Then, just as suddenly, it stilled.

Chloe grimaced, looking over the damage. "Can we drive through that?" she asked doubtfully.

Reed's face tightened as he surveyed the road. "We need the truck if we're going to make it to Bend today. But let's not risk everyone. Take the kids and walk inside the tree line on that side. It looks like maybe five hundred feet to where the road clears, and then you guys can climb back in. I'll meet you there."

Chloe wrung her hands, her nerves creeping up. "I hate this plan. But let's hurry. There may be more tremors any minute, and I've got a bad feeling about Mount Jefferson."

"Watson, go with Chloe. Protect." The golden lab hesitated and whined, but with a glance back at Reed, he trotted after Chloe, keeping close to her side. Reed felt a swell of pride for his dog. Watson had never let him down.

Brett hustled the kids and dogs out of the truck. Watson stayed glued to Chloe's side. Shadow limped along with Matthias while the other four dogs dashed ahead, ignoring the calls to stay close.

"Charlie," Winnie scolded. "Come here. You heard Chloe. We have to stay together."

Darting toward her, the little dog barked, veering off again but never straying too far from her. The group, disorganized and a little unruly, picked their way over the rubble, crossing the highway and entering the shade of the trees. The forest seemed to embrace them, the air immediately cooler and more protective as they moved deeper into the woods.

Chloe had her orange knapsack, and Brett and Matthias each carried two go-bags, leaving the heavy black duffels behind in the truck bed. Brett also left the toolbox in the bed.

With the kids and dogs scattered in front of them, they stuck close to the trees, stepping over the rough forest floor as they made their way through the woods.

Several times, the ground rumbled. Smaller landslides cascaded down the slopes, sending rocks, gravel, and brush tumbling into the road, the thunderous noise echoing through the trees. The truck's engine growled, struggling to push forward over the wreckage of the ancient volcano, its wheels slipping on loose rocks and dirt clods scattered across the mountain pass. Chloe and Brett urged the group onward through the forest, the dogs running in circles, breaking for the tree line and back, barking nonstop.

Reed wrestled with the road. It was bad. He tried to find a semi-clear path, but the uneven terrain made it feel like the vehicle was constantly on the edge of tipping. Repeatedly, he used the truck's bumper to nudge a boulder out of the way. Dust hung like a dry fog and swirled with every movement. Every tremor sent more rock down the hills, and he worried it would be impossible to get past the battered fragments of the extinct volcanic mount.

He hung onto the steering wheel, peering ahead, wincing as another tremor shook the earth beneath him. A shriek of scraping stone grabbed his attention as the vehicle's underside caught up on a rock jam. With a grunt, he threw the truck into park. A breeze whipped through the open window, laden with an undercurrent of crushed pine. Stepping out, the ground still quaking beneath his feet, he squinted at the hillside.

Back in the trees, the others heard the truck stop. Everyone froze, eyes locked on the road. Brett took a few steps toward the tree line as the tremors finally eased.

Reed examined the rock wedged under the truck's running board. He tried to push it with his foot, but it wouldn't budge. Gritting his teeth, he crouched and pressed his hands against the rough surface of the stone, shoving with all his weight.

The sun's heat mingled with the raw smell of freshly broken stone and damp earth, filling his nostrils as he struggled. Sweat stung his eyes, his muscles burning with each push. He shoved one, then two boulders back.

With one last grunt, he rolled the last beachball-sized stone out of the way. Standing upright, he stretched his aching back, hands on his hips, feeling the tension in his muscles.

Brett burst out of the trees, jumping up onto a knee-high shard of basalt. He raised his head just in time to see the top of the hill above Reed suddenly give way. The mountainside cracked, and a jagged line of rock slid down toward them.

The first spray of gravel shot down the hillside—intense, quick, and chaotic, like a thousand billiard balls in motion. Brett screamed, but Reed didn't have time to react. A sudden wave of huge rocks crashed down the mountain with terrifying force, the sound deafening—a blast of stone meeting the earth. Reed's breath caught in his throat, shocked as the barrage of soil and rock rained down on him.

He tried to scramble back, but it was too late. A boulder the size of a barrel slammed into the driver's door of the truck, knocking it sideways and into him. The blow caught him right across the middle, sending him tumbling back onto the rubble as the flow split around the truck, the only thing that kept him from being buried alive. His head struck the ground with a sickening crack. Everything went black for Reed Walker.

Dan and Nadia, Three Forks Air Transport, OR: May 21, 12 p.m.

The Three Forks airstrip was a forgotten relic on the outskirts of nowhere, barely a road's width away from the hills. The cracked tarmac was speckled with weeds and long-forgotten patches of oil stains, the surface so worn down in places it looked more like gravel than asphalt.

A lone, rusted hangar sat off to one side, its corrugated metal sides sagging, held together more by years of neglect than any actual maintenance. The faded sign above it read "Three Forks Airstrip," but the letters were half-worn away. It didn't matter. Pilots used this place because of its isolation, not for its charm.

Dan and Nadia sat in the hangar drinking bottled water with Bill Sheridan, the owner. Bill was as weathered and rough around the edges as the airstrip itself. Short, stocky, with a grizzled beard and a perpetually greasy shirt, he had a permanent squint in one eye. He moved like a man who'd been running from trouble most of his life, a little too quick to look over his shoulder. Despite his worn-out appearance, he was exactly the pilot Dan needed.

Bill owned a helicopter.

"I don't know." Bill waffled. "Mount Hood is pretty close to US 20. The ash is already blowing south."

"Bill, even if we found them, I can't land in my plane. I need your helicopter. You are the best pilot in Oregon, and we have five million reasons to risk it. You know the area like you know the back of your hand. We just need to find my truck." Dan poured on the compliments. Then he got serious. "I'll split it with you. One million dollars to fly us on a search grid until we find my truck. Cash. I'll pay you right there on the spot."

Nadia choked on her water in dismay, but both men ignored her.

"They're probably still somewhere along US 20, heading toward an evacuation site. We heard the emergency broadcast on the way here, and Bend is the closest. If we can find them today before they reach the city, it's just a matter of grabbing the bags."

"Huh? What if they don't want to give the bags up?"

"They're just kids, and I won't be asking," Dan looked grim.

"Okay, you got a deal," Bill worried about the ash from the volcano, but the lure of one million dollars was too hard to resist. He led them outside, around the corner where his bird was parked.

A dilapidated fuel pump stood at the edge of the runway, a crooked handle sticking out from the side. The stench of stale gasoline and the odor of burnt rubber, remnants of the last few planes that had come through, made Nadia sneeze. She threw a black look at both men's backs. This place was a dump.

But she wasn't about to stay behind.

Chapter Fourteen

Miguel and Walter, Cook, WA: May 21, 1 p.m.

Miguel landed the helicopter right outside the USGS Building, where Cook-Underwood Road curved east. It was a neat bit of landing, but Miguel brushed off the praises from the other two, pretending not to care. Deep down, though, a flicker of pride stirred in him.

As the blades slowed, they ran for the entrance. Tau mostly limped, brushing past startled employees. Miguel caught a few wide-eyed stares. The kind that said these guys look bad. In that moment, he didn't give a damn about looks.

"I need to speak to Andy Marsh. I'm Director Santiago of the Corvallis USGS office," he told a guy in a black tie and white shirt who was trying to stop him.

"Director Marsh is in the Emergency Center. Mount Hood erupted a few hours ago, and Mount Jefferson is being rocked with earthquake swarms. It looks like it will blow next." The man loped ahead as he led Miguel toward the back of the building. Walter and Tau followed.

The Emergency Center buzzed with energy as thirty people packed into the room, their voices urgent. Massive screens lined the front wall, each flashing updates and images. Walter's eyes jumped to the middle screen, where President Avery Wallace's face filled the space, her stern expression commanding the room.

He barely registered the other faces at first, but then he noticed Deputy Director Vancris on another screen, talking on the side to his team in Reston, his words firm and steady. On a third screen, Nancy Arnold from FEMA sat surrounded by people with laptops, her focus sharp as she listened, occasionally nodding. The weight of the moment weighed on Walter as the chaos outside seemed to fade away, replaced by this odd, impersonal connection to the nation's leadership.

Vancris was speaking fast. "...the situation on the West Coast is rapidly deteriorating. The earthquakes that began with the seismic activity along the Cascadia Subduction Zone have escalated into a full-scale catastrophe. Since the initial tremors, we've witnessed continuous seismic aftershocks, with the tremor intensity showing no sign of abating. The land continues to sink, particularly in Oregon, with large portions of the coastline and inland areas experiencing substantial subsidence."

"What's causing this activity?" President Wallace interrupted.

"We don't know. This is all unprecedented. To add to the disaster, Mount Hood violently erupted two hours ago, sending lava and pyroclastic flows down the mountain and ash clouds into the atmosphere. It's a disaster almost parallel to Mount St. Helens in 1980. But worse, at this time, we have confirmation that Mount Jefferson, too, is showing signs of imminent eruption. Seismic readings and visual observations show heightened volcanic activity that we cannot fully explain. Given the pattern of instability, we fear a chain reaction of eruptions throughout the Cascades and beyond."

President Wallace looked frustrated. "Nancy, what are your people doing?"

The Director of FEMA looked right into the camera. "As of this morning, the devastation has grown far beyond our initial fears. We are receiving reports from our satellite systems that large portions of the California coastline have disappeared entirely due to massive tsunamis, with major cities such as San Francisco, Los Angeles, and Santa Barbara suffering catastrophic damage. Millions of lives are feared to have been lost, and estimates suggest property damage now exceeds trillions of dollars." She paused and signaled to someone out of their view before resuming.

"We have yet to fully grasp the scope of the damage as the tremors continue to affect infrastructure, water supplies, and basic services. Supplies are running low in many of the emergency camps, and given the scale of the devastation, I must express that we cannot maintain this level of operation for long without more federal support."

The Joint Chiefs of Staff chairman, Willard Q. Brown, was sitting at the president's right hand. He picked up the conversation when the director of FEMA paused. "In terms of response efforts, the military, including National Guard and Reserve units, are performing large-scale evacuations from western California and Oregon. However, the task is monumental, with many of the primary routes to safety now impassable because of landslides, sinkholes, and ongoing tremors. Our emergency camps in Idaho, Nevada, and Arizona are working around the clock, but we are stretched thin. Transportation lines are running 24 hours, but the capacity of these systems is not enough to handle the overwhelming demand."

Deputy Director Vancris cut back in. "I know that you have declared a state of emergency for the West Coast, but I must stress that time is running out. The situation is dire, and the window for large-scale evacuations and relief efforts is closing rapidly. Coordinating rescue and relief operations is the greatest challenge, especially while managing ongoing seismic events and eruption risks. The infrastructure we rely on for communications, transportation, and coordination is failing."

He's right, Madam President." Director Arnold sat forward. "We ask for any additional resources you can allocate to support the evacuation efforts. We desperately need additional military personnel to assist with search and rescue operations, medical response, and evacuation of critical personnel. In addition, FEMA needs greater support to establish new emergency zones further inland. The situation is fluid, and the risks are unpredictable."

"The USGS team is working tirelessly to understand the full scale of these events," Director Vancris told the group. "But the seismic readings and geophysical data are difficult to interpret given the scale of the tremors and volcanic activity. We cannot predict when this will stop. Multiple fronts are experiencing unprecedented geological turmoil. We need all the resources we can muster to manage the response. Real-time updates will continue as they become available. However, please prepare for the worst. Please let us know what we can help with. Our focus remains on saving as many lives as possible and ensuring the safety of those in the most affected areas."

The meeting wrapped up pretty quickly after that. Miguel went forward, looking for Director Marsh. Walter and Tau hung back.

"This is crazy," Walter said, clutching his knapsack as people milled around them.

"We need to find somewhere to work," Tau looked around, frustrated by the crowd. "Before the fire, I think we were getting somewhere with your model."

"Do you want to see a doctor first?" Walter gestured at Tau's right side. The scientist had taken quite a blow from the dueling Komodo dragons. His face was bruised, the scrapes on his hands looked painful, and his limping had worsened.

Tau looked ruefully at his torn clothes. "I'm fine. This morning, your model gave a 94% probability of Mount Hood erupting, and it just blew. That's amazing. What worries me are the probabilities for the other volcanoes on the list. This situation is getting worse by the hour. That was my first volcano, by the way."

Walter laughed, able to relax now that Komodo Dragons, snakes, or walls of fire weren't chasing them. "My first volcano, too. Nothing like your first, huh?"

Then Miguel was there, hustling them back into the hall. "Okay, we're being evacuated to D.C.," he told them. "Even though most of the ash from Mount Hood is being blown southeast, this office will temporarily shut down. There's too much uncertainty about which volcano may erupt next. We're catching the next transport out to Reston."

"We need to look at Walter's model," Tau stopped, refusing to be herded. "It predicted Mount Hood. It could give us an idea of what to expect next."

Miguel stared at him, then at Walter. "We're only forty miles from Mount Hood. Mount St. Helens and Mount Adams are north of us. We should get to safety."

"All I'm saying is let's take fifteen minutes, pull up Walter's model, and see what it predicts. It's been right so far. Then we'd have an idea of what's coming next."

Miguel mumbled something, then threw up his arms. "Okay."

He pushed them to an empty office, and Walter got to work with Tau hanging over his shoulder. It was actually seventeen minutes later that they looked up.

"South," said Walter. "Mount Jefferson and probably Three Finger Jack next to it and then the Sisters."

"Three Finger Jack and the Sisters are extinct, well, all but the South Sister," Miguel protested.

"Nevertheless, the highest likelihoods of eruption run south through the Cascades, and those volcanoes have prospects at this point in time in the 90 percentiles. Whatever's been happening is spreading south now." Tau explained. "To compare, Mount St. Helens and Mount Adams have nearly flat probabilities. So north of us is definitely safer."

"Only if Walter's model is correct." Miguel interpreted the look on both their faces. "I know, I know. It's been right so far. Let's tell Director Marsh and get to the evacuation point. We need to be in Reston and let their technicians get to work."

Outside, they all stopped to look at the sky to the south, frightening with an oppressive gray column hanging heavy on the horizon. Visible above the tops of the towering pines surrounding them, the massive plume of ash billowed, rising high into the atmosphere like a monstrous, dark finger. The cloud was vast, swelling and roiling as it climbed, blotting out the sun and casting a pall over the entire landscape.

It was terrifying to think that more of these monsters could erupt today.

Reed and Chloe, US20, OR: May 21, 1 p.m.

Chloe's heart thudded in her chest, a sharp pulse of anxiety threatening to break through her calm. The woods had gone eerily still, save for the last of the falling rock. Brett's shout broke through her fear, his words frayed with urgency.

Chloe caught Watson's head and looked the dog straight in the eye. "Stay, Watson. Stay with the children."

The Labrador seemed to understand. He woofed once, then walked around all three kids as if he were herding them.

She looked at the girl beside her, appreciating her cool head. "Piper, you, Matthias, and Winnie walk another couple hundred feet through the trees before you come out on the highway. Matthias, you have your compass?"

"Yes, right here," the boy clutched the metal circle hard.

"There's no trail, so you'll have to keep them on course," she warned him.

"No problem," he assured her.

"Okay, I'm going to help Brett and Reed. We'll meet ahead in just a bit. Keep your eyes open, and be careful."

"We've got this, Chloe. Go." Piper urged her.

She crossed between the cedars, stepping fast until she reached the landslide's edge. The fill had spilled ten feet into the forest, but the huge trunks and branches had kept the worst on the road. The truck was just a little ahead of her position.

Chloe's eyes scanned the truck, her breath catching. It sat at an awkward angle, the driver's side door caved in under the weight of a fat, waist-high boulder that still rested against it. Gravel and chunks of stone forced her to pick her way as she approached the scene, her stomach tightening at the sight of Reed's prone body sprawled near the roadside, across the rocks.

Chloe's pulse quickened as she knelt next to him. His face was pale, streaked with dirt, and his chest moving slowly. She pressed her fingers to his neck, her heart jumping when she felt the weak, steady pulse. But still, he didn't wake up. Scared, she gently shook him, calling his name, her voice tight with fear. Brett knelt next to her.

"Reed, come on, wake up," she murmured, trying to hold back the flutter in her voice. There was no response.

Brett's face was set in grim determination, his jaw tight as he glanced at her. Chloe's eyes met his, the unspoken worry between them clear. Reed was too big to carry easily, especially with the mess they had to navigate. They needed wheels.

"Okay, can we even move the truck?" Chloe stood and looked over at the vehicle beside her.

Brett had already assessed the wreckage. "I think we can. If you'll help me, I think we can use that branch to leverage the boulder off the driver's side. The door probably won't open, but I don't think the engine was damaged."

It was a struggle, but together, with a deep grunts and strained muscles, they finally shifted the boulder, using a branch as a pry bar. Its immense weight groaned against the truck's frame, dragging a shower of dust over them. The stone tipped, just enough to clear the way.

Chloe dashed around the F-250, breath coming in short bursts as she climbed into the passenger seat and slid over. Her heart skipped when the engine coughed, sputtered, and then roared to life. She nearly collapsed with relief. Sliding back out, she pulled Brett into a hug, and he patted her back clumsily, not used to hugging anyone besides his mom.

"Let's get Reed to the bed," Chloe said, her voice steadier now, more focused.

Together, they gently lifted Reed's limp body, maneuvering him over the remnants of the landslide. Chloe struggled to keep her grip—he was dead weight—but Brett's strength made the difference. With one final, coordinated effort, they heaved Reed into the back of the truck. He landed with a soft thud between the black bags, a few crumpled bread packages spilling onto the ground.

Brett quickly rounded them up, piling the bread against the truck bed's side, unwilling to risk losing any food, even with Bend so close. As Chloe adjusted the big man's position, the rough fabric of his shirt scraped her sore palms, but she hardly noticed. They couldn't afford to waste time.

In the cab of the F-250 Chloe slid across the canvas to get into the driver's seat, hands trembling slightly as she shifted into gear. Down the road several hundred feet, standing on mostly clear pavement, she could see the kids waving wildly and the dogs running around. The gravel crunched beneath the tires as she eased the vehicle forward, the sound of the truck's suspension groaning in protest as it bounced over the uneven road.

Brett sat in the truck bed with Reed, catching his breath. He clenched his fists, urging the Ford to go faster, his mind racing with the risk of another landslide. Chloe maneuvered around and over the remnants of the rockslide, almost holding her breath. Every inch of the asphalt they crossed felt like it could be the last.

When she reached the kids and the dogs, Brett hustled everyone into the back of the cab except Watson, who jumped into the bed, sniffing and nuzzling a non-responsive Reed. The golden lab let out a low, mournful whine, sensing something was very wrong.

With everybody in, Chloe hit the gas, determined to get to Bend. Mount Jefferson still loomed behind them, and she could feel the weight of its threat.

Mount Jefferson, OR: May 21, 2 p.m.

A week ago, when Bane Rutgers hiked up Mount Jefferson, he thought to himself, "Thanks, Pop, for the years we spent camping at Mount Jefferson. It was the only place I could think to go when I needed to lie low. And thank the freaking calendar; it is the end of May. Decent temperatures at these lower levels are rare before spring." His pops had died many years before, but Bane still remembered his old man's lessons.

Huddled under the craggy overhang, his back pressed against the rough stone, he wished for the thousandth time he had remembered the old man's advice last week before he got into this mess. He looked around and figured he was somewhere between Milk Creek Falls and Woodpecker Ridge. The best way to stay out of sight was to keep moving further up the mountain. If he was right, there was a creek about a half mile north of here. Maybe he'd spend the night there.

Before he stood, he unzipped his knapsack, peering into the interior. The stack of cash was as exactly as he had left it. Every time he checked, it was in the same place, but his OCD wouldn't let him rest. Bane wiped his mouth with the back of his hand. This money was going to change his life; he knew it. $53,410.

If only he had robbed the Agarwal's house while they were out or even after they went to bed. There was no hurry. He had the safe combination. It was the sheerest luck, the first time in his life when something went his way. He had been washing the office windows when old man Agarwal came in and went right to the safe. The old guy never noticed him.

It was a one in a million shot that he could see the pad from his angle. He always had great eyesight. When he realized that he now knew the safe combination and saw the stack of cash sitting inside, he went a little crazy.

Standing, he rambled up the incline. No need to rush. The ground stirred again. He frowned, looking between his feet and around the clearing he was standing in. All day, these tremors had bothered him. He didn't remember all this activity when he was here as a kid.

Killing the old couple had been a mistake. He hadn't meant for it to go that far. He shouldn't have just walked into their house, either. But the sight of the money bewitched him. He blew his top when they both kept yelling at him, screaming loud enough to get the neighbors to notice. It didn't take much. They were a skinny old couple, barely a few inches over five feet. A couple of whacks, and they were both dead at his feet.

He rubbed the stubble on his chin, fingers rough against his unshaven face, feeling the shadow of regret hanging over him. Well, he regretted being forced to run. He didn't care so much about the Agarwal's. The old crank thought he knew everything and his wife was a nag.

He'd planned to camp for a few weeks, lying low, waiting for the heat to pass, and then head east. He had parked his old van down in a gully and thrown branches over it. Not much chance of anyone finding it. It'd be there when he was ready to go.

The mountainside was unnervingly quiet between tremors. He realized he had not heard a bird in hours. Weird. Maybe a storm was coming. Earlier, rumbles from the north had interrupted his meager lunch. He had finished hastily, ready to find shelter, but the sound died away after a while. There was no rain, though. He figured he had just lucked out for once. The weather was nice. It had been warming up all day.

Bane eased down onto a boulder, appreciating its smooth, weathered surface beneath his palms. The ground was littered with fragments of rock, bits of ancient, charred material, and a fine dust that clung to his pants when he shifted. He wiped his brow, taking a slow, deliberate breath as bits of something drifted down from the sky, settling softly around him.

His inspected the ground, then the mountain for a hint of what had caused the sudden flurry. A few pebbles skittered down the boulder beside him, followed by more powdery ash fluttering like fragile snowflakes in the still air.

He scanned the horizon, squinting through the haze until his gaze froze on the sky above the trees to the north. A dark mass had spread across the heavens, blotting out the daylight, and it wasn't just a cloud. This was something heavier.

The sight sent a quiver through his chest. The memory of Mount St. Helens eruption flashed in his mind. He'd seen that same black shroud roll across the sky before, choking the land and blocking out the sun.

Bane pushed himself upright, his palms pressing over the worn surface of the boulder. As he stood, more ash-like particles floated down around him, settling with faint taps against the stone, their weight heavier than snowflakes.

Bane's mind raced. How far away was the eruption? It looked bad. He should have brought his phone, but the fear of being tracked had kept him from it. Now, with no idea of what was happening, he was cut off from everything. He needed water and needed to find shelter. Maybe the creek would offer him some cover, some safe place to ride this out. If he could reach it before the full force of the ash fell...

He didn't waste another moment. Bane quickened his pace. His heart pounded in his chest as he pushed through the dense underbrush, determined to reach the safety of the creek. Breath hitching, it suddenly occurred to him that the rumbling noise he had heard the last several minutes was getting louder. When he broke through the last line of trees and came to the clearing, the sight that greeted him stopped him cold, and his mouth fell open.

The narrow creek, which had once flowed lazily through the landscape, was transformed into a violent torrent. Watery, churning mud surged through the clearing, choked with debris. The flow was like a beast—dark and relentless, sweeping up everything in its path. He knew its name.

Lahar!

He fumbled with the word; too many years since he had watched the news from Mount St. Helens. The flood was easily fifteen yards wide, rushing fast and deep, surging past the trunks of trees caught too close on shore. Branches, twisted bushes, even entire uprooted trees—tumbled by, caught in the violent sweep of the water, scraping, crashing, and churning with sickening force.

The flood had swallowed the ground, the downhill current so strong that even the stoutest trees were pulled from the earth. Lumps of fur, matted with mud, tumbled across the surface, swirling with the violent flow. Boulders, chunks of rock, and fragments of wood swept downstream, carried by the surge of sludge, an unstoppable force in motion.

Bane's pulse spiked with panic as his mind scrambled for direction. There was no way he could get across this; no shelter to be found here. His eyes darted in search of any escape, but before he could move, the ground beneath him trembled violently, the earth groaning as the mountainside cracked open.

With an ear-splitting blast, Mount Jefferson erupted for the first time in thousands of years, sending shockwaves rippling in every direction.

Bane lost his feet, falling backward and landing hard. The air seemed to crackle with energy, vibrating through his body, and the ground shook again, violent and unyielding. He gasped for breath, struggling to push himself up as the eruption sent a massive plume of ash shooting into the sky, blotting out everything above him. Swirls of ash flew around him, each an ember that burned where it landed. The trees swayed in the shockwave, breaking like brittle twigs under the pressure.

Bane's eardrums rang with the force of the eruption, blood trickling down his neck as waves of hot air seared his skin. Steam rose from the ground, filling the air with boiling heat. The tremors beat out a constant, bone-rattling rhythm.

Screaming, with the ground rocking beneath him and his flesh scalding a bright red, in his last seconds, Bane bitterly realized that he would never get the chance to spend his money.

Mount Jefferson erupted around him.

Chapter Fifteen

Chloe, US20, OR: 2 p.m.

When the road started shaking again, Chloe immediately felt the difference in the strength of the jolts. The truck lurched under the force, its tires slipping for a split second on the cracked asphalt as the tremors passed through it. She could hear the truck groaning, the suspension straining against the earth's violent convulsions. This was no aftershock. Detonations echoed behind them, deep *BOOMS* that hit like a shockwave.

"Mount Jefferson!" Piper's voice wobbled as she stared out the back passenger window, her wide eyes locked on the darkening sky.

In the rearview mirror, the sky behind the mountains had turned black over the last hour, as if someone had pulled a shadowy curtain over the landscape. She tried to focus on the road ahead, but her eyes kept returning to the ominous mass rising behind them. Her stomach twisted, dread tightening her chest. She hadn't realized how much she depended on Reed's steady presence until it was gone.

Her heart skipped a beat as she watched a huge curl of steam and ash suddenly billow upwards from one of the peaks behind them—higher, wider, swelling with a terrifying speed. It seemed to balloon out into the sky, sending pillars of cloud to choke the horizon. The rising column twisted in the wind, swirling madly.

Eyes fixed ahead, Chloe pressed on, the truck groaning with every turn of the engine. Since that boulder rammed them, the vehicle kept sputtering, the engine skipping in uneven bursts. It was still moving, though, and she couldn't afford to stop, not for anything. Her instincts told her to keep pushing forward.

Bits of ash peppered the windshield, dusting the glass with a fine layer of sand. Small flakes drifted through the air, falling in ghostly showers, streaking across the road like confetti caught in a breeze. The emergency broadcast on the radio blared warnings about the fallout from Mount Hood, but the reports about Mount Jefferson's eruption were even more urgent. Chloe's thoughts snagged on the possibility. Could Piper be right? Was that Mount Jefferson that had just blown?

She guessed it didn't matter which volcano as long as it was far enough behind them. They needed to get to Bend.

She stole a quick glance in the rearview mirror of Brett and Watson's forms covered by the heavy truck blankets they had found under the big, black go bags. Brett had pulled the blankets over them when the ash began to fall, trying to shield Reed and Watson as best he could. She could see the blankets darkening, thickening with the ash, ratcheting up her concern. The air was growing heavier by the mile.

"Did you see that sign?" Matthias asked, his voice full of excitement. He was sitting next to her, helping navigate the truck around the roadblocks littering the road.

"No, what did it say?" Chloe focused on the front again.

"Sisters – four miles and Bend – twenty miles! We're almost there!" His enthusiasm was contagious, but Chloe couldn't shake the feeling that anything could happen in the next twenty miles.

Shadow licked his hand, and he laughed, giving her a hug. He scratched the dog behind her soft ears. The Clarks had never owned a dog, always too busy for one. But now, with

Shadow, Matthias realized what he had been missing. It was the kind of bond that couldn't be overlooked, and in a few days, the stray had already become part of his small family.

Behind them in the truck bed, Brett's hand hovered over Reed's still form, his fingers patting the edge of the makeshift bandage Matthias had fashioned. The cloth was wet, clinging to the back of Reed's head like a second layer, soaked through with blood.

Brett's heart thudded, heavy with unease. Reed's breathing, slow and steady, didn't reassure him as much as it should. He checked again. No sign of life beyond the rise and fall of his chest. He shifted, careful not to bump Watson, and glanced down at the black bags on either side of Reed's unconscious body. His father's bags.

The dim light filtered by the blankets was barely enough to see by. Brett hesitated, then unzipped the nearest bag. At first, the contents didn't register—a stack of something that looked like packets of cut paper. His pulse quickened, unease creeping through him.

He shifted to his knees and leaned over the bag. Pulling out one packet, the paper felt heavy between his fingers. He couldn't make it out in the low light, but it felt familiar—smooth, slightly textured paper. His mind raced, thoughts slipping and sliding as he turned the packet over in his hands. With a quick pull, he lifted the edge of the blanket and rapped on the rear window with his knuckles. The sound sent Duke into a frenzy, the pug's paws tapping anxiously against the glass, his whining filling the cab. Piper's face appeared through the crack she opened in the window. "What's wrong?" she asked, her voice high with worry. "Is it Mount Jefferson? Or Reed?"

"No, I need a flashlight," Brett said, his voice clipped, more urgent than he'd intended. She handed it to him, and he yanked it through the window, brushing his fingers against hers. Duke's face pushed between them, his panting breath hot on Brett's hand. He mumbled a distracted thanks and ducked back under the blanket.

Flipping on the flashlight, Brett shone the beam directly onto the bag. His breath caught. His heart skipped a beat. The light revealed what he thought he might see. Money. Hundred-dollar bills were stacked neatly, tightly wrapped in uniform bundles. He pulled one out, his hands shaking.

He blinked. They looked real. Too real. His stomach twisted. What was going on? Still shaking, he left the first bag open and hurriedly reached for the second, ripping the zipper open. More money.

By the third bag, Brett's mind was reeling. This bag was full of clothes, shoes, and even perfume bottles, if his nose was any judge. Closely packed layers of silky, gauzy fabrics filled the bag.

Nadia's bag. He remembered her trying to pull the bag from the truck bed when they first arrived at the quarry. But the other two bags? Where had his dad gotten this money? Why had he kept it hidden away like this?

The weight of the discovery hit him like a sock to the gut. He thought of his mom, carefully balancing the budget with four kids to care for, his uncle, pitching in when they needed extra help for activities, even helping him pay for his car.

And all that time, his dad had this money put away. Brett shook his head slowly, the enormity sinking in.

More ash landed on the blanket, each fleck sticking as it landed. He pulled one of the silk blouses free from the third bag. He tore it quickly, fabric slipping between his fingers as he worked, his breath catching in the dusty air. The truck jostled over the uneven road, but he didn't let it throw him over. He wrapped the torn cloth around Reed's head, careful to cover the blood-soaked bandage. It wasn't perfect; he wasn't an EMT, but it would hold for now.

A faint scent of perfume drifted around him, mixing with the dust and the heat. He recognized Nadia's brand. It was a strange contrast to the confusion of the last few days.

Brett sat back, arms wrapped around his legs, eyes fixed on the bags of money. His mind drifted to the thought of his dad. He imagined the fury on his face when he realized they'd left the bags of cash behind. A sharp, humorless smile pulled Brett's lips. It served him right. Not that Brett cared about the money. It didn't mean much now.

What mattered was getting his siblings to safety and keeping them together. He needed to make his mom and Uncle Jess proud. He just wasn't sure how to do that yet.

More rumbles chased them down the highway. He hoped they'd get to Bend soon.

Dan and Nadia, US20, OR: 2 p.m.

The helicopter's blades chopped through the thickening afternoon air as Bill squinted into the distance. His hands, worn from decades of flying, gripped the controls with a steady precision that belied his years. His baseball cap sat low, casting a shadow over his eyes, though it was hardly needed as it grew darker. Clouds spread from the active volcanoes. His raspy voice crackled over the intercom, starkly contrasting the silent tension building in the cabin.

"Don't like the look of that ash," Bill muttered, glancing at the northern horizon. He angled the copter southeast, steering past Mount Washington toward the southern stretch of US 20. "This whole place will be a disaster zone soon. Ain't no telling how far that stuff'll travel."

Beside him, Dan leaned forward, wiping his forehead with the back of his hand. His shirt was sour with sweat, and his hair was stiff and stuck to his scalp. The stress weighed on him. He clenched his jaw, his eyes trained on the landscape below.

"Just keep looking," Dan growled. The old man's constant warnings were wearing on him. "We're not stopping. Not until we find the truck."

Nadia sat behind him, her blonde hair tangled in loose strands and smudged with ash and dirt from the last two days. She was striking even in this state, her features hard and angular beneath the grime. She felt more frazzled than she looked. Her eyes, sharp and focused, were also bloodshot. They darted over the broken landscape below with an edge of panic. Every minute they didn't find the truck gnawed at her insides. Her hands gripped the seat, nails digging into the worn leather.

She wiped the sweat off her brow. "We can find the truck," she said, her voice tight with anxiety, willing it to be true.

The helicopter hummed over the fractured landscape of the Cascades, the sound vibrating through the wind as they passed over the desolation below. Damaged trees stood sentinel over the winding roadways, now dotted with the remnants of vehicles and ragged undergrowth from the recent tremors. There was no sign of the gray F-250 they were searching for, nor the three black bags in the truck bed.

Bill exhaled, his hands steady on the controls as he banked the helicopter away from the worst of the ash. The sky to the north darkened, the air filling with the fallout from Mount Jefferson's eruption. The horizon was swallowed by a gray veil, casting the world beneath them into an unsettling twilight.

"You know," Bill said, his concern growing, "this ash's gonna make it harder to see the truck. It's not gonna be safe to fly much longer. I told you before—I'm not sticking around for some eruption fallout. I want that million, but not at the cost of my life."

Dan shot him an annoyed glance. "We're not stopping, Bill," he snapped, his voice tight. "We're close. I can feel it. Just... just keep your eyes open."

Bill snorted, adjusting his flight path. "Eyes open, sure, but I ain't flying blind into no dust storm. That truck's got to be somewhere out here, but it won't do us any good if we're buried under that ash ourselves."

Nadia pressed her face to the window again, her breath shallow as the weight of the situation settled in. Time was running out. The eruptions raged to the north, and the ash cloud was closing in fast, a huge risk for the helicopter. Soon, visibility would be impacted. But those black bags were worth the risk.

Chloe, Sisters, OR: May 21, 3 p.m.

Chloe had driven through Sisters, Oregon, a handful of times before. It was the kind of town that always felt tucked away, nestled in the heart of the Deschutes National Forest with its artsy, laid-back charm. The streets—lined with galleries and quirky little shops—made everything feel smaller, slower like it was untouched by the world outside. She'd always admired the view of the Three Sisters peaks rising in the distance, their snowy summits slicing through the sky like they belonged to another world. Those towering volcanoes, part of the Cascade Range, made you feel insignificant, even if you were miles away.

The town sat deserted. Quiet beyond the lazy afternoons. No cars lining the streets, no tourists wandering into the galleries, no sign of life at all. She'd passed through it in minutes, the absence of activity making her skin prickle with unease. It had all happened so fast—the evacuation, the warnings, the exodus that had swallowed the town whole.

At least the escape had cleared the road ahead. Chloe made good time as she sped through Sisters, but the truck was sputtering more with each mile. The engine's stutter, still rattled from the landslide, grew more pronounced. Chloe tried to drive faster. The truck groaned under the strain, its engine coughing and wheezing, but she pushed it forward, willing it to go just sixteen more miles.

US 20 stretched out ahead, barren and swallowed by the ever-thickening ash cloud creeping in from the north. She turned down the volume on the radio, the constant stream of warnings grating in its repetition, but just as her fingers hovered over the dial, a new voice broke through the recorded announcement. It wasn't the usual recorded message. This was live, frantic, the announcer's voice full of panic. Matthias jumped, quickly twisting the dial to turn up the volume.

"...interrupting to update you... Mount Jefferson has erupted, but that hasn't settled the abnormal activity of the last few days. Heavy earthquake swarms have spread south, and Mount Washington and the Three Sisters are now shaking. Though deeply eroded and considered extinct, recent movement has scientists issuing warnings. New steam vents have broken through, as well as continuous tremors and ground swelling. The USGS warns everyone to avoid the mountains in that area—head south or east. There could be an eruption any minute!"

As the broadcaster continued, Chloe's heart skipped in time with his words. Her eyes flew to the horizon on the west, her stomach dropping. The words on the radio seemed to blur and fade as the landscape fractured as she watched.

A towering mushroom of smoke and ash unfurled above the mountains, billowing black and heavy against the pale sky. The Three Sisters. One of them was erupting, but Chloe couldn't tell which one. Panic surged, cold and fast. Hoping she was making the right decision, she hit the brakes. The truck screeched to a stop, its tires sliding over the thin layer of ash on the road.

"Get out!" Chloe shouted, her voice urgent and sharp, pushing Matthias, Shadow, Bella, and Coco beside her out the passenger door. "Run! Over there!"

She jabbed a finger towards a patch of ground just off the road. A cow pond, its surface slick with ash, lay nestled beneath the lip of a broad ridge. The ridge was a natural barrier, an ancient geological wall between them and the eruption.

"Now! Hurry!" she screamed again, adrenaline surging through her veins.

Piper's frantic voice cut through the bedlam as she scrambled from the backseat, dragging Winnie along behind her and urging the little girl to hurry. Fur flew around them, the dogs barking in confusion and excitement. When she saw the eruption, her face went pale. "What do we do?"

"Grab your go-bags! Get the kids in the pond!" Chloe barked as she threw the blankets off Reed, Brett, and Watson in the back of the truck. Ash flew up in a cloud. Her hands shook, but she didn't stop. She dropped the tailgate and, without hesitation, began pulling Reed's limp form out of the truck, the dead weight slowing her down. Packages of bread shifted and fell under her feet, but she ignored them.

"Help me!" she snapped at Brett, who stood frozen, eyes wide with horror, staring at the ash cloud that was growing larger by the second. His gaze shot from the sky to Chloe, and with a jolt, he moved to help. Together, they heaved Reed out of the truck and toward the pond, dragging him over the ground. The cold water splashed against their ankles as they stepped in, but Chloe barely felt it, focused only on getting everyone to safety. Brett glanced up again as they dragged Reed farther into the pond, his eyes scanning the sky, the air filling with ash. They didn't have much time.

The first eruption was like a nightmare unfolding in real time. A terrifying arc of smoke and fire twisted into the sky, consuming everything in its wake. The soundless sight of the discharge scared him to his core. Before he could process the first wave, another one followed.

The second explosion, even darker and more ominous, shot out horizontally—a tidal wave of rock, ash, and acid gas. It moved too quickly for his eyes to track, unstoppable, a torrent of devastation. The ground shook beneath him as deafening booms cracked through the air, followed by a searing hot wind that tore at everything in its path.

Terror seized Brett as realization dumped over him like ice water. They weren't far enough away. The flow would reach them.

Without a second thought, he shoved Reed into Chloe's arms and sprinted back to the truck, Jess's voice ringing in his head, giving him instructions. Every second counted.

His heart pounded in his ears as he slid around the tailgate, reaching into the bed of the truck. His fingers fumbled as he yanked the open black go bags from the bed and tossed them onto the ash-covered ground. The money packets fluttered in the wind, spinning through the air before they landed with soft thuds on the dirt. Brett cursed under his breath and grabbed the truck bed liner, wrenching it free from the bed and tipping it to dump the last of the bread. Thank God his dad hadn't fastened it down. He dragged the heavy liner across the ground, the weight of it straining his already fatigued muscles, but he didn't care.

"Chloe!" he shouted, his heart hammering.

Chloe was already in motion, pushing the kids into the cold, murky water, pulling the dogs in with them. The bigger dogs splashed in without hesitation, but Charlie pulled back, unsure. Chloe gripped the pup by the scruff and tossed him to Piper, who caught him with a firm grip.

She left Reed, still unconscious, resting against Watson in the shallows. The Labrador stayed close to Reed, ignoring the commotion surrounding him, whining softly as he nuzzled the man's motionless body. The kids swam toward a half-submerged log at the far edge of the pond, gripping the slick bark for support, pale faces, terror in their wide eyes. Matthias clipped the floating knapsacks to the log, freeing up his hands to help with the dogs.

Choe splashed over and grasped Reed, keeping his head above water as she swam him to the log. Wedging his head between two branch ends, she ordered Watson, "Protect." She hoped the golden lab would understand.

Watson moved close, paws on Reed's chest. Chloe pulled off her sopping jacket and threw it over both their heads, then whirled to help Brett, who was dragging the truck liner into the pond.

The water near the road was shallow but quickly dropped off into a deeper section toward the far side. Piper and Matthias's feet just barely touched the bottom. Together, they worked to keep the dogs afloat, their hands cupping the animals' chests, ensuring heads stayed above water. Winnie, clutching Charlie to her chest, tucked the little dog beneath her shirt, keeping him warm as he shivered against her. His nose, damp with water, pressed close to her face, his breath shaky against her skin, but he had calmed in her arms.

Brett flipped the liner over, and he and Chloe quickly shoved the kids and dogs underneath, jamming the open end tight against the log and stuffing the gap with the damp blankets Chloe had soaked. Each of them grabbed a loop on either side, bracing themselves.

The blast hit like a freight train, a wave of heat and sound that seemed to swallow them whole. The air cracked, and the pond shuddered beneath them, sending ripples through the water with enough pressure to rattle Brett's teeth in his skull. Instinctively, everyone but Reed and Watson ducked beneath the water. The dogs dove down, surfacing only to dip back under, their bodies trembling.

Brett and Chloe fought to keep the liner down, struggling against the force of the blast. The ridge overhead provided shelter, but if it weren't for the liner being mostly submerged, the blast might've torn it away.

The air seemed to warp, vibrating everything around them. Ash rained down in sheets, pattering against the top of the liner. The air grew stifling, the heat searing even in the cool water. Brett's lungs burned as he held his breath, praying the flimsy liner would hold and keep them safe from the storm that raged around them.

The liner sagged and softened, edges beginning to melt under the blast's intensity. The water, once cold and numbing, now clung to their skin like warm sludge, tainted with ash and grime. Brett could taste the sulfur in the air on his tongue. He grimaced but didn't move. They waited, every second stretching into eternity.

Finally, after what felt like hours, Brett poked the blanket with trembling fingers, trying to peek outside. The water was slick with yellow dust, stinking of sulfur. But the air was clearing behind the smoke and heat, just enough for them to see.

He pushed up, careful not to disturb the shelter too much, his arms stiff from holding the liner in place. His palms slipped against the slick surface of the log, and he kept his breaths light, wary of the biting sting of the swirling ash. The heat burned his chest, dry and suffocating. He swam toward the shallow end, crawling out with effort, his body aching with each movement. The world above the water was muted, coated in a leaden gray blanket of ash that clung to everything like a grim fog.

Tiny flecks of ash continued to fall, drifting through the still air. Standing, he stumbled through ankle-high ash drifts, each step sinking beneath his wet sneakers, caking them with gray mud. He reached the Ford, now skewed off the highway, doors still open. Crawling across the passenger seat, he winced as his hands brushed against the hot metal of the seat belts and the chips of glass from the windows. He tried the starter, but it just clicked.

Discouraged, he looked out the hole in the driver's side window and stopped. There, amidst the ash, was one of the black bags lying on its side.

It lay covered in powder but mostly undisturbed. He climbed out of the truck the same way he'd entered, moving cautiously to avoid disturbing the ash any further. He rifled through the bag, relieved to find the clothes scorched but still whole, likely protected by the truck's angle. The deeper he dug, the better they looked.

The money bags behind the truck weren't so fortunate. Their contents spilled out, choked with ash. Most of the top bills were scorched, curling at the edges, and some of the packets were blackened and brittle. He kicked the money bags halfheartedly, the ash swirling. Standing up the first bag, he took an armful of clothes and returned to the pond, where Chloe was helping the others out of the water.

The group was waterlogged and pale, with faces and fur streaked with ash, but everyone was alive. Chloe helped the kids and the dogs scramble onto the bank and then floated Reed across the pond, leaving him resting on the shore.

After a quick exchange with Brett, Matthias got to work, the blade of his scout knife slicing through the silks and satins with practiced precision. He layered the fabrics, the colors bright and smooth beneath his hands, before fashioning makeshift face coverings. One by one, he transformed the materials into crude masks and scarves, cutting and folding them into shape. He also made masks and scarves for Reed and the dogs. Matthias tucked an N95 mask from their go bags into each one to filter out the worst of the ash.

Watson didn't resist, sitting quietly as the mask was tied around his face, but the other dogs weren't as easy. They squirmed, unsure of the foreign fabric. Piper, quick on her feet, helped, and even Duke, though reluctant, allowed her to fit a paper and plastic mask over his nose, though only one layer. They finished the task in minutes.

Standing off to the side, Winnie eyed the fabrics with a frown. "Nadia is going to be mad you ripped up all her pretty dresses," she said, her tone serious.

Matthias glanced at her and shrugged. His glasses were smudged. "She'll be glad we used them to save ourselves."

"I don't think so," his little sister shook her head, unconvinced.

To Chloe's surprise, Matthias had even packed lightweight goggles in the go-bags. When she asked, he didn't hesitate to explain, his voice matter-of-fact. "Uncle Jess and I made lists of everything we could think of; then we narrowed it down to the essentials. He said after watching what happened with Mount St. Helens, any good go-bag in Oregon would include safety glasses."

Chloe slipped the eye protection over her head, grateful for the foresight. The others followed suit—Piper and

Winnie with ease, the little girl giggling as she watched Chloe fumble slightly with her new gear.

"Matthias taught all of us how to use his stuff. We had drills," Winnie said proudly. "He said we had to be ready."

Chloe couldn't help but smile at Matthias, her voice full of admiration. "Your go-bags are amazing, Matthias!"

The boy beamed, his usual quiet confidence shining through as he pulled on his goggles. "We had to be ready for anything."

Ash clung to the fabrics wrapped around their heads and necks, the bright silks and satins now muted by the clotted, gray dust sticking to everything. They were the only touch of color, starkly contrasting with the bleak, ashen landscape around them.

Chloe caught Brett's arm. "We have to get out of here. There could be another eruption. Can you get the truck running?"

Brett didn't meet her eyes. His lips pressed into a tight line. "No. The truck's done. We'll have to walk out."

Shocked, Chloe fell silent, the weight of their situation overwhelming her. Walking wasn't an option—not with Reed unconscious. She glanced at him lying on the wet, soiled blankets and wondered briefly if they could pull him along. But the thought faded quickly. The ash on the blankets had already softened into mud, turning the fabric into a heavy, sodden mess. It would be impossible to carry him that way.

Brett wasn't ready to give up. "I know what you're thinking. Reed's still out cold. Leaving him here would be like sealing his fate. But we can't just sit here. I've got an idea. Let me work with Matthias. We can build something to pull him."

"Pull him? With what?" Chloe's gaze swept the barren landscape. There was nothing. The aftermath of the eruption had transformed everything into a lifeless, broken wasteland.

"Give us fifteen minutes. We can make this work." Brett said, his eyes flickering with a stubborn resolve.

Without waiting for her to agree, Brett turned toward the truck and called Matthias over. He had a plan.

He set to work, grabbing the 10-millimeter socket from the tool chest he had dragged around since this morning at Merry Maple. After bracing the truck's hood, careful not to burn himself on the hot metal, he unbolted the spring supports, leaving the loose bolts in place for now, trying to work fast. Matthias wrapped his hands in more fabric to pad them from the heat. He held up one side while Brett worked on the hood hinges.

Once it was loose, they maneuvered the truck hood, flipping it onto its back. The wet blankets they'd retrieved from the pond were spread over the metal, insulating it from the heat and what would be a rough ride. While Matthias scrounged for a solid branch, Brett wasted no time. He set to work, removing pulleys and belts from the engine. Rigging them together with ropes and the straps he cut off from the black go-bags, he created a crude pulley system. The branch Matthias found would serve as a steer bar.

"Give me a hand with this," Brett said, tying off the last knot. Matthias grabbed the other side, shifting it, and they both stood back, admiring their handiwork. They had a makeshift sled.

While the boys were busy working, and Chloe and Piper fitted a mask around Reed's unconscious face, Winnie sat by the truck, a little removed from the flurry of activity.

Her small fingers traced the edges of the big black go-bag, the last of the bright fabric peeking out against the endless gray dust. Her attention shifted as something hard pressed against her fingers through the soft material. Intrigued, she tugged it free, revealing a jewelry box about the size of a small briefcase. The latch clicked open with ease, and Winnie's breath caught in her throat.

Inside were sparkling necklaces, bracelets, and rings resting on a velvet bed, their stones catching the faint light in a flash of vibrant reds, greens, and blues. Winnie recognized them immediately—the play jewelry she and Nadia pretended with when she stayed at her dad's house. The little girl didn't know these gems were real or what they were worth.

Winnie chortled quietly, her mask muffling her glee. She was relieved that the baubles had survived the eruption. Everything else in the bag—all the pretty clothes and shoes—were stained by the yucky ash, but the glittering jewels still sparkled, even in this dim light.

The go-bag Matthias had made for her before all of this running had begun was sitting on the other side of the truck with the rest of their knapsacks. Their covers were drying from the dunking in the pond. She hurried around the vehicle, her little shoes sinking into the ash, and grasped her bag, pushing aside the stuff Matthias had packed inside. The box wouldn't fit, so she carefully transferred the jewels—one by one—into the bottom of the knapsack, covering them with damp t-shirts and pants as if hiding treasure.

She didn't know when she'd see Nadia again, and a spark of anger pricked at her chest, remembering how Nadia had yanked her arm that morning. But right now, the little girl only cared about the jewels, about keeping the magic of play alive. She tucked the empty box aside by the truck tire, wiped her hands on her pants, and slung the now heavier bag over her shoulder.

"Winnie!" Piper's voice called, breaking her from the moment. Without a second thought, Winnie trotted over, careful not to stir up the ash too much, ready to help her sister.

Chloe stood with her hands on her hips, eyeing the contraption Brett and Matthias had cobbled together. The truck hood, lashed with engine parts, ropes, and strips of the heavy polyester from the big black go-bags, looked more like a patchwork of random materials than a practical solution. But she shoved aside her apprehension. It had to work.

Her brow wrinkled as she asked, her voice tinged with doubt, "Are you sure it'll slide with Reed on it?"

Brett flashed a grin underneath his scarf, but he nodded so she would see. "It'll slide. The dogs—Watson, Coco, Duke, and Bella—will help pull. The hood should glide over the ash, make it easier to move."

Chloe looked over at the Sisters, her nerves tightening as another vibration rippled through the ground beneath them. "Well, let's get moving. These tremors aren't letting up, and with how that mountain looks... we need to go."

She spotted Matthias rifling through the bags of money behind the truck, piling some of the less damaged packets on the tailgate. Brett had explained what he had found and his assumptions about the black bags. He rubbed the burned edges of the cash; his face crinkled with disappointment as fragments fell away.

"What about this?" he asked, lifting one of the currency straps with a mixture of reluctance and longing.

"These are one-hundred-dollar bills. This stack is worth $10,000!"

"Leave it," Chloe replied firmly. "Our lives are worth more than that money. It's heavy, and we don't need to carry any extra weight."

Brett nodded in agreement, though his voice softened slightly, acknowledging Matthias's silent regret. "It's too heavy to carry and won't do us any good now. We need to move fast."

Matthias hesitated, his fingers curled around a flaking stack of cash. With a deep sigh, he let go, letting the packet fall back onto the tailgate. "Fine. Who needs money? Dad would have a stroke if he knew we had his bags, anyway."

Brett let out a short laugh. "No kidding."

With that, Chloe and Brett moved quickly, gently lifting Reed onto the truck hood, his wet body limp and unresponsive. Chloe draped a blanket over him, trying to shield him from the ash that was already thickening in the air. Matthias slid Shadow into position beside the unconscious man. The dog limped more with every step, and he was afraid she'd collapse if she tried to get very far. Her dull coat and weary eyes mirrored the exhaustion that seemed to settle on everyone.

Chloe's gaze lingered on Reed. She bit her lip, worried about his head injury. Her mind sorted through solutions. But she didn't have an answer, and there was nothing to be done right now. Reed was the EMT. He was also the patient with an injury they didn't know enough about to treat. They needed to get him to Bend.

Brett and Matthias harnessed the dogs to the hood. The dogs, eager to work, wagged their tails, oblivious to the destruction unfolding around them. Brett took the lead, holding the branch steady while Matthias encouraged the dogs and guided them along. There were a few initial mishaps—the dogs getting tangled or pulling in opposite directions—but with Brett and Matthias keeping them in line, they soon had a rhythm. Watson led the charge, his steady pace setting an example for the others.

Winnie, knapsack slung over her shoulder and holding Charlie, walked close to Piper. The Sisters loomed ominously in the distance, the ash cloud growing broader and darker in the sky above them as they hurried down the road. Chloe glanced over her shoulder every few steps, her stomach sick with unease. They had no idea what was coming, but they couldn't afford to stop.

Chapter Sixteen

Dan and Nadia, Sisters, OR: May 21, 5 p.m.

Bill eased the helicopter down onto a flat stretch of ground along US 20, the blades slowing with a rhythmic whirr. With one last gust of air, the chopper settled, kicking up a swirl of ash in every direction. Dan was the first to leap out, boots kicking through the fine dust. He headed for the fuel tanks, leaving light impressions in the soft ash. Bill followed behind, muttering curses under his breath.

"Damn stuff's getting in everything," Bill muttered, wiping his brow on his already filthy sleeves. The wind had shifted south, dissipating the particles, but Dan could see the pilot's nerves fraying. If it got much worse, they'd be heading back to Three Forks.

Dan twisted the cap off the auxiliary tank while Bill hooked up the fuel hose, watching the liquid slowly drain into the copter's main reservoir. Bill's gaze drifted nervously toward the mountains in the distance, his face tightening. Too much ash. They were running out of time.

In the back of the helicopter, Nadia shifted uncomfortably in her seat. The dust clung to her skin, making every inch of her feel itchy and raw. Her clothes and hair were coated in the same grimy film, but she remained silent, knowing better than to voice the irritation building inside her. There was too much on the line.

The local radio station crackled to life, and the voice that followed was shrill and frantic, sending an icy shiver down Nadia's spine. She leaned forward, adjusting the dial to hear better, and her stomach dropped at the words.

"...looks like it was only a small eruption from the Middle Sister, based on what the authorities from the USGS are telling us, but the Sisters are still shaking. There may be more violent activity. This may just be getting started. Leave immediately if you are anywhere near Mount Washington or the Three Sisters volcanoes. Bend has evacuation processes running twenty-four hours if you can get to the city. Don't wait. Leave now!"

Nadia turned down the radio and fell back against her seat. She was not sharing that news with Bill or Dan, she thought, though Dan didn't panic easily. She willed them to hurry.

Dan's eyes scanned the sky again, his stomach flip-flopping. He cursed inwardly, replaying the decision to stay behind yesterday. Every minute spent here was a minute lost. They should've been miles away, safe in Montana by now. Instead, they were still stuck in this mess. He helped Bill finish securing the auxiliary tanks, both of them working quickly. Every second felt like it was pulling them further from their goal.

Once the helicopter's engine kicked on and they were airborne, Dan leaned forward, peering through the thickening haze. To the south, a dark plume of smoke spiraled upward. A new eruption. His gut turned over. But he didn't say anything, not wanting to risk setting Bill off. There was no advantage in pointing it out when they had no control over it. They had to focus, follow the grid, find the truck, and keep moving.

The helicopter's blades pushed aside the light ash as they passed over abandoned vehicles. The sight of them—sitting still and empty in the bleak wasteland only stoked his frustration. Each passing car seemed like another reminder of how much ground they were losing. They needed to find it, and they needed to move faster.

"Do you think they'd have stopped in Sisters?" Bill's voice broke the stillness, and Dan looked up as the pilot adjusted the angle of the copter. The small town of Sisters came into view, the haze making it look like a ghost town. "It's up ahead. Should we fly a grid?"

"Do a fly-by first," Dan said, spreading his hand on the glass and leaning so close his forehead was touching. "If we spot something, we can loop back for a closer look."

From the air, the destruction was even worse than he imagined. A blanket of ash muted everything, the world smeared in dull gray. A lahar, a terrifying churning mudflow, had torn through the valley, swallowing Whychus Creek and sweeping over everything in its path.

Surging over the Lodge, a famous hotel frequented by the rich and famous, the brutal wave had then crashed into the city, swallowing roads, buildings, and anything in its path. The overflow snaked around the curve of US 20 and into a subdivision, burying the neighborhood. Trees, rocks, houses— all of it tore away, leaving the land ravaged and unrecognizable.

They circled higher, scanning the destruction, but there was no sign of the Ford. The knot in Dan's stomach twisted tighter. The lahar could have taken the vehicle, but he refused to believe that. Brett was always careful. He wouldn't have left his siblings without a ride.

Bill shook his head, pulling the chopper away from the destruction. "Nothing," he muttered, pointing the aircraft south. The township of Sisters was behind them now, its fate sealed in ash and mud.

Just as the weight in Dan's chest threatened to crush him, his eyes hit upon a dark shape below. His heart stopped. There, half-buried in the mess, was his Ford 250, the gray frame barely recognizable. The hood was missing—maybe it had blown away? The driver's side door was caved in, and the other doors flung open. Most of the windows, including the windshield, had shattered. Ash clung to the wreck, swirling around it like a shroud, giving the scene an abandoned air.

If it hadn't been for Nadia's go-bag, her vivid clothes spilling the only color for miles, his eye might not have caught the shape of the bag or the other two by the tailgate. Before he could comprehend that someone had opened them and that the loose paper blowing in the breeze was his money, Nadia saw her bag and screamed suddenly in anger. Surprised, Bill yelped, jerking the controls. The helicopter pitched sideways, dipping dangerously momentarily.

"That's it. Land now!" Dan barked, ignoring the furious woman beside him.

Bill didn't hesitate. He scanned for a place to touch down, muttering curses as he brought the chopper to rest on top of the ash layer. "If this shit gets in the engine..." His voice choked off as Dan and Nadia were already on the move, shoving the door open and springing out of the helicopter, sprinting in the heat toward the ruined truck.

"Shit, shit, shit," he swore but idled the copter, immobilizing the flight controls. He climbed out and followed the other two across the field.

The bills—stacks of them—scattered across the tailgate, spilling over the ground. The paper was blackened and curled. Some were so burnt they crumbled to dust when Dan tried to pick them up. The bags were torn and mutilated, with their straps slashed clean off, leaving the mutilated covers and contents behind. Dan's mind raced, trying to make sense of it. Why take the straps and leave the money? The thought bewildered him, but there was no time to dwell.

Nadia was already on the ground, her hands tearing through the mess in her bag. The fabrics were stained, singed, and ruined. Burn holes marred the cloth, tattered by the smoke and heat. She dug furiously, her fingers trembling until something else caught her eye. Her jewelry box was half buried in the ash under the truck.

She lunged for it with a cry, scrambling to open the box. She knew before the clasp gave. It was much too light. The contents were gone. She screamed again, long and loud. Bill, just reaching the truck, ducked instinctively. He knew better than to stand in the path of a woman on the edge.

Dan rifled through the bags, desperately searching for bills not scorched beyond recognition. The thin cotton and linen paper had been no match for the heat. Every bill he touched disintegrated into ash, leaving nothing but wasted scraps.

The earth trembled beneath him, another deep, bone-rattling quake. Dan looked up and froze.

Another of the Sisters was erupting!

Bloated plumes of smoke and ash shot into the air, and below, the mountain unleashed a torrent of volcanic fury. Clouds of molten rock and ash surged down the flanks, engulfing everything in its path.

Another violent quake shook the ground, sending Dan's head snapping back. His ears rang from the roar, and his vision blurred as he gripped the truck bed.

Bill screeched as he lost his footing and crashed to the ground. The air pulsed with violent booms, and rocks the size of boulders rained down, smashing into the earth with explosive force.

The sky darkened. Ash absorbed the daylight, instantly turning day into night. Dan couldn't even see his hand in front of his face. Bill's voice cut through the suffocating blackness, his frantic face suddenly inches from Dan's, his breath hot and erratic.

"We have to get out of here!" Bill screamed, his eyes wide with panic. Spittle flew as he clutched Dan's shirt, shaking him once before pulling away. Without a second thought, Bill turned and sprinted toward the helicopter.

The deafening roar of the eruption consumed everything around them. Dan could barely hear his thoughts, let alone Nadia's terrified screams. Reaching down, he caught her arm. He jerked her toward the helicopter, their feet slipping on the shaking earth, trying to stay upright.

Time blurred, stretching, warping into something that felt endless. Moments later, the helicopter materialized out of the gloom. Bill was already in the pilot's seat, the blades spinning up. Dan threw Nadia through the door, scrambling up behind her. Bill launched the copter and the ground dropped away beneath them. For a split second, he felt weightless, his feet barely touching as the chopper surged upward. It took a breath, but with Nadia pulling on him, he made it through the door and banged it behind him.

Bill's curses filled the cabin, a string of angry, frustrated words that Dan could barely make sense of. The heat outside was suffocating, clinging to them like a blanket. Dan's arms stung. Looking down, he was surprised to see red spots where hot bits of ash had singed his flesh. Flying embers had riddled his clothes with holes, fraying and scorching the fabric. Nadia's hair was a mess of charred strands, the odor of burned hair mixed with the sulfur heavy in the air.

Through the haze, Bill fought to keep the helicopter level. It was a battle. The helicopter bucked in the wind, fighting against the violent updrafts, the ash swirling like a storm around them. Bill struggled to keep them level, his body tense as he battled the machine and the pandemonium outside. Without the instruments, he would have been flying blind. They could only keep moving east, hoping the ash wouldn't bring them down.

Dan's ears rang from the eruption. His body tensed, instinctively holding on tighter, knowing they were hurtling through an inferno. Their lives hung on Bill's skills and chance. All he could do was ride out the madness.

Chloe, US20, OR: May 21, 5 p.m.

Chloe's legs felt like lead as she trudged forward. She couldn't be sure, but she calculated they had covered about three miles. The adrenaline that had spurred them early, driven by the fear of another eruption, had worn off. They moved slower now, exhaustion dragging at their feet, every step harder than the last.

Surprisingly, the dogs were the ones to keep them going. Despite the strain, the ash, and the impossible conditions, they'd pulled their weight and more. Brett knew they would never have made it this far without their muscle. Twice, he and Matthias had swapped places, but the dogs had really carried the load. Their steady pace had been the only thing keeping the group moving forward.

The brightly colored fabrics they had used to shield themselves from the ash now hung limp and faded, bleached by the soot and dust. They were a procession of pale figures, shuffling down US 20, each of them too tired to speak, too worn out to look up. The dirty haze that clung to everything made Bend feel far away.

So, when headlights cut through the gray gloom ahead, the sight was a burst of light that made Chloe's heart sing in relief. She hadn't realized how much she was holding on to hope until that moment. A young man in uniform jumped out of the medium tactical truck and hurried over to her.

"Ma'am, are you okay?" he asked, his voice strong with concern.

"Oh my god, yes!" Chloe said, grabbing his hand, her voice breaking with a mixture of exhaustion and relief. "We have children and an injured man. We're trying to get to Bend for the evacuations. Our truck broke down after the eruption, and we've been walking ever since."

Private Henderson glanced over at Reed's still form under the blanket and then at the kids and dogs huddled around Chloe. "I'm Private Henderson," he said, his voice clipped but steady. "We're from the 4th Battalion, part of the Tactical Recovery and Evacuation Team. Our final search of this area is underway, hoping to find survivors. We'll take you to Bend."

Chloe didn't think; she just moved. She threw her arms around him in a tight hug, squeezing him hard. He smiled but urged her to hurry. Two other soldiers appeared before she could pull away, bringing up the rear.

Minutes later, everyone piled into the back of the military vehicle, thankful for the canvas sides filtering out the ash. Reed was laid out on the floor as carefully as possible, and three other evacuees scooted over to make room. Pulling off the makeshift masks and scarves was a sweet relief. Tails wagged, and smiles lightened hearts as they exchanged names. The truck sprang to life with a jolt, and they bobbed forward, bouncing over the ragged pavement.

Suddenly, multiple deafening bangs split the air, shaking the truck to its core. The vehicle lurched forward, speeding down US 20 as if it were in a race. The damaged road barely registered under the wheels. Chloe's pulse hammered.

The rear window slid open, and Private Henderson's face appeared in the gap, grim and focused. "One of the Sisters just blew again!" he shouted over the deafening noise. "Hang on! We're getting out of here!"

The truck barreled down the highway, every bump and jolt threatening to throw them onto the floor. Chloe fell to her knees next to Reed and pinned him with her body, Watson lying over his legs. Brett and Matthias folded the girls between them and held on while the rest of the dogs huddled close. Their fellow evacuees clung to the benches, doing their best to stay steady as the truck swerved and bounced wildly.

The ride was a blur of noise, motion, and fear. Each bump and tilt felt like it would be the one that threw them all off balance. Time seemed to yield, the seconds dragging.

Finally, after what seemed like hours, the truck slowed, the jolts lessening as they moved away from the worst of it. The road smoothed out just enough to allow them to breathe again, but Chloe didn't let go of Reed. Not yet.

Private Henderson peered through the rear window again. "Everyone okay back there?"

"Yes, yes," came the collective answers from the group. They were battered, but they were still breathing.

"We're almost to the evacuation center," he called back, relief evident in his voice. "We'll have you folks out of here in no time."

Chloe rested her head on Reed's chest as she tried to steady herself, then looked up, only to find Reed's brown eyes, hazy and confused, staring at her.

"Uhh, Chloe," he rasped out, his voice barely audible. "Is everything okay?"

Her chest tightened as tears sprang to her eyes. She smiled through them, her hand reaching up to wipe them away. "Yes, everything is fine. You just rest."

Brett leaned down, a big grin on his dirty face. "We made it, thanks to you both."

"Thanks to all of us," Chloe replied, her voice shaky with emotion. She smiled back at him, but tears still tracked down her cheeks. "We make a great team."

Winnie, hanging from Brett's arm, looked up at Chloe, her little face serious, Charlie tight in her arms. "We're not a team," she said matter-of-factly. "If anyone asks, we're a family."

Epilogue

Reston, VA: May 28

Tau was still limping, but the scratches on his face were healing. When he returned to their shared workspace after his last meeting of the day, Walter was eager to show him the latest output from his model.

"Look at this," Walter said, excitement bubbling in his tone. He slid a stack of papers across the desk, tapping his finger over a chart. "The forecasts have fallen almost to zero," He traced the downward curve of the graph. "I think whatever was happening along the West Coast is finally ending."

Tau leaned in, scanning the data. "With the entire West Coast decimated and six different eruptions along the Cascades, I'd say it's about time," he replied, his voice relieved, "It'll be years before they recover."

Walter sighed, scratching his head and leaning over a notebook filled with scribbles and equations. "We need time to fine-tune my model," His eyes scanned the page. "There's still data here I don't fully understand."

Tau's gaze sharpened. Their terrible ordeal hadn't diminished Tau's enthusiasm at all. "We've got the best minds in the country working on this, including you and me. We'll figure it out." He leaned against the table, his expression serious but determined. "That is if you plan on sticking around."

Walter's lips twitched into a grin. "I'm not exactly eager to head back to Oregon anytime soon," he admitted. "Besides, Miguel got promoted to the USGS VP of West Coast Dynamics this morning. He's going to work from here and report directly to Vancris. He wants both of us on his team. What do you think?"

Tau's dark eyes gleamed. "I'm in. Where do we start?"

Condon, Montana: May 28

Dan stepped out of the barn, the heavy door creaking on its hinges behind him. The vast expanse of Mack's property stretched before him—sixty acres of impenetrable forest and rolling hills, with only the cabin and the barn breaking the natural sweep of land. He tucked his plane away in the back stalls, hidden from view, while the plants, safe for now, sat in temporary trays, waiting for something sturdier.

They'd barely made it back to Three Forks Airfield. By the time Bill landed the helicopter, the engine was sputtering and coughing like it was about to die. Hours later, ash fell, blanketing the Ochoco National Forest and Three Forks in fine, gray dust. Dan heard it had made it all the way to Boise, Idaho, and further into the western states. The ash cloud would eventually circle the globe.

But Dan wasn't thinking about the cloud or its global journey. His mind fixated on the money—the bags of cash they had come so close to recovering, only to lose them in the end. The whole thing felt like a cruel joke. They had been so close.

Nadia was in worse shape. Bronchitis had settled deep in her lungs, leaving her bedridden for days. Her body shook with coughs that seemed to drain the last bit of energy from her. She was angry and obsessed over her lost jewels. Every minute she ranted about how Dan's kids must have taken them made Dan's frustration boil hotter.

Mack had called in a doctor, and the man looked concerned. His face creased with worry as he listened to Nadia's rattling coughs. He suggested a hospital, but Nadia refused to go. She stayed in bed, fixating on everything they lost.

Dan kept scouring the online forums from the evacuation centers, hoping for a sign of the kids—anything to point him toward the jewels. He didn't care about the children, but the jewels? He'd go after them. But so far, nothing. Amidst all the turmoil, their names hadn't come up. Maybe they had died along US 20 in the second eruption. If they had, then the jewels were buried with them, gone forever.

Dan exhaled sharply. Starting over without the money or jewels felt bitter, but he couldn't think of another way. He was stuck.

Latah County, ID: May 28

The Latah County Fair and Events Center was a whirlwind of activity. Tents fluttered in the wind, generators hummed, and people hurried from place to place. Cars filled every available space; some were haphazardly parked, while others lined up in rows like cattle awaiting a pen. It was everything Chloe had expected from an evacuation center, yet there was something almost peaceful about it. Far from the madness of the eruptions and hundreds of miles away from Bend, the center felt like a temporary reprieve.

Chloe had heard there hadn't been a new eruption in two days. She hoped they were at the end. The toll of the natural disasters weighed heavily on her. Millions were dead, and countless more were injured or displaced. The worst disaster in the history of the United States would take a massive effort to rebuild.

She'd lost everything—her home and the life she had known before the world turned upside down. Her job, her students, her coworkers—none of them had made it. She checked the survivor lists daily, and each time, her heart sank when she found no familiar names recorded.

It was even more heartbreaking for the children. Every day, Brett joined Chloe, their eyes scanning the lists, hoping to find Jolene Clark or Jess Tate. The reports out of Albany were grim, but they still held onto a fragile thread of hope. That thread was fraying as more news came out of the West. Reports had confirmed that Albany was gone.

Chloe and Reed were trying to help the kids, providing them with a safe space to share their feelings, setting up routines, and encouraging them to share their memories. But it was really the dogs that made the difference.

They seemed to sense the sadness and were a balm for aching hearts. At just the right moment, one would nudge a kid's hand or curl up by their feet, offering warmth without words. When the sadness seemed too heavy to carry, a dog was there, tail wagging, bringing a quiet comfort. Playful barks filled the gaps when the weight of loss was too much to bear. Their calm and steady presence was the glue that held everything together.

At least the survivors evacuated Lebanon in time. Mollie and Oliver were safely up north. When she spoke with Oliver earlier, he mentioned heading to his parents' place in Florida, as far away from the West Coast as possible. He'd invited her to join them, but she knew she couldn't. Not yet.

Despite everything, she had something she hadn't found in years—family.

Walking into the massive meal tent, Chloe's eyes immediately found Matthias and Winnie waving excitedly. Their enthusiasm was contagious. As she made her way toward them, she spotted Piper, Brett, and Reed sitting with them, surrounded by the dogs curled up at their feet. The smiles that greeted her made her chest tighten, warmth flooding her body as she returned the wave.

"Did you talk to Oliver?" Reed asked, his voice still rough but stronger. His bruises were fading, and yesterday, the doctor removed the bandages from the back of his head, leaving a patch of bare skin where his hair had been shaved. The kids thought the scabs and stitches were cool, though Reed secretly hoped his hair would grow back soon to hide the scar.

"Yes," Chloe replied, settling in beside him. "He and Mollie are going to Tampa. They're trying to catch transport out tomorrow. Everyone from his house made it out safely, even Carl. Oh, and Carl asked about Bella, by the way." Her tone made everyone chuckle.

It wasn't just Bella on a leash—every dog had one. The fairgrounds had become a maze of people and animals, and Bella, particularly, was on high alert, her instincts triggered by every cat they passed.

"Did you tell him where to find us?" asked Winnie. Chloe could tell the little girl was still pining for Mollie.

"Yes," Chloe said, offering a comforting smile. "I told him to look for the Walker family in Harrowood, Kentucky. I made sure he knows Royce Walker, Reed's dad, owns a farm there right along the Mississippi River. We'll all stick together, and that's where we'll be."

Winnie sighed contentedly, her expression softening. "Because we're all family and family sticks together." She reached down to pat Charlie. "That makes you Charlie Walker."

Everyone laughed.

Chloe glanced at Reed, her smile bright. "With our IDs gone and everything in an uproar, using your last name for everyone was a stroke of genius. It cut right through the red tape. Do you really think your dad will be okay with adopting a woman, four kids, and six dogs—even just temporarily?"

Reed met her gaze, his expression serious but reassuring. "My dad rolls with the punches. He'll be fine. It only has to be temporary if you want it to be. You and the kids are welcome to stay in Kentucky as long as you want."

Chloe felt a slight flush creep up her neck at the intensity of his tone. She cleared her throat. "Well, let's see how it all works out."

Just then, a loud, familiar bark echoed across the tent. Reed's face broke into a grin as he turned toward the noise.

"Stella!" he stood, yelling.

Sure enough, Stella came bounding into view, her tail wagging furiously. Albert trailed behind her, hanging on to her tether.

"So, you folks made it," the old man said, surprised to realize he was glad to see them. Stella jerked on the rope, tangling herself in the middle of Coco and Bella's leashes. He couldn't help but chuckle as he sat beside Reed.

"I am so glad you made it," Chloe exclaimed. "I wondered how you two fared."

Albert's smile faded into a grimace. "My house came down on us; that's how we fared. But Stella and I managed to get out and head east. We ended up in an evacuation center, and after Mount Hood erupted, they transported us here."

Reed rubbed Stella's head affectionately. "You always were a good girl."

Chloe shifted, a new thought crossing her mind. "Do you know where you're headed now?"

Albert shook his head. "Nope, no family left. I guess we'll catch a transport east and figure things out as we go."

Reed exchanged a glance with Chloe, a silent conversation passing between them. She smiled in agreement. After all, Stella was family.

"Why don't you come with us?" Reed asked, his voice casual. "At least until you find something else. My dad's got a big farmhouse in Kentucky. We're going to help him with the crops. I think you'd get along great with him—especially with your experience growing produce. You could stay as long as you want."

Albert blinked, a bit taken aback by the offer. He opened his mouth, then closed it again, unsure. But the more he thought about it, the more appealing it seemed. The thought of settling somewhere—getting a break from the constant chaos of the last week—felt like a small blessing.

"Well," Albert grumbled, scratching his chin, "we can try that."

Winnie jumped to her feet, pulling on her heavy go-bag and picking up Charlie. "You and Stella can sit next to me and Charlie," she told Albert, beaming.

This was a new chapter for all of them, filled with uncertainty but also with a glimmer of hope. And that seemed pretty good.

Idaho Falls, ID, May 28

Ramona Wellington shifted slightly in the bed, stretching her arms, feeling better today. She hadn't been able to move much just days ago, but today, the pain was manageable, enough so she could stretch her legs out and let them rest on the bed without wincing. She knew she wasn't fooling herself. The sharp bite of burns on her arms and backside still ached. But she was moving, really moving, for the first time in what felt like days.

Every morning, she checked on Barry and Sam. They were improving, too. Their parents had practically worn a path to her bedside, constantly showering her with thanks. But Ramona knew better. People might thank her, but Ramona knew the real thanks belonged to a higher power watching over them.

A monstrous pyroclastic flow rolled down the mountain, but somehow, they survived. It could have caught them in the inferno, consuming them in a surge of lava or scorching ash. The odds had been stacked against them, yet here they were. Deep in her bones, Ramona knew the flows had tilted away just enough to save them.

It was a miracle, no question about it.

So, whenever she felt the sharp pains in her healing skin or heard the familiar annoying sounds of the hospital, she whispered a quiet thank you. For her. For Barry and Sam. And for the second chance they'd been given.

She would be grateful for the rest of her life.

Eugene, OR, May 28

Emmet Shale spun the wheel of his truck as he cruised down OR-58 East. The road was in better shape than he'd expected, the damage nowhere near as severe as he'd seen elsewhere. Behind him, the trailer and his boat, *"THE BIG ONE,"* bounced gently with each bump, a slight sway that didn't bother him. A satisfied smile was plastered over his face.

He replayed the predictions he'd nailed in his head—one after another. The eruptions, the quakes, the disaster unfolding just as he'd said it would. The vindication felt sweet. He'd been ahead of the curve, calling the shots before anyone else. While the world scrambled to catch up, it had been Emmet Shale with the answers and who saw the signs before they were obvious.

But now, Oregon was in the rearview mirror. Time to move on. He glanced over his shoulder, watching the landscape shrink into the distance, a fading patchwork of trees and roads. The horizon stretched ahead—endless and unknown. There were other places, other risks waiting for someone to uncover them. Places he'd yet to explore but had already mapped out in his mind. Patterns no one else had seen, waiting for him to connect the dots.

And when he found the next big story, he'd be ready. He'd share the truth. The people deserved to know what was coming, and Emmet Shale was the man to make sure they did. The podcast would be his megaphone to the masses. The world was just getting started, and Emmet was right where he needed to be.

Thank you for reading Wreckage Road. I hope you enjoyed this story.

Please visit my website bewaretheend.com and sign up for my mailing list for updates and new release information.

Your support is invaluable to me. I welcome and respond to your feedback. Please feel free to email me at bb.bewareauthor@gmail.com.